Alan Golbourn

THE 666 MURDERS

First published in Great Britain in 2022 by Gelbs Publishers Ltd
GelbsPublishersLtd@protonmail.com

ISBN (Hardback) 978-1-9993795-2-0
ISBN (Paperback) 978-1-9993795-4-4
ISBN (eBook) 978-1-9993795-3-7

A CIP catalogue record for this book is available from the British Library.
Formatting by Polgarus Studio
Cover design by Creative Covers

Mog, aka 'Gwurm' ♥

Battle not with monsters, lest ye become a monster, and if you gaze into the abyss, the abyss gazes also into you.
— Friedrich Nietzsche

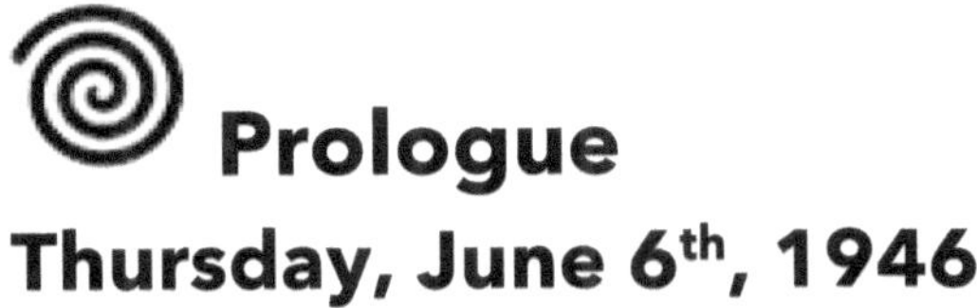

Prologue
Thursday, June 6th, 1946

Western Europe - 5.36 am

He listened intently to what he was told, although he never said a word. He just stood there, listening, understanding everything. He showed no emotion. He was their favourite. They knew that he was special when they had first taken him in. He was chosen and had his own destiny to fulfil — but only when the time was right. He was told to remain patient and to wait for his moment: his 'calling.' When the earth shook, he would need to return. His moment was not now — his time would come. He had been prepared for it.

The hunched-over woman removed his hat and kissed him on his scarred and not fully developed face. She told him that she loved him like he was her own and promised that they would see each other again in time. She then stepped aside and the tall, slim man stepped forward, reiterating the words of his pain-stricken wife. He too, kissed the young boy and then placed the hat back onto the boy's head. They wished him a happy birthday again. The young boy regarded these two as his parents. He had only ever been loved by and felt love from them. The young boy watched the man and woman descend through the opening, to join the other children. He still showed no signs of emotion. He walked over, pulled up the ladder and then closed the trap door shut.

The wood of the building had already been saturated and prepared in advance just before. That included virtually everything inside. The young boy then lit a match and threw it. The flames grew instantly and fiercely, burning bright and hot. Only then, did the young boy show a sign of emotion; a tear formed from one eye and rolled down his right cheek. He slowly left the burning building with the dawn breaking on the horizon. With the wooden building burning and crackling, the young boy walked off in the twilight; the flames danced orange and green behind him.

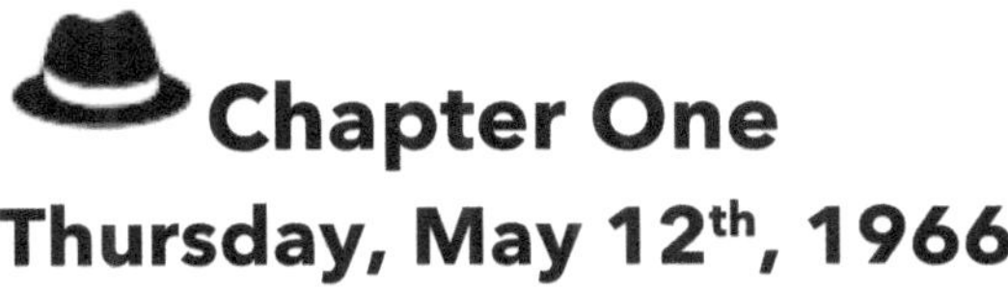# Chapter One
Thursday, May 12th, 1966

Carnaby Street, London – 10.12 pm

"Hit me again, Max."

The bar was full of smog. A haze of greyish white sat and hovered in the air. The smell of a recently lit cigar came from nearby. Above the chatter, came a few coughs.

"Rough day again, huh?" Max replied, from behind the bar.

Max Munson had taken over Teresa's, formerly known as Ray's, and had been running the bar for what would be twelve years in the fall. Previously run-down, it needed much work and renovation. Max had renamed it after his beloved mum — she was pushing eighty.

"You could say that," the man answered, stubbing out one of his cigarettes into a dark blue, Murano glass ashtray. He coughed a couple of times before lighting another of his Winston Lights.

Max laughed sympathetically. "We've all had that, I'm afraid."

"Some more than others …"

"True!" Max said, taking the empty glass away from the seated man and pouring another large whisky. "Perhaps you better take it easy, Randy. That's your fourth in half an hour." Max was a little concerned.

"What are you, my *mother*?" The man glanced up. The cigarette hung from his mouth. He forced a smile. "At least you're making money from me. That's more than can be said about myself …"

Max smiled. He had known Randolph for several years now. He was a frequent customer. Particularly of late. He had been in every night for the past week, even during the day. He had become a bit of a barfly. But tonight, Randolph seemed to be knocking the whisky back faster than usual. He had also come in much later this time. "I'm just saying, maybe you should slow it down some? We're closing in around half an hour anyway."

"Time to get a couple more in at least!" Randolph took a large swig. He liked his whisky neat. Yet he never got used to the burning sensation as it washed down his throat, which was tickly no doubt caused by the smoky atmosphere and his own smoking. His grey fedora sat on the bar. His matching trench coat was draped over one of the stools with a pale orange cushion poking out from underneath.

Max half-smiled, with empathy this time. He more than understood Randolph's financial struggles. He'd been there himself in the past, like many others; these were difficult times for all.

Randolph himself, wasn't one to share his problems with someone else. Nor did he want to bore anyone with them. He wasn't like that; he didn't seek attention. But he had opened up a little more during the past week, due to the influence of the alcohol. Max was a good listener as well. It probably came with the territory, listening to other folk spill their problems and issues, along with their drinks.

The overweight man who had lit the cigar, started a coughing fit. He was sitting by himself at a table, reading a newspaper, not far from the bar entrance.

"You seriously need some more windows open, Max ..." Randolph mentioned, turning around on his stool to briefly watch the man cough.

"They're all open as it is! No luck on that missing dog, then?" Max remembered Randolph telling him about some old dear's little Chihuahua that had gone missing the previous week. *Peanut*, had been his name. He had escaped so it was believed, from a hole in one of the back garden's fences. The hole had gone unnoticed due to the overgrowth.

Randolph shook his head, taking a sharp drag from his cigarette. "Nothing yet. The mutt's probably run off for good ... can't say I blame the little fella. I don't think the owner is *quite* the full ticket."

"Why's that?" Max frowned, wiping up some spillage from the bar with a dirty cloth.

"It doesn't matter. She just seems a bit odd; that's all." Randolph rubbed a finger in the corner of his eye; both his eyes were sore and itchy, stinging from the smoke and tobacco fumes.

"Well, let me know how it goes. I'm sure you'll find him. Or he'll just return home eventually of his own accord."

"Possibly. At least I got paid upfront for my efforts. I'll get paid more *if* I actually find him."

"No 'leads' then?" Max attempted to joke, smirking.

"Idiot," Randolph replied, but couldn't help but grin. "That's actually quite a good one, for you!"

"I try." Max held his hands up, laughing.

Randolph shook his head some more, before finishing off his drink.

*

"Shit!" said Randolph, exiting Teresa's.

It was raining heavily. He did up his trench coat tightly and pulled his collar up, and his fedora down to cover his face the best he could from the downpour. He then scurried to his office. He decided to spend the night there as it was raining; it was a little closer than his flat, which served as a poor excuse for a home. Poor as it was, he had been struggling to afford it for the past three months.

Despite the nonstop rain, he chose not to run. He was tired from lack of sleep lately and his head felt fuzzy from the whisky he had sunk in such a short space of time. At least he had stopped after the fourth, following Max's advice and his own intuition.

He swayed a couple of times as he hurried. The streets were pretty much dead on this spring night, as were the roads, apart from a few other passers-by with their umbrellas up. They were returning to their homes, most likely *better* homes than what he called his own.

He picked up his pace, cursing and grimacing as his black shoes splashed on the worn, uneven pavement. His dark grey trousers became soaked on his lower legs where his trench coat didn't protect him. He swore again when he splashed his right foot into a deep puddle, where a hole had formed over the years in the pavement slabbing. He wished that he had brought the car, rather than gone to the bar on foot. Although he felt a little drunk, he would have been fine to have driven back — or so he believed.

*

It took Randolph less than ten minutes to reach his office on Hopkins Street. He climbed and almost stumbled up the decaying steps to the main entrance of the large office building. His small office was on the ground floor. He had chosen it because he couldn't be arsed to walk up and down the flights of stairs. He would also have to go down the other end of the large corridor to reach them. Yes, there was a lift halfway down, but it was often out of order. An office on the ground floor was more than fine with him. With the lack of work lately, he wondered why he still bothered paying for an office at all.

Randolph had opted for an (albeit cheap) office because he didn't want strangers coming to his home, if he needed to interview them; they could be a strange bunch and he didn't want them to know where he lived. With some, he would prefer it if they didn't even know where his office was. It also seemed more professional.

Randolph took a right and walked down a narrow corridor to his office. The hard-white flooring had brown and black speckles that seemed to blur his vision. His office was the last one on the left. Half of the lights weren't working. The few that were on, seemed to flicker and dim above him. It was typical. He paid for the office and things didn't even work properly. The lights had been fixed twice before, in as many months. Now they were out again. Useless pricks.

Standing at his office door, he gazed at the fading chipped frame and read his name. It was printed in black on the frosted glass, as was the office number and his title. The lights seemed to be fine down this end:

40
RANDOLPH LANDON
PRIVATE INVESTIGATOR

A couple of letters of his name were peeling off.

"Humph ... Private investigator, my arse ..." he muttered to himself as the lights above him now dimmed slightly. He glanced upwards.

He had had no new proper cases for months now. Just small things here and there. He considered getting a 'proper' more reliable paid job, whatever that meant.

His past few cases had all been owners' pets that had gone missing, including his current case, Peanut, wherever that little shit had got to. Him still being lost was costing Randolph money. If he found him, dead or alive, there would be another payment in it for him. The other animal cases had been two cats and another dog.

He had located a cat in someone's garage, where it had been stuck for around a week. He had found another pet runover and dead, much to the owner's distress, and another dog had travelled several miles back to its old home, from where the owners had recently moved house. How he had even known the way back, only the dog knew.

Randolph had seen him sitting outside the back garden gate. The American owners hadn't even considered the possibility that Zippy, a cross between a Cocker Spaniel and Poodle (a Cockapoo), might have returned to his old home. They thought he had been stolen from outside their front garden, where he had been chewing a bone when they last saw him. It was no wonder they were concerned, seeing as it was a designer dog. Not that it probably mattered to them financially — they could afford it. But Randolph was glad they hadn't checked. He had made money from it, and the owners were more than generous when they got their Zippy back. He was a cute dog too.

Randolph had rarely worked pet cases before. He usually had bigger fish to fry. He had helped the police out on a couple of occasions, when they had asked for his assistance, and they paid well. Either way, Randolph was desperate for the work and needed the money. He was never ungrateful, even if a little peeved. At the end of the day, money was money.

His last big case involved a young boy aged eight; little Felix Geoffreys, with Randolph working alongside the police force, even leading the way at times. Although rare for a PI to work with the police, the young boy's parents knew of Randolph, and had hired his help; they were distraught. Randolph and the police ended up collaborating well.

That was well over a year ago now. Felix had gone missing one morning, while he was out shopping with his parents. They had only turned their back for a matter of seconds. Felix had wandered off unhappy and with the hump, because his parents had refused to buy him the latest toy. He was missing for over a week before he was found.

It was Randolph's expertise that had led them to an old house, where the boy was found in a basement, tied up. He had been fed very little and was dehydrated. He had been held captive by a convicted child molester, named Peter Gibbs, who had been released a few weeks before. The poor boy was enticed away to the man's white van. Thankfully, the boy had remained unharmed; the police and Randolph arrived just in time.

There had been much debate about releasing Peter Gibbs early and whether he should be released at all. Those who disagreed with his release were soon proved correct. Needless to say, Mr Gibbs would not be seeing anything other than the inside of a prison cell for quite some time after Randolph and the police caught up with him. The story had been on the news as well as in the papers, including Randolph himself. Randolph and the police earned well-deserved recognition for their efforts.

Opening the office door in the semi-dark, Randolph reached for the light switch on the wall to the right and flicked it on. The ceiling light inside his office dimmed, before lighting up in full. He almost stepped on a brown envelope with his name written on it, lying on the square red and black welcome mat. Someone had slid the small envelope underneath the door. Randolph bent down to pick it up and then wiped his shoes a couple of times on the mat, adding to a few scuffs of dried dirt and mud already residing there.

Holding the envelope gently between his teeth, he took off his wet hat, shook it ferociously a few times, and hung it on the tall wooden coat stand next to the door, along with his soaked trench coat. He walked over to his desk and sat on the vintage tan leather chair. At least his coat protected most of his clothing from the rain. It was only his lower legs that were still wet and had fallen victim to the downpour. He could still hear the rain from outside, hitting against the office window. The office light dimmed and flickered a few more times, before returning to normal again.

Randolph used an old stainless-steel, canteen cup as a pen holder; it had survived from the army along with him, from World War II. Like him, it had seen many locations. Apart from a slight dent in its side, it was in almost perfect condition, which was, perhaps, surprising. He took out a letter opener from the cup and carefully sliced the envelope open. The contents were a thank you letter and an apology, along with a cheque. "About time!" Randolph said to himself.

It was a letter and payment from a middle-aged gentleman, who believed his wife was having an affair with a much younger guy; his suspicions had been justified. When Randolph investigated the matter, the wife did turn out to be seeing a man twenty years her junior. This had been three months ago. Randolph had had to chase the payment numerous times, until he practically gave up. The man kept apologising and continually stated that he was having money difficulties. He ended up filing for a divorce and the cheating spouse had not been entitled to anything. Period. As it turned out, the younger guy then ditched her for someone else soon after. It served her right — a double whammy. Karma. The cheque was for a little more than the quoted sum and he wrote at the bottom of his letter that it was interest. Although not an awful lot, it would keep Randolph ticking over for a short while.

Randolph smiled to himself. He placed the cheque, empty envelope and letter to one side on the green leather-topped desk. He would pay the cheque in first thing tomorrow morning; the sooner the better. He then picked up the newspaper from his desk, immediately turning to the back page and the sports section.

"Yeah, right," Randolph said sarcastically. He was reading an interview with the Sheffield Wednesday manager, Alan Brown. Brown was claiming how he rated his team's chances against Everton on the coming Saturday, in the FA Cup Final. "No chance!" The paper also stated how there would be a full preview on the eve of the

Final in tomorrow's paper. "Can't wait," Randolph said aloud sarcastically. He wasn't exactly interested, being an Arsenal fan.

After scanning through the rest of the newspaper, Randolph stretched up to the ceiling and yawned, feeling even more tired. The reading made his eyes heavy. He looked over to the small blue sofa bed in one corner of his office. Unlacing his black shoes and leaving them under the desk, he got up and made his way over to the sofa bed, where he would rest for the night as he often did. He lay down fully clothed and he fell asleep instantly.

 # Chapter Two
Friday, May 13th, 1966

Hopkins Street, London – 9.04 am

Randolph woke to an annoying ringing sound. His mouth was dry and his neck throbbed. Last night's whiskies had taken their toll. In his younger days, he had never suffered from hangovers at all. As he got older, even just having a few now made him feel crappy, when he woke up. Not that it was exactly a full-blown hangover. He often thought how it should be the opposite; your body should get used to the booze.

He checked the time from his wristwatch, an old Onsa. It was the longest he had slept for a while. The alcohol had probably helped, even if it came at the cost of him feeling a little worse for wear for a good couple of hours. He'd be fine. "Ugh …" Randolph uttered, holding his neck that hurt from the way he had slept. He made his way to his desk and picked up the telephone. "Hello?" He then sighed, grimacing. "Oh. Mrs Tennyson!" Randolph rolled his eyes. His neck hurt further and now his forehead. "Yes … I know how you are feeling. I would be the same, too if it was *my* dog that had gone missing … Yes, I know … I am still working on it … I know you paid me for my services … Yes, I know Peanut is a sweet dog …"

The phone call lasted for almost ten minutes. Mrs Tennyson kept repeating herself, much to Randolph's annoyance. She was a little frantic and irritable. But to be fair to the widowed woman, she didn't really have much else after her husband had died six years ago. Peanut was all she had left; they had never had the good fortune to have children.

Randolph had insisted several times that he had a couple of leads.

He remembered the joke that Max had made the previous night and smiled to himself. He had a couple of places and people that he needed to check some more.

One was an Asian man Randolph had dug up some information on; he lived and hung about in the West End area and was known to have allegedly stolen dogs or picked up strays and then sold them to Chinese restaurants for food. These might just be vicious rumours. There was no recorded proof per se. Regardless, it was worth checking out, although even if the Asian had taken Peanut, he wasn't likely to admit it.

Another potential lead had arisen a couple of days back from some gypsies who had parked up at Hyde Park. They were rumoured to have stolen people's dogs in the West End area. Randolph had checked the area yesterday morning and again in the afternoon. No one was home. He had also done the same regarding the Asian; he wasn't home either. Randolph would try again later today, once he had paid his cheque in.

Randolph took out a tin of St Joseph aspirin from one of the draws of his desk, swallowed two without the need of water. He picked up a small bottle that sat next to his Devil's Ivy pot, and sprayed it with some much-needed water. He couldn't remember the last time that he had watered it. It must have been over a week ago.

Once he was done, he scooped up the cheque and made his way to the office door. He retrieved the still damp trench coat and fedora from the coat stand and put them on. The dampness didn't bother him. The smell of the bar smoke still clung to his clothing, and emanated from his hair, when he ruffled it while putting his hat on.

He left the beige blind pulled down on the door. Although it seemed pointless having one, with a frosted glass door, it gave him a sense of a little more privacy. He took a cigarette from the damp packet and lit it with a silver Zippo. He locked the office door and made his way down the dark corridor to leave the building.

*

"Get yer papers, get yer papers!"
From the bank in Soho Square, Randolph walked towards the

newsstand where he heard a familiar Cockney voice. "You're back, then?" Randolph smiled. "How are you feeling?"

"Indeed, I am!" the elderly man greeted Randolph with a smile, holding an almost burnt-out cigar between his teeth, where he was missing a couple; one at the top, one at the bottom. He was holding today's edition of the *Evening Standard* high up in his right hand.

It was old Tom Galton. He had run his own newsstand for years. Randolph had known him for around nine of them since the relocation. Tom used to own a stand at the East End of London, but the crime rate that side of the capital had spiked at the time. He preferred it here now, on the other side.

Like Randolph, Tom had fought courageously in World War II, deservedly earning the George Cross. He narrowly missed out on the First World War and married at an early age. His wife, Lesley, had convinced him not to sign up; although he met her wishes, he did so with reluctance and felt guilty. He became a father for the first time, at the end of the Great War. As well as a fondness towards each other, there was also mutual respect between the two, not to mention some banter between the fellow ex-soldiers.

Tom had been off work for weeks following acute appendicitis and surgery. One of his grandsons had taken over the stand until he returned.

"The surgery all went good? Your grandson said you were recovering well."

Tom removed the almost finished cigar from his mouth. The end was chewed, dark and wet. "Yep! I'm still a little stiff and sore — the pain was really bad. I guess I'm used to it, after being shot during The War. *Another* scar to add!" Tom laughed. "The doctor insisted I wait another week or so, but I got bored just sitting around for days at a time. There are only so many light walks you can do. Plus, the wife was doing me bleedin' 'ead in!" Tom laughed further. "I suppose the breakfast in bed was nice — being waited on hand and foot and getting me pillow plumped up for me," Tom joked.

"I'm surprised she didn't smother you with it, putting up with you for weeks on end."

"Ha! Whatever you say, you private *dick*!"

Randolph grinned. He looked around the newsstand.

Copies of numerous newspapers were neatly stacked. There was a separate section for magazines that covered movies, music and sport. One had The Beatles on the front cover.

Randolph noticed the latest copy of *Speedway Star*, with Olle Nygren on the front cover on his motorcycle. A group of comics hung above the main stand at a slight angle via a wooden peg and line. Randolph was sometimes partial to a comic, despite his age. Especially *The Beano*. He considered buying one but decided against it for now. "I'll take the usual."

"You can have this one," Tom replied, offering the *Evening Standard* that he had held aloft. He then took a deep drag from his cigar, making himself splutter. "Me lungs aren't what they used to be!"

"Yeah. I really need to cut back." Randolph handed over 4d in four single pennies.

Tom dropped the coins into his worn, denim money apron — his grandson had also used it in his absence. "Thank you kindly, my dear Sir," Tom joked, but still genuinely grateful. He dropped the cigar butt to the ground and stamped it out, squashing it with his old heavy boot.

"No worries," Randolph replied, folding the newspaper in half. He had already noticed the main headline of the paper, printed in large black letters:

ANOTHER BODY FOUND!!

"I see there's been another body ..." Tom said seriously, his face matching his tone.

"I saw that just now. I'll read it properly when I get home."

"It's the second one in a month." Tom shook his head. "Poor bastard had their heart cut out — throat slashed ... just like the other victim. He was also nailed to a wall. Like he was crucified. Seems like the same thing; a ritualistic murder. Looks like it's a serial killer."

"It has to be three ..."

"Three?" Tom frowned.

"It's only really classed as a serial killer, when it becomes three or more victims."

"Ah, I see. I guess you'd know!"

Randolph gave a slight understanding smile. He then looked above him at the grey skies. "I ought to get home. It looks like rain again."

"Yep. It sure does. At least I've got a bit of cover under here."

*

Randolph missed the rain this time. He got back to his flat on Shaftesbury Avenue just as it began to tip it down again.

He climbed the old wooden stairway that always creaked. His flat overlooked the Shaftesbury Theatre. A recent playbill had been added, advertising *Big Bad Mouse*, although it was still months away in October. A large black mouse stood upright on a red background. It was holding a pitchfork in its right hand. The name of the play was emblazoned in white on the body of the mouse.

Randolph often gazed out of his flat window, watching the hustle and bustle of people walking and driving past, including some with their skinhead fashion and others with their mod subculture whizzing past on scooters. He almost felt envious of late, seeing other folk go about their business and to work, while he sat twiddling his thumbs due to the lack of work coming his way. He'd look out from his flat on a Friday or Saturday night, usually smoking a cigarette — unless he was out there himself, watching some of the scantily dressed women with their miniskirts and boots. The sexual frustration added to his depression.

Blue wallpaper with yellow flower heads covered his living room walls. It had been there when Randolph moved in fourteen months ago. He never took to it but couldn't find the energy nor be bothered to change it. It had already begun to tear in places, revealing the dented, blackened walls underneath. The wallpaper seemed to have deteriorated further in the past few months. The damp air and moisture in the winter had played its part. It had always seemed cold in the flat even during the summer months, and now despite the heating being on.

The light grey carpet that was turning up at the sides of the skirting boards, was darkened in patches, from numerous spillages by the previous occupant. The ceiling was white but with yellow stains, no doubt due to smoking, both by Randolph and the previous occupant. Small pieces of furniture were situated around the main living area of the flat, including a small bookcase with a cupboard and a table with the telephone. A television on legs sat in one of the far corners. Randolph had to repeatedly thump down onto the top of it, to make it work and show the picture. Fucking thing! He really needed a new one. But again, he had no real desire to pay for one, nor spend what money he did have.

The worn, dark green sofa and two armchairs, were also not free from previous spillages from the past owner. It was of no surprise, that they had left them behind. One of the chairs had a rather large tear down the side of it, like someone had slashed it with a sharp knife. Randolph had hoped there might be a stash of money slipped down there. No such luck! Obviously.

Randolph untied his shoes and kicked them off. He took off his hat and coat and slung them on the sofa, before making his way to the small bathroom to take a long, hot soak. He took the newspaper with him.

The cold tap continued to drip like it always did — constantly. It splashed onto the bathwater. Randolph had considered fixing it himself as he had time on his hands but he couldn't be fussed with it. Nor could he be bothered to get the landlord to call out a plumber to fix it. One of the taps in the kitchen was the same. Randolph shed his clothes into a heap on the black and white chequered bathroom tiles.

He lay soaking in the bath, with steamy mist around him. He was reading about the latest murder. It hadn't mentioned the victim's name, only the sex. The body was yet to be identified. The front page had a black and white photograph of the body covered up by a black plastic sheet.

According to the report, the corpse was found in a dead-end alleyway off Upper St Martin's Lane. Randolph shuddered; that wasn't too far from his flat. The man, believed to have been in his twenties, was stripped completely naked. The heart had been removed from his body. There was no trace of it — and his throat had been slit. His body was discovered early the previous morning by two schoolchildren. Poor kids!

The dead body was nailed upside down by the feet and wrists onto a wall, with one foot placed on top of the other, and his arms outstretched. The killer had avoided puncturing any major arteries. Randolph suspected this was deliberate and that the throat had been slit first, whilst the man was still alive, and the heart removed afterwards. But how did the killer manage to overcome the man and nail him up like that? Surely the victim must have struggled and fought. An inverted pentagram had been drawn perfectly on the stone ground in red chalk in front of the nailed-up body. Numerous black candles had been placed on each of the points, burning a mysterious green and orange. The victim's clothes had been neatly folded and placed in a heap on the ground nearby.

The first victim — a woman, was found a few weeks earlier. She had died in a similar fashion. Sheila Davies was twenty-four, Randolph recalled. Her naked body was found at the back of the All Saints Church on Margaret Street, on the ground near to some piled up empty boxes and rubbish. Again, there was another red chalk inverted pentagram drawn to perfection. Only this time, the body was laid upside down, legs and arms positioned and spread over the symbol at each point. Her head was placed at the bottom point; her heart removed — throat slit. Black candles were placed at the end of her hands and feet as well as her head. Again, still lit and burning green and orange, at the time the body was found. A pile of her clothes lay folded close to her naked body.

The report itself, as well as the police, had insisted for people to remain calm. With this being the second murder, people would no doubt start to panic. The police apparently had no leads. No evidence was found at the scene of either crime. No knife, no fingerprints — nothing. There also didn't appear to have been a connection between the two victims, other than the same modus operandi. There were even unconfirmed reports of London proposing to have a curfew at night.

There were a few more photos of the crime scene, showing the inverted pentagram and candles, but no photos of the bodies themselves. Just like last time, the press and police obviously believed that it would be too distressing and even disrespectful, particularly to any next of kin, to show them — too graphic.

Randolph felt saddened for the victims and any potential family members. Reading about the murder wasn't helping his depressed state. He scanned through the rest of the paper and moved on to a slightly lighter read. He half-smiled to himself, while reading the small comic strip of *Billy the Bee*.

*

Randolph parked his light blue Hillman Imp near Hyde Park. He lit one of his Winston Lights. It was after two in the afternoon. It had kept trying to rain again. Randolph didn't fancy walking, nor did he trust the weather. He had ditched his long trench coat for a lighter jacket, sufficient to keep him dry, if it started raining. He wore a newly purchased, wool black trilby. It felt soft and snug on his head and kept his combed black hair tidy. He noticed of late, several more greying hairs coming through, both on his head and on his face. He wondered if it was down to his age or to stress. Perhaps both. The thought of getting older had also fuelled his depressive slump, although at forty-eight, he still looked good for his age.

He approached the same area as yesterday, where there were two large trailers and a smaller caravan. It appeared that some of the gypsies must have been home, because a couple of kids aged between ten or eleven were kicking an old flat football about. A couple of lurchers sat nearby, watching the boys and the football from under a large tree. Randolph took a final two sharp drags from his cigarette and flicked it on to the grass.

The two boys stopped and stared at Randolph as he made his way to one of the trailers. The bottom half of it was a green colour, the top half, a dirty looking white. One of the windows to the left of the half-opened dented door was also open.

A couple of female voices speaking in a foreign tongue came from inside. The two boys whispered something to each other, before going back to their kickabout. One of the lurchers joined in, running after the ball and trying to bite it. Randolph gave a couple of firm knocks on the door of the trailer. The conversation between the two women tailed off and one of them came to the half-opened door.

"Yes? Can I help you?" The woman sounded a little abrupt in her thick accent. Randolph was guessing it was Romanian or possibly Italian.

She must have been in her late thirties. With her dark skin, blue eyes, mascara and eyeliner, the first thing Randolph immediately noticed, was how attractive she was. Large golden loops hung from her ears. The top of her earrings were covered by a silk and paisley head scarf that hid most of her thick dark hair. Her forehead had some kind of sparkly jewel on it and there was a smaller one on the left side of her nose. Randolph could smell her perfume; it was almost seductive.

"Good afternoon, Madam. I was hoping to ask you some questions, if I may, please? If you have the time? It won't take long ..."

The attractive lady frowned and stared mesmerisingly at Randolph. "I have a few minutes. What is it about? What do you want?"

Randolph felt stupid, asking about someone's dog, like it was important business. But to Mrs Tennyson, of course, it was. "I am just investigating the disappearance of a small dog ..." Randolph handed over his private investigator ID card. It had a black and white photo of him, along with his name, office address and phone number.

"What, no *badge*?" the woman mocked in her heavy accent, giving a wry smile, taking the ID card. She looked at it with disinterest, before handing it back.

"No, Doamnă ..." Randolph returned the wry smile with one of his own, taking back his ID. He noticed her fingers and the long nails of the woman, which were varnished in a deep purple colour. There were a couple of rings but no wedding ring. He thought he'd try to lighten the situation a little. He went with his hunch that this woman was Romanian. "I don't require one."

"Ah ... So, you speak Romanian, do you, Mr Randolph?" She gave a seductive look this time, folding her arms across her curvy chest. She was wearing a loose-fitting turquoise blouse. Around her neck she wore a glittering necklace that had a silver cross hanging from it. What looked like moons and stars in gold and silver were also attached to the silver chain.

"Just a few words," Randolph replied, averting his eyes from her necklace and cleavage.

The woman gave another wry smile. "And what makes you think that I have *seen* this dog?"

Randolph felt a little awkward. "I erm —"

"Let me guess … someone had told you us *gypsies*, like to steal people's dogs … am I right?"

Randolph raised his eyebrows. "Well, do you?" he said with a hint of sarcastic cheekiness.

"Why, of *course* … we've got our trailers *full* of them! Those two over there, are just a couple of them …"

Randolph could tell that the woman was being sarcastic. He didn't feel the need to check. He had no real authority anyway. "I am sorry … It is my job to check these things. Here …" Randolph took out a coloured Polaroid of Peanut from his trouser pocket and handed it over.

"Sweet doggy," said the woman, taking note of the photograph. "I am afraid, that I haven't seen him. I doubt the others here would have done, neither. The small group of us here, have a few dogs, two of which you can see over there. We do sometimes spot 'strays' – is that the word? – walking about. But not one like this." The gypsy woman handed back the small Polaroid. "I can check with them, once they get back."

"That is the correct word, yes." Randolph smiled. "Please, take this. If you do happen to see him in the park, don't hesitate to contact me."

The woman took one of Randolph's stained white, business cards. "I shall do. I don't have a phone here, but I can find one." Her mood seemed to be a little more friendly.

"I appreciate it, Mrs …?"

"Albescu. *Miss* Albescu," she simpered.

"Have a good afternoon!" Randolph smiled and gave a tip of his trilby.

Miss Albescu said goodbye and called the two young boys over, presumably her sons, and they jogged towards the trailer leaving the ball behind. The two lurchers first hesitated and then trotted in tow.

Walking away, Randolph could hear the woman speak further and shout the word *"Mamă."*

While making his way back to his car, Randolph lit another of his cigarettes. He wondered if this gypsy woman was a fortune teller because of the way that she dressed and how she looked, but it was hard to know, as many gypsy ladies wore clothes like that. If only she could use her so-called powers to find Peanut! Randolph never believed in such things, however.

He was curious as to how many of the gypsies there were. It couldn't have been many, seeing there were only the two trailers and a caravan. Did they have permission to stay in Hyde Park? Were they in the country legally? He started pondering on these questions, but they were of no concern to him and he didn't care.

*

Randolph watched when an attractive woman in a pair of cat-eye sunglasses walked past him with her dog; he was sat in his car, parked not too far from the Chinatown Gate. He needed to question the Asian guy, who lived in a tower block of flats on Wardour Street.

Randolph checked his face in the rear-view mirror, which had a couple of large smeary thumbprints on either side. His brown eyes stared back at him. He had well over two weeks' worth of facial hair; it brought out more of the grey. He had forgotten the last time that he had shaved. He hadn't even thought about it. Underneath his eyes were dark circles. He took a huge yawn, before getting out of his car.

He looked up at the tower block and stood in the dark shadow that was cast from it. It was now almost a clear day. He left his jacket in the car. He waited for a couple of cars and a bus to pass, then made his way across the street to the tower block. Cheng-Lei Wu, lived on the eighth floor.

Cheng-Lei Wu was a Chinese immigrant who had come over not long after World War II with his parents and was known for a few dodgy dealings. He had a criminal record from selling stolen goods, counterfeit watches and things like that, only petty crimes and he had never served time. He was thirty-eight years old.

Where the rumours of his selling animals to Chinese restaurants came from, Randolph didn't know. He was told about it via a couple of men who co-owned a pet shop on Greek Street, where he had questioned them for both the Zippy and Peanut cases. The pet shop was also known to take in strays and find them homes. The two men had not said they believed the stories about Cheng-Lei, only that they had heard them on the grapevine.

Making his way down the corridor, Randolph could smell sausages cooking from inside one of the flats. The red and black, zigzag patterned carpet looked old. Randolph noticed a stain that looked fresh. It was black and felt sticky when he walked over it. It hadn't been there when he visited yesterday.

Cheng-Lei's flat was just a little further than halfway on the right. Randolph knocked on the door firmly. An elderly man and woman walked out from next door. They said "afternoon" to him and walked on past. Randolph acknowledged them with a nod of his head and a brief smile.

Waiting for an answer, he knocked again, a little more forcibly and gave an extra knock to boot; still no response. Randolph considered knocking a third time but assumed that Cheng-Lei wasn't home and decided to leave. As he turned, at the end of the corridor, he noticed a man approaching wearing a black trilby hat like his own. The man frowned at Randolph when he got closer. He was wearing a caramel coloured, ribbed top, with dark brown stripes across it, over black jeans and boots. By his ethnicity, Randolph guessed that this was Cheng-Lei.

"Afternoon?" the man posed, more as a question than a greeting. The accent was Chinese, with a touch of English. On his face was a Van Dyke styled beard. He stopped a few feet away from his flat and Randolph.

Randolph cleared his throat. "Cheng-Lei?"

"Who's asking?"

"My name is Randolph Landon. I'm a PI."

"Good for you! What do you want?"

Miss Albescu's lack of welcome was nothing compared to Cheng-Lei's; Randolph already felt that he wouldn't get much information out of him, if anything at all.

Randolph sighed, feeling awkward. "I'm looking for a lost dog. He goes by the name of Peanut ..."

Cheng-Lei laughed. "What sort of name is that?"

Randolph raised his brow and laughed in response. "Yeah, I know!"

"So, you aren't a *rozzer*, then?"

"Nope! Preferred doing my own thing."

"Good," Cheng-Lei replied. He seemed more than a little relieved.

Randolph knew that Cheng-Lei was most likely on the fiddle and guilty of something. He doubted that his having a criminal record would stop him.

"You think that I have this dog?"

"I'm just doing some checking about and asking people."

"And it just so happens that you are asking me. And you know where I live?"

"Look, it's my job to look at possible leads. Even if I don't believe certain stories, I still have to look into things."

"So why me?" Cheng-Lei rubbed his beard.

Randolph didn't beat around the bush. He decided to be up front with the guy. "I was told that you capture dogs and sell them to Chinese food outlets."

Cheng-Lei couldn't help but laugh. "I knew it! I know I have a history — I won't deny that. I'm sure you are aware of my record. But I would *never* do that to animals! No matter how much money I was offered ... It isn't like I would admit it, anyway." He laughed again.

"This is true."

"Besides, I would never touch a dog by that name: I'm allergic to peanuts!"

Randolph smiled somewhat awkwardly. He knew Cheng-Lei was telling the truth. He had an investigator's hunch.

"You are most welcome to look around my flat? Just in case I have him."

"No, it's fine. I apologise. It's like I said. I have to follow up on these things. Even if a lot of the time the accusations are false."

Randolph moved out the way as Cheng-Lei walked past him and opened up his flat.

"You can still check if you want?" Cheng-Lei stood in the doorway, gesturing.

"Nah, you're fine."

"Suit yourself … You want to know how those rumours started?"

"Sure, why not." Randolph removed his hat, scratched his head, then replaced the trilby.

"A few years ago, I stole from someone. They owed me money for a job I did for them."

"What job?"

"It doesn't matter. Let's just say that I would have gotten into trouble for it! Anyway, I waited for weeks to be paid. I was more than patient with him. So, I took matters into my own hands, and took some items from him that were equal to the cost of what he owed me."

"Yeah, I know how you feel. I didn't resort to anything like that, but I have had clients who have taken weeks to pay me."

"Yep. Total bastards, I tell you! Naturally, they were pissed off with me, so they started to spread the rumour around about me stealing folks' animals and selling them on to the Chinese food outlets … that I was unofficially working for them." Cheng-Lei shook his head, grinning.

"What happened after that?"

"Nothing, really. But the rumours are still floating about to this day. Not that it affects me. The guy in question never tried to retrieve his items from me. He let it be. He started the rumours, then buggered off up north or somewhere. Stupid, fat bastard!" Cheng-Lei chuckled. "Guess you have to give it to him."

"I guess."

"The rumours even changed a little at times. A bit like Chinese whispers! Get it?" Cheng-Lei beamed.

"I get it." Randolph held back a grin of his own.

"Some people believed that I was even skinning and eating the animals alive. Thankfully, I'm thick-skinned. *Yellow*-skinned!" Cheng-Lei laughed at himself.

"Here …" Randolph took out the photo of Peanut and showed Cheng-Lei, anyway. "In case you have seen him about. Or do. Take one of my cards, as well …"

"Nah, I haven't seen him. I've seen a few walking the streets. But no dog that breed. Where did he disappear from?"

"Shelton Street … he belongs to some old woman. He's been missing almost two weeks now."

"I know it … It's not nice. I am sure she is missing him. Hopefully he'll turn up or you find him."

Randolph seemed a little taken back by Cheng-Lei's genuine empathy. Perhaps he wasn't *too* bad a person, despite his background.

"Anyway, I'm going to cook myself something to eat. That smell of those sausages down the corridor is making me hungry!"

"I hear you. Thanks for your time. And if you come across this dog or something, you've got my card. My office address is on there as you can see, along with my work number and my home one." Randolph didn't always spend a lot of time at his office, certainly not of late, so he had made sure that his home number was also on the card, although not his address, for obvious reasons.

There were times, when people would ask for help in letters pushed underneath his office door, particularly if they hadn't been able to reach him by phone. He'd heard about answering machines coming out in the UK soon, but they would no doubt cost a fortune for him.

"I will do," Cheng-Lei said.

"Keep out of trouble," Randolph joked.

"I always do!" Cheng-Lei winked and shut the door to his flat.

Randolph made his way back up the corridor. The smell of sausages was now making him hungry; he could smell the onions cooking too now.

*

After another dull and uninteresting day in his life as a private eye, Randolph had gone back to Teresa's for just a couple of whiskies, around an hour or so before they closed. Max had finished earlier that evening; one of his employees had taken over from him.

Randolph sat quietly at the bar in his usual seat. He didn't speak — only when he ordered his drinks. He really needed to sort his life out. Spending money at the bar wasn't doing him any favours. Nor was it doing his liver any good for that matter.

He was disappointed that nothing had come up about Peanut, his only current and ongoing case. He kept thinking how pathetic it all was, as well as himself. He hadn't expected to find the dog at the gypsy site or at Cheng-Lei's. Even if he had, it wouldn't have made him feel any better about things, although he would have been pleased for Mrs Tennyson. His motivation wasn't just the extra money that he would receive from the woman: he sincerely wanted to find the dog for her. He knew how much the little thing meant to her, and what it was like to lose someone or something you love. Like with all his cases, he would do his best. Even more so, when someone had entrusted him with his services. He hated the idea of failing, but this Peanut case was one he might just have to admit defeat in.

Chapter Three
Saturday, May 14ᵗʰ, 1966

Hopkins Street, London – 9.01 am

The next morning, having slept in his office, Randolph took out one of his cigarettes. Smoking was something else that he wished to cut out; he lay on his sofa bed, with his head resting on one of the arms. A clear glass ashtray rested on his stomach. He stared up at the dirty ceiling, blowing out a few smoke rings that faded as they dispersed in the air. "Christ, I'm bored," he said quietly. He laid there a while longer, even after he had finished his cigarette. The butt was squashed as much as it could be into the base of the ashtray, along with several pieces of ash and some chewing gum that had been there a few days.

He eventually got up and watered his plant. He had no idea what his plans for the day were going to be. Pretty much the same shit as always, he expected. He was completely at a loss how to find little Peanut. It was like finding a needle in a haystack. He could be anywhere by now. Particularly in a city the size of London. That's if Peanut was even still alive. It felt like it was becoming an obsession because he hated the thought of letting people down. He never failed with a case. Even when searching for a missing person who he didn't find per se, he usually discovered their whereabouts, whether miles away from the city, or even in another country for that matter.

He knew that Mrs Tennyson was getting desperate and at her wits' end. He'd have to try harder somehow. He had no other case or work to focus on. This was it. Finding someone's pet was much more difficult than finding a missing person.

In his office, he had a small table where he made coffee. An old brass tap was nearby. When turned on, it noisily shook and vibrated the water pipes within the old walls. Randolph made himself a large mug of piping hot coffee, using an old stainless-steel kettle that was full of limescale. His jar of Maxwell House was almost empty but he needed the caffeine. He added a couple more spoonfuls of sugar to his mug than usual and stirred it. He was already out of biscuits.

He took his time with the coffee and was careful not to burn his mouth. Randolph stood near the window and stared aimlessly, watching the world go by — it was an overcast morning. He looked at his watch; it had gone half past nine. He saw a red, Routemaster double-decker bus drive past. It had a jean advertisement on it. The bus was pretty much empty.

Finishing his coffee, he went back to the table and placed the empty mug back down. He'd usually take any dirty mugs and cups back to his flat to wash-up, as there was no sink in his office and he needed them sometimes for clients, when they came in.

He'd once had to scrub a woman's lipstick off one of his mugs; she'd been an attractive woman in her early fifties who wanted to know if her husband was having an affair with his boss. As it turned out, he wasn't. Instead, he had been seeing an estate agent about buying a new home for him and his suspicious wife. It was meant to have been a surprise and he had explained all, after she had confronted him with Randolph's evidence.

After his coffee, Randolph was so bored, he decided to give his office a clean, using an ostrich feather duster. He racked his brains to solve the case of the missing Peanut. He had already interviewed the neighbours, like Mrs Tennyson had done. He wasn't sure who else to ask, now that he had interviewed the gypsy woman and Asian guy; he had no clues.

He removed a huge cobweb from a corner of the room and then dusted off his filing cabinet, when his phone rang.

"Randolph Landon, PI?" he answered trying to sound upbeat.

"Dad!"

"Matthew?"

"How are you, Dad? I tried phoning your flat, but there was no answer. I thought you might be at your office."

Matthew 'Matty' Landon was eight years old. Randolph absolutely adored his son. It killed him, not being able to see him regularly. He hadn't seen him since the start of April, when he had gone up to Lincolnshire for a long weekend to spend some time with him. It had been a week since they last spoke on the phone.

Randolph was still on good terms his wife, Thelma. He was also still very much in love with her. Randolph knew that love was never an issue for either of them. Although separated, they had never filed for a divorce. They both still thought that they could work things out but being so far apart, it was always going to be difficult.

Thelma had taken Matthew up to Lincolnshire sixteen months ago to stay with her parents. She and Randolph had decided to separate after Christmas, after New Year. They wanted to spend Christmas together as a family, for Matthew's sake.

They used to rent a three-bedroom house in South London but it was too expensive for Randolph on his income alone, so he had moved out two months after they split up. He wanted to be closer to central London and thought he would get more business there, especially as PIs were a rarity in the area. Flats were cheap there too.

Randolph's job had put a strain on their marriage, back when business was good. It came at a price. In hindsight, it seemed ironic now that he had so little work. He wished he had been less busy back then. Lack of financial income would have been an issue, but he could have jacked the PI malarkey in and found something else. Things may have worked out fine. He had resented the fact that Thelma had taken their son up north, and still held a grudge at times. She kept on insisting that she still needed time. Eventually, they had stopped discussing getting back together.

The 'trial' separation was only supposed to last a few weeks, or so they had hoped, so Randolph hadn't kicked up too much of a fuss at the time, when she took Matthew to her parents. But Thelma's father had fallen ill, and she had found employment locally there through an old school friend. She was now working in a sewing factory and was a very skilled seamstress.

Randolph wasn't happy about Matthew changing his school and Matthew hadn't been too pleased either at first, leaving all his friends behind. He had moved to a new school not far from Thelma's parents in the new term.

Randolph had been considering quitting his job as a private investigator and finding a place closer to his son and wife, particularly of late, with no real work coming his way. Thelma perhaps, wouldn't be too keen on that though.

"I'm good, Matty! What are you up to this weekend, buddy?" Speaking to his son, immediately lightened Randolph's mood; he smiled over the phone. It was fantastic hearing the sound of his voice again.

"Me and Mum are going to the cinema in a little while. We're going to watch *The Ghost and Mr Chicken*! We've heard it's really funny ... I wish you could come with us ..." Matthew sounded excited at first, but then sad. "We're going to watch the FA Cup Final as well later, with Nanny and Grandad."

"I know, mate. I wish I could come as well." Randolph's smile soon went from his face. He felt saddened. Although he had seen his son numerous times since the turn of the year, he was still missing out on doing things with him. He was only playing a bit part in his eyes. It was horrible. He still wanted Thelma back as well. To be a family again.

"Are, are you and Mum going to get back together, Dad?" It was not the first time Matthew had asked that question. It wouldn't be the last time either.

Randolph had lost count of how many times Matthew had asked. "I honestly don't know, Matty. I certainly hope that we can sort something out. But we will catch up soon and do something. I'm due to see you in a couple of weeks, and your mum. We can definitely do something together as a family ... I can get us tickets for Arsenal again ... that obviously won't be until the new season now, though."

The last time Matthew came back down to London had been in March. Randolph had taken him to Highbury to watch Arsenal play Tottenham. It had finished in a one all draw in the North London Derby.

"Yay! Up The Arsenal!"

Randolph came over all emotional, listening to his son cheer and sounding happy. He had to clear his throat before he could speak again. "H-hopefully, we can win next time we go!" He wiped a couple of tears from his eyes.

"I can't wait! I really miss you, Dad …"

"I miss you too, Matthew."

Father and son chatted for a few more minutes before Matthew had to get ready for the cinema.

"I love you, Son."

"I love you too, Dad."

They both said their goodbyes and hung up.

Randolph picked up a small-framed photo from the corner of his desk and stared at it for a while. It was taken in the summer of 1964, in the back garden of their house. Matthew was smiling broadly, wearing an Arsenal colour red T-shirt, with his foot resting on a football. "I miss you, Matthew." Randolph sniffed, placing the frame back in its place.

*

Randolph had searched the streets that Saturday morning. He showed the small photograph of Peanut to more people than he could remember. Not one person claimed to have seen him. He had even showed the photo to a few people who he had already asked before — they still hadn't seen him. He particularly asked around at Soho Market, where there were crowds of people and he thought he might have better luck. He hadn't. It was pretty much pointless. Even if someone *had* seen the lost dog, it wasn't likely that Peanut would stay where he was last seen. Not unless someone specific had him.

Randolph overheard a few people talking about the latest murders whilst walking past them. One was paranoid that they might be the next to be murdered.

Randolph took a nap early that afternoon and then watched the FA Cup Final on and off; he had to bang the top of his television numerous times to sort out the picture.

*

That evening, Teresa's was packed to the rafters, although it was still early. That could only mean one thing as well; more smoke.

A few of the punters were Evertonians — they were more than buoyant. They were celebrating their team's 3-2 victory over

Sheffield Wednesday in the Cup Final, cheering, singing, shouting. Plenty of spillage of booze. It was all good-natured.

Randolph had gone outside the front into the street to get some fresh air and to smoke a cigarette on the pavement. He wasn't the only one.

"EV-ER-TON!" A drunken fan came stumbling out of the bar.

Randolph looked across and smiled to himself.

"Fucking hell, it's hot in there!" the Everton fan said to whoever heard him. His face was flushed and he was sweating heavily. He wore a blue and white rosette on his white T-shirt that had several stains of beer on it. His slight beer belly protruded.

More cheers and shouts came from inside.

The Evertonian made eye contact with Randolph. "All right, mate? You watch the game?" His Scouse accent slurred from the consumed alcohol.

"I'm fine. Is hot in there … smoky as hell, too. And yes, I watched most of the game."

The Everton fan had a cigarette tucked behind his left ear. He searched his pockets for a light. "Shit … left me lighter inside."

"Here …" Randolph offered his Zippo.

"Ta, mate!" The fan took the lighter from Randolph, lit his cigarette and handed it back. "You like footy, then?" The fan took in a huge drag, looked to the evening sky and exhaled.

"I sure do."

"Who's your team?"

"Arsenal."

"Ah, right … When was the last time you won anything, eh?" the Everton man teased. It was asked in a light-hearted manner, but he had a smirk on his reddened face.

"A while back. 1953."

"I remember now … won the League, didn't you?"

Randolph nodded, dropping the butt of his cigarette to the pavement and squished it with his right foot, next to a couple of old dried pieces of chewing gum.

Randolph wasn't really in the mood for chatting. He just nodded and answered when needed when the Everton fan chatted about nothing in particular in his drunken state. Randolph didn't wish to be rude.

Once he had finished his cigarette, the fan told Randolph he would catch him later and he went back inside and shouted, "Come on The Toffees!"

*

By 9 pm, the bar was even more rammed. Randolph hadn't recalled it being quite as busy as this for a while. The smoky atmosphere was almost unbearable, even with all the windows fully open.

Randolph, drunk, was standing in the pool room watching a couple of guys play their third game. It was too crowded in the main area or where he usually sat at the bar. People had been pushing up against him trying to get served. Despite the alcohol, he still didn't like being in confined places. In here, it was less packed.

The green felt of the pool table had faded down the years. It had its fair share of stains and patches from spilt drinks. It was the same table as when the bar had still been Ray's; Max had decided to keep it as it was still in fairly good nick.

Randolph was considering making a move soon. It was getting too much for him. The smoke, the noise. His head was starting to hurt and he felt dizzy. He had had a good few drinks and considered making his current one his last for the night.

"Any leads on those murders, then?" asked one of the men, stretching his body out onto the pool table to take a shot … "Shit," he added. The red ball ricocheted missing the pocket.

A man in his late fifties, who was seated behind him holding a pint of beer, replied, "You already asked me that a couple of hours ago!"

"I know … but you hadn't had much to drink at the time!" The man playing pool grinned and looked at the seated man whilst chalking his cue. He blew some of the blue dust from it. "Care to divulge?"

Some of the other folk in the room smiled and looked towards the seated man.

Randolph didn't want to appear too obvious but he too, looked and listened.

The seated man in his green and white short-sleeved shirt, shook his head and drank some of his pint. "You know I can't discuss anything with you lot … you're wasting your time. You won't get anything from me no matter how much I drink! The only thing you'll get to know about, is what you read in the press."

"Spoilsport," said the other pool player, potting a ball off the far cushion.

"Jammy bastard," said the other, causing his friend to smile, before he sunk another. "You have any clues to go on? The reports said that there wasn't anything found. Apart from the two bodies, candles and a symbol, whatever it was."

"Do you think there'll be another murder? It has to be the same killer, surely?" Having missed his next shot, the pool player walked to a table and gulped at the dregs of his pint.

"You don't give up, do you?" The seated man sounded a little annoyed, but he couldn't resist a slight smirk. He didn't blame the others for asking questions and being curious; it was a worrying time. It wasn't just the fact that there had been two murders inside a month, but the manner of the victims' deaths.

"Well?" This time another seated man spoke. He was in his sixties it seemed, with balding grey hair and a heavy salt and pepper beard to boot. He was puffing away on a pipe.

Randolph assumed the man they were questioning was a detective or policeman. That much was obvious. He didn't recognise him from when he had been working with the police force in the past.

"You're wasting your breath." The detective/policeman necked back his pint until it had almost gone. "I'm off in a bit as well."

"Have you ever had to deal with anything like this before, though? The way in which they were murdered?" a different man in his twenties asked this time. He was stood next to his girlfriend holding a glass of Coke or at least Randolph assumed it was his girlfriend. They had been displaying numerous signs of affection toward each other — but had no wedding rings.

"I've seen some things in my time … but no, not quite like this."

"It's very disturbing. Gruesome. Those poor victims and families," the 'girlfriend' said.

"They don't know any different now. It's the relatives I feel sorry for. Having to carry this for the rest of their lives. All thanks to some *sick* bastard. I just hope you fucking catch him!" someone else said. "Has the latest victim been identified yet?"

"Not yet." The detective/policeman rose from his seat and finished the last of his pint. "I'm going to head off. Before the *wife* starts moaning!" he joked.

*

A few more drinks later, Randolph finally decided he had had enough. Unlike the Everton fans, who were still rampant; the booze fuelled their buoyancy further throughout the course of the night. It hadn't shown any signs of letting up. Some of the Everton fans had persuaded Max to have a 'lock-in' after the official closing time.

Before he left, Randolph briefly asked someone in the pool room who the seated man had been. They weren't completely sure, but stated he was leading the murder case.

Leaving Teresa's, Randolph walked down Carnaby Street. Saturday night was busy, like usual. The bright lights and lit streets were filled with people, couples, groups of friends, all on their way home, or eager to pop in somewhere for a quick drink before last orders sounded. It left Randolph feeling especially sad and alone. The alcohol wasn't helping, acting as a depressant; he was thinking about his wife and son. He had walked past a busy restaurant, where a couple and their young son, who was around Matthew's age, were sitting and laughing about something at a table near the window.

"Sorry!" a blonde-haired woman said, after she stumbled into Randolph in her red high heels, while walking with her friend.

"It's fine." A weary eyed Randolph smiled. He then looked back at the pair and checked them out in their tight jeans. They were giggling, no doubt about the stumble. He could still smell the scent of their perfumes.

The mild night had now turned cold. Randolph, in his short-sleeved blue and white shirt, felt his arms gooseflesh. He could smell the smoke from the bar on him again. Damn smoke. He felt hypocritical as he smoked there as well. They should all smoke outside really. He wondered if smoking would ever be banned in public places. Perhaps, one day it would.

He decided to take a slight short cut on his way back to his flat on Shaftesbury Avenue, via Greek Street. Well, it wasn't really a short cut at all, more a detour. He wasn't even sure why he took that route. It meant going underneath a small arched alleyway — about thirty yards long. His head began to hurt.

The large crowds on the streets had thinned out by now. Entering the dark archway, it seemed that he was the only one about. He needed to urinate but wanted to wait until he was out of sight before relieving himself.

Although the alleyway was fairly dark, it was lit by two old gaslights that were fixed to the old crumbling brick walls, spaced apart from each other. Randolph decided to take a leak under one of them. A few moths and midges were attracted to the lights. He unzipped his trousers, and pressed his left hand hard against the cold surface of the wall, while he urinated. He screwed his face up when it touched a spider's web.

His eyes felt tired and heavy. He was swaying a little, when the two gaslights seemed to shimmer and dim. He thought nothing of it and turned to progress to the end of the arched alleyway. He then came to a stop, just as he was about to walk out of the archway.

Standing there and swaying on the spot again, he had the sensation that he was being watched. He thought he heard the sound of someone walking behind him. Footsteps? Frowning to himself, he turned around and faced the other end of the arched alleyway; there was nothing there.

He stood staring into space for a few moments … It was, no doubt, the alcohol and tiredness playing tricks on him. He did, however, suddenly remember about the murders. It had completely slipped his mind, when he decided to take the alleyway route. Careless. Risky of him.

Turning back around, he was suddenly startled by a shout and echoing footsteps racing through the alleyway. He spun back, to see two young men chasing after a third, shouting and laughing. Idiots.

Randolph picked up his pace to quickly reach an area with more night-time crowds and eventually reached home and his bed.

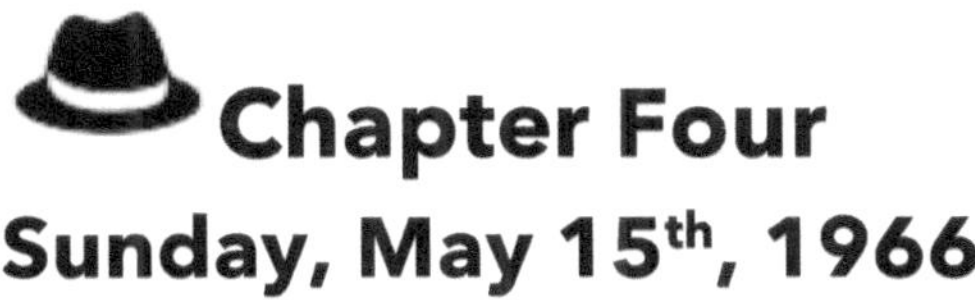# Chapter Four
Sunday, May 15th, 1966

Shaftesbury Avenue, London – 12.28 pm

Hungover and severely depressed, Randolph had spent most of Sunday morning sobbing like a baby, which had made his head pound even more, so he had to take some painkillers. It had taken almost three hours for the pain to virtually subside. While waiting, he became concerned that the pain wasn't going to stop. Laying down wasn't an option; it only made it worse. He just had to stand in his bedroom waiting for the pain to go. Any sudden movement aggravated it further. Despite feeling nauseous, he hadn't been sick.

Apart from the hangovers themselves and feeling like shit, he dreaded the 'hangover depression.' It was potent and raw. It was like a vicious circle and he hated himself and the self-inflicted aspect of it. It enhanced his depression. He felt so God-damn lonely, empty and lost. More than usual. He kept thinking of his wife and little Matty, and not being able to hold them both. To say that it was emotional agony was an understatement.

He was usually careful not to drink too much for this reason. But he had relapsed somewhat last night. Failing to find Peanut had compounded his misery. It was almost two weeks now since the dog had gone missing. He felt a complete and utter failure. He didn't remember an awful lot about last night. But he had recalled a few things and remembered asking some people in his drunken state if they had seen Peanut.

*

Randolph had always found it almost impossible to sleep with a hangover. He did, however, manage to get in a couple of hours. It made him feel better on waking. At least his headache had completely gone. His depression had worn off a little too.

He made himself some hot coffee and managed to eat a couple of slices of buttered toast, just something light. He then smoked a couple of cigarettes before taking a bath.

*

Still a little worse for wear, Randolph decided to get some fresh air at Regent's Park. He thought that it might do him good, now that he was over the worst of his hangover. He really didn't want to stay inside his dark flat all day. It would just make him feel more depressed and closed off. He'd spent a lot of time lonely and depressed of late.

Randolph decided to walk, as it wasn't far to Regent's Park from his flat anyway; he welcomed the walk in the afternoon warmth of the sunshine.

He sat under the clear blue sky on a bench, from which he could feed some ducks close to the lake. He sat alone and it was pretty quiet. He listened to the soft sound of the water and numerous birds chirping, which relaxed him. A few Sunday afternoon joggers went past and then a couple of rowing boats.

Randolph looked down and smiled at a few of the ducks. "I'm sorry, guys. That was the last of it." He screwed up the empty plastic bag that had held several slices of bread.

The innocent faces of the ducks still looked up at him. A couple looked back down on the empty ground and pecked anyway.

"I'm sorry," Randolph said again, smiling.

The ducks eventually got the message and waddled off to underneath a tree.

Randolph got up from the bench and put the empty bag into one of the nearby bins. He looked up to the sky. He then turned his attention to a family sitting on a white picnic blanket. A young couple sat holding their two children and laughing. They had been enjoying a late lunch. Randolph started to feel sad again. Now that he was feeling better physically, he considered going to Teresa's, just for a couple. Hair of the dog. But after a while contemplating, he thought better of it. In the end, he went to check his office, just in case a miracle had happened and someone required his skills and expertise. Chance would be a fine thing.

He walked down the path casually, with both hands in the pockets of his pleated, navy-blue trousers. He smiled and nodded at an attractive female who went past jogging. She smiled so he turned to watch her progress.

*

He walked up the steps and into the office block, where the cleaner was busy mopping away at the large area in the entrance. Randolph had decided to stop off in a nearby newsagent on the way to his office and picked up a copy of the *Sunday Mirror*. He held it folded in half just under his arm.

"Randy!" the cleaner said. "I don't think I've ever seen you here on a Sunday, before?"

Randolph smiled. "I know. I just thought I'd check in on my office. I've got nothing else better to do … I didn't think you worked Sundays?"

The cleaner laughed and said, "Saturdays are included in the contracted hours. But it can be flexible. As long as the cleaning is done over the weekend, it doesn't really matter. I had some things to do yesterday. I would have been in this morning. But let's just say that I had a 'few' drinks last night." He grinned.

"You and me both." Randolph smirked.

Randolph had known Greg for a good couple of years. He did the cleaning three days a week. The fifty-four-year-old Greg often liked a good old chinwag. Randolph was more than happy to talk to him. He liked him. He was a pleasant enough chap.

"They still haven't gotten you a machine yet, to do the floors?"

"Nah … I won't hold me breath. The tight bastards." Greg laughed. "Mopping alone does a decent enough job, anyway … Try and be careful down your corridor though, mate. It's still wet down there. Some of those lights are still out."

"Still?"

"Yep. They're supposed to be coming to fix them again. Useless prats."

"Tell me about it. Wasn't too long ago, they repaired them before … Sorry for having to walk over your wet floor. My shoes are clean, anyway." Randolph checked his rubber soles.

"You're all right, mate. Can't be helped. I've done me job, anyway. If it gets shitted up again, tough!" Greg laughed again.

Randolph laughed too. He walked past an old metal bucket towards the dark corridor. A yellow, metal warning 'Wet Floor' sign was placed on the floor. "If I slip over, I'm going to sue you, *and* the company who own this building!" Randolph joked.

"Fine by me. I'm worth jack shit, anyway!" Greg laughed.

Randolph shook his head and smiled. He carefully walked to his office and checked down on the mat upon entering; there was nothing. No notes, nor any envelopes. Not that he was expecting anything. He went over to his office window and opened it to let some fresh spring air in. Taking off his khaki-coloured trilby, another from his collection with a few fedoras – he loved his hats – placed it on his desk and sat down to read his newspaper. He gave the paper a shake and started to read the front page, with his crossed legs up on his desk.

The front page of the newspaper covered the murders. The second victim had now been named and his age officially confirmed; Christophe Livingston. He was twenty-five years old. Poor bastard. He was half-French and half-English. He had recently fathered a little boy; he was only a few months old. His wife, now widow, wasn't named. Poor woman. She must be completely distraught. Such pain. Many thoughts went through Randolph's mind. He could feel the pain of the family and that of the previous murdered victim.

Randolph had seen the murders covered on the news, but he hadn't really paid too much attention to it all. He had his own problems. According to the newspaper report, people were getting frustrated and annoyed with the police. The police were coming under fire for their lack of investigation skills. The public believed the police should be doing more. Randolph could understand their fears but if the police had nothing to go on, what more could they do? It was possible, however, that the police were keeping their cards close to their chests and knew more than they were letting on to the public. Completely understandable. Randolph knew how they worked.

On the second page of the paper, was a black and white inset of the man responsible for leading the case: Detective Chief Superintendent Kendall Quincy. It took a few moments before Randolph recognised him. It was the man being questioned in the pool room in Teresa's last night. Despite his drunken state, Randolph remembered.

The report carried on for a few more pages. Nothing new had been written, other than what had been said previously. The words: *These are very worrying times for all of us. God help us!* finished the report. There was nothing like the media to spout more fear and panic into people but on this occasion, they were right. Anyone could be next. Especially if these killings were random. Nothing was confirmed nor denied by the police department.

Randolph flicked through and read the rest of the paper. He turned it over and saw on the back page, a photo of some of the Everton players celebrating yesterday's Cup Final win. Captain Brian Labone beamed with the FA Cup held on his head by two of his joyous teammates. Randolph wondered if and when he'd be able to celebrate Arsenal winning a trophy. He couldn't help but feel a little envious and bitter.

*

Having made himself a coffee and after smoking a cigarette, Randolph decided to head off home. He said goodbye to Greg who was finishing off and smoking a cigarette himself. He then trotted down the old steps but not before pretending to slip on the floor, making Greg laugh. He had also offered Greg his newspaper. Greg happily took it.

Chapter Five
Monday, May 16th, 1966

Shaftesbury Avenue, London - 8.33 am

Hangover free and sleeping in late, Randolph woke up refreshed. It was definitely the best he had slept in a long time. He didn't feel too bad for a change. After a smoke and a coffee — like his usual routine, he decided he would treat himself to a breakfast fry-up at one of his favourite cafés; Beanz & Eggz. Not exactly the most original name, but the food was good and cheap. The owners were more than generous with their servings. The café was less than a five-minute walk from Randolph's flat. Last week, he had even got the owners to put up in their window, a photocopied photo of Peanut, along with his contact number and that of Mrs Tennyson, for anyone to contact them if the missing Peanut was found. That included other shops and places. Randolph couldn't help but think if someone else had found the dog, that it would mean him missing out on extra payment. But to him, he just wanted the dog found for Mrs Tennyson's sake. He had also paid out for the copies to be made.

Already before heading out for breakfast, Randolph also decided he would wander the streets afterwards. He never believed it for a second; but he might get lucky and come across the dog. It's not like he had much else to do neither. It would also do him good to be out and about at least.

*

Earlier that night, he had decided to go to Teresa's again. Just for a couple of drinks. Nothing more. After returning, he laid soaking in the hot bath before bed. Randolph could hear his phone ringing. He

42

quickly stood up, wrapped a towel around him, and made his way into the living room, dripping wet. "Hello?" He wondered who would call at such a time.

"Mr Randolph?" the heavily accented woman replied.

"Erm. Yes?" Randolph recognised the voice.

"It's Miss Albescu …"

"Oh."

"I am sorry, for calling you so late."

"It's fine." Randolph checked the clock that hung on his crappy-coloured wallpaper. It was almost ten-forty.

"I'm just ringing about that little dog that you were asking me about the other day …"

"Peanut?"

Miss Albescu gave a slight laugh at the name. "Yes … I think I may have spotted him. It's why I have called so late."

"What? Really? *Where?*"

"I am in a phone box on Maddox Street, Mayfair … do you know it? I have been keeping your card on me, in case I spotted the dog."

"That's kind of you, and I know it, yes."

"We have been out for a meal and drinks. We were driving in the taxi, when I spotted a dog matching your description. I asked for the driver to stop. I got out to try and catch him. But unfortunately, he ran down some alleyway and disappeared. It was too dark; I don't know where he went. I am sorry. That's if it indeed *was* the same dog."

"Please, don't be sorry. Thank you for trying to catch him. I can come check for myself. How long ago was this?"

"A matter of a few minutes. I can wait for you, and show you, if you wish?"

"No, no. That's fine. You get off home, as you are using a taxi, too. I can check by myself. Where was this alleyway?"

"If you walk down Maddox Street from the Hamleys' end, there is a fruit and vegetable shop called *Frank's*, about halfway down on the left side … An alleyway is just before it."

"Okay. Thank you. I know it. I'll go check it out immediately."

Randolph quickly dried himself and got dressed. Even if Peanut had disappeared, he might still be in the area. Time was of the essence. Of course, it may not have been Peanut at all. Either way, he needed to check. This was the closest he had come to potentially finding him.

Accelerating off to Maddox Street, he remained hopeful.

*

The streets were empty. There was more than a nip in the air. Randolph hadn't considered taking a jacket. The Waning Crescent Moon hung in the air above the city, shining down brightly. Perhaps a little surprisingly, for a moon not full. Randolph had found the alleyway straight away; it wasn't exactly difficult. He had taken a torch from the glove compartment of his car. He shined the torch repeatedly over the dark alleyway, 'Peanut' was nowhere to be seen.

"Peanut?" Randolph called again, more forcibly this time. He felt a total idiot, calling out to some dog he didn't even know in an alleyway in the night. Not that there was anyone about to have heard him.

The alleyway went off to the left. On the left-hand side were the backs of the buildings and shops and a couple had backdoors, quite likely fire exits. The other side consisted of a brick wall with some graffiti painted over it. One part in yellow, lit up emphatically in the torch light;

BRETT GIBSON IS GAY!

"Mature." Randolph half-smiled and shook his head.

He came to near the end of the alleyway. It stunk of piss down this end. He wondered where the dog had disappeared to.

Shining the torch lower down in one of the corners, Randolph could see some rubbish and a few bushes coming through the bottom of the brick wall. "I wonder ..." he muttered to himself. Bending down, Randolph could see a hole small enough for Peanut to fit through, just behind the bushes. "Little shit ... you certainly like getting through these small holes, eh."

Getting back up, Randolph could feel the temperature drop. He went back to the street where he had parked his car by the alleyway. He walked around to the other side of the brick wall, with the hole and bushes. A small patch of grass was on the other side, with a couple of swings and a seesaw; they looked old.

"Peanut ... *Peanut!*" Randolph called out. Though he didn't believe Peanut would respond if he heard him. Perhaps he could hear him and was ignoring him.

Randolph checked around some more, before finally giving up. The one big chance to have possibly solved his latest case now appeared gone. Once again, the dog could now be anywhere. Randolph sighed with annoyance. Fucking dog. Shaking his head, he went back to the car.

He put the torch back in the glove compartment and was just about to close the car door, when he heard a sharp scream of a man from somewhere not too far away ... He heard it again. Then again. He frowned. His eyes then widened. He got out the car and stood there. He then heard another scream ... Nothing but silence. The streets still appeared dead — there was no one else about, other than him. What if it was someone in trouble? What if it was the murderer? Randolph grew uneasy fast. His heart rate went up. He was now genuinely concerned for someone else's well-being. They could be in severe trouble, unless it was someone larking about. He considered calling out, to see if anyone responded. But what if it was the killer, and they became alerted to his presence? Randolph wasn't even certain exactly where the screams had come from.

Looking around, Randolph didn't know what to do. He sensed it was perhaps coming from the Savile Row direction ... Taking the torch back out from the glove compartment, he dashed over that way ...

Standing at the top of an empty and dark Savile Row, which had some of its streetlights out, he hesitated, breathing heavily and gripping the torch. He swallowed. He had heard another scream whilst running; he was fairly certain that the scream came from this direction. He then heard the scream again. This one seemed fainter than the previous ones. It now came from somewhere to his right, on Conduit Street? The hell? Despite it being late, he still thought it was strange that he was the only one out, apart from the man screaming.

Instead, he ran further down Savile Row to the police station there. It was worth checking to see if anyone was there. Considering the previous murders, his concerns regarding a scream were justifiable, even if there was nothing to worry about. Better to be safe than sorry. The large wooden doors were shut; no lights on. No sign of anybody working late. He tried an old buzzer — nothing. He thought he'd call the police from an old phone box opposite but it was out of order. Typical. He wasn't sure where any other phone boxes were. He would waste time checking the streets, if someone was in danger. He was on his own.

He tried following the screams of the distressed person. With his heart pounding in his chest, Randolph walked down an eerily quiet Conduit Street. Even more of the streetlights were out here. Randolph turned on his torch. He resisted the urge to call out. His mouth became dry. He felt even colder. Nothing but silence. He walked past another darkened alleyway, stopping. He heard a few rustles and scratches. Struggling to swallow due to his dry mouth, he turned to check out the sounds. Hesitantly, he shone the torch down the alleyway. "P-Peanut?"

The torch lit up part of the alleyway and a stack of old damp cardboard boxes to the left. A Chihuahua was scratching ferociously at one of the bottom boxes. It seemed determined to try and pull something out from underneath it. The dog then stopped, looking over at Randolph who walked slowly. The Chihuahua's ears pricked up, staring straight at Randolph and the torch beam.

"Woah … Easy, boy," Randolph said calmly. "Don't be scared … Don't you run …" Randolph had almost forgotten about the screams he was so excited to find Peanut.

Getting within touching distance of the small dog, Randolph carefully crouched down. The last thing he wanted to do was scare him off. The dog seemed startled. He slowly backed away from Randolph. Randolph shone the torch over the bottom of the boxes. He could see that the dog was trying to claw out a chicken bone. Randolph thought he'd try and use it to his advantage. He picked up the old bone. Reaching out his hand, trying to entice the dog towards him, the Chihuahua darted past Randolph into the street and ran off to the right.

"Shit!" Randolph got up and chased after it. Doing so, he slipped on something that had oozed out of one of the squashed boxes. He lost his footing and fell into the sodden boxes. Cursing, he quickly got up and ran to check the street. The dog had gone. Randolph cursed under his breath again. He then remembered why he was down this street in the first place, the man's scream.

Coming to near the end of Conduit Street, he decided to head back the way he came. No sign of the Chihuahua. Nor of any distressed man. Walking back up the dark street to the other end, he caught sight of an orange glow with a hint of green, flickering in one of the buildings upstairs on the other side of the street. He hadn't noticed it before. He decided to cross over. He was curious, as he knew that this building had been abandoned for almost a year. It used to be an old television shop; Tony's Televisions. Tony, who ran the business, had owed the proprietor a considerable amount of rent. He ended up doing a runner, along with his stock. As it happened, the proprietor died a couple of months later. Then most likely kids had ended up trashing the windows and other parts of the old shop. The empty building remained just that; empty and trashed.

Approaching the building, Randolph wondered if it was a tramp upstairs, using the derelict building as a bedsit. Or was it something else? A strange feeling washed over him. He became wary again, standing in the doorless frame with splintered wood around it. Above the shop front, some of the blue lettering remained on what was left of the white background:

T NY' TEL VI I NS

There were large and small debris and broken glass covering the dirty floor, including numerous old newspapers. To the left, was what was left of the counter. Straight ahead, were two flights of worn stairs. Walking towards them, Randolph shone the torch. He could see part of the glow from upstairs flicker onto the crumbling back plastered wall. Looking down at the bottom steps, he could see small footprints of blood.

Randolph swallowed. It looked like a small animal had injured themselves, perhaps on the broken glass. The footprints had come down the stairs. He wondered if they belonged to Peanut, or the Chihuahua that he had recently seen. The footprints trailed off to the right. Randolph followed them slowly, his shoes crunching on the debris and glass under him. He stopped at a small damaged, white cupboard. The door was half open, hanging off the hinges. Hesitating and nervous, he bent down and opened it fully, shining the torch. He was half-expecting something to jump out at him. "Peanut! Is that you?" Randolph whispered sharply.

Inside the old cupboard, was most likely the same dog Randolph had seen a short while ago. It certainly looked that way. It would have been too much of a coincidence if it was a different Chihuahua. The dog was hunched up inside the cupboard, shaking. Randolph wasn't sure if the poor thing was hurt and frightened by something, or cold. It looked terrified. This time, the dog didn't run away. It allowed Randolph to scoop up its limp body; it was a boy. It definitely looked like Peanut. Randolph held the torch in his mouth as he examined the poor little dog. Holding him up, the dog was completely submissive.

"What's got you so spooked, eh?" Randolph said softly, biting down on the torch. "I guess this is you, Peanut. Finally!" Randolph was certain the Chihuahua he held in his hands was Peanut. He recognised the 'heart' shaped marking of dark fur on his breast from the photos that Mrs Tennyson had shown him.

Examining the four legs and paws of Peanut, and the rest of his body, it was evident that the dog was unhurt physically. The blood was from somewhere else. Peanut had obviously stepped in it. Upstairs, perhaps? Randolph swallowed. He needed to check the light source from upstairs and where this blood had come from. He decided to carry Peanut up with him, even at the risk of getting some blood on his top. He didn't dare leave Peanut by himself down here. He couldn't risk losing him again and there was nothing to tie him up with. The poor thing was frightened as well, so he didn't want to leave him alone. The debris crunched further underneath Randolph's shoes, despite his treading carefully.

Holding Peanut, who was still cold and submissive, under his right arm and with the torch in his left hand, Randolph slowly walked up the hard and cracked stairs to the top, where the trail of blood led to …

Randolph almost dropped the torch in shock at what he saw, and even loosened his grip on the shaking Peanut, who made a slight whimper, staring in front of them. Peanut had indeed walked in blood. There was enough of it. Randolph froze on the spot. He was now completely certain of who the screams he had heard belonged to.

The floor above was similar to below, with numerous cracks and rubbish strewn across it. There was one major difference though … a completely naked man was half-lying on the floor. His upper back and neck were unnaturally bent backwards and over, his spine and neck snapped. His upside-down head with dead eyes stared widely at Randolph. It freaked the shit out of him, although he'd seen many horrible things during the war. The victim's throat was freshly slit. Blood covered the poor man's back, buttocks and legs. Blood had even gushed from his open mouth. A gaping and bloodied hole covered the dead man's sternum. A pair of blue jeans, a brown jumper and a green jacket were folded neatly in one corner of the room and were accompanied by a pair of brown shoes with the socks tucked into each one.

Above the body on the severely cracked wall, in between where two windows used to be, was a perfectly drawn inverted pentagram in red chalk, somehow avoiding the cracks and crevices. Five black candles, creating the glimmer of light Randolph had seen, were placed around the dead body, resembling the five points of the inverted pentagram on the wall. Out of nowhere, came a gust of wind that blew through the abandoned building, blowing out the candles.

*

It had taken less than ten minutes for the first of the police to arrive at the latest crime scene. It had taken Randolph a while to find a phone box on Bruton Street and frantically call the police. He was in a state of shock, still holding Peanut under his arm throughout the call. Peanut never struggled at all. Randolph made sure he didn't touch the dead body, or any of the evidence. Ironically, a new police station had recently been built on Conduit Street. It just hadn't been a hundred per cent completed.

"I know this is tough on you … but you never heard or saw anything, apart from those screams?" the DCI asked again.

Randolph hadn't paid much attention when the DCI mentioned his name and showed his ID. The DCI was writing down notes and Randolph's statement.

"Nothing … only what I've already told you." Randolph had explained everything that happened that night, including Peanut's case. Peanut was being looked after by a female police officer in one of the police cars, whilst Randolph gave his statement.

The Detective Chief Superintendent was upstairs with a few others. They didn't wish to contaminate the crime scene and were waiting for forensics to arrive. The DCS eventually came down and approached Randolph, issuing a sympathetic and understanding smile. "I think that's enough for one night, Mr Landon. You should go home and get some sleep. We know it's late. Perhaps you can come in tomorrow morning, to the station?"

"I can. But is it really necessary? I've told you everything already. There really isn't much else to say." Randolph felt annoyed and was still in a state of shock.

"I know." The DCS smiled again. It was the same guy Randolph had seen last Saturday night and in the paper, the man responsible for leading the murder case. "It won't take long."

Randolph sighed and reluctantly agreed. "Okay."

"Shall we say, nine?"

Randolph gave a slight nod. "I even tried you guys on Savile Row. You were shut."

The DCI sighed. "It's always the way. We'd been working late, and left after ten."

"If only I got here in time, sooner … I might have been able to save the poor man."

"Don't beat yourself up. You could have ended up risking your own life, had you encountered the murderer," the DCI added.

Randolph shook his head.

*

Randolph barely slept a wink that night. He had taken Peanut back with him to his flat. It was too late to have reunited him with Mrs Tennyson, although it probably wouldn't have bothered her that time of night, seeing as she was getting her beloved Chihuahua back. Nevertheless, he decided to wait until morning. After cleaning him up, Randolph had let Peanut sleep on his bed with him. He seemed a bit more active and affectionate, licking Randolph's face and snuggling up to his body and slept fine during the night, perhaps getting over his ordeal.

Chapter Six
Tuesday, May 17th, 1966

Shelton Street, London – 8.31 am

Feeling like crap that morning, Randolph needed a shave. Perhaps he would sort that out later on. Mrs Tennyson, still in her nightgown and slippers, cried with happiness as Randolph stood holding Peanut at her front door. Peanut licked furiously at her face. She kept thanking Randolph over and over. Randolph had started having doubts in case it *wasn't* Peanut and he was wrong. Mrs Tennyson invited Randolph in for a "nice cuppa and few biscuits" but Randolph politely declined. He was due at the police station soon. He was in two minds whether to tell her about last night's events. He thought he'd be straight with her, seeing as she obviously wanted to know where Peanut had been found. However, he left out the more horrific details of the dead body.

Mrs Tennyson was shocked and genuinely felt for Randolph. He insisted that he was fine, and she went to write another cheque for him. She was grateful and felt bad that Randolph had been the one to find this latest dead body. Randolph said she didn't need to, but she insisted he took the cheque with a "little extra" added to it, smiling when she gave it to him. Randolph reluctantly accepted. After all, he could do with a cash injection. Putting the cheque in his pocket, he realised that this finalised his latest and last case. Now, he had nothing. He then got back in his car and headed for the police station.

*

"I'm sorry for keeping you waiting, Mr Landon." The DCS smiled.

"It's fine, honestly." Randolph yawned. He was sat in the office of the DCS.

"Did you sleep okay, considering?" Detective Chief Superintendent Kendall Quincy pulled out his desk chair and plonked down in it.

"Not exactly."

"I know how you feel. I've been the same, since all this started … The bodies being found like that. It's one thing to find a murdered dead body. But like that …" DCS Quincy looked glum, shaking his head.

"Tell me about it. I've seen a few things during the war, but last night, that's going to take a *long* fucking time to get that one out of my head. If ever!"

DCS Quincy gave a caring and understanding smile. "Yep, same … How's the dog?"

"He seemed fine and a lot better this morning. All right for some, eh?" Randolph half-smiled. "The owner was more than grateful. Peanut seemed happy to be reunited as well. I just hope the little shit doesn't run away again! I'm pleased he's back, though. It wasn't nice for the old woman after he'd gone missing. She's delighted."

"I bet." DCS Quincy smiled again. "It's quite possible, that this little dog saw the murderer. He could be the only witness so far … if only dogs could speak, eh?"

"If only … Listen, I don't mean to sound rude or anything. But I gave my statement last night. It's not like I have anything better to do, but I really don't need to go over it all again. I don't understand why I need to be here … unless, I'm a suspect?" Randolph quipped.

DCS Quincy gave a slight laugh. "No, of course not! I just thought that maybe you might have remembered more this morning, seeing as it was late and you were quite rightly shocked. I wanted to see how you were doing, too. I've been over your file as well. You seem to be quite the private eye. I read about the case last year, involving Mr Gibbs. You did well, helping the police out."

Randolph detected genuine sincerity in the DCS's voice. He didn't feel patronised. DCS Quincy seemed warm and a genuinely caring man. He wasn't trying to blow smoke up Randolph's arse. "Ha. I haven't been that much of a PI of late. Only minor cases, and a lack of them too. The Peanut case was probably the biggest I've had in quite some time," Randolph half-joked.

DCS Quincy smiled. "I understand ... swings and roundabouts. I'm sure things will pick up for you soon enough."

"Thanks," Randolph replied. "About last night, though ... I didn't see or hear anything other than those screams. It was strangely quiet out. I know that it was late, but even so ... it was almost as if the victim was being taken over to Conduit Street — the way the screams changed direction. If that was true, why there? Why not just kill the man where he had him? Why take him to that building and risk being seen? Did the murderer carry a full-grown man like that? Or was the man running from the murderer? Maybe I would have seen the killer, had I not been in that alleyway with the dog, before I slipped and fell into those boxes."

DCS Quincy sighed. "I know ... We've never seen anything like this. We're trying our hardest — we're working day and night. We've found nothing concrete, other than what's been at the scenes of the crimes."

"I mean, was the killer in that building with that poor man, whilst I was in that alleyway on the street opposite? Jesus ... I saw no one. And it must have happened quickly. How could they have done what they did, so fast? Why didn't the man scream out more? Frightening." Randolph gave a shiver.

"There might be an explanation behind that ..."

"Oh?"

"Forensics arrived not long after you left us last night. We saw upstairs anyway, before they came ... the victim's tongue had been removed along with his heart. There was no sign of them, just like the other two victims. Though, this is the first time the tongue has been removed. It could explain why you didn't hear any more screams. Saying that, it is still possible to scream without a tongue."

"Jesus. That poor guy. That would explain all that blood from his mouth. I was too shook up to take a closer look. I didn't want to risk messing up the crime scene, either ... I called you guys straight away. Well, after the initial shock and finding a phone box."

"You did good. You left it to us." DCS Quincy half-smiled.

"How do you bend back someone's body like that? Remove the heart? It must require some kind of *strength* to do such things."

DCS Quincy shook his head. "You're asking the same questions we've all been wondering. Right now, we have no answer to that."

"Has the man been identified yet? What did forensics say?"

"Not yet. And we're still waiting for the full results. It's not looking good, though. Like the past two cases — no weapon, no fingerprints, no footprints, other than the dog's."

"No leads, then …? What's with the candles and inverted pentagram?"

"Nothing. We have no real idea as to why this person or persons — it could be more than one, is drawing this symbol and committing these heinous acts. We're in contact with someone who might know of these things. We can only assume that it's some kind of ritual … We are working on it. There are a few people we intend on questioning. Potential suspects … but I am not at liberty to say. Obviously, I can't tell you too much. I hope you understand?" DCS Quincy smiled. "It is a police matter."

"Of course. Completely … I was there in Teresa's last Saturday night, in the pool room when those guys were questioning you." Randolph smiled.

"Ah … those guys! Yes, they've been trying to get some information from me. It's all classified." DCS Quincy smirked and shook his head. "I fully understand their concerns. I can't blame them."

"Yep. It's a worrying time for all of us. I feel for you guys, getting criticism from the press and people, the victims' families. It must be tough."

"For sure … Would you like some coffee?"

"Erm, sure. Why not?" Randolph was a little surprised. He thought the DCS would want him gone fairly quickly, so that he could get back to work.

They chatted a bit more about the case, though only briefly. DCS Quincy didn't want to disclose too much. There wasn't an awful lot to tell anyway, seeing as there were no leads or strong evidence linking the crimes to anyone. Randolph was still saddened and upset too, by the fact that things could have been different had the police station not been closed. Or maybe he should have phoned as soon as he first heard the screams. They were most likely from the latest victim. DCS

Quincy insisted he shouldn't beat himself up over it. The chances were, it wouldn't have made any difference. He wasn't at fault, period.

They conversed more in general. DCS Quincy offered Randolph a cigarette and they both smoked for a while. Randolph had forgotten to bring his own.

Kendall Quincy was another brave veteran who had fought during the Second World War, a former lieutenant, promoted to captain who had served in multiple countries. He had earnt the Victoria Cross and rightly so. He considered hanging it on his wall back home or in his office here, but decided against it. Although he was honoured in earning the highest military award, he felt humble about it. He didn't believe he deserved it, when so many of his friends and fellow soldiers were just as brave as he was — if not braver, not to mention the ones who gave their lives for our freedom. He never declared himself as 'brave.' He was just doing his job. Anyone in his position would have done the same. If he had earnt the Victoria Cross, then so should everyone who fought under him and in the war.

The previous DCS, who Randolph had known a little during the Peter Gibbs case, had retired several months ago. His DCI had since transferred. Kendall Quincy had transferred himself from Manchester soon after, not long before bringing down his own DCI, Burt Sommers. DCS Quincy was fifty-seven years old and his DCI, Burt, forty-six.

An attractive secretary came to inform DCS Quincy that the press were waiting outside the police station in their masses.

"I better go address the press. I'm dreading it to be honest with you." DCS Quincy rose from his seat.

"Good luck." Randolph got up too. "Rather you, than me." He half-smiled.

"Thanks. I'm going to need it. They're already out for blood as it is, demanding answers and when we're going to catch the killer … it's definitely a serial killer now. That's for sure. And you just *know*, there's going to be another body soon. It's gut-wrenching, knowing it's going to happen again, and we can't currently stop it. Awful."

DCS Quincy swallowed, downcast.

Randolph felt his pain. He knew that he and his team were doing their utmost best to find out who was doing these god-awful, heinous acts and why. He wondered if that was why DCS Quincy asked him to stay for a coffee; he was someone to talk to before the press. "I know. Hopefully, something will come up. Perhaps the murderer gave something away, somewhere?"

DCS Quincy sighed. "Hopefully … we're going to go back to the abandoned building, like we did with the previous other two crime scenes … return to turn the place upside down, if we have to. It's going to be all over the news again later, and in the papers tomorrow."

"I'd appreciate my name staying out of it. I don't fancy being mentioned as the person who found this latest body. I don't want the press turning up at my office or flat either. Although I told the old lady, when I brought Peanut back."

DCS Quincy smiled. "Your secret's safe with me. Don't worry about that at all."

Randolph looked again at the large map of London on the wall to his left. It had three large drawing pins marking the locations of each of the murder sites; the alleyway off Upper St Martin's Lane, behind the All Saints Church on Margaret Street and now Conduit Street … He wondered how many more of these killings there would be and drawing pins put up.

DCS Quincy went to use the loo before facing the press. Randolph walked past the seated secretary and smiled; she smiled back. He then made his way out of the police station, seeing the hordes of press with their cameras, microphones and notepads. Several police officers were already pushing them back. Rather you than me, Quincy.

Getting back in his car, Randolph pulled out another cigarette that the DCS had given him and lit it using the car's cigarette lighter. He headed off to the bank to pay in his latest cheque, sensing it would be a while before he paid another one in.

Trying to get the image out of his head from last night, Randolph decided to go for a drive around the city. He kept seeing the face of the poor dead man in the abandoned building, not to mention the blood. He wondered how Peanut was coping — no doubt better than he was. He then decided he ought to thank Miss Albescu and headed off to Hyde Park.

*

"Ah. Mr Randolph. How nice it is to see you again."

Randolph wasn't sure if this was sarcasm or if Miss Albescu was serious. Perhaps it was a bit of both. "I'm sorry for disturbing you. I just wanted to pop by and thank you for last night. I found Peanut."

"That's good to hear! Was he okay?"

Randolph sighed. He didn't exactly want people knowing what he had found last night, yet wanted to be honest. As long as the papers and news weren't aware of him finding the body, he guessed it didn't matter too much.

"*What? Really?*" Miss Albescu's blue eyes enlarged and she frowned. A serious look etched upon her face. "I've heard about these killings … but did not realise there had been another one. *Doamne Dumnezeu.*"

"I am afraid so. You'll no doubt see it on the news later and all over the papers tomorrow … Peanut was really frightened. It was possible he saw the murderer."

"Poor little doggy … I am sorry that you encountered that. Truly, I am."

"It's fine. To be honest, it's the last thing that I needed." Randolph looked at the ground. He considered knocking back a few at Teresa's. Where else? "Thanks again, anyway. If it wasn't for you, Peanut would still be out there somewhere. He may not have ever been found and returned to the old woman."

"You're most welcome. I'm sure you would have succeeded in time."

"Take care!" Randolph gave a sad smile and nodded, turning to leave the trailer.

"Perhaps, you'd like a reading?" Miss Albescu suddenly said. She sensed his negative energy.

"Excuse me?" Randolph turned and frowned.

"A palm reading …"

Randolph screwed his face up. "Erm. Maybe? I can't say I have ever had one. I don't have any money on me."

Miss Albescu smiled. "It is fine … this one is on me. It might make you feel better. I'm with another client at the moment." She looked over her right shoulder, standing in the doorway of her trailer. "If you don't mind waiting, that is? I'll be about another ten minutes."

"Sure … why not?" Randolph half-smiled. "I did kind of guess you did something like that."

"Good intuition, Mr Randolph … that's why you are a private detective, yes?" She had a seductive look in her eyes again.

Randolph wondered if Miss Albescu had sensed his 'negative' energy. Though it wasn't exactly difficult. He also wondered if the other client inside the trailer overheard him talking about last night. He wasn't exactly fussed if they had.

Whilst waiting, Randolph decided on another cigarette, then remembered he had none on him and searched his jean pockets anyway. He walked around the area of the gypsy site, hands in his pockets, waiting for Miss Albescu to finish with her client. He felt nervous. A palm reading? What the hell was that going to achieve? He most often gave anything a try. Besides, it wasn't like he had much else on. It wouldn't hurt. It seemed too, that Miss Albescu was being nice towards him, sensing his gloom.

Randolph also wondered who occupied the other trailer and caravan. He was about to find out. Coming nearer to him, were the two boys he'd seen the previous week playing football, no doubt the sons of Miss Albescu. The two lurchers were with them, an older woman, another woman a similar age to Miss Albescu, and two grown men, most likely in their early thirties.

Randolph felt awkward, only glancing at them briefly. He cleared his throat and smiled at the group. One of the men nodded and went into the other trailer; the younger woman followed behind him. The other man went into the caravan, whilst the old woman stood outside Miss Albescu's trailer with the two young boys and lurchers. The boys giggled, looking again at Randolph. The old woman turned to look at him seriously.

"Friendly bunch …" Randolph muttered sarcastically under his breath.

The old woman knocked on the trailer door, saying something in Romanian. Miss Albescu's voice came from inside. After a couple of minutes, she came out, followed by a young girl, who must have been around nineteen or twenty. She made her way to behind the trailer and reappeared riding a bicycle and set off across the park.

A brief conversation between the old woman and Miss Albescu seemed to annoy the old woman, who wore a purply patterned head scarf tied underneath her chin. She threw her arms up in the air; then she and the boys, along with the lurchers, went off across the park too. She didn't seem happy.

"Come, Mr Randolph …" Miss Albescu encouraged Randolph to join her inside.

Randolph turned and looked at the others walking away.

"Ignore my mother … she often gets annoyed easily." Miss Albescu smiled.

"We can do this another time; I don't want to intrude or anything."

"Nonsense. Come!"

Randolph sat down on one side of the trailer's sofa. It was patterned with a cream background with pink and white flower heads on their stems. A table sat between him and Miss Albescu. It had a small, dark red cloth over it. Incense burnt from an old brass lantern hung from the beige ceiling. Randolph wasn't overly keen on incense scent in general but this was mild and pleasant enough. The trailer was fairly large, and just about big enough for Miss Albescu, her two sons, mother and the dogs. A small kitchen was in the middle and then at the other end were the beds. It felt fairly cosy. A dreamcatcher with blue and pink feathers also hung down from the ceiling, up against the window to Randolph's right.

Miss Albescu saw Randolph glance around her trailer. She smiled. "This is only temporary. It isn't ideal. Especially with two young children."

"I was half-expecting the inside to be full of gypsy ornaments and trinkets. Stuff like that. Or even a horse outside … at the risk of sounding stereotypical." Randolph smiled.

Miss Albescu laughed. "You do amuse me, Mr Randolph." She had that look in her eyes again. "We aren't all extreme like that."

Randolph smirked. "How long have you been here? Who are the others with you?"

"In England, or Hyde Park? The former, long enough!" She smiled. "Hyde Park; almost a month now. We should be off here by the end of the week. The others are my sister, her partner, and their friend."

Randolph was tempted to ask her if she had permission to be on the land, just out of curiosity. He didn't bother. Why would he care?

"Anyway, shall we start before my mother comes back moaning, again." Miss Albescu gave a little laugh. "She doesn't speak English and understands very little."

"Sure." Randolph grinned, holding out his hands, palms facing up. At least Randolph wasn't distracted by her cleavage this time. She was wearing a pink blouse which covered her up more.

Miss Albescu placed her own hands with her large painted nails underneath Randolph's. Her nails were still the same colour as last week, purple.

A few seconds of silence passed. Randolph suddenly caught a scent of her sweet perfume as well as the incense.

Randolph felt a little awkward. "Do I need to lace your palm with silver, first?" He smiled.

Miss Albescu looked up and half-smiled. "This is your first time then, having a palm reading?"

"It is."

"I guess I am honoured, then." Miss Albescu glanced up and gave a wry smirk.

"Likewise." Randolph smirked back.

"I believe you are right-handed?"

"I am."

"The right hand is considered to be the 'major' hand. The 'now' hand, of everyday life. If you were left-handed, it would be the other way around. Your right hand would be the 'past.'"

"I see." Randolph tried not to patronise her. She was being nice to him and who was he to doubt her 'abilities' and beliefs?

"Your left hand represents your characteristics and past events, and your right hand is what is around you now … Are you spiritual?"

"Not exactly. I'm certainly not a religious person! Can't stand it."

"You have many lines here, Mr Randolph. I sense that you have great intuition. Your, how do you say … 'gut' feelings are usually correct and strong. The more lines a person has, the more they can sense and feel … even worry and have more concerns …"

"That last part is definitely right. Particularly after last night!"

Miss Albescu frowned a little, concentrating on examining his left palm. "Your heart line is a little jagged … you've had some issues lately? Marriage problems, have you not?"

"I guess you could say that …" Randolph screwed his face up and made a clacking sound with his mouth.

"Yes … things haven't gone the way you wished for them to. I feel that things will become more positive for you. You come across as cautious, which is good. You don't rush into situations without thinking … you've learnt from past mistakes. Or you certainly will do."

Randolph listened intently. What she was saying was virtually all correct. But that didn't mean she had some 'psychic gift.' Some people were just good at picking up on other's energy and emotions.

"You are certainly very sharp as well … I guess that's why you are a good investigator?" Miss Albescu flicked her eyes up quickly, raising a slight smile.

"I do my best." Randolph returned the smile.

"You certainly have many lines … These are your 'life lines' and 'lines of destiny.'" Miss Albescu pointed.

"I'm not going to die anytime soon, then?" Randolph joked a little. The way things were going, he might end up drinking or smoking himself to death.

"I don't think so." Miss Albescu smiled.

"That's all right, then."

"I thought you might be able to find Peanut earlier, if you were psychic or something … though technically speaking, you did!" Randolph laughed.

Miss Albescu's face, however, became more serious. She frowned and swallowed.

"What is it?" Randolph felt concerned now.

"I, I am not sure … I just sense something."

"Something bad?" Randolph frowned himself, becoming uneasy. At first, this had all felt light-hearted.

"Maybe … perhaps it is nothing. I just sense something negative … *dark*. That involves you."

"But you just said things would get more positive?"

"I know … I just sense … something. I am sorry. I don't wish to scare you."

It was the first time that Randolph had seen her more serious like this. Her dark skin went pale. "Are you all right?"

"I, I don't know." Miss Albescu let go of his hands, pulling away and jolted back. She gasped slightly.

"Now you've got me worried! What is it? What did you see?"

Miss Albescu swallowed. She quickly went to the kitchen and poured a glass of water, drinking it down quickly … "I just came over a little nauseous. I didn't mean to scare you. Th-that was never my intention."

"What was it?"

"Just … just something dark."

"Am I in danger?"

"I am sorry. I do not know."

"Jesus!" Randolph got up too. He now wished he hadn't agreed to this. Although he had never believed in psychics, mediums, clairvoyants or palm readers, this genuinely worried him, even more so, from Miss Albescu's reaction.

"Just be careful … *please*, Mr Randolph …. use your intuition. Be cautious."

"What does that even mean?"

"The symbol … look out for the symbol. Be cautious."

"Symbol … *What?*"

They were startled by a loud *thump* against the side of the trailer, followed by two boys laughing.

Miss Albescu, annoyed, walked hastily to the trailer door and opened it. She shouted at her two boys in Romanian; they stopped laughing and looked sheepish. They had kicked their football up against the trailer. Her mother was a short distance away with the two dogs.

"Please? What did you see? Saying something like that — no wonder I have more 'worries' and 'concerns!'"

"I am sorry. I didn't really see anything. It was just a very quick flash … I just sensed … saw something like a symbol … the circle — an eye … I am not sure. Just please, be careful. And you will be okay."

Randolph didn't know what else to say. He just moved his mouth slightly and frowned. Miss Albescu wasn't making any sense. She even sounded contradicting.

"I, I have some things to do; I have to make lunch soon. The boys will be getting hungry … I hope you understand. I also have another client."

"Jeez! I hope they have a better reading than I do!" Randolph said sarcastically.

"I, I am sorry."

Leaving the area, Randolph had a seriousness etched across his rugged face. He remained frowning when he returned to his car. Bloody woman! Whether or not she was right or wrong, Randolph now had something else to concern himself with. Things would get 'positive,' but then she had said something more like the opposite and she had reacted so strangely. Did she mean things would get better temporary, and then worse or what? What did she mean about a circle and symbol, an eye? Getting back in his car, he slammed his door shut and headed off home to his flat. He would spend that afternoon thinking about the latest murder and his palm reading with Miss Albescu.

*

It began to rain that evening. Randolph watched the news. Virtually the whole news was about the three murders and how it was now definitely a serial killer. Randolph's name was never mentioned regarding finding the latest victim. DCS Quincy was shown addressing the press this morning, straight after had Randolph left. Some were almost heckling and hounding him, demanding answers from the DCS, and at least wanted to know what the motive behind the killings was. Quincy remained professional and calm throughout, saying that the investigation was ongoing internally and asking for calm. Easier said than done. Quincy asked them to let the police do their job.

Randolph felt for the man. A dead body turning up here and there once in a while was bad enough, but three inside a month. And the manner of the killings was something else. One of the newspaper journalists had asked DCS Quincy if this was like another Jack the Ripper case. Quincy tried avoiding the question by saying he couldn't disclose too much. In other words, the police hadn't a damn clue.

Randolph finally had a shave. Despite being careful not to cut himself, he accidently nicked his top lip. It took a while to stop bleeding. Once done, he lay in a hot bath drinking a glass of whisky. He winced as the whisky stung his cut. At least he looked tidier.

He still couldn't help thinking about the body he had found and Miss Albescu's 'warning.' Making Randolph paranoid, the latter was perhaps worse. Now he just had to live each day, fearing that something bad was potentially going to happen. Things were bad enough. He half wondered if Miss Albescu, being a gypsy, had put a curse on him.

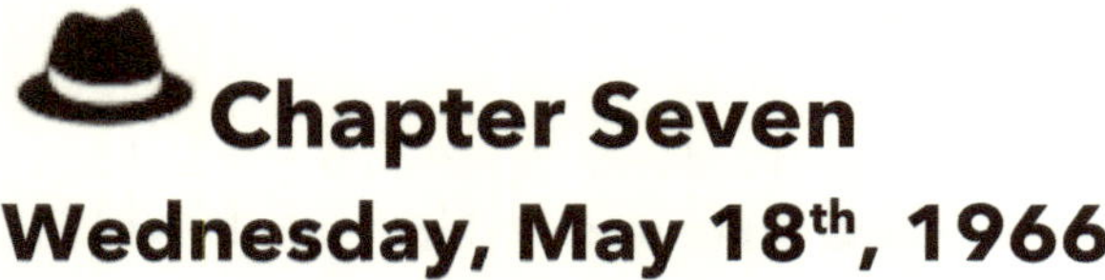

Chapter Seven
Wednesday, May 18th, 1966

Shaftesbury Avenue, London – 8.08 am

Randolph had tossed and turned throughout the night. He woke up sharply in a cold sweat. His body and his plain white flannelette sheets were soaked. He had a nightmare about the dead naked man in the abandoned building. *Not my idea of a wet dream,* he thought. He breathed heavily, trying to return his breathing to normal. He rubbed his now clean-shaven face with the palms of his hands.

In his nightmare, he was back on Conduit Street chasing after Peanut, who was playing silly buggers and running around the dark street. Randolph was trying to catch him. Peanut ran around Randolph a few times, before disappearing into thin air. Randolph then went into the old building and then up the stairs.

It was the same scenario as before; the dead naked man lay abnormally on the floor. Only this time, staring at Randolph, he tried to speak from his bloodied and tongueless mouth — groaning and trying to get the words out. All of a sudden, the man slid across the floor and jumped up to Randolph's face. That was when he woke.

Slowly recovering from this nightmare, Randolph got out of bed in just a vest and his underpants. He made his way to the kitchen and made himself some coffee, then went and sat in the living room for a while. He smoked a couple of cigarettes with a lot going through his mind. He couldn't stop thinking about the palm reading, amongst other things. He was now officially jobless. Maybe it was time that he started looking for a different job. Perhaps he could ask Greg, to see if there were any cleaning jobs going with his company? It wasn't just about the money — it was about occupying his mind. He needed to get out and do something on a regular basis, though he lacked the motivation, especially now he had no cases to work on.

*

Randolph dressed and decided to stretch his legs. He hadn't seen Tom since last week, so he went to see him at his newsstand. It didn't take a genius to work out what was plastered all over today's newspapers …

"Come on … *Get yer papers!*"

Randolph could hear Tom's voice before he even turned the corner. It was the same familiar sight; Tom holding up a newspaper, smoking and chewing on a cigar.

"Morning, Tom." Randolph tried to smile.

"Randy! I was just thinking of you, earlier … I haven't seen you for almost a week. How you been?"

Randolph sighed. "Don't ask, Tom."

"Ah, I get you … just be thankful you haven't ended up like *this* poor bastard!" Tom pulled the cigar from his mouth and pointed to the front page of the newspaper he was holding up. "That's your number *three*, Randy … serial killer, now! Not that it wasn't obvious before. It's just a question of *who* it's going to be next!"

"Yeah, I know."

"Same kind of thing, too … *ritualistic.* Heart removed. Throat slit. Only this time, the poor bastard had his neck and back broken *and* his tongue removed."

"I know, Tom … I was the unlucky person that found him …"

Tom Galton frowned and half-smiled at Randolph. He looked confused. "You what?"

Again, Randolph didn't exactly want people knowing he had found the latest body, however, he didn't mind telling a couple of people who he had a connection with. Besides, it felt like he was keeping it from them, if he didn't tell them, so he told Tom the story.

"*Shit!* I'm sorry, mate. I don't blame you for not wanting folk to know. Don't worry, I won't say anything."

Randolph smiled. "I know, Tom. I saw some things during the war, like we all have; you're certainly no exception … things we'll never forget nor fully heal from … but this, this was something else. The whole sensation of it all. The victim's eyes … How do you *snap* a man's neck and back like that, you know?"

"I'd feel the same, Randolph. Whoever it was must have been bloody strong, to have done that!"

"Exactly. Even that little dog, who I mentioned was petrified. I don't get why he hid in that cupboard, rather than leaving the building, full stop."

Tom puffed away on his cigar, before removing it from his mouth. "Shit … You say you spoke to that Chief Detective?"

"Yep. I feel for him — all of them involved. The pressure from the victims' families and press and that. Having to see them bodies like that … He seems a decent enough guy, too. And again, he saw more than enough shit during the war. He was a lieutenant and then captain. Earnt the Victoria Cross."

"Wow. Brave man … they didn't give them out to just anyone!"

Randolph nodded. "I'll take the usual anyway, Tom. I think I'll buy one of those comics as well. Gives me something to read and take my mind off things. Temporarily, at least."

"The Beano?" Tom smiled.

"Yep." Randolph smiled back.

*

After buying some more smokes, Randolph headed back to his flat on Shaftesbury Avenue. It looked like a miserable day, both weatherwise and as the day in the life of a so-called private investigator. It had started to drizzle not long after Randolph said his goodbyes to Tom.

Randolph put his gas fire on, not that it gave out much heat. It had become fairly cold from late in the morning.

He chuckled to himself as he read *The Beano*, lying on the old sofa. He had only skimmed through the latest murder report in the *Evening Standard*. He didn't want to depress himself any more than he had to. At least his name wasn't mentioned, which was a minor consolation. The report had been almost repetitive, like previously. The latest victim was yet to be named.

Finishing the comic, he sat up and placed it down on the sofa next to him. He stretched up and yawned. Rather than throw the comic out, he would save it for Matthew to read, when he came down next. He often did this, the few times he'd bought one. "Fuck, it's cold!" Randolph got up and turned the setting up to high on his gas heater. He hadn't remembered it being as cold as this for a few weeks at least.

He then picked up his dirty ashtray from the table and made his way to the kitchen. Emptying it into the bin, he washed it out under the tap and made some more coffee. That was when his phone rang.

"Mr Randolph? It's Miss Albescu …"

Great. He temporarily forgot about her and her palm reading, and then she called him! 'Mr Randolph,' she called him, rather than his first name or Mr Landon. Must be a foreign thing. He hadn't asked what her first name was.

"I, I am sorry for calling you … I just wanted to apologise again, for what happened yesterday."

Randolph paused before answering her, "Don't worry about it … it's fine. Though, I can't help but worry now."

"I know. I am sorry. It's never happened to me before. Not like that. I didn't mean to scare you. I've been thinking a lot about what it meant as well. I can only get these *sensations* … and at times, very brief images. It's why I couldn't elaborate further on things, or on that circle or symbol. I am sure you will be fine. But as I said, *trust* your instincts, your inner intuition. *Look before you leap*." Miss Albescu gave a nervous laugh.

It made Randolph feel unnerved again. He sighed. "I guess I'll just have to watch out for *something* …"

Miss Albescu paused. "I just wanted to call you, and just explain a bit more. We are moving off Hyde Park in a couple of days … it was a pleasure meeting you, regardless, of yesterday."

"I'll be okay. Thank you again, for helping me find Peanut. It was a pleasure meeting you, too. Take care."

"You're very much welcome. You too, Mr Randolph. *Take care.*"

That 'take care,' didn't help Randolph. The way she emphasised it. He wondered what on earth it all meant. Maybe she was just a bit of an eccentric woman and he shouldn't read too much into it.

*

That Wednesday night grew colder; it was more like winter. The fear that had further gripped the city added to the chills in more ways than one. It still hadn't stopped people from going out. They believed there was safety in numbers.

A trumpet and saxophone were playing near to the entrance to the pool room at Teresa's. Jarvis James was the trumpet player. His partner in the duo, on this customary Wednesday Jazz Night at Teresa's, was Leroy Joseph, blowing passionately into his saxophone. The two popular black men had been playing there for almost four years now. Sometimes their performances would stretch to another day of the week, and they'd be accompanied by a skilled drummer; a Brummie by the name of Adrian Perks.

Randolph had often wondered what the smoky atmosphere did to the pair's lungs, inhaling it all through their instruments.

"How have you been, Randy?" Max asked. He had a pint of beer for himself, enjoying the music.

Randolph, sat at the bar in his usual seat. He looked up. "Wonderful," he said sarcastically, followed by a smile. He didn't tell Max about finding the body. He didn't want to offload onto Max, any more than he had done these past few weeks.

Max, who lived above his bar, had recently come down to take over from one of his employees. "That great, huh?" he replied sarcastically himself, smiling. "See there's been another one ..." Max was referring to the murder victim.

Randolph nodded, staring into his whisky. "Yep ... there's some sick people about, Max."

"Makes you wonder, doesn't it? It could be anyone committing these atrocious crimes. It could be someone that frequents my bar. Hell, they could even be in here now! It certainly causes fear and paranoia."

Randolph sipped some of his whisky. He had been there for almost two hours but it was still his first one. "It's no doubt what this bastard, or *bastards*, want. Leaving the bodies the way they do, they're injecting fear and worry into people. If they're careful and don't leave behind any clues ... they probably get off on it."

Max sighed. "I get that, well, from their point of view. I can't understand how anyone can do such twisted and God-awful things. It's terrible … I hadn't even thought that it might be *more* than one person doing this, until you just said that."

"It's quite possible, Max." Randolph took out a cigarette. He tapped it a couple of times on the bar.

Leaving out the 'dead body part,' Randolph eventually updated Max on the Peanut case, claiming he had found him safe and well and returned him to the grateful Mrs Tennyson. Max was genuinely pleased for him and insisted that the next whisky was on the house.

Jarvis and Leroy took a break from their performing and headed over to the bar, where Jarvis ordered a large brandy and Leroy a large whisky. They were familiar with Randolph; Leroy didn't live too far from him and they would often pass each other in the street. Randolph was fond of the pair and they likewise of him.

"You okay, Randolph?" the tall figure of Leroy asked with his large smile.

"How you doing, Leroy? I'm good," Randolph lied, although his mood had improved since he got to Teresa's.

"Good, good," Leroy answered.

"Jarvis …" Randolph smiled and shook Jarvis' hand.

Jarvis was shorter and stockier than Leroy. "Rando! You been keeping well?"

"Yeah, so and so … Some different tunes tonight, then?"

"We thought we'd mix it up a bit!" Leroy grinned.

"Sounds good, guys." Randolph smiled.

"It certainly makes your mouth dry, all this blowing! Certainly need to wet yer whistle," Leroy stated.

"I really don't need to hear about your two's sex life …" Randolph joked.

Leroy, Jarvis and Max all laughed.

*

Shortly after nine, coming back from the gents, Randolph caught a glimpse of a couple of men in a corner of the bar. It was DCS Quincy and DCI Burt Sommers. Both were taking off their trench coats, which were wet from the rain outside. DCS Quincy took off his matching grey fedora, placing it on the bar sofa next to him as he sat down.

Randolph retook his seat at the bar and saw the DCI walk over.

"What's it to be?" Max smiled.

"Just a pint of bitter and a lager, please," the DCI replied.

DCI Burt Sommers hadn't seen Randolph at first. He paid for the drinks and turning, noticed him. "Evening, Mr Landon." He half-smiled, before returning to the table.

"Detective." Randolph nodded.

Max looked over at the pair from across the bar. "Guess they're taking a break from their investigations … can't say I blame them, poor bastards! Must have their work cut out."

"Do you know them, then?"

"Not overly. The main one, Kendall, he comes in quite a bit of the time. As for the other one, not so much."

"Yeah. I saw DCS Quincy in here last Saturday night in the pool room. People were trying to get him to spill the beans on the case. He wasn't giving anything away. If there was much *to* give away."

"Rather them than I. They're no doubt under severe pressure and scrutiny. Especially with the press demanding answers."

Randolph and Max stared over at the detectives for a moment. They were in deep discussion, most likely talking about the case. They were sat a little apart from anywhere else, probably for privacy. The volume of the jazz music would make it harder for people to overhear too. Others briefly looked over at the two sitting there. DCS Quincy lit a cigarette. He nodded in agreement to something his DCI said.

Randolph and Max heard someone from across the room utter a few obscenities, something along the lines of "useless pricks."

Harsh, Randolph thought, but he couldn't blame them. These were unprecedented times. Nothing quite like this had happened in London since Jack the Ripper. Not to mention the ritualistic side to the murders. Some people interviewed on the news were suggesting that Jack the Ripper had returned from the grave, or even that it was still the same killer.

Randolph thought this highly unlikely for obvious reasons: these latest murders didn't involve prostitutes neither. Randolph was curious as to what the police did know. What linked the victims, for example? Was there a connection between the three victims? The police were keeping what cards they had, if any, firmly to their chests.

About twenty minutes after the DCS and DCI had sat down, the guy who had made the offensive remarks earlier started again. He began talking in a loud voice, talking over the live music so they could hear him. One of his friends at their table seemed to be trying to calm him down.

"No, I won't keep it down! They're sitting having a fucking pint, when they should be working their arses off, trying to catch my cousin's killer!"

The two detectives looked across the hazy room, between groups of other people standing; some were dancing to the music.

"Come on, mate! Everyone needs a break. I'm sure they've been working hard all through the day," his friend said, trying to reason.

"Fuck off, Jake!" The man then got up and pushed through the dancers and confronted the DCS and DCI, directly.

"Shit … here we go …" Max said, watching on.

"This is how you go about catching this sick fucker, *eh*? Sitting around and having a pint, smoking a cigarette, with your thumbs up each other's arses!" The man was average in height, in his twenties, with dark hair and receding hairline; he didn't hold back.

The two detectives just looked at each other for a moment. The man stood and glared wildly at them, demanding an answer.

Max stepped in, walking out from behind the bar before the detectives could answer. "Hey! Come on, now … that's not fair. You know the police are working day and night on catching this killer."

"Yeah? Well, they ain't working now, are they!"

The man's friend, Jake, with another friend got up and tried leading the enraged guy back to his seat.

"Fucking useless, I tell you!"

"Come on, mate! They're entitled to a pint and a break," the other friend said.

The two detectives still didn't say anything. They no doubt felt the pain and frustration of this man, having heard that he was a relation to the latest victim.

Randolph remained seated on the bar stool, watching.

By this time, Jarvis and Leroy had stopped playing. The rest of the bar had fallen silent.

"I'm not the first one to think it! I'm just saying it for what it is … There's a fucking sick cunt out there, and he's getting away with it, because of *their* incompetence!" The man viciously pointed at the two detectives.

Nothing they could say would calm this guy down. DCS Quincy tried anyway. "We're sorry for your loss. But believe us, we are trying *everything* to catch this killer and bring them to justice …" he said calmly, looking straight at the man.

"At least tell me why this killer is doing it? What is the motive behind it?"

"I'm sorry … I can't tell you that," DCS Quincy answered.

"Or you don't know… Fucking pigs!" The man's eyes had tears of anger.

"Right, that's enough … you're out of here. Now!" Max said sternly.

"Ah, fuck off! I'm done here, anyway." The upset man walked back to his table to knock back the remains of his pint. He slammed the glass down almost breaking it and stormed out the door.

"I'm sorry about that," one of the friends said to the detectives. The two friends then ran out of the door after their friend and into the pouring rain.

Less than a minute later, the jazz duo started playing again and the bar returned to normal, but not before some muttering. The two detectives looked sheepish. Max apologised to them and they insisted it was fine: they completely understood the man's anger.

"Who was that guy?" Randolph asked Max when he returned to the bar.

"I'm not sure. I don't think I've seen him in here before. He's certainly not a regular. I get why he's pissed off, but I won't tolerate that in my bar. Not when it isn't warranted."

A woman bystander approached the bar. She was carrying a black jacket. "That man left his jacket here. He was obviously too enraged and he forgot about it. His friends missed it, too."

Max thanked the woman. He checked the pockets for a wallet and some form of ID. He also pulled out a driving licence. "Jeremy Brixton … he lives in Blackfriars." He placed the wallet and licence back in the inside pocket of the jacket.

Just then, Jeremy Brixton returned wet from outside, he stormed straight up to where he had been sitting. Seeing the jacket had gone, he approached the bar. Before he could say anything, Max held up his jacket. Jeremy snatched it and marched out, glaring back at the two detectives.

"You're welcome," Max said sarcastically.

Randolph asked for the whisky Max had offered on the house.

*

Randolph parked his car in the garage at the back of his flat and made his way up the old creaky stairs. He wasn't sure why, but he was certain he had heard Jeremy Brixton's name before.

Chapter Eight
Thursday, May 19ᵗʰ, 1966

Shaftesbury Avenue, London – 9.32 am

Randolph checked the time on his watch. He looked out of the window to a bright morning and drank a cup of coffee. He frowned, thinking about the confrontation between this Jeremy Brixton and the two detectives last night. Maybe he was mistaken and he hadn't heard the name before. It certainly seemed to ring a bell. It took his mind from other matters. He shook his head, drinking some more of his coffee. He had definitely heard the man claim that the latest victim was his cousin. He would get today's paper again, to see if the latest victim had been named. He had considered asking the two detectives last night; they wouldn't have told him anything. It wasn't his place to ask.

*

"No Tom, today?" Randolph asked the boy. He was around thirteen, give or take a year.

"Nah … he's taking my nan out for the day," the boy replied in his young, Cockney accent. It was Tom Galton's grandson.

"Ah, okay." Randolph smiled. "Just a copy of the *Evening Standard*, please."

"Sure thing, Mister."

Walking down the street, Randolph checked the paper for any updates on the murders. The latest victim had indeed been formally identified; Reece Brixton. Same surname and cousin of Jeremy Brixton, no doubt. Reece Brixton was twenty-three. No wife was mentioned. Nor kids. He had worked in a warehouse near to the

76

docks before his 'untimely demise.' Randolph suspected that his cousin, Jeremy, was a few years older. Going by his looks.

Skimming through the paper as he walked, he almost bumped into a woman pushing a pram. He apologised. He then decided to head back to his office on Hopkins Street, just in case he had anything underneath his door. Yeah, right!

*

Greg, the cleaner, was outside smoking a cigarette.

Randolph trotted up the steps. "Morning, Greg."

"Hey, mate! You okay?"

"Yeah, I'm all right … You almost done?"

"Almost. Just got to do the downstairs."

"Don't suppose those morons have sorted out the lights yet, eh?" Randolph smiled.

Greg laughed. "What do you think? Useless, I tell you." Greg smoked the last of his cigarette and dropped it to the floor. He didn't bother stamping it out. He scratched his balding crown. "I doubt they'll get around to fixing them anytime soon. Some on the top floor have gone out as well now."

Randolph shook his head. "Doesn't surprise me, mate … I was thinking. Does your company have any cleaning jobs going? Even if it's part-time?"

"Cleaning jobs? You thinking of giving up the PI work, then?"

"Ah, I don't know, Greg. If I'm honest with you." Randolph scratched his right temple. "Work's scarce at the moment. It's hard to tell if and when something is going to come up again. I was just thinking of doing something to keep my mind occupied. I need the money as well. Ideally, something flexible perhaps."

"I can ask for you, mate, when I see the supervisor next. I know there isn't an awful lot about at the moment, mind. Not just cleaning, but in general."

"Yeah, that's fine, Greg. Thanks. Hopefully something *big*, will come up soon for me."

"Fingers crossed, mate. I'll ask for you, anyway."

"Appreciate it."

Greg went back to work and Randolph headed back down the dim corridor to his office.

Stopping at his office door and unlocking it, he heard someone walking in heels down the corridor. He turned to see a woman, around five-nine tall, coming towards him.

"Are you Mr Landon ... Randolph Landon?" the woman asked. She stopped a few feet away from him.

Randolph saw Greg grin with both his thumbs up, back in the foyer. Randolph tried not to laugh. Although the corridor wasn't well lit, the woman appeared to be quite attractive. "I am he. Yes."

"I hear that you are *quite* good at checking on potential 'cheating' spouses?"

"I've had some successful cases. I guess you could say that."

The woman smiled. "Then, I have a case for you."

"Then, we should talk. Come in ..." Randolph smiled. He opened his office door and gestured with the folded-up newspaper for her to enter.

The woman walked past him. Greg made a brief humping motion with his hips. Randolph grinned and shook his head, following the woman into his office. He closed the door behind them, after checking the mat.

"Please, sit." Randolph gestured again. "Would you like a coffee?"

"Please, thank you." The woman pulled out a chair and sat down. "Black. No sugar."

Randolph placed the newspaper on his desk and walked over to the small table where the coffee was. He filled the old kettle from the brass tap and it made its familiar vibrating sound.

The woman was more attractive in clearer lighting. She was around early forties. She wore a slim fitting, dark blue dress and a matching pillbox hat with a black birdcage veil, that covered the top off her face. Her blue eyes looked through it. Around her neck, she wore an expensive looking diamond necklace. Her earrings looked the same. A black leather shoulder bag hung over her right shoulder, which matched her black high-heeled shoes.

"Would you mind if I smoked a cigar?"

"No, no. That's fine," Randolph replied, looking over at the woman who crossed her legs.

She took out a silver patterned, engraved cigar case from her shoulder bag. Opening the case, she took out a short cigarillo and a holder. She put them together and then placed the cigar between her red-painted lips. She checked her shoulder bag for a light. "Damn. I seem to have forgotten my lighter …"

"Here …" Randolph walked over and took out his Zippo from his grey trousers. He lit the cigar for her.

"Thank you." She inhaled, then raised her chin up and exhaled. "I phoned you earlier. As I was in the area, I thought I'd check if you were by any chance at your office. Looks like I got here in time."

She was an elegant woman, not just how she looked, but in the way she spoke. Sophisticated, not posh. Nor rude or abrupt, although she could easily be interpreted that way. Randolph felt a little intimidated, not least because it had been a while since an attractive looking woman had been in his office, or anyone else, for that matter. He waited for the kettle to boil. "Won't be long." He smiled.

"That's fine." She half-smiled. "I'm in no rush."

Randolph didn't fancy a coffee for himself. He walked over to his desk and placed the hot mug down in front of the woman, being careful not to spill any. The smell of the cigar had already started to fill the room. He wasn't overly keen on cigar smoke. However, he wasn't going to refuse the woman for smoking. He did, however, open the window to let some fresh air in.

"I'm sorry. I can put the cigar out, if you wish? You should have said if it was a problem me smoking."

"It's fine, honestly … I'm a cigarette smoker myself. Rarely touch a cigar." Randolph gave a slight smile, sitting down at his desk to face the woman. He breathed out. "So, what can I do for you, Mrs?" He moved the ashtray on his desk nearer to the woman.

"Andrews … *Claret* Andrews," she emphasised her first name. Pronouncing it as *Cla-rette*.

"That's a nice name, Mrs Andrews. I've not known anyone by that name before."

Claret Andrews lifted her chin again and blew smoke into the air. "No need for flattery, Mr Landon." She gave a wry smile.

"I honestly wasn't trying to flatter you." Randolph smirked and adjusted himself in his old leather chair.

"My mother named me … she was fond of purple and red roses. She thought of me as her *little rose* when I was born …" She brushed back some of her dyed blonde hair from underneath her hat with her right hand.

"Your mother … she lives in London?" Randolph had no idea why he just asked that question.

"Not quite. She's dead … a car crash. Back in '57. She's buried here in London. It's been a while since I visited her grave."

"Oh. I'm sorry to hear that."

"It's fine … you weren't to know."

Randolph cleared his throat. "Anyway … I'm happy to help you …"

Claret Andrews was forty-two. She sat and talked about her marriage to her husband, Timothy Andrews. They had been together for twelve years and married for almost ten of them. He was forty-six. He had inherited his father's business of a luxury hotel chain, *Clarets*; the hotels were in numerous countries around the world, including one in Knightsbridge, central London. Randolph knew the prices. There was no chance he'd ever be able to afford a room there. Timothy's own mother had passed away whilst he was in his twenties. As a wedding present, Timothy had renamed his hotels from The Andrews' Hotel, with an apostrophe, to Clarets, dropping the apostrophe.

Claret described most of the marriage as having been excellent; great sex, luxurious holidays, gifts, and pampering. All was more than great. Randolph didn't wish to know about Claret's sex life, due to his own lack of one. Claret and Timothy had no children and for the past couple of months, things had begun to simmer down somewhat; their marriage had lost its spice. Claret's husband had been spending more time abroad since the start of May, and acting secretive about things. He seemed closed. They didn't talk nearly as much and Timothy was also dismissive at times. Her suspicions were aroused even more, when she heard that people had recently seen him with an attractive brunette — the same woman each time. When Claret questioned Timothy, he said it was business. Claret had joked slightly, suggesting it was most likely 'dirty business.'

Claret mentioned there were other things that pointed to her husband having an affair, although she didn't elaborate, apart from saying the phone often rang. She would answer it, yet the caller would hang up. Claret wanted concrete evidence that Timothy was cheating.

Randolph wrote all this down in as much detail as he could. He filled out a form he used for new clients: he usually added to the forms as needed later on in cases, and attached photographs etc. He turned the form over. His right hand had cramped. He gave it a shake still holding his favourite pen, a platinum sheep leather fountain pen, dark grey in colour — Japanese made. It was a wedding gift from his father-in-law. It hadn't come cheap.

"Perhaps, you should use a typewriter?" Claret jested. She had finished her cigarillo. The small butt was neatly squashed out in the ashtray.

Randolph laughed. "Believe me, I've considered it in the past. I guess I just like doing things the 'old-fashioned' way. Besides, it's not like I've been overly busy of late." He gripped his hand slightly, before returning to the form.

"Oh? Not many cases?"

"Not too many of late." Randolph didn't look up; he carried on writing. He tried to make his handwriting as neat as he could so he wouldn't struggle to read it later. "Just a few things here and there."

"I'm sure things will pick up for you, Mr Landon. Besides, you have *my* case now." Claret smirked.

Randolph briefly looked up at her. The way she looked reminded him of how Miss Albescu had looked. He then remembered the palm reading and her reaction to it. He shivered slightly.

"Are you okay?" Claret asked.

"Fine. Just adjusting myself." Randolph half-smiled, looking again at Claret.

"At least you don't have to worry about solving these awful murders that are being committed in the city ..."

"Yes. That's quite true." *If only she knew what I'd seen the other night,* Randolph then thought.

"What is it you do, Mrs Andrews?" Randolph looked up again at Claret.

"*Claret.* Please. I'm not sure I'll be a 'Mrs' for much longer, if my suspicions bear fruit." She smirked further. "Although I play a part in my husband's business, I have my own fashion brand and business. Many of my clothing and designs are sold throughout the country and internationally, as well."

"Did your husband aid you in that?" Randolph asked.

Claret laughed. "I'm not completely reliant on my husband, you know, Mr Landon."

"I apologise. I was just curious. And please, call me Randolph."

"You're fine. To answer your question, no. He's never paid a penny into my side of things. Of course, he offered but I do all right for myself. I'm not anywhere near *his* wealth, of course." Claret gave a wry smile.

Randolph jotted the details down. He then placed the pen on his desk next to the form, which was now completely filled.

"When can you start investigating?"

"Straight away. I have nothing else to work on. I am all yours."

"Interesting ..." Claret smirked some more. She sipped her coffee.

Randolph cleared his throat and felt a tingling sensation in his lower half. "You say your husband is due back this afternoon, from Switzerland?" Randolph hadn't even discussed the rate. He hadn't even thought of it.

"Correct. Naturally, I can do certain things myself. I can always follow him and that. Although, he doesn't tell me much nowadays. I am sure you are more inconspicuous and experienced than I, in these matters. Besides, I am busy with my business. Amongst other things."

Randolph nodded.

Mrs Andrews then discussed payment and asked how it all worked.

More often than not, Randolph would charge a flat-rate fee up front for his work. Sometimes he would ask for half now and half later. It varied depending on the case and what he believed was needed, or how long the client needed him, or whether it was ongoing. He also included expenses for travelling. If he needed to do more or travel further afield, he would then inform his client and request for more payment up front. Sometimes he was lenient and accepted payment afterwards. Of course, there was always the possibility of being paid an extra sum, if he was successful, as had happened with some of his latest cases, like a bonus. Certain cases were also tailor made. Either way, Randolph was more than reasonable, fair and flexible. His generosity and leniency occasionally went against him, if clients took advantage by delaying payment.

Before Randolph had estimated the cost, Claret spoke again. "You can start at my address I've given you. I shan't be home in the morning … I know he has a couple of meetings tomorrow. We can go from there. Perhaps, just for a few days to start. Even if he isn't having an affair behind my back, I'm curious as to what he's up to. I'm usually right with my gut instincts." Claret gave a crafty smile and reached back into her shoulder bag. She took out a black leather purse with a gold rim and bobble clasps. She opened it.

Randolph wondered if it was real gold. It wouldn't surprise him if it were.

Wetting her finger, she pulled out several pound notes. She handed them over. "I think this will be enough to get you started, Mr Landon — Randolph."

Randolph reached over his desk and took the notes. His eyes widened a little. It was over double what he would usually charge for a few days' work. "It's erm, quite a bit more than I would have estimated, Mrs Andrews — Claret."

"Maybe … but I believe you will be worth it … there maybe a little more in it for you as well." She looked straight into Randolph's eyes.

He felt a sensation down below again. He swallowed. "Rest assured, I will do my best. I can't always guarantee results, or the information that you wanted. I hope you understand that? Or, you might not like what I do find, if anything."

Claret smiled. "I understand … there are no guarantees in life. Not even great sex and marriage, it now seems …" She smirked.

Claret and Randolph finalised a few details. She pulled out a photograph of her husband. Randolph asked for her signature at the bottom of the form and they both signed it.

After she had left, Randolph sat in his chair going over the details on the form. He looked at the empty mug Claret Andrews had drunk from and her stubbed out cigarillo butt in the ashtray. They both had some smears of her lipstick on them. He then looked at the small pile of banknotes. It could be an interesting case. This was one positive thing of being a PI. He got paid for his work, regardless of whether it would return results. Again, Randolph hated the thought of failing. It never made him feel happy, just accepting people's money. Any case, big or small, he wanted to make sure he got what the client wanted. Even if their worse suspicions were true.

Claret seemed more than generous with her payment. Randolph didn't want to fail and disappoint her. It was more of a 'proper' case than he had had for a while. He also relied on his reputation. He had forgotten to ask Claret where she had heard about him. Chances were, a third party had recommended him to her, not that it mattered. She had come to him and he was good at what he did. *Great* some might argue, when he had something to investigate. He enjoyed his job, except for the fact it had put such a strain on his marriage.

*

Folding up the newspaper he had read and stubbing out his cigarette into the ashtray, Randolph decided to head home to his flat. He looked forward a little, to tomorrow's new case. Before Claret had left, he had offered to start the case straight away, today. Claret, however, stated it wasn't necessary, and to start tomorrow with the first meeting. She also never said what time Timothy would be returning home from Switzerland this afternoon.

Greg was finishing up mopping the foyer again. He saw Randolph exit the corridor stepping awkwardly. He had made a few muddied footprints on the floor.

"Sorry, Greg."

Greg didn't care. He stood grinning. "I'm often fighting a losing battle … don't worry about it. What did that woman want? You give her a good 'investigating' over?"

Randolph looked up and smiled. "Wouldn't you like to know!"

Greg laughed, holding his mop in his right hand. "You got a new case, then?"

"Seems that way. Just a few days to start." Randolph stopped near to Greg.

"Not worth me asking you what she wanted, eh?"

Randolph smiled. "Nope … client confidentiality."

"She was quite something …"

"Yeah, I saw you doing your 'thrust' thing out here." Randolph smirked.

"Ha-ha! I saw her strutting her stuff. She even gave me a smile when she left. I watched her go down the steps, too. Great arse. Have to admit!"

"Can't say I really noticed."

Greg laughed again. "What are you, blind?"

Randolph grinned and shook his head. "Here …" Randolph affectionately slapped the folded-up newspaper against Greg's broad chest and held it there. "Read this when you've finished."

Greg laughed again and Randolph made his way out of the office block and down the steps.

*

That evening after six, Randolph had another phone call from his son, Matthew. They spoke longer this time. Matthew couldn't stop laughing about the movie he had seen last Saturday; *The Ghost and Mr Chicken*. Randolph wished he had gone with the two of them, but he was happy that Matthew had enjoyed himself, even if it was bitter sweet. Randolph asked him how school was going. Matthew said he enjoyed it and had even made a new friend, a boy who had recently started there. Randolph couldn't help but laugh when Matthew called his new friend a 'brown' boy. Randolph corrected him by saying he should be called 'black' or perhaps 'of colour.' Matthew didn't mean anything malicious: it was just an innocent mistake a young child would make.

Towards the end of the call, Matthew once again asked his dad when he and Mum would be getting back together. Randolph just said they'd have to see. They ended the call both saying they loved and missed each other. Although it made Randolph feel sad, being apart from his son, he felt slightly optimistic after the call. He had a new case to start on, even if it was only for a few days. He was also due to see Matthew a week on Saturday. Both these things made him feel better, until he remembered what Miss Albescu had said. *And* the dead naked body of Reece Brixton. He also remembered where he had heard the name Jeremy Brixton before. It was from a flyer put through his letterbox before Christmas. It was advertising a removal service or something along those lines. Of course, it could have been a different Jeremy Brixton entirely.

# Chapter Nine
Friday, May 20th, 1966

Shaftesbury Avenue, London - 7.34 am

Randolph had slept fine after an early night. He made himself some cereal, drank some coffee and smoked a cigarette. He made his way into the bathroom to wash and brush his teeth. Claret Andrews had told Randolph that her husband had a meeting for 9.30 am. He intended to get to their home in Chelsea, roughly an hour beforehand. That was more than enough time. Randolph had asked if Claret was certain of this meeting; she told Randolph to "trust her" and smiled. She had said that her husband, Timothy, was usually late for most of his meetings so would probably be late leaving. Even if Randolph missed him leaving from home, Claret had already informed him where the meeting was due to take place: Bromley.

*

Gilston Road, Chelsea, London - 9.10 am

Randolph sat in his car on the opposite side of the road to Timothy and Claret's large and expensive looking home, which was a short distance away. There was a light green, 1962 Aston Martin DB4 GT Zagato, in front of him, and a dark blue, 1960 Porsche 356B Super 90 Cabriolet, parked up on a driveway to his left. They were a *lot* costlier than his own car. Trying to remain inconspicuous with his light blue Hillman Imp was perhaps a little difficult: he might stick out like a sore thumb, but he doubted that Timothy would suspect anything even if he saw him. Besides, there was a red Ford parked by the Andrews' house so they weren't all posh cars.

Randolph had sat patiently for just under an hour. He was dressed casually with no hat. Sitting there, surrounded by wealth and large houses made him feel meek, particularly the house next to him.

The Andrews' mansion appeared to be the largest on the street. The house stood a little more on its own than the others. The façade and exterior of the house were white and there was a five-foot wall that ran alongside the edge of the wide pavement. Above the wall grew several green, neat looking shrubs. A small red gate to the right side of the wall had white pillars on either side. A large main gate was open in the centre so that the Andrews could drive their cars into their driveway. Claret hadn't mentioned cars, but Randolph assumed that they had two cars at least.

A fountain decorated the middle of a large strawberry and cream, flint gravel driveway. Randolph couldn't tell from the outside, though he suspected that the back garden was also large, possibly with a pool. He couldn't imagine living such a luxurious lifestyle; he'd never cared for being wealthy. His own house and family with a steady income would be more than enough to make him happy.

Randolph checked his watch, just as two men came out from the house to his left with the Porsche on the driveway. With his window half-down, he could hear them; they sounded quite posh and laughed. One of them even pointed to Randolph's Hillman Imp when they came closer, joking that was his car. They laughed more, until they saw Randolph looking back at them from inside. They then dropped their smiles. The one who had pointed was wearing some grey and blue, chequered golfing trousers and a grey vest cardigan and a white cap.

"Yeah, you can laugh. You rich pricks," Randolph muttered, when they walked past his car to the Aston Martin. Randolph watched them chat. He didn't have anything against rich people, unless they were arrogant and up their own arses with it or if they had done sod all and had inherited it. He respected people who made their own wealth and worked hard for it, although it was often still down to a lot of luck. Not everyone had the right tools and luck needed to succeed, regardless of how hard they tried.

Randolph checked his Onsa again. Still no sign of Timothy

Andrews. He was cutting it a little fine. The man in the golfing trousers pulled out a golf bag and showed his friend some of the clubs. His friend seemed impressed. The golfing guy put his clubs back inside the Aston Martin. He said farewell to his friend and drove off. The other guy looked seriously at Randolph when he came back past. No doubt he was wondering why Randolph in his 'average' car, was sitting outside his home. Randolph tried not to make eye contact.

Less than a minute later, Timothy Andrews finally left his home. Randolph pulled out and was on the move. Timothy drove a BMW 507. Randolph couldn't help but think how these socialites liked their sports cars.

Randolph tailed him carefully, making sure at least one or two cars remained between him and his target.

Despite Claret's suspicions of Timothy cheating, she still believed that her husband's meeting was for business, to expand his hotel empire. It was likely he was working to expand into smaller hotels through mergers. Regardless, she still wanted confirmation of this meeting and for Randolph to follow him. It was still possible that her husband had lied. She hadn't explained too much detail, but stated that Timothy had his 'fingers in several pies.' Randolph believed that Claret was holding back and knew more than she was sharing with him.

*

Timothy was late. Randolph detected some arrogance in the man. He suspected this was a tactical move, to keep any potential clients on their toes. Randolph doubted that Timothy would be too fussed if a potential deal collapsed or didn't materialise; it wasn't like he and Claret needed the money.

The scheduled first meeting was to take place at a business centre that had opened back in '64. Randolph had driven past it a few times since it had opened.

Randolph held back whilst following Timothy Andrews, always keeping his distance, but enough to still have him in his sights. It didn't matter too much, because he knew where the meeting place was. However, it would have been awkward if the information was false, and he had lost Timothy.

With the detachable soft-top on, Timothy parked with several other cars at the front car park of the business centre. Not surprisingly, his motor looked the most expensive there.

Randolph temporarily drove past, with Timothy making his way inside through the double-glass doors. He was wearing sunglasses and a grey suit, no doubt both designer — no tie. Randolph swung back around at the end of Florence Road and pulled into the car park, parking several cars down from Timothy's car. The entrance was still in view.

Randolph sat in his car for a few moments, contemplating what to do next. He rubbed his face with his right hand. His stubble was already beginning to grow back fast. He had never been inside this business centre before. He wondered if he would be allowed in there. It may be for arranged meetings only, so he couldn't just waltz in there. Or could he? It was worth a shot. He didn't know where Timothy would be inside the building. If he could somehow get inside and perhaps be in earshot of Timothy and his meeting, he might learn something. He couldn't start taking photos either. It would look too suspicious. So, leaving his Kodak Brownie Cresta 3 camera on the passenger seat, Randolph opened his car door and got out. Making sure he had his spiral notebook and pen pushed in the ringed metal spine, from inside his jacket pocket, he made his way to the business centre entrance.

"Good morning." A seated, middle-aged woman wearing black, thick rimmed glasses, looked up at Randolph from behind a small reception desk to the left when he walked in. There was a telephone and a grey and white typewriter on the desk. An appointment book lay open. A green and white plant pot held a rather tall Dracaena, with its dark green, glossy leaves.

Randolph hesitated and then stopped. He wondered if he could just walk on past the reception desk into the main foyer and down the brown carpeted corridor. "Good morning."

"Can I help you?"

Randolph was about to say that he had an appointment with Timothy Andrews, but he thought better of it. It could backfire on him. He also wasn't exactly dressed for a supposed business meeting. "I erm. I'm just waiting for someone who's in a meeting … I just thought I'd pop in to use the loo," Randolph lied.

The woman gave a slight smile. "Oh, okay. Unfortunately, you aren't really allowed to use the facilities of the building, unless you have a meeting here. Silly, I know. But Mr Porter, who owns the building, is very strict and adamant about that." The woman gave an awkward clearing of her throat.

"I see. That does seem rather *strict* now, doesn't it?" Randolph replied sarcastically.

The woman looked a little sheepish. "I know. I am sorry. It's all kind of confidential here. Although there are a number of private rooms … He isn't here right now. But I could get into trouble if he found out."

Randolph thought it was a stupid rule. Obviously, it wasn't a public toilet, and it was understandable that they wouldn't want random members of the public just *strolling* in to use the loo. But considering Randolph gave the impression he was waiting for someone who was *meant* to be here, surely it wouldn't matter, especially when all the meetings no doubt took place in separate rooms, privately from each other.

"I'm sorry," the woman said again.

"Honestly. It's fine. You don't make the rules. And I'd hate for you to get into trouble." Randolph gave an understanding smile.

The woman did the same. "That reminds me; I better put this on. I can get moaned at about this, if I don't wear it …" She opened up one of the draws from the wooden desk, pulling out a small name badge and pinned it to her blue and white, gingham check blouse.

"This *Mr Porter*, sure does seem a very strict man," Randolph said in another sarky tone. He gave a smirk. What Randolph really meant to say, was how this Mr Porter seemed a right petulant arsehole. He looked at her name tag.

The woman, Coleen, going by her small name tag, couldn't help but smirk back. "He certainly can be … What time does the meeting end, for this person you are waiting for?" She glanced down at the opened appointment book for a moment, before looking back up at

Randolph with her slightly enlarged brown eyes through the glasses.

Randolph thought he would try charm. It had worked numerous times before in cases. He hadn't recalled a time it hadn't. "You know what, Coleen? I honestly can't remember." He gave a slight laugh. He jokingly tapped his forehead. "*Coleen* … That's a lovely name. It's also my mother's name," he lied again.

"Really? It was the name of my grandma. My mother named me after her."

"Well, fancy that." Randolph smiled, looking straight at Coleen. "I hope you don't mind me saying, Coleen, but that's an interesting necklace you have …"

"Oh?" Coleen frowned and looked down at the gold necklace that hung from her neck. At the end of the charm necklace was a cute boat propeller. Coleen held it. "Thank you … My father gave it to me. He used to love his fishing. He would sometimes take me when I was little … He, he was killed during the Second World War. He was a merchant seaman. He gave me this necklace for my birthday. Just before he went away …"

Randolph felt a pang of guilt for humouring the woman. "I'm really sorry to hear that, Coleen. I fought in the war. It was awful. I lost many friends. The things that I saw, too."

Coleen looked up at Randolph and smiled. "His crew and boat were attacked. They were helping with supplies, ammunition and food, amongst other things. He was a very brave man. Like all of you that helped and fought for us."

Randolph smiled. "I'm sure he was, Coleen. God rest his soul. *All* of them that died," he said sincerely.

"You know what? I'm sure it won't hurt for you to use the facilities. Mr Porter isn't here. I'm sure it will be fine."

"Really? As long as you don't get into trouble."

"It will be fine." Coleen smiled, touching her glasses. "If you go into the main foyer straight on, there is another corridor to the left. The toilets are at the end."

"Thank you." Randolph smiled.

The main foyer was hard floored and white. It was bigger than Randolph had anticipated. A large crystal chandelier hung from the ceiling and there was a bar there to the far end of the foyer. A couple of black leather couches were positioned by it as well as some tables and chairs. It looked very smart to Randolph, again, not what he had expected. A man from behind the bar wiping a glass, glanced over and smiled. Randolph smiled back before heading down the corridor to the left, past some wooden stairs that led up to the floor above.

Zipping up his jeans, he had no idea what to do next. He wasn't even sure which floor Timothy Andrews was on. Even if he had known, there wasn't much that he could do. He couldn't just barge in and ask to take notes and demand what the discussion was about. He was at a loss. He didn't even know how long this meeting was going to take or how many attendees there were. He was stumped. After staring briefly in the mirror and shaking his head to himself, he exited the toilets.

As chance would have it, Timothy Andrews came down the corridor towards him, past the other closed doors. Randolph started to feel a little nervous. What if he had been rumbled? Shit. He swallowed as Mr Andrews came closer. He said nothing and casually walked past Randolph, giving just a brief acknowledgement with his eyebrows. Randolph gave an awkward half-smile back. He turned his head to see Timothy enter the toilets. Randolph then had an idea; he could wait in the foyer to see where Timothy went. One issue though, would be that Coleen the receptionist might start to wonder where he was, and what was taking him so long — he decided to take that chance.

A couple of minutes later, Timothy Andrews came out of the toilets and returned to the foyer. Randolph stood at the top end of the foyer, looking out through one of the large windows. In the short distance, he could see an allotment where a few people were digging away in the now overcast day; it looked like rain. The man behind the bar had since left.

Trying not to look suspicious, Randolph turned to watch Timothy climb the stairs. He disappeared into a corridor above. Randolph then quickly made his way up the stairs in pursuit. Christ knows what he would say if Timothy *had* sussed him out. Regardless, Timothy seemed oblivious as Randolph saw him open up a door on the right near the end of the corridor, disappearing into one of the business centre rooms — but what next?

Randolph carefully and silently walked down the corridor, towards the room. He was just winging it now. Going on his instincts. He was hoping that he could somehow hear through the wooden door. He winced a little, approaching the door Timothy had entered.

Placing his ear a couple of inches from the door, he could hear several voices and then laughter. It was a little muffled. He hoped that no one would catch him and that the door wouldn't suddenly open. The other doors he had walked past were all closed and it seemed like they were vacant as there was no other noise.

Randolph wasn't even sure what Timothy's voice sounded like; he soon found out …

"My wife rarely puts out nowadays," a voice said, followed by laughter. "What about your sex life, Timothy? Any good? There's no point asking you, Peter. We know you don't have one!"

More laughter came from the room.

"I'm not one to divulge. But Claret's a great wife, really. She's always adventurous. That's all I'm saying on the matter."

Randolph stood listening, moving his right ear so it touched up against the door.

"Lucky bastard!" another voice replied. It was different to the other two. It could have been the one called Peter. Randolph had no clue as to how many people were inside.

"In more ways than one." Timothy Andrews laughed. "Anyway, let's get back to talking business … Our initial offer that was discussed, was thirty per cent. I'm thinking now, of fifty."

"Half? That's more than I was willing to go!" a reply came. It sounded like it was from the same man who had asked Timothy about his sex life. "Shit, Timothy. It's not like you need the money! It does seem a bit unfair. Can't you come down?"

There was a moment of silence.

"Forty? I don't think I'm being unreasonable. With my resources and reputation, I believe that it's fair. You'll gain more in the long run," Timothy offered.

The man sighed. "Shit … I guess you are right. Deal!"

Randolph sensed that the two men inside the room shook hands with this deal done, whatever 'deal' that may have been.

"I think we should have a drink to seal the deal? What do you say?" the voice of Timothy suggested. "Although it's early, I can grab a bottle from the downstairs bar. I know Ken Porter. He won't mind."

"Sure," the man who agreed to the forty per cent replied.

"I'll be right back."

Randolph quickly moved away from the door and jogged to the end of the corridor, then back downstairs. Coleen entered the main foyer at the same moment.

"Are you okay?" Coleen asked, frowning. "I thought you got lost or something." She gave a slight laugh.

"Sorry." Randolph smiled. "I got chatting to the person I am waiting for, outside the gents … they're not going to be too much longer. I'll wait in my car."

"Oh, okay." Coleen smiled back.

Timothy Andrews glanced at the pair, making his way back down the stairs and headed towards the bar.

"It was nice meeting you, Coleen," Randolph said, when Coleen sat back behind the desk. "Thank you for letting me use the facilities."

"You are most welcome."

"Have a nice day." Randolph made his way back to his car.

*

Randolph sat in his car for almost forty-five minutes. A few other people had left in the meantime, followed by others entering the building. He looked again at his notebook:

Timothy Andrews – forty per cent?
Who agreed to the forty per cent and what was it for?
Peter?
Three of them in the meeting?

He tapped his pen on the page, thinking. It had started to rain. If it wasn't for Coleen, he could perhaps have eavesdropped some more; he couldn't go back in there now. He decided to wait for Timothy to leave, along with the others.

Timothy soon came walking out of the business centre into the pouring rain, along with another man. Randolph managed to take a couple of photos as the two dashed towards Timothy's car. Randolph then added to his notebook:

Forty per cent guy? – 5'10" – balding – slim – early fifties?

"I'll see you two, soon," a voice called out, also exiting the building, before making his way to his own car, a brown colour Rover P5 Series.

Randolph took a photo and wrote down the number plate for reference:

Rover P5 Series – AOL 183B.

"No worries, Peter!" the man with Timothy called back, getting inside the BMW.

Peter – 6ft – dark hair – chubby – late fifties?

Randolph had no idea who this Peter was, nor the name of the other guy now in Timothy's car, but it would at least be some information for Claret. It was all he could do right now.

Tailing Timothy again, Randolph followed the car for several more miles where it stopped off in Lewisham. Claret had requested for Randolph to track Timothy after the meeting, though Randolph had already planned on doing that anyway.

After a few minutes, the 'forty per cent guy' got out of Timothy's BMW and hurriedly made his way to his presumed house in Clarendon Rise. The detached house, despite being fairly large, was nothing in size or style compared to Timothy and Claret Andrews.

Randolph added the address to his notebook and waited for

Timothy to leave. Timothy didn't hang about. He drove straight back home to Chelsea.

*

After following Timothy back home, Randolph decided to park up opposite to the Andrews' house. Again, a little further down. He had sat there for over three and a half hours, waiting to see what Timothy's next move was. Claret, herself, then returned home, driving her white Rolls-Royce Silver Cloud III. She only just spotted Randolph in his car. They conversed through the cars' windows; albeit, only briefly. Claret said they would discuss things later on by telephone and not here, including details of this second meeting. Of which, she wasn't sure herself where it was and what for — yet. She insisted on relieving Randolph of his 'spying' duties for now.

*

Randolph had decided to take a nap before tailing Timothy again that evening for his second meeting of the day. Wherever this was. Well, that was his plan, until he received a phone call from Claret Andrews not long after he woke up. She informed him that Timothy was staying home tonight, and that his other 'meeting' was cancelled. Timothy never disclosed what this meeting would have entailed.

"… So yes, Randolph, do not worry about this second meeting tonight. What did you find out from earlier?"

"That's fine … About earlier, I didn't learn too much from the meeting. It was a little difficult to get too much information, but I noted a few things, before Timothy returned home."

"That's good. What did you learn?"

Randolph explained to Claret about earlier and the two men's descriptions.

"Ah, yes. I know of these gentlemen. Peter Strong is a lawyer. Not ours, though. And this man who agreed to the forty per cent is most likely George Taylor. He owns several small businesses and hotels throughout Southern England. He is looking to expand his chain with my husband's help, further north … Timothy actually confirmed this earlier on, when I got back home."

"I see. Pretty much as expected, then?"

"Yes. Although I knew about this meeting in advance, I do not know what the second meeting would have been about. The cancellation is unfortunate." Claret sounded disappointed.

"What do you want me to do next, Mrs Andrews? Continue to tail him tomorrow? After all, you have paid me substantially in advance for my services."

"No. That's okay for now. I will be in touch. I don't want you to be at my beck and call, I will be in contact, though." Claret gave a slight laugh. "We can leave it be for now."

"Honestly, it's fine. I'm available for whenever you need me."

"I shall let you know."

Randolph was a little disappointed himself after this second meeting was cancelled. He was looking forward to following Timothy again. He was also interested to see what he was potentially up to. Instead, he ran himself a hot bath and drank a couple of whiskies and smoked a couple of cigarettes. He then watched some TV before heading off to bed. Wondering if tomorrow would bring about anything.

Chapter Ten
Saturday, May 21ˢᵗ, 1966

Hopkins Street, London – 9.26 am

Randolph bought his newspaper from Tom. He then went to his office to read it and saw Greg again, walking into the building. Although Greg's days and hours were flexible, his usually preferred days of working, were Tuesdays, Thursdays and Saturdays. The contract was for three days a week. Sometimes, things didn't even need doing much. He never had to worry about cleaning each individual office neither. Just the main parts of the building. Though sometimes, someone who was working there, would 'tip' him, for giving their office a clean whilst he was there. It was basically the person's job of whoever rented the office, to keep it clean themselves.

"Ah. I was hoping I would see you." Greg smiled. "I spoke to my supervisor and asked if there were any cleaning jobs for you. He said he would check with his boss and let me know. He thinks there might be something available."

"Thanks for that, Greg," Randolph replied.

"No worries, mate. There's some office building opening up at Charing Cross Road, soon. They're looking for people to clean there. Hopefully, I'll get to clean there, too. More money. We could even end up working together!" Greg laughed.

"Nice," Randolph replied, a little less enthused.

"Hopefully, it will be better than this old dump of a building, eh?" Greg laughed again. "Oh, at least they fixed the lights. They came yesterday, apparently. They're all working now."

"About time — until the next time they go out."

"Ha-ha. Yeah!"

Randolph then made his way down the corridor to his office. He checked the mat and then sat with his feet up on his desk, reading the paper.

Half the paper was about the London killings. There was an interview with some well-known psychotherapist on why they believed the killer was doing these things. His comments included a 'poor and abused upbringing' and maybe believing that Satan or even God was telling the murderer to commit these atrocious crimes, seeing as they had a ritualistic method to them.

*

After filling out half a crossword puzzle, Randolph's office phone rang.

"Hello again, Mr Landon — Randolph."

"Mrs Andrews …"

"Claret, please. I tried your home phone and then thought you might be at your office."

"I'm usually here or there. Though not always working." Randolph gave a slight chuckle.

"Well, I think I can help further with that, Randolph … How would you like a trip to France?"

"*France*? Excuse me?" Randolph frowned over the phone call.

Claret gave a little laugh. "Yes … Have you been, before?"

"Apart from during the war, I took my wife and boy to Paris for a few days a few years ago."

"Ah, sweet *Pah-rhee*," Claret said in a French accent. "Beautiful city. I can speak a little French … Anyway, yes. How would you like to go to France for a couple of days?"

"I don't understand?"

Claret laughed again. "I'm sorry. I'll get to the point. Last night, I heard my husband speaking to someone in his study. I have a feeling he may be taking the woman he is cheating with to France, or she is there already. Regardless, he was acting suspicious, when I brought him a coffee, and he quickly ended the phone call. I would like for you to go there, to see what he is up to."

"Erm. I can do. I didn't expect that I would be leaving the country, though!"

"Is it a problem, Randolph? It doesn't matter if it is. We can wait until he arrives back and go from there."

"No. No, it's fine. I'm just a little surprised, that's all. Besides, after all, you have paid me in advance for my services."

"You won't have to worry about any further expenses. Everything will be paid for you."

"Well, how is this going to happen? When do you want me to leave, exactly?" Randolph didn't know why, but he felt a mixture of excitement and anxiety. Perhaps as well, it was because he wasn't keen on flying.

"Timothy already left this morning. I know where he's staying. You can take a private jet, later this afternoon from Fairoaks Airport, in Surrey. I can send a car to pick you up."

Randolph knew of this small, private airport. It was used by the military during the war. "Erm. Sure."

"I know it's short notice, but at least it gives you something to do, and perhaps a change of scenery, yes ...? I'm sorry, Randolph. I didn't mean to come across as patronising."

"No. It's fine. It might do me good! I just wasn't expecting a trip to France. Or anywhere for that matter." Randolph laughed awkwardly.

"I believe it will only be for a couple of days. The driver will also bring some francs for you ... I know of a hotel not far from where Timothy will be staying, not one of our own hotels, though. A car will also be waiting for you to hire. It will be paid for, along with the hotel — once I arrange it. I know the owners of the hotel and the car hire company."

"I guess the big question is, where in France will I be going to?"

"*Limoges*. It's in Southwest France. Again, another lovely city. Timothy will be staying in one of our villas just outside the city there."

"Yes. I've heard of it."

"At this time of year, the UK shares the same time as France, too ... There's a private airstrip just outside the city. That's where you'll be picked up, Randolph. The driver this end will give you more details. I could go myself, but as I said before, I'm busy."

"I see," Randolph said. It seemed overkill that Claret would send him over the Channel to spy on her husband, especially if he wasn't being unfaithful. At the same time, however, it might be justified. And who was he to complain? A short trip away, all expenses paid for. At the end of the day, she was the client. Plus, he could do with a break away even if he would still be technically working.

"As I said, it should only be for a couple of days. When you are ready to return, phone me from the hotel and I will arrange your flight back and for the driver to collect you."

"I'm fine with that. I best pack a few things, then."

*

Fairoaks Airport, Surrey – 4.30 pm

Despite discovering someone had moved abroad in previous cases, Randolph had never travelled abroad per se for any of his investigations; this was a first for him.

He sat alone drinking a whisky on a light blue couch in the airport building that had a small bar. His small, brown suitcase sat on the floor next to him, containing a few items of clothing and his investigating tools, such as his camera. He even threw in an old pair of binoculars.

He got up to order another whisky — his third. Although his fear of flying wasn't too bad, he wanted to settle his nerves a little with alcohol.

"Same again?" The barmaid smiled.

"Please."

*

Forty minutes into the flight, things got a little bumpy. The private jet started to rock from side to side and Randolph started to fear for the worst. Even the stand-alone air stewardess looked concerned after she took a seat and buckled up. Randolph's whiskies, including a fourth in-flight, weren't helping him.

"Don't worry. We should be fine," the air stewardess said, looking nervously back at Randolph.

Randolph wondered if she was trying to convince him, or herself. Randolph didn't answer. The private jet seemed to drop several feet and he felt his stomach also drop. *Shit.* He looked out through one of the circular windows. The aircraft flew into a dark and menacing cloud. Several splashes of rain hit against the window. He gripped the seat arms and closed his eyes.

Thankfully, after a few minutes, the jet stopped rocking when it flew out of the cloud and the sun could be seen.

*

Hôtel de Limoges, Limoges – 7.32 pm – Local Time

The hire car, a Renault 16, was more than late, when it had finally picked up an annoyed Randolph from the private airstrip a few miles north of Limoges. The driver had kept apologising in his broken English. After dropping Randolph off, he had then made a phone call at hotel reception and sat down in the lounge waiting to be picked up himself. He would leave the hire car at the back of the hotel for Randolph.

Limoges was an attractive city. Randolph hadn't been here before, though he knew of it. He had travelled to France during the war, where the circumstances had been different then, with too much bloodshed. He hadn't fully appreciated the beauty the country had to offer.

He wasn't overly keen on heights but he had enjoyed looking out of the small private jet window, as it descended. He had admired the pleasant and vibrant countryside and the grazing cattle down below. It was certainly a contrast to the city of London.

The hotel itself seemed quaint enough. It was situated in the city centre. A couple of red canopies hung over the beige stone paving that lined the façade of the hotel. A French flag blew in the warm evening breeze from a pole above the entrance. Above both, a sign read *Hôtel de Limoges* in blue. Further up were the bedrooms. Several had small walk-out balconies with black railings.

Randolph wondered if the Andrews had their own chain of hotels here. He assumed not, seeing as he was staying in a different hotel to theirs.

After Randolph had been checked in by a rather camp Frenchman, Patrice, Randolph was shown upstairs to his room on the third floor, by a female employee.

Randolph sat on the huge hotel bed. He opened the white envelope with the franc notes in it and read Claret's note:

This should cover you for a couple of days – Claret.

She had been more than generous with the money, considering his stay in France was only supposed to last for two days.

Randolph pulled out another note with some details on it, along with Claret's number:

Timothy bought this villa back in 1961. We have stayed here numerous times down the years. This is the third time since the start of the month he has flown out there, which I can only assume is with or to see his 'woman-friend.' Even if I am wrong about an affair, he is most definitely up to something! Find out what you can, Mr Landon. When we are not using the villa, it is usually looked after by a couple we know down there. I include the address of our villa with a map on the back of this note, and if you need anything else, please don't hesitate to phone me. All calls will be paid for.
Claret

Randolph turned the piece of paper over and saw the black and white copy of a map and address of the villa below, attached with a blue paper clip. The villa was in a place called Verneuil-sur-Vienne, some seven miles or so, west of Limoges.

Placing the envelope down on the small chest of drawers, he considered taking a nap. His head hurt from the whiskies and the flight, not to mention the frustration of having to wait for the hire car. He then reconsidered. He took a couple of painkillers from his

St Joseph aspirin tin in his suitcase and washed them down with water from the tap in the bathroom. Claret wasn't paying him to sleep, dammit.

*

Getting nearer to Verneuil-sur-Vienne, Randolph again admired the countryside and hills, while driving the red Renault 16 through the old country roads in the setting sun. It was very rustic and rural — peaceful. He had his window down, welcoming the warm fresh air. He almost made the mistake of driving on the left-hand side of the road; he also had to get used to the steering wheel being on the left-hand side of the vehicle.

He wasn't sure what he would do once he arrived outside the villa, or if Timothy and his alleged mistress were there. He felt, however, that he may as well get out to work and appreciate the view. Fortunately, his aspirin was kicking in. In his soft grey trilby, Randolph smiled and nodded at an old French farmer on horseback, pulling a large metal trailer of fresh manure: the smell from it picked up in the breeze as he drove past.

Verneuil-sur-Vienne was a quiet commune in the Haute-Vienne department. Randolph followed the map and had no difficulty finding the Andrews' holiday villa. It wasn't quite as big as he had expected, though obviously worth a lot, nonetheless. It was certainly something that he alone would never be able to afford. The Andrews certainly had it made. He couldn't quite help feeling a little envious, once he pulled up the Renault 16 not far from the entrance that had a palm tree to its right.

A slabbed driveway led up to the square-shaped, beige looking villa at the end: there were numerous red and yellow daffodils along each side. A large, lush lawn with a couple of small trees, was laid in front of the house. The villa had two floors. All windows had light blue shutters; one below and one above were open, along with the rectangular shaped windows. The villa doorway was on the left of the building. Randolph watched some birds land on the brown, slated roof that over hung the villa.

After admiring the villa, Randolph drove on a little further down the old country road, out of sight, where he passed an old blue camper van. He then saw a red and white, 1960 Ford Zephyr, coming down the other side of the road and realised that it was Timothy Andrews. A brunette wearing sunglasses sat in the passenger seat.

"Shit ... " Randolph quickly took his left hand off the steering wheel and raised his arm to cover his face. He didn't want Timothy Andrews to recognise him from the business centre.

Regardless, Timothy paid no attention driving past, pulling into his villa.

Randolph continued a little, before coming to a lay-by and a large oak tree, where he swung the car around. He cursed when he struggled to get the car into gear, making a rather loud grinding sound.

It now seemed that Claret Andrews' suspicions were right. But Randolph wasn't jumping to any conclusions just yet. This woman in Timothy's car could literally have been anyone. Even just a friend. Randolph made his way slowly back down to the villa, where he saw the Ford Zephyr parked up on the driveway. The big question was, what would he do now?

Randolph pulled over just past the villa and sat thinking as the sun slowly went down behind him. He made clacking sounds with his mouth, considering what he could do next. Out of the car window, he heard voices chatting. It was no doubt Timothy and the woman. The Andrews' villa was pretty isolated, distanced from other residents, similar to their main home back in Chelsea. The Andrews perhaps valued their privacy more than most.

Slowly getting out of the hire car and closing the door as quietly as possible, Randolph walked slowly to the back of the villa via the right side, which was protected by numerous fresh smelling bushes and trees. He sometimes suffered with hay fever, but he resisted the urge to sneeze. He pulled a white napkin from inside his trouser pocket and wiped his runny nose. Fucking hay fever!

Cowering whilst listening and watching, he felt like some kind of obsessed stalker, and technically speaking, being a PI was like that. Randolph could see Timothy through the bushes on a patio. There was a more than adequately sized outdoor pool. Timothy was holding a glass of what looked like red wine, smoking a cigarette and the woman was walking over to be near to him.

"… It's been over two weeks now since she went missing. It's not like her at all. She isn't one for letting people down regarding work. Something isn't right. Sorry, I know I keep repeating myself."

Randolph peered on, frowning.

"It's fine. I do the same, Mr Andrews. I'm only her assistant. As I say, I don't really work too much on site. I do more of the paperwork side, arrange meetings, things like that. It is a concern. She's never gone quiet for longer than a few days before. This time definitely feels different," the woman replied, now taking off her sunglasses.

Timothy sighed. "I'm going to have to try someone else, other than the police and gendarmerie. I'm not bothered about how much it will cost; I just want her found."

"I understand. I'm really worried, too. She isn't just my boss, but my friend as well."

Timothy drank some wine and shook his head. He then threw what was left of it into the swimming pool.

"I'll look into things more tomorrow, when I arrive back in Paris. I'm doing my best, Mr Andrews."

Timothy turned and smiled. "I know you are, Christine. And I really appreciate it. And you can call me Timothy."

Randolph wondered what the two were talking about.

"I've got some business calls to make, anyway … It's gotten a little chillier out here now."

"Yes. It has. Thank you for letting me stay the night."

"It's the least I can do."

As Timothy went to make his way back indoors, Randolph stepped on a huge twig, snapping it. It caught the attention of both Timothy and Christine. Neither of them said anything.

Randolph winced and carefully made his way back to the hire car.

Chapter Eleven
Sunday, May 22ⁿᵈ, 1966

Rue Louvrier de Lajolais, Limoges – 8.17 am

Randolph looked at his wristwatch. He had tried phoning Claret from his hotel room after he got back the previous night. Despite trying several times, there was no answer. He'd try again after breakfast. Perhaps Claret would know about this Christine, who Timothy was speaking to at their villa yesterday evening.

Randolph was sat in the breakfast lounge where a few other people had joined him. Behind him on the right near to the entrance, was the bar. He already thought ahead to this evening when he might have a whisky or two.

"Would you like a refill, Monsieur?" a young waitress asked, smiling.

"Please." Randolph looked up, smiling back.

The waitress smiled again, carefully pouring the hot coffee.

"Merci." Randolph winked and gave a grin. She looked a nice girl.

Randolph waited a little while before having his second coffee of the day. It was *damn* good coffee. His mind pondered about his latest case. It was still possible that Timothy Andrews was having an affair, even if it wasn't with this woman at his villa. But Randolph started to doubt that now. Timothy was definitely concerned over some missing woman and up to something. That much was evident. The question was, who was this missing woman? Why the secrecy keeping it from his wife? Unless, Claret knew about all this. Either way, he'd ring her after he was finished eating, and when he'd finished this really good coffee.

*

Randolph had a shower and wrapped himself in a dark green bath robe, courtesy of the hotel. He sat on the edge of the bed, with his hair still partially wet.

"Mrs Andrews. *Claret* ..." Randolph finally managed to reach her by phone.

"Mr Landon. *Randolph*," Claret replied a little sarcastically. "You have some news for me, already?"

"I think so. I need to ask you some questions, though."

"Feel free to ask away."

"I tried ringing you last night, but there was no answer. I found your villa without any problem. The area is a lovely place. Anyway ..." Randolph told Claret about the conversation between her husband and this woman.

"Interesting ... Judging by your description, it most likely is the same woman others have reported seeing with my husband in London. I have not seen her for myself. Whether he is being unfaithful or not, it is clear he is up to something."

"You don't know of the name, *Christine*, then?"

"I am afraid I don't, Randolph. I'm in the dark as much as you. But I believe you will find out. Although I do not like snooping, I've searched through my husband's things in his study — I can't find anything."

"Who could this woman be, who your husband is intent on looking for? Any theories? Any at all, might aid me in my investigation. Or *investigations*, I should say."

There was a sigh and pause from Claret. "I honestly don't know. My husband knows a *lot* of women. Who doesn't, when you are a rich businessman? Just as I know many men. But he hasn't told me about any missing woman or person. I honestly don't know. This is all new to me. I am sorry ... Of course, it could even be a different woman to the one others saw him with in London."

"It's fine. I'm going back to the villa. Hopefully, he'll still be there. I can perhaps go on a stakeout." Randolph laughed slightly.

"Do what must be done, Randolph. If you need anything, anything at all to assist you further, don't hesitate to call me."

Randolph detected that she was concerned. "I will do my best,

Mrs Andrews — Claret. I always do."

"I know you will."

*

The Andrews' Villa, Verneuil-sur-Vienne – 9.20 am

It was a nice morning — more than warm already, with a clear blue sky and the sound of the birds chirping. Timothy's car hadn't moved since last night. Randolph pulled over past the villa and kept his eyes peeled. He wondered if Christine was still there. She had said the previous evening that she was due to fly back to Paris today.

Randolph sat thinking. He wore a dark brown trilby. He had given up the fedoras of late. He felt his head start to perspire. He took off his hat and placed it on the dashboard. He sighed and got out of the car. He lit a cigarette and walked around the car a couple of times, before leaning up against the front of the Renault 16; feet crossed.

Taking his time with his cigarette, he closed the car door and made his way down the road to the villa. He could hear the gentle sound of splashing as he took up the same position as yesterday evening. Ducking his head under a few branches and minding not to get scratched by the bushes, he peered into the garden.

Timothy Andrews was in the pool, doing several laps of breaststroke. He then got out and picked up a red towel to dry himself from one of the nearby wooden deck chairs.

Randolph gave a slight smirk and shook his head. He felt like some kind of pervert.

Christine came outside. "I'm ready to leave when you are, Mr Andrews."

"Let me just get dressed … You can't beat a nice morning swim." Timothy smiled.

*

Randolph tailed Timothy and Christine to the same airstrip where he had arrived yesterday. An orange windsock blew in the breeze.

Randolph took some photos when the pair got out of Timothy's car. He tried to listen in, but Timothy was parked up across the car park.

The airstrip was just that. A basic airstrip in the countryside with one small building that included an office.

It was hard to understand what was being said between Timothy and Christine. Timothy placed what seemed like a sympathetic hand on her left shoulder. A small jet soon landed. It was a different one to the one Randolph had arrived in. Timothy then carried Christine's suitcase over to the jet as the small steps were coming down. Randolph wondered if these private jets were owned by the Andrews themselves. Or perhaps they just hired them for when they wished.

Timothy started to walk back and turned his head around, raising his thumb to the pilot.

"What the heck is going on," Randolph muttered to himself.

*

Randolph had followed Timothy back to the villa. He had sat for almost three hours in his car out of sight from the entrance. He now started to become hungry and his stomach rumbled. This was one of the worst things about the PI job, having to wait and be patient. It could become painstakingly boring. But Randolph had to remain calm and patient when in these situations, careful not to doze off at times, particularly throughout the night. There were times when he had drifted off and had almost missed where someone needed to be tailed, or followed on foot. Randolph however, did become a little more accustomed to it down the years.

He considered going back to his spot in the bushes; currently, there was no point. No one else was in the villa besides Timothy. It could be a few more hours before Timothy himself left again, if at all, for the rest of the day. The case could become even more mind-numbing.

*

Over an hour later, Randolph's stomach started to hurt. He was craving for food in spite of the big breakfast that morning. He sighed and muttered under his breath. A blue gendarmerie car drove past him. The gendarme was wearing a dark navy hat and looked over at the parked-up Renault 16. Randolph hoped he wouldn't pull over and question him, not that he was doing anything illegal. Instead, the car turned into the villa up ahead. Interesting. Randolph frowned.

Randolph hesitated. He opened the car door. He intended to eavesdrop. Risky or not, perhaps he could find out something further …

"Monsieur Andrews …" the gendarme said in his thick accent.

Randolph stood at the end of the entrance to the villa. He peered out slightly from the bushes opposite the palm tree.

The thin, moustached gendarme stood at the door at the side of the villa. "I hope you are well today, oui?"

"I've been better — have you any news?" Timothy quickly asked. He remained out of sight in the doorway.

"Sorry, I am afraid not, Monsieur Andrews. We are still looking into the woman's disappearance. I was driving through the area and thought it would be common courtesy to see you, again, oui. Seeing as I wasn't available when you met my colleagues yesterday."

"Thank you, Arnaud. That's kind of you. Christine is going to do more on her side, once she's back in Paris."

"Again, I wanted to let you know in person that we are doing all that we can. The police in Paris, too."

"Thanks … I'm thinking of hiring more people to look into Natalie's disappearance."

Natalie? Randolph frowned.

"It is most understandable. We do not believe that she is in the area, non. So, it would be good to widen the search. We are doing all that we can."

"I know you are. I appreciate what you are doing and you coming here in person, Arnaud. Hopefully, she is safe and well somewhere, wherever somewhere is."

"We will of course let you know of any further updates, oui," the gendarme added.

Randolph continued to listen; nothing much was said, other than brief casual talk. The gendarme talked about his newborn child keeping him and his wife up at night, and how the lack of sleep was making him feel like *la merde* at work.

The gendarme nodded his head and said goodbye. He slowly turned and walked back to his car. Randolph quickly jogged back down to his own car.

*

"Natalie, eh?" Claret sounded suspicious.

Randolph had driven straight back to the hotel and rung Claret Andrews, again from his room.

"I think I know who this Natalie is. Of course, it may just be a coincidence and a different one …"

"Well, who do you think she is?"

"Timothy's ex-partner …"

"What? Really?"

"He was actually engaged to a Natalie. He had proposed in his twenties. Things didn't work out. But they still remained on good terms. Though, I didn't realise they spoke anymore."

"I see …"

"As I say, it could be a different Natalie. But it's most likely to be her."

"But if it is her, why the secrecy? Why would he not tell you that she has disappeared? Why would he be so concerned after all these years?"

"I've met this Natalie a few times. We didn't always see eye to eye. Although I didn't think that Timothy still loved her, he had some feelings for her. That might explain the secrecy, unless they were having an affair behind my back. As far as I'm aware, she never married." Claret let out a sigh over the call.

"Interesting … I wonder where she's disappeared to?"

"She's an archaeologist, Randolph. She specialises in a few ancient artefacts and things and knows her history. She has quite the reputation. I know that Timothy helped fund one of her projects a couple of years after we married, over in Mexico. I wasn't happy about it, but he said that it was a one-off … I know he felt bad about how their relationship ended, despite there being no hard feelings."

"If your husband funded her again, and she got herself involved in something, it would make sense that she might disappear like she has …" Randolph sat on the edge of the bed and made some notes in his notebook.

"I certainly hope she's okay. I wouldn't wish her any harm … Well, unless she *was* doing the dirty with my husband." Claret gave a little laugh. "Obviously, something has happened."

"You have no idea where or what she was working on? Do you still want me to track Timothy until he leaves France? Will you contact him, demand answers?" Randolph took the lit cigarette that was resting in the glass ashtray on the chest of drawers. He took in a couple of large drags while Claret paused.

Claret sighed again. "I am afraid I don't know what she's working on. I didn't know he was still talking with her … Stay to keep an eye on him until he leaves for home, which should be tomorrow. I will confront him once he returns. But see if you can learn more, Randolph. After all, he might not tell me anything if I do confront him. I'm still not ruling out an affair, either, with his ex or somebody else."

"Okay. I can head back to the villa. There isn't much else that I can do, other than wait to see when and where he goes next — if he does … The patient and frustrating game of being a private investigator." Randolph chuckled and breathed out some smoke.

"Yes, I can imagine it requires much patience … but I believe you're doing your best. Take care, and don't hesitate to call me again."

"I won't. Speak soon, Claret."

*

After getting some late lunch at the hotel, Randolph headed back to the villa. He parked in the same place as before. He hoped the gendarme station wagon wouldn't pass him again, in which case he would look suspicious. Randolph yawned and looked at his wristwatch. The nice day had now turned overcast and droplets of rain splashed over the windscreen. Randolph sighed and shook his head. At least he was getting paid for this. Or had been paid. He considered taking an afternoon snooze in the car, but thought better of it.

Feeling the urge to urinate, he got out the car and relieved himself in some overgrowth. Getting back to the car, he saw Timothy leave the villa in his car, turning left.

Not for the first time, Randolph followed behind …

*

With the country roads quiet, Randolph kept his distance from Timothy. He again admired the rural scenery and old houses, which were now dowsed in heavy rain. Randolph wondered where Timothy was heading to this wet afternoon. He hoped it wouldn't be too far.

They had driven through the small commune of Veyrac — a few miles or so from Verneuil-sur-Vienne. Before exiting Veyrac, Timothy pulled over at a small roadside florist. He bought some bright flowers from the elderly woman who stood in a wooden hut near to an old stone house, probably her own. Randolph could hear Timothy thank the woman in French.

A few minutes later, Timothy indicated right and turned through some black wrought iron gates into an old cemetery. Randolph frowned. Still keeping his distance in the downpour, he slowed down on the opposite side of the road further up. With the flowers just bought, it was evident that Timothy was visiting someone's resting place. Tapping his fingers on the steering wheel, Randolph considered what to do next. Was it worth following Timothy into the cemetery, or should he wait until he came out? He didn't wish to be seen. It was highly unlikely Timothy would be meeting someone. Surely he was just visiting a grave. Randolph's curiosity got the better of him.

He could already see some of the graves and tombs from where he'd parked the Renault 16. He reached into the back seat of the car and grabbed a black umbrella he had brought with him. Rather than drive through the large gates, he walked. The entrance sloped upwards. Black iron fencing lined the top of the overgrown embankment. Going through the cemetery entrance with the umbrella up and his head bowed wearing a grey trilby, Randolph noticed Timothy's car parked up to the right. His was the only car there.

The cemetery was a little larger than Randolph had expected. A large stone crucifix was mounted high up on concrete ground, in front of some old uneven steps, which led further down to the main part of the cemetery. Keeping his eyes peeled for Timothy, who was nowhere in sight amongst the masses of tombs, graves and crosses, that were surrounded by patches of grass, Randolph slowly walked down the steps. The rain started to fall even heavier. He stopped at the bottom, underneath a large yew tree. There were a few other old trees scattered around the cemetery. He wondered where Timothy was. The last thing that he wanted was to be seen.

After a moment, Randolph carefully walked out from under the yew tree and down the pathway that separated the cemetery. With his umbrella tilted down more, protecting him from the rain that was blowing in his face now, he saw Timothy to his right standing over a grave, also holding an umbrella. Randolph quickly moved on so that Timothy wouldn't see him.

Taking cover under a smaller tree, a little further on, Randolph remained out of sight, but in a position to be able to watch Timothy. After several more minutes of waiting, Randolph saw Timothy walk up the steps and disappear back to his car. Randolph then made his way across to the grave where Timothy had been standing. It was whiter and more preserved than the other graves or tombs nearby, despite the age of it; it had a stone angel positioned next to the headstone, looking down at the ground, where Timothy had placed the fluffy looking white and pink flowers. Randolph read the headstone:

IN LOVING MEMORY OF A
BEAUTIFUL DAUGHTER AND SISTER
TAKEN TOO SOON, BUT LOVED FOR EVER
TIFFANY IRENE ANDREWS
03.03.1922 – 18.04.1932
FLY HIGH WITH THE ANGELS

Randolph frowned for a second. This young girl who was laid to rest here, was obviously Timothy's younger sister. Claret had never mentioned Timothy had a sister or any siblings for that matter. Certainly no mention of this poor, young girl, who had died at the age of only ten. Unless it was a cousin or other relative. There was that possibility. And why buried here, in this isolated cemetery, in west-central France? Thinking it over, it wasn't exactly relative for Claret to mention of it anyway. Randolph just assumed that Timothy was an only child, seeing as he inherited his father's hotel chain. Randolph rubbed his chin, underneath the umbrella, just as the wind picked up, ruffling the flowers.

*

Back at the hotel that evening, Randolph sank a whisky at the bar after he had eaten. He would phone Claret soon and ask about 'Tiffany,' and arrange his return to England for the next day. After visiting the cemetery earlier, he had followed Timothy back to Verneuil-sur-Vienne. Staking out the villa, Randolph had deduced that Timothy had retired for the evening. There wasn't much else that could be done and Randolph was due to fly back tomorrow.

"Another please," Randolph said, when the barman walked over.

"Oui, Monsieur."

Randolph took out a cigarette. "Merci."

The barman placed the small whisky glass in front of him.

Randolph took his time with his second whisky. He wondered again, what all this meant; the missing Natalie — Timothy's missing ex-fiancée, and a possible deceased sister buried in that cemetery. He also wasn't looking forward to the return flight tomorrow. He started to feel a little anxious and finished the last of his whisky. "Merci," Randolph said, getting up from the wooden bar stool.

"Good night, Monsieur," the barman replied and smiled.

Randolph walked up the hotel stairs to his room.

*

After taking a long and hot shower, Randolph sat on the edge of the bed in a white towel and called Claret from the telephone on the bedside table.

"Hello?"

"Mrs Andrews. Claret. It's Randolph. I hope you're well, tonight?"

"Ah. Randolph. I'm fine, thank you. I'm just about to take a long soak … You have any news?"

"Nothing new to report, I am afraid. Although, there was one thing …" Randolph told Claret about the cemetery and resting place of Tiffany Andrews.

"Mhm … Yes. It was most tragic. Timothy did have a younger sister that unfortunately died all those years back, when he was only young himself. The poor girl had an aneurysm. She died right in front of him. I know of this cemetery … They used to visit the area on holidays as a family, back then. As a young girl, she used to like this cemetery. So, they buried her there."

Randolph still thought it seemed a little odd. "I guess that makes sense. I did wonder. I thought it was strange that she was buried there. That hers was the only 'Andrews' one there. At least from what I could see. I checked around before I left. Most of the headstones were in French, of course. Not many were in English."

"To be honest with you, Randolph. It hadn't crossed my mind to mention it before. I didn't think that it was necessary."

"I get that. It has nothing to do with the current case … What happens next? You still want me to return home, tomorrow? What are the arrangements?"

"Yes. I need to question my husband upon his return. I still may need your services, Randolph. But you have acquired enough information for now. There's no need to beat around the bush any further. I need to know why Timothy is trying to track down his ex-fiancée, Natalie."

"Do you think he will be honest with you, Claret?"

Claret sighed. "I think he will be, Randolph. When I tell him what you found out, I don't think he will deny things. He's usually honest about things, even if he doesn't always tell me everything. He rarely lies."

"Well, just as long as he doesn't come after me or something!" Randolph semi-joked.

Claret chuckled. "You will be fine, Randolph. Timothy is usually laid back, although he has appeared a little stressed of late. He's clearly concerned about this Natalie's disappearance, it seems. I guess we will have to see … About tomorrow, your return flight is booked in the afternoon at two. Feel free to do what you like in the morning. I included some money in the expenses for you to enjoy. Perhaps check out the area some more? Enjoy yourself. There are some lovely shops in the city and some great cafés."

"Thank you, Claret, but I don't think it's right to spend your money. You've already been more than generous for my services."

"It's fine, honestly. You've earnt it."

"Thank you."

"You're most welcome. You can leave the hire car at the airstrip, and it will be picked up after you've left."

Chapter Twelve
Monday, May 23rd, 1966

Central Limoges – 10.00 am

After breakfast at the hotel, Randolph decided to walk through the city of Limoges before his return flight at two. It was certainly a lovely city, quaint with its attractive historic buildings, perhaps, a hidden gem. Although busy, it wasn't hectic. The streets were kept clean, compared to London. The city was fair on this glorious, warm, sunny morning. Randolph felt it was a shame that he couldn't stay on for longer. Locals smiled warmly and greeted him as he walked the streets, saying "Bonjour." In return, he nodded his trilby at them, trying to fit in. He couldn't speak French, but he knew some of the basics, including a few swear words learnt from the French Resistance during the war.

He checked out a few shops and went into an old bookstore that had been established way back in 1898. He wasn't sure why he went inside, especially as most, if not all of the books were likely to be in French. He was greeted with a friendly smile from an elderly gentleman, who looked almost as old as the bookstore itself. A much younger, attractive woman also greeted Randolph in French as he perused through an old dusty book. She seemed to work there, and was going around some of the bookshelves, wiping dust away from the books. She blew on a couple, so that the dust particles dissipated into the air.

Next, with Limoges being renowned for its porcelain, Randolph entered an old porcelain shop. He was greeted by a middle-aged woman. Randolph smiled.

Taking his time and looking at the porcelain on sale, Randolph noticed a cute looking elephant that was half the size of his hand. It had a small price tag attached to one of the stumpy back legs. The original price had been crossed out and a lower one written in its place.

Although perhaps a little dear, Randolph thought this porcelain, trumpeting white elephant with blue markings would be an ideal gift for Matthew. Matthew was fond of elephants, and often mentioned about how he would like to ride on one. Randolph picked it up to examine. It was fairly heavy. On the underbelly were the Limoges porcelain markings. He decided to buy it, so he walked over to the counter and smiled at the woman, handing her the elephant.

The woman carefully took the elephant from Randolph and asked him something in French.

"I'm sorry. Erm. Je ne parle pas Français."

The woman smiled and asked in English this time, "Would you like a bag, Monsieur?"

"Oui. Please. Merci." Randolph smiled.

The woman smiled again and wrapped the elephant in a small brown paper bag and Randolph handed over the money.

Exiting the small shop, Randolph placed the bagged elephant in his right trouser pocket and continued down to the end of the street, where he noticed a café, Le Central. Several people were seated outside in the sunshine. There were a few spare tables so Randolph sat at one. He took off his trilby and placed it on the patterned metal table.

After a few minutes, a waitress came and served him. He tried ordering in English, but the waitress smiled awkwardly and said something in French, clearly not understanding Randolph's requests. Instead, he gave an understanding smile and pointed to a small menu on the table and ordered a coffee and a couple of croissants. Some of the items he understood in French.

Whilst waiting, Randolph took in the scenery some more. A breeze flowed down the street. He welcomed the soft chatter from nearby tables, where others smoked and drank their coffees. Some enjoyed a breakfast, sitting under yellow and dark blue, triangular shaped parasols — his own table didn't have one. He looked over at the Saint-Martial arched bridge that crossed the Vienne River. In the distance, he could see the towering cathedral beyond some trees, with the sun shining down onto the old brickwork, illuminating it. He smiled to himself, just as the waitress returned with his hot coffee and freshly baked croissants that were still warm. On the plate was a tiny pot of jam and a knife, along with a few strawberries.

"Merci beaucoup," Randolph said, smiling.

"De rien." The waitress smiled back.

Everyone seemed so friendly. It made Randolph feel warm and happy. He thought how nice it would be to live somewhere like this, or just outside Limoges, compared to the hustle and bustle of London. Well, if he could afford it. It seemed the perfect place for a family — for him, Thelma and little Matthew. But then the reality hit Randolph. The brief warmth and happiness he had felt, soon vanished. They weren't even a family anymore. He doubted they ever would be again. Randolph stared into space for a short moment, then stared down at the wedding ring he still wore; he had never taken it off since he had married Thelma. He sighed and gave a shake of his head, before taking a small sip of his coffee.

The two croissants, flavoured more by the jam, had been the best Randolph had ever tasted and the coffee was delicious. He took his time eating and drinking. Afterwards, while smoking a cigarette, he was joined by a stray dog, or so it seemed. The black Scottish Terrier wasn't overly large and looked quite young; Randolph guessed it was around one or two. A few other customers had stroked and petted the dog, but Randolph made more of a fuss of him, when he started licking his hand. Randolph looked around to see if the dog belonged to anyone. The dog was lying on the ground with his tongue out and Randolph was concerned he was thirsty.

A different waitress this time had come out of the café and Randolph called out, "Excusez-moi ..."

She walked over to the table.

"Puis-je avoir une carafe d'eau?" Randolph wasn't too sure if his French was accurate enough. He pointed towards the dog and gestured drinking to his own mouth, shaking his hand a little, mimicking a glass.

The waitress smiled, held her index finger up and then went back inside the café. She returned shortly after carrying a metal bowl full of water and placed it down in front of the dog's face. The dog quickly starting lapping up the water. The waitress smiled and then quickly went to serve someone else who had caught her attention.

"You certainly look thirsty, little fella." Randolph smiled and bent down, stroking the dog's furry head gently. "Bless ya."

"He often hangs around here. No doubt for the free food and water," an English voice explained, making Randolph look up at another table. The man, who was sat by himself, was chomping on some toast with jam. He washed it down with a large gulp of his tea. He must have heard Randolph speaking to the dog.

"He's a stray, then?"

The large man wiped his mouth clean with a white napkin and smiled. He must have been in his late fifties. "Yep! He first started coming here a few months ago. He's no bother. The locals often feed him some scraps and give him water. He's pretty much well looked after." The man finished off his toast.

"That's good, then … at least he's not starving."

"Nope. I would have given him some of my toast, but he was too late!" The man grinned, with a couple of black gaps showing from lost teeth.

"He doesn't look too old."

"Yeah. He can't be much older than a year or so, I'd say."

"No one has offered to take him in?" Randolph stopped stroking the dog.

"Nah. I considered it. But the wife wouldn't be too keen. We already have three cats and two dogs as it is!" The man laughed.

"I see." Randolph half-smiled. "You're a local?"

"Oui. My wife is French. We live on the outskirts of the city. Been here since just after the war ended. Lovely area."

"Yes. It most certainly is. It's a shame I don't have more time to explore and take in the area some more. I fly back to England later on this afternoon."

"That's a shame. How long were you staying for?"

"Just a couple of days. Been here on business. Perhaps I'll get another chance to come back." Randolph laughed slightly.

"I hope you do! There's plenty more to see. Beautiful place."

Saying goodbye to the man and finishing at the café, Randolph walked along the river Vienne, staying in the shade under the cover of the trees that formed an arch above him. He was trailed behind by the Scottish Terrier who had decided to follow him from the café. Randolph looked back and smiled. It was certainly a sweet little dog, trustworthy. Randolph hadn't encouraged the dog to follow him, yet blamed himself for making a fuss of him. He felt a little guilty, especially if the dog was leaving his known territory.

Randolph found a grassy area close to the river and sat down. He enjoyed the soft sound of the water and the birds singing and the sun was shining brightly. The dog lay close by and Randolph smiled. He removed his trilby and used it to cover his forehead and eyes. He put his hands behind his head, resting on them. He still had a good few hours before his flight this afternoon, so he closed his eyes and relaxed.

*

After his nap, Randolph had walked back through the Limoges city centre, albeit, taking a different route. He admired more of the historical buildings, including the town hall with its large fountain. The dog had continued to follow him. Randolph felt bad leaving him outside the hotel, but there was nothing he could do. He wished he could have taken him back across the English Channel. Later, when Randolph had checked out of the hotel, the dog was gone. It made him feel a little sad, but he had some comfort in knowing that he was fed by the locals. He knew he would never see the dog again. Not unless he returned to Limoges one day.

Randolph had parked the hire car at the airstrip to be picked up. The same private jet he had travelled to France on had landed. Boarding the aircraft, he had become a little more nervous.

*

Shaftesbury Avenue, London – 6.18 pm – Local Time

London was grey and miserable in comparison to France. The return flight had been smooth — no turbulence. Randolph had felt fine once the small jet was up in the air. The couple of whiskies possibly helped. The car Claret had arranged to pick him up at the other end was on time. Randolph had called her not long after he returned home to his flat. She again thanked him for his help and would let him know what Timothy had to say. Timothy himself, was due to return home in the evening. Claret also told Randolph to keep any expenses he had left over from his short trip, at least for now. It was still possible that she would need his services, after demanding answers from her husband. Although it wasn't exactly Randolph's problem(s), he was still intrigued to know about the secrecy behind everything. Once a case was settled, Randolph would usually shut his mind off from it, moving on to the next job. But then, that was the problem — there was no *other* job.

Randolph had also picked up today's paper upon his return and he had also watched the news. He had only been gone for the weekend but was curious to know whether there had been any more brutal killings and learn of any updates on the previous murders. Not much was mentioned; it was mostly information which had been in the papers already. At least there had been no more killings since the last one, the one Randolph himself had encountered first-hand. The trip away had also taken his mind off Miss Albescu's palm reading. However, now lying in the bath and smoking a cigarette, it quickly came back to him.

Chapter Thirteen
Tuesday, May 24th, 1966

Hopkins Street, London – 11.03 am

It was another drizzly and overcast day, when Randolph went up the steps of the building to his office. The change of scenery and temperature still felt like a dramatic change compared to France. Randolph wondered if Claret had questioned Timothy yet. He was tempted to call her. However, he would let it lie until Claret got back to him. It wasn't any of his concern right now.

In his office, with no mail nor new cases to look at, Randolph made himself a coffee. He filled out some paperwork ready to file regarding the Andrews' case, for his records. He always did this after each case and kept the files in his cabinet in alphabetical order. He then lit a cigarette and sat down. The telephone then rang.

"Mr Landon. Randolph."

"Claret."

"I have managed to obtain some answers from my husband. We discussed things this morning, before he left for work."

"Really? What did he say?" Randolph took a drag from his cigarette, flicked some ash into the ashtray and leant forward.

Claret sighed. "Christine — Natalie's personal assistant or PA, contacted Timothy, concerned that Natalie had gone missing. Timothy knows her through Natalie. Natalie had been working on a dig over in France, near to where you were staying. Timothy insisted he hadn't funded nor heard from Natalie for ages, and I believe him. Christine became worried and contacted my husband. She was the woman people saw my husband with in London.

"Timothy kept it from me, because he was worried how I might

126

react, and how it would seem; him concerned about his ex-fiancée when they are no longer together. Especially when I wasn't happy, he had funded Natalie that time for one of her digs, and me and her didn't see eye to eye when we had met in the past. It really wouldn't have bothered me. I told him it's worse that he kept it from me. Not to mention I thought he was having an affair! I would have understood his concerns. I'm not a monster. If the woman is in trouble and missing, she needs to be found."

"Why would Christine contact Timothy, if they hadn't spoken for a long time?"

"Timothy said it had been a few years since he and Natalie spoke. I guess Christine knew they had a history and thought that Timothy might be able to help. My husband has a lot of contacts, Randolph."

"I can believe that, as a rich businessman."

"Exactly … Anyway, she went missing after the digging had finished. There were a few other people working for her, and they are also stumped as to where she is. Timothy was concerned, too. I guess it's understandable, because of their past. I don't believe anything is going on between the pair. The gendarmerie are looking into things. However, they are stumped too, and have no idea where she is. The Paris police have also been involved."

"This seems really strange, Claret. What was she working on exactly, this Natalie? And where? Are there are no clues as to her whereabouts? Has anyone checked her home for clues?" Randolph flicked some more ash into the ashtray.

"I told my husband I'd hired you and that I was concerned he was having an affair. He joked that he was flattered I would go to the extreme I did. He insisted that he would never cheat on me, despite the spark being lacking from our marriage right now. I told him you were a good PI, and someone who can be relied upon."

"Erm. Thanks. But in all honesty, Claret, anyone could have done what I did. It wasn't exactly difficult. And it isn't like I've found out very much."

"Nonsense, Randolph. You've done well, and I know of your reputation. Work not coming your way of late isn't because of your lack of qualities."

"Thank you, I guess." Randolph laughed a little awkwardly. He had always been humble about himself.

"You're welcome … I can explain more about what Natalie was working on over in France, but it would be better to get Timothy to explain things himself. It would be better coming from him. I have to leave shortly, as I have an important business meeting to attend … You can ask him more when he meets you."

"Wait. *What?* Your husband wants to meet me? Why?"

"He's considering taking you on to investigate Natalie's disappearance, based on your reputation."

Randolph laughed awkwardly again. "What? I'm really confused, Claret. How on earth can I help? There's no clues as to where this Natalie is, or even if she is alive for that matter? I wouldn't know where to begin. I've only ever worked in and around London and other parts of the country. Never abroad! I'm not sure what I can do that the French police haven't already done."

"Have more belief in yourself, Randolph. Timothy will pay you well. I'm sure you will do your best, if you choose to accept his offer, that is. I have to admit, I'm not overly keen on my husband fretting about an ex-fiancée from many years ago, but I have to support him and understand his concerns. After all, Natalie could be in trouble. If it had been any of my exes, I don't think I would have gone to these lengths." Claret laughed.

"Shit. I don't know. It all seems rather odd, if I'm honest with you. Though, I can see it from your husband's point of view … When is he supposed to be contacting me?"

"Some time this evening. Most likely after seven. He has your office and home number, Randolph."

"I really wasn't expecting any of this, Claret. I thought we would probably be closing the case after this phone call. I would appreciate the money, but it isn't about that. This is a completely different case to any I have ever worked on before, not to mention in another country. I've never worked abroad before."

"I understand your concerns. However, I'm sure you will do your best."

"I'll always try. I mean, I'm free. I have the time. I just don't know what Timothy would expect me to do or how long it might take. This Natalie might not even be found! Or maybe, she doesn't want to be found. I also have my son and wife coming down to see me at the weekend. I really can't afford to cancel that. I've been waiting weeks to see them again. I'm still hoping I can sort my marriage out. Sorry, I don't mean to babble on. I just miss them like crazy."

"It will be fine, Randolph. I understand that you miss your family. Timothy may be a shrewd businessman at times, but he does have a heart and sympathetic side to him. He will understand — trust me."

"Okay. Well, I look forward to meeting him for proper and chatting to him."

"I'm sorry I can't tell you more right now. Timothy will fill you in on everything later, or when you meet in person."

Ending the call, Randolph got up and finished his cigarette. He stubbed it out in the ashtray and then drank the rest of his coffee. It was rare, if at all, that Randolph felt unsure or uneasy about a potential case yet for some reason, this unnerved him. He didn't doubt his credentials or abilities as a PI, but this was different. It obviously meant going back to France. He didn't know where in France, Natalie's archaeological dig had taken place. He was concerned about what he might be getting himself in to.

*

"I was getting worried," Max said half-serious. "It's been a few days since I last saw you in here."

Randolph was sat on his usual stool at the bar in Teresa's. "I'm fine, Max." He told Max he had been busy on a case, though not the details of what or where.

"I'm happy for you, Randy. Really. I told you things would pick up! You've just got to hang on in there."

"Thanks." Randolph looked up and smiled. "I only popped in for a couple. I've got someone ringing me later on, so I'd best be going soon."

"It's all good." Max smiled, before serving a couple of customers.

Randolph soon finished his second and final whisky. Getting up, he happened to look over to a corner of the bar, where a seated man was chatting quietly to another. One of them was Cheng-Lei, the man who was rumoured to sell animals to Chinese restaurants for food, and who Randolph had questioned almost a couple of weeks back about Peanut.

Randolph frowned. He saw Cheng-Lei take out a couple of watches from inside his leather jacket and hand them over to the other guy, who in return, pulled out a small brown envelope that no doubt contained money. Randolph half-smiled to himself and shook his head. It seemed that Cheng-Lei was still up to no good and into dodgy dealings. It didn't concern Randolph. It had nothing to do with him. He had his own business to attend to.

*

Back at the flat, Randolph paced anxiously around the small living room, biting his nails. It had gone half seven. He kept looking over at the telephone, waiting for it to ring. He had made himself a bacon sandwich for dinner, something light. He wasn't overly hungry. He went to the kitchen for a glass of water and the phone finally rang.

"Is this Mr Landon?"

"It is, yes."

"It's Timothy Andrews … Claret said you'd be expecting my call?"

"She, erm, did. Yes."

"That's good … I hear you've been quite busy, checking up on me?" Timothy laughed, trying to ease any awkwardness.

Randolph laughed too. "Yes. I'm sorry, I was only doing my job and what I was being paid to do."

"It's fine, really. No need to apologise, Mr Landon. Claret told me of your abilities, and I know about that little boy you helped find last year, the one you saved from that sick pervert."

"Yeah, it was a while ago, now. And please, call me Randolph."

"Okay … I know Claret's given you brief details. I'd like to hire your services. We can meet tomorrow morning, if it's okay with you? I'd rather meet you face-to-face and go through everything with you in person. Perhaps say, 9 o'clock, at your office, if that's convenient for you?"

"That's fine … but listen, Timothy, Mr Andrews. I'm not sure what you want me to do exactly?"

"Well, you're good at finding people, aren't you?" Timothy joked a little sarcastically, then laughed.

"Yes. But it's just this case is different. As I told Claret, I know nothing about the French systems. It's a completely different environment. And this Natalie, may not even still be in the country. Not to mention, I don't speak the language!"

Timothy laughed again. "I don't speak French, either, only the small basics. And believe me, I've spent a *lot* of time over there! It shouldn't matter. A fair few of the French speak a little English. But we can speak more tomorrow morning. You will be well paid for your services, by the way."

Randolph appreciated the money, even he was still doubtful about it all. "I'll look into things for you. I'll do my best and see what I can find. Again, as I said to Claret, and to all my clients, I can't guarantee results. Or the results may not be the answers you're hoping for."

"It's fine. And I accept that. As long as you try your best and do what you can do, I don't have any issues with that … So, we are all good for tomorrow morning? Claret gave me your office address. I know the building."

"It's fine. I'll be there."

"Great. I'll see you tomorrow, then. Have a good evening, Mr Landon. Randolph."

"You too, Timothy." Randolph put the receiver back down and stood thinking. He breathed in through his nose and out of his mouth. There was something about this case that concerned him, especially when he started thinking again of that palm reading. Shit!

Chapter Fourteen
Wednesday, May 25ᵗʰ, 1966

Hopkins Street, London – 8.59 am

Still feeling anxious, Randolph waited in his office for Timothy to arrive. He had applied a little whisky from an old steel hipflask to his now lukewarm coffee; a morning tipple was not his usual style. Finishing the coffee, he placed his empty mug on the desk and heard a knock at the door. He went over to open it.

"Randolph Landon?" Timothy Andrews smiled and held out his hand.

Randolph smiled and shook hands with Timothy. "Pleased to meet you. Properly, this time," Randolph joked.

"Ah, yes … I remember your face. We passed each other at that business centre, that morning, when you were no doubt doing your surveillance on me." Timothy laughed and let go of Randolph's hand.

Randolph grinned. "That was me!"

"It's all good. You were only doing what you were paid to do. No problems from me."

"Please. Sit down. Would you like a coffee?" Randolph walked back to his side of the desk.

"I'm fine, thank you. I've not long had one. I've actually just come from another meeting, early this morning … No rest for the wicked!" Timothy joked, sitting down.

"I guess I'm not wicked enough, then," quipped Randolph, thinking of his lack of work lately.

Timothy smiled. He looked smart but casual in a grey suit with no tie. "I'm sure things will pick up for you, Mr Landon. Claret mentioned that you were having some bad luck with work not coming your way. I'm sorry to hear that. Perhaps it's just as well, as you can focus solely on what I'm offering you …"

"And what exactly is it that you propose, Mr Andrews?" Randolph cleared his throat.

"Call me Timothy, please. As you're aware, my ex-fiancée has been missing for a while now. She'd been working on a dig over in France —"

"Oh, wait. Hold on. It's best I start making notes for my records. It also helps me keep on top of cases."

"That's fine." Timothy watched Randolph pull out some paperwork from his desk drawer.

Randolph gave his favourite pen a shake and then started to write … "Please. Continue!"

"Yes. Natalie Conners was working in west-central France, not too far from Limoges in a place near to Oradour-sur-Glane. My villa is not too far from there, as it happens."

Randolph frowned and stopped writing. He looked up at Timothy. "Oradour-sur-Glane? The village that was destroyed and where hundreds of people were massacred during the war by the Nazis? By the SS to be precise."

"Correct. It's awful what happened. A new village has since been built nearby. But yes, the dig is around a couple of miles or so east from there. It's not far."

Randolph sighed. "Yes. We all heard about what happened there, during and after the war. I knew a few soldiers who witnessed the dead bodies there. Including those of young children. A most distressing and sadistic tragedy. Completely needless." A serious Randolph shook his head.

"Totally. War is bad enough as it is, without that happening. I didn't see any combat myself, thankfully. I was a part-time cooper and worked some kitchens for our soldiers. I was still fairly young back in the forties. It was before I got fully into the hotel business. My father helped supply our forces and the allies with food too, using his contacts and his reputation."

Randolph nodded his head slightly. "How did this archaeological dig come about?"

"Natalie lives in France. She moved to Paris several years ago. Her assistant, Christine, who you obviously saw at my villa, helps Natalie run her office." Timothy gave a knowing smile.

Randolph, who had continued to write, glanced up and smirked.

"The dig came about after some locals discovered some strange artefacts that had resurfaced from below the ground."

Randolph stopped writing and frowned again, looking up at Timothy. "Strange artefacts? What like?"

"Oh, a few things. I think there was a goblet, some strange gemstones and a doll. Things like that. It's believed they were used in black magic or witchcraft or for the 'dark arts.' To perhaps worship The Devil. Anyway, Natalie and her team investigated the area. They dug down and found an old cavern, where skeletons of two adults and several children were found, along with more strange artefacts. The bodies have since been removed and are being investigated."

"Shit. Really?"

Timothy nodded. "One theory, is that it was some sort of pact suicide. The details are sketchy, to say the least. Christine is still waiting for the results on that … I saw a few photographs and some of the items for myself, which Christine showed me in Paris. I have to admit, it made me feel unnerved seeing them. Perhaps even more so, when me and one of the gendarme officers checked out the cave for ourselves. Christine was too afraid to go down there. Not that I blame her. The archaeological team were also deeply disturbed by what they had discovered."

"And when did Natalie disappear, exactly? What of her team?"

"It wasn't a large dig. She had a team of three. Four, including herself. She disappeared not too long after, after the artefacts and skeletons were removed. Her team know nothing of her whereabouts. Nor do the gendarmerie and the French police. When you saw Christine at my villa, she had wanted to meet the gendarmerie and speak with them in person."

Randolph didn't say anything for a moment. He just carried on writing with Timothy looking on. Randolph assumed that when he first saw Timothy and Christine near the villa in the car, they were coming back from seeing the gendarmerie.

"It's most peculiar." Timothy gave a shake of his head.

"It certainly seems that way. Who else is looking into her disappearance? Could any of her associates, team, be behind this, perhaps be covering something up?"

Timothy sighed. "No. We don't think so. But I guess it's a possibility. Hopefully, you can look into things and find something out … The police and the gendarmerie have been looking for her. I've contacted some other people I know, too. She's been missing for like three weeks."

"Yeah. I saw a gendarme turn up last weekend at your villa. I tried to eavesdrop." Randolph couldn't help but smirk again slightly.

Timothy did the same. "You were certainly doing your job well! Claret was right about you."

"It was nothing, really."

"Even so."

"I have to ask, though … and I don't mean to cause offence and seem out of line, here, but why the concern over your ex-fiancée, I mean to the extent that you would lead an investigation like this? If I've understood correctly, you haven't been together for many years now."

"No offence taken, Randolph. Claret asked me the same thing. She was my first proper love, although it ended long ago. When we broke up, there was no real bitterness. It was sad, but it ended amicably. I still care about her well-being. As you already know, I helped fund one of her digs in Mexico a fair few years ago now. But it's not what you think. I love Claret and she's the only one for me," Timothy answered sincerely. "Things have been a little strained of late – business is great, but stress comes with it and of course on top of that, Natalie's disappearance.

"I must admit that for the past two or three months, I've been neglecting Claret's needs and my personal life. I've travelled abroad for work when I should have focused more on what's important. I'll be the first to admit that. Our marriage has lost some of its spark, but that's only temporary …"

Randolph believed Timothy was being sincere and felt somewhat uncomfortable, as he had done when Claret had confided the same. "I can understand that. Claret also informed me of your sister that died, where I saw her grave in that cemetery. I know it was a long time ago, but still, I am sorry for your loss. I can imagine it was tough on you … I assumed you were the only child and had inherited your father's business."

Timothy sighed and scratched his forehead. "Thank you. As you say, it was a long time ago. Though it still pains me, thinking about her. The same with my parents that I unfortunately both lost, too. I think about them all every single day. I always try and remain positive and look ahead. No point in looking back. My father was already dying and had died from cancer a few weeks after I married Claret. They both got on really well.

"As a wedding gift, I renamed the family name in honour of Claret. But I was in two minds and torn because at the same time, I still wished to keep it as my family name. Especially after losing my mother and sister, already. I considered changing just a few names of our hotels. However, it was my father, himself, who had encouraged me to change the name period, saying that change is always good. He totally approved." Timothy gave a sad smile.

"I understand. I'm sorry for your losses."

"Some people think that just because you are rich and fortunate, it automatically removes or stops pain — that you are immune to it. We are all human at the end of the day. I would say that Tiffany's death perhaps hurts the most." Timothy surprised himself, opening up a little to Randolph.

"How did she die? If you don't mind my asking?"

"It's fine … We were staying in one of our villas at the time in France. We were in the garden one morning, chasing each other about. She suddenly stopped and cried out in pain, holding her head. The next thing, she suddenly collapsed …" Timothy's eyes welled up and he looked down to the floor.

"It's okay. You don't have to continue." Randolph felt Timothy's pain.

"The doctors believed she was born with it. Perhaps some defect that was basically a ticking time bomb. There were no warnings. No headaches, nor anything like that. Tiffany appeared in perfectly good health. Or so it seemed."

"I'm sorry."

Timothy held his hand up. "It's fine. It happens … As for the cemetery she was buried in, we used to stay in the area there. For some reason, Tiffany was always drawn to it whenever we went past it. She used to like walking around the grounds there, particularly in the spring with the blossom on the trees. She said she had a dream a couple of times, about seeing an angel there. Ironically, it was not too long before she passed away …"

Randolph didn't know what to say. He could tell it was hard for Timothy talking about his sister and his family. "You don't mind if I smoke? Would you like one?"

"No, thanks. I'm not really a smoker, only occasionally. But it's your office! Don't mind me." Timothy laughed.

Randolph smiled and took out a cigarette, before lighting it. "So, what happens next? Where do I start? I'm happy to help you. I guess it means going back to France? How long am I supposed to stay there? It could be quite a lengthy task."

"It's a tricky one. Perhaps you could start in Paris and meet Christine, there? There's another member of the team who lives in Paris as well. Christine can fill you in more than I've done. She obviously knows more. I won't overload you with all the details. Maybe we can then get you back to west-central France, to take a look at the dig yourself, although, that may not be worth your time, as there's nothing left there."

Randolph took a drag of his cigarette and then tapped some ash into the ashtray with his forefinger. "Yeah, that's erm, fine … I'm still not sure if I can be much use. If the police can't find anything, it could be like looking for a needle in a haystack, Mr Andrews."

Timothy smiled. "Timothy, please. We can get rid of all these formalities."

Randolph grinned back. "There's one problem, though … my wife and I are currently separated. She's coming down for the weekend with my little boy. I have to check whether it's Friday or Saturday morning. It's been weeks since I've seen them. I miss them both very much. I still haven't given up hope of maybe fixing things with my marriage."

"Claret mentioned that, Randolph. There's no immediate rush. Natalie could be in trouble, but maybe she'll turn up safe and sound. We can start Monday, next week, or I can get you a private flight to Paris later this morning or this afternoon? Or tomorrow? Whatever you're happy with, I'm happy with."

Randolph felt a little anxious at the sudden suggestions. "Erm." He puffed out his cheeks, holding the cigarette in his right hand. "I guess I can go today, whatever works for you."

"Let's say this afternoon. I can arrange it right now, if you don't mind me using your phone, that is?"

"Erm. Sure. It's fine," Randolph replied. It must have been nice being able to afford to make such arrangements when and where you wished -- an advantage of being well-known and rich. Randolph couldn't help but feel a little envious.

After the phone call, Timothy confirmed with Randolph, "It's all good. My pilot can fly you out at around three this afternoon from Heathrow. We'll lay on a car to pick you up from your flat or office, whichever you prefer. Another car will pick you up from Orly Airport. We can book you in at one of our hotels near the airport. We'll cover any expenses. It won't come out of your pay. Christine will also be able to help you with anything."

"Thanks. It just seems a little strange that everything is being paid for. I'm not used to this hospitality and stuff. It makes me feel guilty. Usually for the cases I take on, the expenses are included in the cost."

Timothy smiled. "It's fine. No need to feel guilty. Although you'll be paid well, you'll still be well looked after, too. Claret mentioned you had some francs left over – keep those and we can add a bit more if need be."

"Thanks. It just seems, like I say, strange. I'm not used to this kind of treatment!" Randolph laughed awkwardly. "I need to check with my wife, but I'll need to be back by Friday or Saturday at the latest, though."

"Totally fine, Randolph. I wouldn't expect you to miss seeing your family."

Timothy seemed more compassionate than Randolph initially expected. He wasn't ignorant nor arrogant.

They chatted some more and Randolph finished writing his notes up and asked Timothy to sign the paperwork. Timothy pulled out a chequebook, writing out a cheque for a generous amount for Randolph's services, saying "with perhaps more on the way."

At the very least, the payment would look after Randolph's rent for the next few months, for both his flat and his private office. But the most important thing to Randolph, was getting results: the money was secondary. Timothy used Randolph's phone again to arrange a car to pick Randolph up from his flat later on.

They shook hands warmly and Timothy left, giving Randolph time to phone his wife and also pay in his cheque.

Apologising to Thelma for calling her at her work place, Randolph was informed that her and Matthew were coming down some time on Friday evening, after Matthew had finished school. They were to stay until late Sunday evening. Ending the call, Randolph was still sceptical about what he had to offer regarding Natalie Conners' disappearance, unless he found something the police and others had missed. It could be his biggest and most challenging case to date. He still couldn't shake off the worried feeling he felt though.

*

Randolph's flying nerves had disappeared not long after take-off. He had refused an onboard whisky, although he felt apprehension about what to expect in France. He looked down below at Paris as the small jet lowered its altitude, in preparation to land at Orly Airport. He could make out the Eiffel Tower below. He reflected on how only a few days ago, he hadn't been expecting to travel to a foreign country anytime soon in his life, and here he was on his second trip.

After the short flight across the English Channel and landing at Orly Airport, Randolph was picked up on time by a black 1965 Cadillac Fleetwood Limousine, to take him to the hotel. The male chauffeur was in uniform, wearing a dark suit with tie and hat. It all felt very surreal and over the top to the humble Randolph. He felt like James Bond and reminisced back to seeing *Dr No* in the cinema with Thelma, when it had first been released back in 1962.

It was roughly a thirty-minute drive from the airport to the hotel. The traffic was fairly busy and the driver tried to make small talk. Despite being French, he spoke perfect English. He had worked for the Andrews for almost six years. He told Randolph that Timothy and his wife were nice people to work for and generous with their Christmas bonuses. They always made sure that their staff were well looked after. There were apparently three Clarets hotels in Paris and possibly a fourth in development. The driver, Maurice, pointed out the Louvre Museum on the way to the hotel. Randolph and his family had visited it on a previous trip to the French capital a few years earlier.

*

Clarets Hotel, Rue de Rivoli, Paris – 4.44 pm Local Time

The Clarets hotel where Randolph would be staying briefly was in central Paris. The limousine pulled up outside the steps of the hotel, which overlooked the Tuileries Garden on the other side of the street. Randolph looked up at the white façade of the posh looking hotel, getting out of the car. Above the large archway entrance leading into the lobby, was the name *Clarets* in maroon. Randolph wondered if the colour referenced Claret's mother having named Claret after her fondness of purple and red roses; if so, it was a nice touch. The windows at the front were also huge, giving the impression of lush and large rooms inside. They were no doubt ridiculously expensive, at least for Randolph's wage packet, or lack of. Either side of the archway were two flags hanging from poles. On the left was the French flag, and on the right, the Union Jack representing the United Kingdom.

"I will pick you up at 7.45, Mr Landon?" the driver said, getting out the limousine.

"Thank you. That will be fine," replied Randolph, turning to face the driver. He had never been chauffeured about before. It made him feel guilty for some reason. He wasn't sure why. The driver no doubt earned more than Randolph, as he was in a stable job.

Timothy had previously confirmed to Randolph, that Christine was happy to meet him in Paris; at Natalie's office on Rue Saint-Rustique. Timothy had brought Christine up to date regarding him having hired Randolph's services. She was to go over everything she knew with him, and to show him photographs and the artefacts that had been found at the dig.

"Do you need any assistance, Mr Landon?" the driver asked politely.

"I'm fine, thank you." Randolph smiled and grabbed his small suitcase from the black leather seat of the limousine.

The driver smiled warmly. "They'll be expecting you at reception."

Randolph nodded and walked up the steps under the archway entrance. A pretty brunette came out through the glass door and Randolph stepped aside, letting her pass. They smiled at one another, and Randolph made his way inside.

The hotel lobby had a large maroon-coloured mat in the entrance, which contrasted with the shiny grey-tiled floor. It was clean and immaculate like the rest of the lobby. A security guard in a grey suit and hat, wearing a black tie, stood to the left near the entrance with his hands held behind his back. He looked briefly at Randolph. Randolph, still carrying his suitcase, walked towards the rosewood reception desk, where a clock set presented times of the major cities around the world, including: New York, London, Beijing, Tokyo and Paris. A huge oil painting of Paris and the Seine with the Eiffel Tower in the background was positioned below the clock set. The lobby smelt clean and fresh and was well lit.

Four large and gold looking crystal chandeliers hung from the ceiling and on each side of the lobby were large plinths mounted to the floor, each holding a small tree. A few maroon-coloured sofas lined the walls.

"Oui, Monsieur?" one of two receptionists addressed Randolph, in his smart dark suit.

"Hi there. Erm. I have a room booked for me? My name is Landon ... Randolph Landon ..."

The receptionist checked the maroon reservation book. "Oui,

Monsieur. Yes. You are in a luxury suite on the fourth floor …"

Luxury suite, eh? Randolph thought to himself. Timothy was really spoiling him.

After confirming his reservation at the front desk, the male receptionist pulled out a small brown envelope with some francs in for Randolph's expenses. Randolph was then shown to his room on the fourth floor by a bellboy, a young French man, who asked if he would like him to carry Randolph's suitcase. Randolph politely declined.

The luxury suite had a plush double bed with white covers and maroon plumped up pillows, and another large chandelier. A white desk and chair were positioned near to the tall windows that looked out on to the Tuileries Garden. A large mirror with gold trimmed patterns was fixed to the wall opposite the bed. Over the bed itself, hung a large black and white photograph of Montmartre in a gold-coloured frame.

"If you need anything at all, don't hesitate to use the telephone, Monsieur," the young bellboy said. He smiled, pointing to the gold and white decorative telephone on a wooden bedside table.

"I won't. Thank you." Randolph smiled, placing his suitcase down. He took off his trilby and placed it on the edge of the bed.

The bellboy bowed his head and left Randolph alone.

Randolph sat on the edge of the bed next to his hat and sighed. He ran his right palm over his stubbly face and then checked his watch. He still had some time before his meeting with Christine, Natalie's assistant. He had been down on his luck with work and in general for so long, he found it difficult to believe how things had suddenly changed. He couldn't believe he was in France for a second time in less than a week.

*

Rue Saint-Rustique, Paris – 8.08 pm

The limousine driver had dropped Randolph off outside Natalie's office. Randolph had insisted on waiting outside, in spite of the light drizzle. He stood under the small arched porch of the office building.

He was due to meet Christine at eight. Randolph checked his wristwatch again, just as he heard from his left the sound of heels scurrying along the wet, old stone pavement. Looking up, he recognised the dark-haired woman he had seen at Timothy's villa. She was carrying a dark blue umbrella.

"Randolph Landon?" Christine asked, when she got to a few feet away.

"That's me!"

"I'm sorry I'm a little late. I had some things to attend to and my babysitter was late. I hope you weren't waiting for too long?" Christine lowered her umbrella and gave it a shake, before closing it up and stepping under the porch.

Randolph smiled. "It's fine."

Close up for the first time, Randolph could see that Christine was attractive; she appeared to be in her late thirties. She smiled at him and reached into her coat pocket for a key. "Let's get ourselves inside. We have a *lot* to go over."

Randolph stepped aside and Christine unlocked the front door to the office for them to enter. Randolph scanned around the neatly kept office. The painted, light blue walls were covered in numerous framed photographs that consisted mainly of archaeological digs and people working there. Some were photos of them posing with certain finds and relics, beaming for the camera. Most were in colour, but there were a few black and white photographs too.

"That's Natalie, there," Christine suddenly said, noticing Randolph paying attention to one of the photos. She pointed to a coloured picture of Natalie holding a stone statue and smiling to the camera. "It was from a dig some years ago, over in Mexico. You can see a Mayan pyramid in the distance."

Randolph moved his head closer to the photograph on the wall to examine it further.

"Her work takes her all over. It's one of the perks of the job, to experience other countries and their cultures. I get to go along too, some of the time." Christine took off her coat and hung it on a peg on the wall next to the door. She propped up her umbrella inside a decorative, brass umbrella stand. She then opened the blinds with a cord, to allow the gloomy light from outside to enter. She walked over to a chair and sat, giving a shiver as she did so. "The temperature certainly seems to have dropped this evening. Though of late, it's often been cold. It's been raining a lot, too. This is my desk. Natalie has hers out the back when she's here."

Randolph looked down a doorless corridor to the back of the old building. Now the blinds had been opened, he could see a little more into the other room. "Have you worked for Natalie, long?"

"Over nine years, now. It can be hard work but I really enjoy it, apart from of late, of course." Christine dropped her head. "I don't just regard Natalie as my boss: she's a good friend as well. We've become close. Please, take a seat." Christine smiled and gestured for Randolph to sit opposite her on a light brown, Danish leather chair.

Randolph pulled out the chair and sat. "So, what is it you actually do?" He smiled. He pulled out his notebook and pen and placed them down on the desk. He noticed a small framed photo of Christine, bending down and holding a young boy; both were smiling for the camera.

Christine saw him look at the photo. She smiled again. "That's my son, Henry. He's only six. We moved to Paris about four years ago. We used to live in Kent."

"Cute boy." Randolph smiled. "I have a son, too. He's a little older." Randolph noticed that Christine wasn't wearing a wedding ring. He wondered if she was married, or separated, or divorced though didn't ask about Henry's father. It wasn't any of his business.

"Yes, he is cute. When he's on half-term with school, I've sometimes taken him along with me to one of the digs we've been working on. He gets on really well with Natalie. She's very fond of him, too … Anyway, to answer your question — and you must have many. I'm Miss Conners' personal assistant; I basically arrange meetings for Natalie and clients, or potential clients, when something comes up. I'm also responsible for the financial side of things as well. I'm pretty good with mathematics and stuff like that." Christine gave a little laugh.

"I do many things. Natalie does things as well, but obviously her work is more about being on site and dealing with things out in the field — that side of things. I also assist in report-writing, publications and just overall checking and looking into things. I won't go into too much detail, as I doubt it's relevant to you."

"It's fine." Randolph smiled again. He then opened his old notebook and jotted a few things down for reference. "And how did Natalie disappear? If you could start from the beginning. Timothy only gave me the briefest details."

Christine sighed and shook her head. "She just upped and vanished one day. I'll get to that, but it basically started back in early March. Natalie had just come back from Ireland, working on a dig, an excavation over there, some Celtic ruins. There's a photograph of some of us up there, behind you ..."

Randolph turned his head to where Christine pointed. Half a dozen of them were holding up some old relics and again, beaming for the camera. They seemed proud of their finds. And why wouldn't they? It must be a highly satisfying job, Randolph believed.

"Anyway, I had a phone call, one Tuesday afternoon. Natalie had popped out for some lunch. A few strange artefacts had been randomly found by a couple of local residents, down in the Haute-Vienne department."

"How did the residents find these artefacts?" Randolph continued to make some notes.

"They weren't deliberately looking for them. They just saw a dip with some cracks in the earth and some objects were sticking up from the ground. It's sometimes the case; they can resurface due to the weather or where there's a sinkhole or if there's an earthquake. In fact, some of the locals mentioned feeling tremors now and then just before the discovery so that might have caused it."

"What sort of objects are we speaking about, exactly?"

"I can show you. We have some here out the back. The location is about two miles or so east of Oradour-sur-Glane, that poor village that suffered at the hands of the Nazis during the war."

"Yes. I'm aware of it. It was terrible what happened to those poor people and families."

Christine nodded her head. "There really are some twisted people in this world. I'm aware about the murders back in London, too.

They are obviously ritualistic as well."

Randolph nodded too. He didn't tell Christine he had witnessed the latest murder victim himself. It wasn't relevant to the case at hand. "Tell me about it. It's certainly scary: uncertain times."

"The dig itself is in an unfarmed field. There's nothing there now, although going back, it's rumoured that there was an orphanage there. It was run by a married couple, supposedly an English husband and his French wife."

"Rumoured? There are no remains or building left out there? No names?"

Christine shook her head. "Nothing … but I'll get to that. The only ones who might have known for sure, have long since passed away. I think one rumour was that it burnt to the ground one night, again, we're not too sure as there were no bodies found, well … apart from what I'll get to, if you bear with me."

"So how did Natalie get involved?"

"Her reputation precedes her." Christine smiled. "She's lived in France for quite some time now. She has always liked Paris, which is why she lives here and set up her office here. She used to have one back in Kent as well. She can speak French and a few other languages fluently. I guess you have to, when you work abroad like she does. Her line of work requires it. As for my French, let's just say it isn't quite as fluid as hers." Christine gave another little laugh.

Randolph smirked.

"The locals who found these artefacts weren't sure if they were of any value. Regardless, they wanted to check anyway, just to be sure. So, they contacted our office here in Paris, and spoke to Natalie. Someone had recommended her to them. They mailed them for Natalie to have a look at. She confirmed that they weren't valuable or even very old; she believed they were witchcraft related."

Randolph frowned. "Witchcraft, eh? Timothy mentioned a few things."

"Uh-huh … Although witchcraft isn't Natalie's main specialty, she knows quite a bit about the occult and beliefs of other cultures. It's part of her job to know. After Natalie had phoned back the folk who had discovered these artefacts, they said not to return them.

They didn't want to keep anything witchcraft related, especially if they weren't of any value. They said they'd often heard stories of witchcraft in the area as children. Though, nothing of an orphanage."

"I see … Well, I guess it makes sense. I'm interested to see these findings."

"I will show you … A month or so later in early April, after Natalie spoke with these people, there was another phone call. More objects had been found by another couple there, whilst walking their dogs. One happened to be a gendarme and friends with the previous couple, and he was also aware of witchcraft stories in the area over the years. He had a hunch that maybe something sinister was buried deep in the ground there. So, again, they contacted Natalie …"

Randolph didn't say anything for a few seconds. He wrote down more notes. He frowned. "Interesting … From what Timothy had told me, I gather that you did *indeed*, uncover something? Skeletons, wasn't it?"

Christine swallowed. "Indeed, we did …" She opened one of her desk drawers and took out some coloured photographs, placing them in front of Randolph. "Natalie and her team travelled down there a few days after. They didn't have any other projects to attend to. I remember Natalie had said beforehand, something about how she had a 'feeling' and 'urge' in regards to going down there to investigate. And that's when they started surveying the area, before finally starting to dig …"

Randolph's face became more serious. Frowning further, he looked down at the photographs. "Jesus. I guess the rumours about witchcraft were true?"

Christine gave a nod, removing a damp strand of hair that had fallen down her forehead.

The photographs showed a fairly large underground cave walled in white stone. Symbols in blood were marked over the walls and ceiling, including on the white stone floor. One photo showed an old wooden table with an inverted pentagram carved into it, along with two crescent moons carved either side. On the table were some artefacts and lit candles. The main item was a fairly large metal figurine of what appeared to be Satan, with large wings and horns on its head. It was positioned in the middle of the inverted pentagram.

Other photographs showed some dried herbs hanging from the ceiling, and another photo showed an old black cauldron in a carved-out hearth in the stone wall. Randolph felt his blood freeze, as the two final photographs showed the skeletons of two adults and some smaller skeletons of several children. These bodily remains were encircled by a neatly drawn, inverted pentagram in blood. Black candles had been placed on the five points, all lit and burning orange and green — the same colour as the table candles.

"My God … What is this? What happened?" Randolph looked up ashen-faced at Christine.

"Tragic. Isn't it? As of yet, we don't know. Not for certain. Only theories. The remains have been sent off for investigation. One theory is that the two adults are perhaps the couple who ran the orphanage and those are some of the children. There were ten young skeletons found. No clothing. The adult skeletons appeared to have been holding one another. The symbols you see over the cave are in blood. We don't know for definite how they died."

Randolph swallowed again. "But why or how were they underground like that?"

"It seems like it may have been deliberate. Like some kind of mass suicide. The team say that the cave is made from limestone, both natural and man-made … You want to know another creepy thing about it all?" Christine swallowed nervously.

"Go on …"

"Those candles in one of the photos on that old table, and the others on the points of the inverted pentagram on the floor where the skeletons were …"

Randolph checked the photos again.

"When Natalie and her team were about to climb down there, they could *swear* they heard some children's cries and some other groans … and those black candles were already *lit* and burning an orange and green colour!"

Randolph's eyes widened. *"What?"*

Christine gave a shrug of her shoulders.

"How the hell is that even possible? Had someone else recently been down there?"

Christine let out a sigh. "There were no other passageways or catacombs, nothing like that. Natalie and her team were the first ones down there in years — for the ground was all covered up before they got there. Apart from a few cracks in the earth. It makes no sense. I couldn't find the courage to go down there myself."

"Jesus." Randolph rubbed his face.

"It's possible that an orphanage did exist, and what was found was situated directly below it or nearby."

"Yet no remains of a building?"

"Nothing at all … We're still not completely sure how long the bodies were down there for. Natalie and her team believe that the cave is possibly a few hundred years old, judging from the stone."

"And the bodies, the skeletons … no results have come back yet?"

"Not yet. Not officially, anyway. Natalie spoke to whoever was in charge, just before she disappeared. It was suggested that they may have suffocated down there or been poisoned. Some dried black remains were found in the old cauldron you can see in one of the photos, together with a stained wooden ladle: they've all been sent off for investigation. It seems that their teeth also had black stains on them, potentially relating to what was in the cauldron. There didn't appear to have been any bone damage, so force or weapons weren't used on them."

"How far down were they found?" Randolph briefly took off his trilby to scratch his crown.

"Roughly fifteen feet, it was … An iron torc which is a kind of necklace or neck ornament, was also found on one of the adult skeletons, believed to have been the female. Their spine didn't look in the best shape, either."

"I wonder how these artefacts, objects — whatever they are, got to the surface the way they did, if the ceiling of this cave was stone … unless they were placed above it, in the earth. Or were from the remains of the orphanage?"

"Quite possible."

"Those poor children, and the adults, too, if they weren't behind it … How many of Natalie's team are there? Excluding you, the ones who help more out in the field?"

"There are three main people who always help Natalie. Sometimes, depending on the size of the site, Natalie hires outside help, if she needs it. They are mostly people who she already knows, or sometimes volunteers from the country where they are working … The main ones who worked on the latest find are Pierre Monet, who acts as her assistant archaeologist, when out on digs and excavations. He's in his sixties. Sixty-four to be exact. He's worked for Natalie since the beginning. She learnt a lot from him when she started out. She used to work for him before she started up on her own. The roles reversed, when Pierre semi-retired. Now he helps Natalie most of the time. He's the most experienced of the group. He's a really nice guy, too. My Henry also gets on with him, like all of Natalie's team."

Randolph started writing again.

"There's Jarrod Robbins, an Englishman — thirty-eight and another half-French, half-English gentleman, Peter Dupont. He's fifty-eight. They've been with Natalie for ten and twelve years respectively. They all know their stuff. Being the elder and more experienced, Pierre is often a 'go to' for things, if the others are unsure about certain finds."

Randolph rubbed his hand. He felt it cramping up. "What do they make of their latest discovery?" He didn't look up from his notebook.

"Even they were shocked by what they found. There was just a bad feeling about it all, when they were down there in the cave. Pierre was physically sick when they first saw it all. They've never come across any witchcraft findings like that before. And they're all worried about Natalie, naturally, especially Pierre, who has known her the longest. She was his protégé."

"Where do these three live?" Randolph glanced up.

"Pierre lives in Paris, in the Latin Quarter. Peter lives in Troyes, and Jarrod lives in Spain. Usually, they return home after a job has been completed. They often do their own things in between jobs, to keep themselves ticking over."

"You get on with all of them, then?"

"Oh, yes. Christmases are the best!" Christine grinned.

Randolph smiled across the desk, but soon saw Christine's smile disappear from her pretty face.

"I wonder if we'll ever have a Christmas together again," Christine added glumly.

Randolph wanted to reassure Christine. Though he didn't want to patronise her, or give her false hope. "They haven't heard anything from Natalie? Tell me what happened, when she just vanished."

"None of us has heard anything. We have no idea where she might be. Natalie's disappearance has even been mentioned on the news over here and in the papers. After the excavation, the skeletons and artefacts were removed, naturally, and there wasn't much more that we could do out in the field. I guess we'd done our job. The police spoke to them as well, of course."

"It would be good to speak them, too. Although it's perhaps not worth it, seeing as the French police have already spoken to them. What about Natalie's friends and family; are they in England?"

"Yes. All her family are in the UK. Some of her friends, too. And here, in Paris. Again, no one has heard anything, unless they're not disclosing something for whatever reason. But I don't believe that to be the case. Jarrod is back in Spain for now, so it may be a bit difficult to meet him. I can arrange a meeting with Peter and Pierre, if you wish? Pierre is in Paris so that's easy. They'd be more than happy to talk with you. Anything to help."

"We'll see." Randolph looked up and smiled. "Talk me through when you realised Natalie had disappeared?"

"After the dig, Natalie returned to Paris with her team. They did their post field work before they headed home. Then, one day, she just didn't turn up at the office. It was the 4th of this month. Around a couple of weeks or so after the excavation — exactly three weeks ago. She still had some work to do related to the dig, some paperwork and finalising a few things. She even had a couple of interviews lined up for this week. One was for a newspaper and the other, the *Archaeology* magazine. They've run articles before about her and her team and their findings. But workwise, we didn't have anything else on. Natalie was also in talks with a publisher in London. They were discussing bringing out another book on archaeology and her projects."

Randolph put his pen down and flexed his right hand. "You don't think she's away on some kind of business, then? Maybe something personal or private?"

Christine frowned. "Erm … I guess it's a possibility. Though I would have to say no. There's no reason for Natalie to keep anything work related private. She's very open about things and honest with the team. Me included. She wouldn't just go quiet on all of us. She would know we'd worry."

"Perhaps that's true. But it's quite possible that she could be dealing with something. Not necessarily work stuff, but non-work related. It could be that something came up, or has been happening behind the scenes, so to speak. Maybe she needed to do something whilst the work side of things had gone quiet?"

Christine sighed, shaking her head. "What you say could be true and it would make sense, generally speaking. The police said the same thing … but no. If that were the case, and even if she wanted to keep things private, she would at least have been in contact with me or her family, who she's close to, to warn us she'd be away for a while. She wouldn't let the publishing editors down either, not without an explanation. She isn't one to let people down, Mr Landon. It's completely out of character. There's still some things to finalise with what we found too in that cave."

"What about her home? I take it someone has searched there. Had anything been disturbed? Were there any signs of clothing gone, or other signs that she might have gone away?"

"The Paris police looked into that less than a week after she went missing. Pierre and I joined them. Someone had to pick the lock to her apartment. There was nothing out of the ordinary evident. Her belongings hadn't been taken. Her suitcases were there. We checked her things. There were no signs of her going away anywhere. Even her passport was on the table there … Pierre had been there the evening of May 3rd. He had said that her apartment looked the exact same as the previous week. I honestly don't know what to think. We're racing to all sorts of theories. Each day that passes, we become more and more concerned for her well-being.

"It's just such a helpless feeling, you know? The police have been checking her apartment regularly, to see if anything has been disturbed. I also have a key and checked. I got one cut from Natalie's spare inside her apartment. Everything has remained untouched. I even checked her diary in her apartment. There's literally no indication of where she has disappeared to."

"I empathise. It is awful … What about confrontations. Anything like that? Anyone she may have annoyed, even indirectly?"

"No. Not at all. Well, I don't think so! Natalie was, is, always polite and friendly with everyone. I can't imagine her making enemies! The complete opposite. She always got on with the locals, too, joining in with their culture and activities. Like there, when she was in Africa on a project …"

Randolph turned his head again and looked at the wall. There were a couple of photos of Natalie playing with some of the young African children.

"I just can't help thinking that she's … she's dead."

Randolph saw Christine's eyes well up. "I'm sorry. Truly, I am. But we can't jump to conclusions. We have to try and remain positive. Sorry if that sounds patronising, but the chances are, she's safe. For whatever reason, she clearly decided to up and leave, possibly on the night Pierre last saw her, or early the next day, perhaps? Her passport still being in her apartment means she is still quite likely here in France, somewhere. I promise you this; I'll do my utmost to find her."

Christine gave a half-hearted smile. Randolph's consoling words seemed to help a little. "Thank you, Mr Landon."

"Please … *Randolph*."

They both laughed.

Christine spoke a little more and Randolph noted everything down. He asked if Natalie had children or was currently seeing anyone, or if she had any exes that she didn't get on with. Natalie who was almost forty-four, was happily single — no children and had no issues with anyone that Christine knew of. Randolph asked for her height and double-checked her age. Christine then asked if Randolph wanted to see the artefacts …

"Witch bottles were usually used for protection against spells and evil. To this day, people still use them, although they were first used centuries ago, if someone thought they were bewitched for example. Ingredients would have been prepared and put into a bottle. It would then be placed inside a person's home to counter the effects of the bad magic. They'd usually be prepared by someone with a medical background and someone who knew of magic and spells. Such people were known as 'cunning folk.'

"However, these bottles are kind of different. According to Pierre, these were used to *encourage* and invoke dark spirits, dark magic, or even *The Devil* himself. These bottles were placed next to each skeleton. Each had strands of hair and dried blood in them, quite likely belonging to each person. There were some nail clippings and thorns, along with a mysterious black powder and small pieces of bone — perhaps not belonging to these bodies, but to someone or something else. Perhaps animal bones."

Randolph screwed his face up somewhat, cringing as he held one of the bottles in his hand. It was made of clay and had a couple of symbols carved into it; no doubt related to witchcraft. He then placed it back down next to the other eleven bottles on a table. On the wall above the bottles was a copy of the painting *The Archaeologists* by Giorgio de Chirico.

They were out the back where Natalie had her desk. Another three desks also filled the room, for when Jarrod, Pierre and Peter worked there. Christine had opened the blind allowing a little light to enter. The rain battered harder against the window during this cold and wet, late Parisian evening.

Randolph picked up another witch bottle.

Christine shivered. The room seemed colder in the back than the front. "Witch bottles in general can be made of glass or ceramics. They can depict symbols or faces on them. The one you hold and others here are believed to be around a couple to a few hundred years old."

Randolph frowned, examining the bottle in more detail. He looked at the bottom of it; another marking was carved at the base. "Perhaps the same age as the cave itself, then?"

"It's what the group believe, yes … Even looking at these bottles gives me the creeps. I certainly don't like touching them, or the other artefacts!"

"I know what you mean. It's pretty grotesque. All of it." Randolph carefully returned the bottle back down next to the others on the table. He wiped his hand on his trousers a few times.

"The contents have since been removed and went with the bodies to be investigated, together with some of the other objects. We got the bottles back so that we could do some more research on them." Christine put the bottles back into a large wooden cupboard near the table. Bending down, she picked up a heavy item and placed it on the table. She pointed to the metallic figurine of what was believed to be The Devil, with its arms held out. It was around twelve inches in height. "It's fairly heavy. This is what you saw in one of the photos. It was on the table in the cave and found by the team once they went down there … I really don't like touching it. I don't like any of these things being out the back here." Christine shuddered. "I don't like being alone here with them, in the office."

"What happens exactly, to the finds from an archaeological site?"

"Once brought back from the field, the team and even I sometimes help clean them up. Then they are analysed, sorted and catalogued. Most artefacts, especially if valuable, are eventually sent to an archive at a selected museum, and some are put on display. The team have analysed these and done some reports, but they were waiting for Natalie to confirm what to do next. To be honest, all of the team, including Natalie, were reluctant to touch these finds; we tried not to do any more than we had to. There really is an uneasiness about all of this. Pierre reached out to someone who might know more about the artefacts, but he hasn't heard back from him yet."

Randolph frowned again and picked up the heavy winged figurine to examine. He felt uncomfortable too, holding this evil looking thing in his hands. "It feels strange and unnaturally cold. This is supposed to represent The Devil? Is it meant to be some kind of idol?" Randolph scrutinised the figurine further; The Devil's head had two horns at the front and two larger ones growing out a bit further back at the side of its head. It also had an inverted pentagram carved into its forehead between the two smaller horns. A long beard grew from its chin. The Devil was sat cross-legged on a rock, wearing some loose trousers and was bare foot with long, sharp claws. Its arms were held out as if demanding something; the palms were face up, with sharp claws pointing upwards. A couple of occult symbols were carved into each palm.

Christine swallowed, watching Randolph put the grey shiny figurine back down. "That's what the team believe, yes. Whoever was responsible for this awful act was worshipping or idolising The Devil using witchcraft. It's quite possible that they sacrificed themselves to him, for whatever they believed in. As I say, we don't know for certain how they died. It's just speculation for now, but still, a strong possibility." Christine gave another shudder. "It makes me uneasy, just looking at it. And yes, it does feel strangely cold. There really is something about it. And believe me, I've seen many similar things that the field team have brought back over the years, but nothing like this!"

Randolph looked at Christine and gave an understanding smile, before she continued.

"It appears as though this Devil figurine was looking down at these people from the table before they died. Or during."

"What of the other things that were found, particularly those found by the locals, that started all this?"

Christine put back the figurine and took out several other objects. Again, placing them on the table … "As for the other objects that you see, this was one of the first things that was found near to the surface by a couple of French residents …"

Randolph looked on. Christine first showed a goblet made of steel. It had become tarnished. Again, there were a couple of symbols related to witchcraft engraved on the goblet. Christine identified one as a sign of the witch and another, a spiral-like shape, as being the sign of 'rebirth,' or something along those lines. She said that she didn't know much about witchcraft or symbols herself, other than what Natalie's team had told her, particularly Pierre. Another couple of creepy-styled goblets with similar or the same symbols had also been found in the cave itself. Other objects that were found at the surface included an old ceramic bowl, some gemstones and an old wooden, horned doll, that again represented Satan. The wood had rotted somewhat. None of these finds held any economic value.

"So, it's possible that these objects or artefacts belonged to this orphanage that burnt down? When was this supposed to have happened?" Randolph stared at the table.

"Most likely they were from the orphanage, yes, if it existed. Again, anyone who knew the place is likely either no longer alive or has since moved. If it did exist, it was in the middle of nowhere, surrounded by open land, so not many people may even have known it existed at the time."

"Interesting."

"Some unconfirmed reports suggest it was there from around the 30s to the 40s. If it burnt down, there's no indication of how. No remains were reported. I know it all sounds confusing, but that's all we know. Though, according to some people, Natalie and the team spoke to, claim that the lands out there are or were, down the centuries, sacred and special to witches."

"Yes. It's all rather strange." Randolph scratched his cheek and picked up a couple of the black, shiny gemstones. They too, felt strangely cold to touch.

"The findings that were found above the ground are most likely twenty to thirty years old. Similar or the same sort of things found below, which are older, are likely the same age as the cave itself."

"What are these gemstones, exactly? What do they represent?" Randolph held one in his hand close to his face, examining it thoroughly.

"Again, linked to witchcraft and the black arts. Apparently, there are 'good' gemstones and 'bad' or 'evil' gemstones. They are Opal. Pierre claims that during the 19th century, Opal was often called the *witch stone*. Some Opal gemstones have other colours embedded inside the main colour. But as you can see with these, they are completely black." Christine swallowed.

Randolph picked up another gemstone. He held the two towards the light from the window and then returned them to the table. There were six in total. He then turned his attention to the ceramic bowl with symbols. "What about this?"

"Again, the same; linked to witchcraft. A similar and older bowl was found next to the skeletons. Just inside the inverted pentagram on the floor. It was possibly used for drinking and maybe part of a ritual. There was still some black residue leftover, perhaps linked to what was in the cauldron. They both have that rebirth symbol on it, along with an archway, which represents possibly, a gateway or 'allowing something in.'"

"Jesus."

"A few larger black gemstones and some children's toys were also found on the surface. They were found by the gendarme and his wife, a few weeks after the initial finds."

"Children's toys?"

"Yes. Here ..." Christine returned to the cupboard, knelt down and pulled out an old plastic baby doll which she handed to Randolph.

The doll had several large cracks over its face and limbs. The head had a large chunk missing from its left side. The doll had no clothing, and only one blue eye remained; the other appeared to be scratched out.

"Creepy. I've never been fond of dolls. Though I guess, I am a male." Randolph gave a slight smirk, looking up at Christine, who returned a wry smile. Randolph turned the doll over to see a few occult symbols drawn on its back and bare buttocks in red paint. Not blood.

"Pierre said that the symbols represent death and pain, something along those lines. The dolls found are from around the 1930s."

Randolph handed the doll back to Christine. "And a child possibly did this, maybe? Either way, what kind of an orphanage *was* this?"

"Not a normal one it seems, that's for certain!" Christine put the objects back, then pulled out a couple of toy trucks and cars. "These were also found and a couple of plastic toy planes." Christine returned the toys to the cupboard. "I don't know why, but it seems wrong, strange, showing you these things. It makes me feel most uncomfortable. I'm sorry for repeating myself."

"You're fine. I don't really need to see much more. My focus is on finding Natalie. As long as I know the gist of things, it's enough." Randolph smiled warmly. He really didn't wish to see anything more.

It disturbed him, making him feel most uncomfortable.

Christine went on to state again, that some of these artefacts were sent back early from testing for the archaeological team to continue to work on them. No fingerprints had been found neither on any of the artefacts found in the cave. Relaying what Pierre and the others had told her, Christine mentioned and showed Randolph briefly, two 'magical' blades from inside the cave. One was an athame, a ceremonial blade with its decorative handle, used traditionally in witchcraft and also linked to Satanism. The other blade was a ritual knife; a boline. With its white handle and curved blade, shaped like a crescent moon, it was used for cutting things such as herbs and cords, and for carving candles — not flesh. It had one unknown symbol on the still sharp blade, that had tarnished a little less than the athame.

"There are a few more things in the cupboard, if you want to see them? There are also some old ceiling herbs and a couple of symbolised boxes — which were empty."

"No. No, it's fine." Randolph smiled. "I've seen enough. To be honest, like you, it creeps me out seeing these things. I doubt anything here will help us find Natalie. You guys have obviously examined everything anyway."

"Indeed, we have. There's nothing here to help us."

"I have to ask, though; what happened to the table? Was it removed?"

"Yes. It's being held in a storage place here in Paris. The team sometimes keep things locked up until they are dealt with, particularly larger artefacts. With Natalie's disappearance, things have been delayed. We're still waiting for clarification and for the final results from the forensic anthropologist's unit here in Paris — they are also forensic archaeologists. I know they were busy when Natalie spoke to them last, and several of the team there went down with an illness just after they started working on the remains."

"Was there anything of note about the table?"

"It wasn't too heavy. As you saw in the photos, the inverted pentagram was carved into it, along with a couple of crescent moon shapes either side. There was like a raised platform or a book holder mounted just behind the symbols. Though no book was found down there. The table was possibly as old as the cave itself. There wasn't anything else of note. Well, not to us, anyway."

"What do the crescent moons mean?"

"Fertility, it's believed. But with witchcraft, like a lot of things, they can have different meanings to different people. It can all be subjective." Christine gave a couple of loud sneezes.

"Bless you." Randolph smiled.

"Th-thank you." Christine pulled out a tissue from her pocket, before sneezing again. She wiped her nose. "You never seem to sneeze just the once. It's always at least twice or three times. I hope I haven't got a cold coming. I've been sneezing quite a lot of late." She smiled lightly. Sneezing a couple more times, she locked the cupboard back up.

They were then startled by a loud *thump* on the back window.

"What was that?" Christine asked worriedly.

"I'm not sure." Randolph walked over to the window and looked out into the rain; there was no one there. "Maybe something blew against the window or a bird hit it. I can't see anything. Either that or someone ran past hitting the window."

They walked back to the front and Christine placed the cupboard key back in one of her desk drawers. Her nose was now running and she wiped it nervously.

"Are you okay?" Randolph asked, noticing Christine screw her face up.

"I'm fine. I just feel a headache coming on. It could be a cold or the lack of sleep and stress of everything, you know?"

Randolph smiled sympathetically.

"I know Henry had a cold a couple of weeks back. I've probably caught it from him. Bloody germs!" Christine laughed and then sneezed a couple more times. The phone rang on her desk. "Hello?" she answered, wiping her nose. "Evening, Pierre!"

Randolph looked at the photos on the wall as Christine chatted. A couple of note were in Scotland: a field in Stirlingshire where some Viking artefacts had been found. Natalie was smiling with a shaven-headed black man. Randolph could sense that the group were close.

"Yes, I have, Pierre. I've not long shown him …"

Randolph looked at Christine, who smiled. Randolph scanned the photos further. He glanced out the window where the rain showed no signs of stopping. A cyclist went past, their face grimaced with the rain hitting them face on. Randolph then noticed someone on the corner across the street, standing in the rain, in a black hooded jacket, with their head bowed, facing the office. The figure didn't move.

"Randolph?" Christine repeated.

"Eh?" Randolph turned to face Christine, who smiled again. "Oh. Sorry. I was miles away." Randolph grinned.

"It's okay. That was Pierre. He seems to have fallen a little unwell, too. He's been sneezing a lot and has a cold. He was also feeling nauseous earlier on. It seems that something is going around, some virus, perhaps. Either way, he'd still like to meet you tomorrow, if that's okay?"

"Sure. If he's feeling up to it? I might have to keep my distance, though!" Randolph joked.

"He said he should be — after an early night and a hot beverage. Obviously, he won't want you to catch anything. We can keep our distance. It's up to you, really?"

"It's fine. I'm flying back early Friday morning so it's best to make the best of my time here. It would be good to meet him, although he'll probably only confirm what I have from you so far. What time and where did he have in mind?"

"A café not far from his home, actually. In the Latin Quarter. Is 9 am okay for you?"

"Yeah, it's all good with me."

"Okay." Christine smiled.

As an afterthought, Randolph half-suggested about checking on Natalie's apartment. Despite knowing it had already been checked, he considered he wouldn't have been much of a PI if he hadn't at least looked for himself. As it wasn't far, Christine offered to take him straight there, seeing as she had a spare key and had been checking on the place since Natalie's disappearance. She insisted she was fine, in spite of her symptoms.

Christine offered Randolph a spare umbrella from the office. Whilst Christine locked up under the arched porch, Randolph looked to the street corner; the hooded figure had gone. They made their way hastily out into the rain with their umbrellas up, disappearing round the corner.

*

Natalie's apartment was on the fourth floor, over on Rue Duhesme. As suspected, Randolph found nothing of interest, leading to the disappearance of Miss Connors. A spacious, bright and expensive looking apartment, it had been well kept and was clean. There was quite literally nothing, indicating on where Natalie had disappeared to. Once done, a sniffling Christine had driven Randolph back to the hotel and wished him goodnight.

Chapter Fifteen
Thursday, May 26th, 1966

Rue de Rivoli, Paris – 7.59 am

Having enjoyed a hot shower, Randolph wrapped the hotel's soft thick towel around his waist and made his way to the bed where his clothes were laid out. His trilby sat on top of his navy-blue trousers along with his Onsa wristwatch. He pulled out a small bottle of aftershave and dabbed some onto his left palm a few times. He rubbed his face quickly and winced where it stung after his early morning shave. He put on his watch and walked over to the window and opened the pink curtains fully. The bright sunny day illuminated the room, making Randolph wince as his eyes adjusted. The road and pavements still looked wet from last night's rain. The trees and shrubs of the Tuileries Garden glistened in the sunlight. It was certainly a pleasant view.

Randolph breathed in, let out a huge sigh and stretched his arms wide. Turning, he paused momentarily and frowned. He then turned his head back. Across the street, stood the hooded person, head bowed. Randolph continued to stare and swallowed. He wasn't one for being paranoid; was this person following him? Was someone watching him? Maybe it was someone checking up on him … perhaps someone hired by Timothy, making sure that Randolph was doing the job he was paid to do. Randolph felt a little annoyed. Timothy had a right to do so but it still pissed him off. Would Timothy Andrews do that? He wasn't so sure. Whoever this person was, it certainly unnerved him. The figure stood frozen. A lady walked past with a dog. The dog paused, sniffed the person's leg, then jolted back to continue. The unfaced person still remained still. There was a knock on the hotel door, which made Randolph jump a little.

"Room service."

Randolph's morning coffee and breakfast had arrived. He still had some time before his driver would take him to his meeting with Pierre and Christine this morning. Christine had offered to collect him herself but he said he would use the driver appointed by Timothy. The meeting wasn't far from the hotel. Randolph didn't know the streets of Paris well, so he opted to go by car.

The room service waiter held a metal tray with a jug of hot coffee and a rack of several slices of warm toast, some jam and butter. Randolph gave the young man some change as a tip. The server took the money and smiled, but not before noticing a scar on Randolph's right shoulder, a bullet wound from the war, where he had bravely taken a round.

After the server had left, Randolph immediately returned to the window. The mysterious person had gone. Randolph had lost a little of his morning appetite. Still, he sat down at the table and managed to eat a few slices of toast and enjoy some hot coffee with fresh cream. He ate slowly and pondered. Who was this person? What the hell is going on? Everything seemed to have happened so quickly. One minute he was depressed about the lack of work coming his way, now he was starting to feel more worried about the fact he *did* have a big case. Be careful what you wish for! While pondering on this, similarities suddenly struck him between the findings of what might be a witches' lair, near to Oradour-sur-Glane, and the ritualistic killings in London: the inverted pentagrams and candles. Was this a strange and sick coincidence? Surely it *had* to be! He then shivered a little remembering Miss Albescu's warning.

*

Le Procope, Rue de l'Ancienne Comédie, Paris – 9.06 am

Sat on the lower level of the oldest café in Paris, the smell of fresh coffee and morning food was strong and appealing. The menu looked a little pricey to Randolph, sitting at a table across from the sniffing

Christine. Her nose was red and she kept wiping it. She again pulled out another tissue from the small pack inside her red jacket. Despite this morning being fairly warm and being indoors, Christine had an extra couple of layers on at least. She didn't exactly look awful, but she didn't look well at all. Especially now that her eyes had started watering. Randolph started to doubt if it had been worth coming to meet Christine again with Pierre — who was running late. Christine had explained everything last night. The last thing he wanted was to catch a cold on a new case and when Thelma and Matthew were coming down tomorrow for the weekend. Then again, perhaps it needed to be done. He needed to know as much as he could. Pierre might know more than he was letting on to Christine or the others, Jarrod and Peter. Christine reassured Randolph that she had spoken to Pierre earlier, and despite feeling terrible, he had promised he would make it.

"Perhaps you shouldn't have come," Randolph said, smiling. "I could have met Pierre alone to save you the trouble. You should really be in bed."

Christine tried to smile. "I know. But I have to go to the office afterwards anyway for some paperwork. At least I've stopped sneezing and my head isn't hurting as much. Maybe this hot coffee will help." Christine carefully warmed her hands on her coffee. "I can barely taste it. My throat's sore, too." Christine winced when the hot beverage went down her throat. She coughed into her tissue.

Randolph had opted against another coffee just yet. "This is Pierre's favourite café, then? I can see why. Perhaps he couldn't make it after all?" He stretched his back and glanced at his Onsa, then around where they sat.

A waitress served an elderly couple on the next table down: they were having pancakes. Randolph felt tempted to order something but he resisted. He didn't fancy the idea of Christine coughing opposite him whilst he was trying to eat, nor Pierre for that matter, if and when he arrived. He didn't want to stay any longer than he needed to.

"It is, yes," Christine replied, dabbing her nose. "I'm sure he'll join us. He lives less than a ten-minute walk away. He usually likes sitting in the same place." Christine tried to smile, giving a couple of small coughs. "Excuse me. I'm sorry."

Randolph leant back slightly from the table, giving a caring half-smile. "It's okay."

After a few more minutes, Pierre, joined their table. He greeted the pair and pulled out a wooden chair, sitting next to Christine on her right. He looked even worse than Christine did. "Forgive me, if I don't shake your hand," Pierre said to Randolph. "I don't want you to catch what we have." His eyes were watering, red, sore and puffy, behind his circular glasses. He also seemed to be perspiring. His face was clean shaven except for a white bushy moustache giving away his age. Pierre took off his white trilby, revealing his white hair combed to one side. He placed it opposite Randolph's hat on the table. He adjusted a blue scarf around his neck as though his throat hurt.

Randolph sat opposite the ill pair. Watching them both, he felt something was wrong. He felt uncomfortable and awkward.

"I am sorry for being late. I really struggled to get out of bed this morning," Pierre said in his strong, French accent. He sniffed, pulled out a red handkerchief with yellow pheasants on, and blew his nose. "I'm even worse this morning. I hoped that I would wake up feeling a little better. I've now got the chills, too." He sneezed loudly into his handkerchief, turning his head away from Randolph. Pierre's eyes watered further.

"You two really shouldn't have come. We could have spoken over the phone."

Christine started to shiver now too. She sipped her expensive coffee.

"I really don't feel like eating or drinking anything. I can't even taste anything. One minute I'm hot, the next, cold — or both!" Pierre stated.

"I'm starting to feel worse now as well. And I can't taste anything, either."

"Maybe we can do this another time?" Randolph suggested. "I already know enough for now, unless you have other information that can help, relating to where Natalie may be, Pierre?"

Pierre coughed into his handkerchief a few times. "Forgive me but unfortunately, no. Only what Christine has told you already. I thought it would be polite to meet you and in case you had any further questions to ask?"

A male waiter came over and asked them if they wanted to order anything else. The three declined. The waiter frowned at the two unwell customers, before walking upstairs to the second level.

"I'm not really sure whether I do have any further questions … Christine told me pretty much everything last night. In most cases, I've always had some form of a lead, even if small, something I can go on. But I'm struggling with where to start with all of this. Not to mention, I know nothing about France! I can't help but feel I'm out of my depth here. Is there nothing you can give me, Pierre?"

Pierre sniffed and wiped a couple of tears from his eyes. "I'm how do you say, *stumped*, Monsieur Landon. The gendarmerie and police know nothing. France is a big country. Natalie could still be in Paris, somewhere. Or elsewhere. Our country is very big! That's if she's still in France? Though her passport was still in her apartment."

Randolph nodded. "It could be a small consolation, perhaps that Natalie is somewhere at least, in the country … The last time you saw her, would have been the night of May 3rd?"

"That is correct, Monsieur. I left around 9 pm — just after. When the police checked her apartment less than a week later, everything was the same as I had seen it that night, the last time I saw Natalie."

"And she was fine? She didn't act strange, or anything like that? Anything at all, that didn't seem right with her? The way she acted?"

Pierre looked at Christine, then back to face Randolph. He shrugged and sniffed. "No. Nothing at all. We had dinner, and chatted about what we had found in the cave, just general chit-chat. She was concerned about our latest find — like all of us."

"Concerned how? Did she give any hint or clue, anything about maybe having to go away? Boyfriend problems? Family issues?" Randolph pushed. He felt his nose begin to tingle. He really hoped it wasn't the start of whatever these two had.

"Nothing at all. We are close. She wasn't seeing anyone. She had no family problems. She would confide in me, if she were. She's an open kind of lady, Monsieur. And as for her concerns, it was just how awful and disturbing it all was, finding what we did down there, and of course, those skeletons. It affected all of us and we've seen a lot over the years."

"She had no conflicts with anyone? Anyone that she may have annoyed, anything like that?"

"No, Monsieur Landon." Pierre shook his head and glanced at Christine, who shook her head in agreement.

Randolph could tell from their pale, ill faces, that they were being sincere. There was no way that they were hiding anything from him. He usually had good instincts and could tell when someone was lying from their body language.

"And your take, your theory on all this? I know the results of the bodies are yet to come back, but what do you believe happened? What is your own expert opinion?" Randolph placed an elbow on the table, placing his index finger knuckle to his lips.

"Like Mademoiselle Reynolds — Christine, has told you, we believe, or I believe, that this orphanage existed. It most likely burnt down somehow, despite there being no evidence of it. It's quite likely that the two adult skeletons were the husband and wife, who ran the orphanage, and no doubt dabbled in witchcraft and worshipped Le Diable. I believe it was some kind of suicide, offering themselves to him. As for why, we cannot answer that, not yet, anyway. There is a strong chance that they were poisoned. Perhaps the children were poisoned against their will or maybe they were brainwashed?" Pierre sneezed into his handkerchief.

"And the inverted pentagram? What's that all about?"

"A common and prominent symbol used in witchcraft and Satanism. One of the most powerful symbols there is. Arguably, the most powerful. Whether or not the magic is used for good or bad — *evil* or if it is inverted or not, it has been used throughout history, and adapted by many cultures and religions around the world. It can be used for numerous methods, depending on the reasons."

Randolph ran a hand over his face a couple of times. His hand rested over his mouth, perhaps subconsciously to protect himself from any germs when Pierre spoke.

"I wouldn't say that I am a thorough expert in witchcraft or

Satanism, but I know a few things, from my working life. It isn't my main specialty, Monsieur, but generally speaking, the pentagram or pentacle, which it can also be called, depending on a persons' terminology, represents the five elements: earth, air, fire, water and spirit. The circle that you see around the pentagram or pentacle symbolises eternity and the unity of all life."

Randolph nodded. It all meant nothing to him, yet it was interesting to know, at least. It certainly wouldn't help find the location of Natalie though. However, he wanted Pierre to carry on, in spite of the sniffing and suffering.

"In Wicca, or witchcraft, the symbol is perhaps more commonly upright, when used to cast spells for example and not necessarily for bad purposes. An upright pentacle or pentagram is believed to represent dominance that the spirit world has over our more 'materialistic' world. When it's inverted, it symbolises the opposite. When used upside down, it's usually for more sinister, negative and evil reasons, 'pointing' down. Again, individuals and cults vary in their beliefs, methods and tradition. It's confusing, I know, even contradictory." Pierre started to cough quite heavily into his handkerchief.

Randolph screwed up his face. He was glad that Pierre bent down with his head away from the table. Christine begun to sneeze. The elderly couple who had half finished their pancakes, looked at the two coughing and sneezing. Randolph gave them an awkward smile.

When Pierre had recovered, he again apologised. "The more technical term for an inverted pentagram is a pentacle — with a circle around it. But ultimately, it's all the same thing regarding magic, spells and summoning, things like that. A pentacle can also be a talisman, but if it's on the ground, it's regarded as a pentagram."

Randolph frowned and shook his head. "Talk about confusing."

Pierre gave a half-hearted grin. "Yes, I know. It's hard to explain with me feeling so ill. But you get the general idea of it all, yes?"

Randolph nodded in acknowledgement. "And what about the symbol representing 'rebirth.' Christine had mentioned about a gateway, too?"

"The gateway symbol, again, can differ in meaning, depending on who is using it. It could be for allowing themselves — or their spirit, to enter into a realm or to allow or summon, something from the other side. Or perhaps, both. Although it has yet to be proven, limestone, which the cave was formed from, can absorb and release psychic energy and magic, acting as well, as a conduit. The fields and land out there are rumoured to have been used by witches dating back centuries, Monsieur Landon."

"I see." Randolph scratched slightly underneath his chin. "It's all pretty sinister."

"Of course, yes." Pierre sneezed a couple of times. "As for the rebirth symbol, it most likely represents reincarnation. To be born again."

Christine sat finishing her coffee, listening.

Pierre reiterated their *deep* concerns for his close friend and boss, Natalie. He got a little emotional. Randolph could see the pain in his eyes.

"I can tell it's difficult for you to be here. The same for you, Christine. It's best I don't keep you for much longer ... Christine mentioned someone you knew, who might know more about these symbols and witchcraft in general?"

"Ah, yes. He's an old friend I have known for many years, Jean. He's quite a bit older than me. He lives in Montazels, which is in the South of France, near to Rennes-le-Château — another place that is steeped with much mystery. I contacted him a couple of weeks ago. I've yet to hear anything back. I must try again, when I'm better."

"When did you become ill, exactly?" Randolph asked.

"I had the sniffles last week for a day or so. I was fine until a couple of days back, when I started to feel more poorly. Why do you ask, Monsieur?" Pierre frowned behind his red handkerchief, while wiping his nose.

Randolph paused before answering, "I don't know. It could be a coincidence. Just a virus, cold, you've picked up, the two of you. But maybe you picked something up when you discovered that underground cave? Or from researching the artefacts in the office. Maybe, it's related somehow. I'm sorry. I don't mean to worry you. I'm just thinking out loud."

Pierre and Christine looked at one another, then back at Randolph.

"It's plausible." Pierre looked thoughtful.

"What about the other two — Peter and Jarrod? Have you spoken to them of late? Have they been unwell?"

"I spoke to them last week and they were fine, apart from being worried about Natalie, of course," Christine answered.

"Yes. I spoke a few days back to both. They didn't complain of being unwell," Pierre confirmed.

"If they're fine, then it isn't perhaps related to what you discovered," Randolph replied, still not certain.

Pierre coughed quite violently and had to excuse himself, making his way to the toilets.

"I think we're done here, Christine." Randolph smiled. "It's not fair on you two being here. You need to head on home and back to bed. Maybe worry about your office work for another day?"

Christine started to cough herself. She struggled to swallow. "Perhaps it is best. The work can wait. Some of it, I can't really do anything without Natalie, anyway."

"Yeah. You really need to rest up. Pierre as well. Hopefully you should both be okay in a day or two."

A couple of minutes later, Pierre returned. They decided to call time on the meeting. Exiting the old café, Pierre said it had been nice to meet Randolph and that he'd be in contact if and when he knew anything useful. Pierre set off for home on foot. Christine said the same and made her way round a corner to her parked car. As the weather was nice and warm, Randolph decided to walk around the streets of Paris, checking out some more of the city's shops and culture, before heading back to his hotel room.

*

Walking past the reception desk at Clarets, Randolph stopped when a female receptionist called out to him. He hadn't heard her at first, due to being deep in thought.

"Monsieur Landon? You had a telephone call from Monsieur Andrews."

Randolph walked over to take a small piece of paper from the woman; it had a telephone number on it. "Merci." He smiled.

Back in his room, Randolph looked again at the number to call Timothy back on. It wasn't one he'd already used for Timothy. He picked up the gold, brass-coloured telephone receiver and dialled the number using the gold and white, rotary dial. It rang a few times before Timothy answered.

"Randolph! I just rang earlier, to see how you were getting on? I hope my staff are treating you well?" Timothy laughed. "I'm spending time at one of my golf clubs. Hence the different number. I just thought it would be good to get updated."

'One' of his golf clubs ... how many does he have? Randolph thought. "I'm doing fine, Mr Andrews — Timothy. It's a lovely hotel you have and the room is superb. The staff are extremely polite. I've got a great view of the gardens, too."

"Thank you, Randolph. How did your meeting go last night with Christine?"

Randolph explained what he had learnt from the two meetings. He also mentioned that Pierre and Christine had fallen ill, together with visiting Natalie's apartment.

"That's not good news. Hopefully they'll recover soon. Are the other two okay?"

"As far as they know the others are okay. Unfortunately though, I still have no idea where to go with this, Timothy. Like I told Pierre and Christine, usually, I have something or someone to go on. At least not long after I start my investigations. Even if it's a small thing. But there really is no clue to Natalie's whereabouts. Maybe, she doesn't want people to know for now. She might come back if and when she feels like it." Randolph heard Timothy sigh over the phone.

"Yes. It's difficult."

"To be honest, I feel guilty being here, being paid for my services, when I'm not really doing much. I'm not sure it would help, even if I interviewed the other members of the team or Natalie's friends and family. They'll probably only say the same as they told the police. I'm stumped."

Timothy sighed again. "I know how you feel, Randolph. But you still deserve to be paid. You are still working, after all. We'll have to come up with something else."

"Obviously, I'm returning home tomorrow for the weekend. It's up to you after that, what you want me to do next. Whatever you want, I'll do it. I really want to find Natalie. I'll do whatever it takes. I'm *damn* curious myself by all this."

"I appreciate your tenaciousness, Randolph. I'm curious, too. Spend today in Paris and come home tomorrow as arranged. A lead may come up: Christine or Pierre may have some more information. I'll see what else I can come up with over the weekend."

"I'm not sure whether it would help, but I was thinking of checking out the excavation site for myself. Everything has been removed and I don't want to risk catching anything. Yet, it might be useful."

"I understand your concerns, Randolph. Though, me and Arnaud, the gendarme, seem to be fine, and we went down to that cave … We can see after the weekend what our next plan of action might be. Thank you for what you've done so far. Enjoy the rest of your day and have a safe flight home tomorrow morning."

"I will. Thank you, Timothy." As Timothy said goodbye and was about to end the call, Randolph suddenly thought. "Oh wait — sorry!"

"What is it?"

Randolph didn't really want to ask Timothy about the hooded person, however, it concerned him. He wanted to know. "I don't mean to offend, but erm, did you have someone check up on me?"

Timothy laughed. "What do you mean? Did I hire someone to check up on you, to make sure you were doing your job you mean?"

"Er, yeah." Randolph laughed awkwardly.

"What makes you think that? I have complete trust in you, Randolph. It's not my style to do something like that. Not unless there was a really valid reason. To answer your question, no. I'm curious as to why you would think that?"

Randolph explained about the hooded character that he had seen twice, once from Natalie's office and once from the hotel.

"That's pretty odd. Are you sure they were looking at you?"

"Well, not exactly looking. I don't know. They were wearing a hooded jacket — their head was bowed. I couldn't exactly see a face.

It creeped me out: it just seemed a bit of a coincidence."

Timothy gave a laugh. "I wouldn't worry about it. The chances are you were mistaken. They could have been watching someone else, or just by chance happened to be outside the hotel. It could be some weird or homeless person. I've come across some in my time when I've been in Paris. You get them everywhere!"

Randolph knew Timothy was telling the truth; he hadn't hired someone to keep tabs on him. He wished that he had because he still felt sure that this person was watching him. On the plus side, he was returning home tomorrow. He would soon see his much-loved wife and son.

*

That evening, Randolph received a phone call from Christine. She wasn't feeling any better; if anything, she was worse. She even found it hard to talk towards the end of the call. She informed Randolph that she had spoken to Peter and Jarrod earlier during the day — they had virtually the same symptoms. They had fallen ill in the past couple of days. Randolph grew concerned; was this just a normal virus that they had all caught by chance, or something more sinister — relating to their discovery? He hoped it wasn't serious and would soon pass, whatever it was. He also hoped that he hadn't caught it. It could be something highly contagious but take a good couple of weeks or so to rear its ugly head. He had so longed for a case. Be careful what you wish for!

After the call, Randolph went to sit downstairs in the dining room for dinner, a French omelette avec frites et légumes. At least he hadn't lost his appetite. He also sunk a large beer. He smoked another cigarette, sitting there in thought and clicking his tongue. He flicked some ash into the ashtray. He was one of around thirty people seated at a circular table each. Most were still eating. A few others were sat at a bar to the left of him, chatting.

At the front of the dining room was an elevated, shiny stage and an expensive looking white piano in one corner. It seemed that the hotel held special occasions, no doubt costly ones at that. A large maroon curtain framed the stage. Randolph wondered if any famous celebrities had performed there, being unveiled once the curtain pulled back. No doubt Timothy and his management team had arranged such events. Timothy probably knew several famous people, with him being rich and all his business connections. Stubbing out his cigarette, he looked up at another large crystal chandelier. Alone, it probably cost more than he would ever earn in a lifetime. Getting up, he tucked his chair under the table and picked up his silver Zippo. Dropping it in his back pocket, he left the dining room and made his way up to his hotel room for an early night.

Chapter Sixteen
Friday, May 27ᵗʰ, 1966

Shaftesbury Avenue, London – 11.06 am Local Time

When he arrived back in London, Randolph wanted to give his old flat a tidy. He wanted his place to look a little more respectful, if that was possible, for when Thelma and Matthew arrived that evening. The hoover seemed to make more of a noise than usual. It gave off a large rattling sound as something metallic got sucked up between its worn yellow brushes, probably a screw from when he'd tried to fix a small clock a few weeks ago. Just after finishing the hoovering, his telephone rang.

"Randolph. How are you?" Thelma's voice asked.

"Hey! Yeah. I'm not too bad. You okay? Matthew?"

"He's good — we both are. You're still okay for us to come down this evening?"

"Of course! I wouldn't miss it for the world. What time are you thinking of?"

"We're going to leave after Matthew has eaten after school. We should hopefully be there by seven, or half seven at the latest, if that's good for you?"

"It's fine — all good. You and Matthew can have my bed again. I'll sleep on the sofa."

"Okay."

There was an awkward pause before either spoke further.

"Your parents doing okay?"

"Yes. They're well. Though I think Matthew and I could do with a little break away from them." Thelma laughed. "You know how it is!"

"I do!" Randolph grinned.

"Has work picked up for you?"

"Actually, it has. I won't go into details over the phone, but I've got a pretty big case I've just been assigned to." Randolph knew he wouldn't be able to tell her about the case and didn't really want to anyway with this one.

"Oh. That's great! I'm pleased for you," Thelma replied sincerely.

"Thanks. It's keeping me busy."

"Good, good. I best be going, anyway. I have the day off and I'm about to pop out with Mum in a bit for some shopping. I just wanted to give you a quick call to confirm for tonight."

"Appreciate it. Enjoy your shopping and I'll see you both tonight. Make sure you drive down safely."

"We will."

Randolph felt a rush of further joy about seeing his family and having them stay over for the weekend. His happiness soon wore off, when he thought of them heading back up to Lincolnshire on Sunday night. It would mean saying goodbye to them again and it would be weeks before he'd see them again. He would just have to make the most of the situation for now. Randolph stood with his mouth curled up glumly. He then went to unplug the hoover and coiled the wire around its metal hook. He placed it back in the old cupboard near to the kitchen entrance.

After drinking some water, he used a feather duster to remove some cobwebs from around his flat. They seemed to appear as soon as he had removed them. With the number of cracks in his walls, it probably wasn't surprising that so many spiders sneaked in. They clearly didn't have standards, invading his run-down excuse for a home. Randolph chuckled to himself. Once done, he lit a cigarette and stared out at the street below. What had been a nice day earlier was now grey and overcast. Randolph watched when a car almost hit a motorbike across the road. The driver gave a sharp blast of his horn and shouted aggressively out of the car window. Randolph gave a slight smirk and took a longer drag of his cigarette. Someone else then caught his eye.

Once again, just standing there, was the hooded figure, standing to the left of the Shaftesbury Theatre entrance, across the street from Randolph's flat. Only this time, his jacket was red. It *had* to be the same person. Randolph stared back, feeling unsettled and nervous. Who was this person? Surely now, there was no mistake that whoever it was, was following Randolph. What concerned Randolph further, as he continued to stare down at the mysterious figure, was that they had followed him from another country. Had they followed him first from England to France and then back? Or started from France and followed him back to London? Despite their bowed head, Randolph could still feel that this person was staring straight at him. He swallowed. Randolph snapped from his stare, his cigarette burnt the tip of his index finger and he dropped it in reflex. He quickly bent down and picked up what was left of the cigarette and stubbed it out in the ashtray that was on the window sill. He returned his gaze to the unnerving, unmoving figure.

Swallowing again, Randolph saw this person slowly raise their head. Although the face was still covered inside the pulled in hood, the mouth could be seen a little. Randolph could just about make out a grin from under the hood. Randolph had had enough. Not only was he now fearing for his own safety, he wanted to know who this person was. He quickly dashed out of his flat and down the stairs outside, where he stood on the pavement across from the theatre. The person had vanished.

*

Randolph sat on the edge of the sofa, thinking to himself. A large glass of brandy was on the small table in front of him, although it was still early. Any pleasure in looking forward to seeing Thelma and Matthew later had now gone completely. Something wasn't right. He considered ringing the police, yet what good would that do? Maybe he was just being paranoid? Maybe it wasn't the same person. Who was he trying to kid! It was the same person. There was no doubt. He nearly rang Timothy to say he couldn't continue with this case — it wasn't like he had anything to go on anyway. But no. He couldn't do that. He couldn't let Timothy or the others down. Natalie's team were desperate for her to be found, even if she was dead. They at least needed closure. Randolph picked the brandy up, necked it in one go, then slammed the glass back down.

Finding the latest ritualistic murder victim, Miss Albescu's fucked up palm reading, this sinister case he had gotten involved in, and now being stalked by a creep in a hooded jacket — it was all too much. He'd rather have no case at all and rather be unemployed or finding people's missing pets. *Be careful what you wish for!* He thought yet again. He felt like getting wasted, but he couldn't do that, with Thelma and Matthew coming. The last thing he needed was to be drunk when they arrived. It sure as shit wouldn't help with any hope that he had left of getting back with his now estranged wife. Instead, he got up and looked out of the window again. At least the weather was brightening up a little. He decided to head to his office.

*

Walking towards the steps to the office building, Randolph saw Greg sitting slouched over on the top step, smoking a cigarette.

"Hello, mate!" Greg said, dropping some ash to the ground. "I'm glad I've seen you."

"All right, Greg? Why's that? I didn't think you worked Fridays?"

Greg chuckled. "I don't usually. I wasn't feeling too great yesterday, so I'm making up for it today. Anyway, my supervisor checked with his boss about any jobs going for you. He said there's a couple available — cleaning some office blocks like this one." Greg thumbed behind him. "It's near Regent Street, and an old launderette over on Oxford Street. I'm not sure about the hours, but I can check, mate? I can get my supervisor to give you a buzz?"

"Cheers for doing that, Greg. I really appreciate it. I just don't know right now. I've got a case I'm working on that's probably going to take up a lot of my time for now. I'll hold off if that's okay?"

"No worries, mate. And no problem! Your case. It wouldn't be to do with that hot bit of totty that walked in here the other week, was it?" Greg grinned and flicked his eyebrows up and down.

Randolph couldn't resist grinning back at him. "Something like that. But tell your supervisor I still might be interested, just not at the moment."

"Sure. I can do that. I know the job is only cleaning but it pays the bills. It's easy enough. I mean, I can do it!" Greg laughed.

"Yeah. A job's a job at the end of the day."

Randolph left Greg to finish his cigarette and walked down the corridor to his office. He checked the mat as usual. Nothing had been slipped under the door. Perhaps it was just as well for now, while he was working on the Natalie Connors case. Randolph still couldn't get the hooded figure out of his head. He assumed that it was a man. But not being able to see their face clearly, it could be a woman. The grin had given him the shivers. He wondered if he was just being paranoid. He soon quashed that thought. Perhaps on a slight positive note, at least there had been no more murders for eleven days in London, not since Randolph had experienced the misfortune of finding the last victim.

He sat at his desk and scanned the newspaper he had bought from old Tom Galton. He found it difficult to focus. There wasn't much mentioned about the killings. Randolph knew it was only a matter of time before the next mutilated body was found.

He lit a cigarette and took a couple of strong drags. The phone rang on his desk. He coughed a couple of times before answering, "Randolph Landon, PI?"

There was nothing but silence.

"Hello?" Randolph coughed again, swiping some smoke from his face. He really needed to kick this filthy habit. His smoking seemed to have gotten worse in the past few weeks.

Again, silence.

Randolph could hear someone breathing at the other end of the line. "Can I help?" Randolph frowned and shook his head. "Hello?" he said annoyed this time.

Still nothing but silence and heavy breathing.

Before Randolph could say anything else, the person hung up. Randolph frowned again and looked at the receiver, shaking his head. "Fucking idiot!" Placing the receiver back down, Randolph reflected that it was the first time that he had ever had a bogus phone call like that in his office. He'd sometimes had wrong numbers but nothing like that. He flicked some ash into the ashtray and closed the newspaper. His mind was too occupied with things to read further.

After finishing his cigarette, he locked up his office and made his way out to the main foyer. Some cleaning products were stacked in one corner but Greg wasn't to be seen. Randolph walked over and placed the paper down next to the products for Greg to read, and left the building, trotting down the steps into the sunshine.

*

Later that afternoon, Randolph ate at Teresa's. It was good to see Max again. He couldn't share much about his new case but Max repeated that he was pleased for him and glad to see things were finally picking up — though Randolph wasn't sure he agreed with *that* sentiment. After his meal and a small whisky, along with some chit-chat with a few bar regulars, Randolph made his way home, to eagerly await Thelma and Matthew. He started to feel excited. He had managed to put the case and this strange, hooded person to the back of his mind for now. He had no intentions of anything ruining his weekend with his family. He had waited for what seemed like ages to see them again.

Randolph looked at the wall clock; it had just gone ten past seven. Thelma and Matthew should hopefully arrive any minute. After a few minutes more, he saw Thelma's car, a light green Ford Cortina, indicate and make its way to the parking spaces at the back of the building. Technically speaking, it was Thelma's father's car but she drove it more now that her father was in his seventies and had lost some of his confidence driving.

Less than a minute later, Randolph heard Matthew excitedly scamper up the old staircase towards his flat. He could hear him laughing and calling out "Dad!" even before he had reached the flat door. Randolph opened the door and held out his arms, with a huge grin etched across his face. Matthew leapt into his father's arms, and they embraced tightly. Randolph couldn't help becoming emotional and tears filled his eyes.

"I've missed you, Daddy!"

"I've missed you too, Matthew," Randolph said softy. He sniffed and wiped a tear from both eyes with his hand.

Matthew put his legs on the floor, still gripping Randolph tightly. His head tucked firmly into Randolph's midriff.

Randolph smiled and stroked his son's brown hair. He then looked down the staircase. Thelma was carrying a small suitcase in one hand, and a couple of jackets in the other. Thelma looked up and smiled at the still embraced duo. Randolph beamed back.

Thelma greeted and kissed Randolph on the cheek at the top of the stairs.

At least that's a good sign, perhaps, Randolph thought to himself. He was a little surprised by the peck. He knew he shouldn't read too much into it and besides, it wasn't like he and Thelma were on bad terms, not now, anyway.

*

"I can do that?" Randolph said, sitting on the sofa with Matthew cuddled up next to him.

"It's fine," Thelma replied, getting up and putting on the kettle for the three of them.

Matthew never used to like tea or coffee but since the start of the year, he had acquired a taste for it, since becoming friends with another little boy at school, who he sometimes stayed over with and vice-versa.

"The teabags are in that cupboard there." Randolph pointed.

Thelma turned and smiled. "I know; I remember."

Matthew was a little sleepy after the long drive.

"The journey was okay, then?"

"It was. There was a bit of traffic as we came into London — as expected. It's why we're a little later than planned."

"Your folks doing all right?"

"They're good, though Mum had a bit of an upset stomach earlier but nothing too bad." Thelma stood in the open doorway with her arms folded, waiting for the kettle to boil. She smiled at her son. "The long drives always seem to make him sleepy."

"Nothing new there." Randolph smiled, before kissing his son's head. He gently pulled Matthew away from him. "I need the loo."

Matthew sat up and yawned, making his eyes water.

It felt so natural and warm, getting reacquainted with his son and wife. He still felt a little resentment towards Thelma for taking Matthew away from him up north, but he never showed it, for Matthew's sake. Seeing them made Randolph forget about his current case and concerns — as soon as they arrived.

After their hot teas, the three sat sharing some laughs and chatter, before Matthew fell asleep on the sofa with his arms wrapped around his father.

"I best take him to bed." Randolph looked down at his son who was fast asleep. He looked across at Thelma, who sat on the armchair. They smiled at one another. "I'll take him into my room for the night. I'll sleep on the sofa again."

"Okay," replied Thelma. She watched Randolph carefully carry their son into the bedroom.

"He's certainly out like a light." Randolph grinned, walking back into the living room, and sitting back down on the sofa. "I'm feeling a little tired, too." He let out a yawn.

"Same here. Your new case taking its toll on you?" Thelma asked.

"You could say that, yeah."

Thelma frowned. She could tell from the way that Randolph's face fell, that something was up. She also knew that Randolph couldn't disclose anything. "Everything okay?"

Randolph sighed. "Yeah," he said unconvincingly.

"You want to talk about it? I know you aren't at liberty to share details, but if you want to talk, Randolph?"

"No. It's okay. I've just been racking my brains about it all. I've been back and forth to France a couple of times, too." Randolph didn't think, mentioning France could matter.

"France?" Thelma said surprised.

He gave a little chuckle. "I know. It's the first time I've ever had to travel abroad for work. I guess I shouldn't complain. It's the first proper case I've had in quite some time."

Thelma was more than curious now. "Is it a big one, then?"

"Ah. It's just a woman that's gone missing. One of her ex-partners is concerned. She'd been working in France. Long story!" Randolph yawned again. He was tempted to tell Thelma everything that had been going on, including the body he had found in London. He didn't however, want to ruin their weekend together as a family. He wanted to enjoy the precious time he had with them and then get back to working on the case.

"Well, I'm here if you want to talk about it?"

"Thanks." Randolph smiled. "I know."

The married couple spoke more into the night. Though neither of them talked about getting back together. It was still an uncomfortable topic. They chatted casually and enjoyed each other's company, before Thelma retired for the night, joining Matthew in the bedroom for some sleep. It took a while for Randolph to get comfy on the sofa. He eventually drifted off into a welcome sleep.

Chapter Seventeen
Saturday, May 28th, 1966

Shaftesbury Avenue, London – 8.06 am

Randolph opened his eyes, squinting and blinking a few times. He heard Matthew come running out from the bedroom. Before Randolph could sit up, Matthew jumped onto him, making him wince. "Argh! You *big* lump!" Randolph joked and held his son who giggled.

Thelma came out from the bedroom into the living room — she smiled, before yawning.

Randolph sat up. He and Matthew held each other. "You two fancy a fry-up? I've got some bacon and eggs in the fridge. There's a few sausages left as well." He looked at his wristwatch.

"I'm up for that. What about you, Matthew?" Thelma walked over and kissed her son on the head.

"Please!" Matthew said excitedly.

"I'll make it," offered Randolph.

"It's fine. I'll do it." Thelma smiled.

"So, what do you want to do today, Matty? Anything you want!"

"Can we go to the zoo? *Please!*" Matthew asked again excited.

"If that's what you want … I've heard they have a new animal there, or *monster* that has escaped. They call it *The Tickle Monster!*" Randolph playfully pinned Matthew down on the sofa and tickled him.

They all laughed. Matthew giggled and writhed as his father tickled him all over.

"Matthew has been saying for a while that he'd like to go to London Zoo. It's been almost a year since we last went. You can take him if you like? I might stay here and do some reading. Or see if Linda's free." Linda was an old friend of both of them, but mainly Thelma. She lived in South London.

Although Randolph would have liked some alone time with his son, he was disappointed that Thelma suggested they went without her. He knew though, Thelma had good intentions. She no doubt wanted him and Matthew to spend as much time as they could together. "Can do. It's up to you, though? It would be nicer if you came, too." Randolph eased up on tickling Matthew.

"We'll see after breakfast." Thelma smiled, before making her way into the kitchen to start the fry-up.

Matthew also asked for his mother to come to the zoo, but he wasn't too fussed when Thelma insisted on staying back. She would ring Linda to see if she was free. It would be nice for a catch up. She hadn't seen her for a few months. Failing that, she'd do some shopping in London or some reading at the flat.

*

Matthew laughed when some monkeys in the cage started swinging on a couple of branches. He held Randolph's hand tightly. The pair had taken their time walking through the zoo and admiring the animals. Randolph's problems washed away further, while holding his son's hand. If only things were like this all the time. He dreaded the next evening, when they would go and he wouldn't know when he was going to see Matthew and Thelma again. He really needed to talk to Thelma about things. The last serious conversation they had had was a few months ago. It hadn't ended badly, but there was no conclusion. Perhaps the only plausible solution would be for him to move up to Lincolnshire. He couldn't see Thelma moving back down to London now, not after she had settled up there and Matthew too. He couldn't let her leave her parents behind either, not now they were getting older.

After laughing at a few more animals and their antics, Randolph and Matthew sat at a table and bench to have some lunch. Despite the breakfast earlier, they had worked up quite an appetite, so they tucked into their packed lunch. Matthew munched on a ham sandwich that Thelma had made the two earlier. He happily swung his legs under the table in a pair of red shorts.

Randolph watched his son and smiled to himself. He had to stop himself from getting emotional. He was starting to miss him already, although he was still there with him. "You're still enjoying it up in Lincolnshire, Matthew?"

"Yeah. I really like staying with Nanny and Grandad. I've made a couple more friends. One is a girl, too."

Randolph smiled, although he grew a little sad. It wasn't just the fact that Matthew appeared more settled up there, but that Matthew had grown closer to Thelma's parents. He was genuinely happy for Matthew but his own parents were no longer alive; they had missed out on having a grandchild. It might not have made much difference anyway, now that Randolph didn't see much of his son himself. "Who's this girl, then?" Randolph winked.

"Her name's Donna. We sometimes play kiss chase in the playground." Matthew giggled and then drank from a small carton of orange squash through a green straw.

Randolph laughed. "I hope you aren't breaking *too* many hearts, Matty?" he teased.

Matthew chuckled, biting a different corner of his sandwich this time.

Randolph began eating his own sandwich. He looked up at the now clear blue sky. The day grew warmer. He thought about what the two of them could do after lunch and the zoo. Thelma had told them to take as long as they wanted.

Matthew laughed when he started to get some hiccups, making Randolph laugh too.

"There anything you would like to do next?"

"I'd really like to see Arsenal play later, Dad!"

"I know, mate but the season's finished now. We'll have to wait until at least August and the new season before we can get to see them again."

Matthew's face turned glum.

Randolph half-smiled. "I'll tell you what! What if we go drive around Highbury, instead? It's obviously not the same as watching the team play, but it would be something. We can park up and have a walk about?"

"Yay!" Matthew liked the idea.

Over lunch, the two laughed and chatted. Then Matthew brought up a more serious subject, which Randolph had hoped to avoid — at least for now.

"When are you and Mum, getting back together, Dad?" Matthew asked softly with his innocent, brown eyes. He had the same eyes as his father.

Randolph didn't know what to say. "I don't know, matey. Me and your mum need to sit down and chat about it. Hopefully we can sort something out."

"That's what you always say, Dad. Are you getting a divorce?"

Randolph was a little taken aback. Matthew had never used the word 'divorce' before.

"A boy I know at school said that his mum and dad are getting a divorce. He said that his dad is 'doing it,' with a younger lady."

Randolph couldn't help but snigger at the 'doing it' comment. He doubted whether his son even knew what it meant.

"Are you 'doing it' with another lady, Dad?"

Randolph laughed and held his son's hands over the rough, wooden table. "No. I'm not *doing it* with another woman. Me and your mum still love each other, Matthew." That's what Randolph still hoped, anyway. She hadn't said it to him for as long as he could remember. The last time he had told Thelma he loved her, was before she took off with Matthew.

"What about a divorce?"

"No. I don't think so, Matthew. We still need to work through our differences. But I *promise* you, we're going to try." Randolph squeezed his son's hands tightly.

"Okay." Matthew looked sad, lowering his face. "Will you move up to live with us and with Nanny and Grandad? So we can all live together?"

Randolph felt sad again, looking at Matthew. "I, I don't know. We'll see. Let's finish our lunch, anyway. Yeah?"

Matthew nodded, his head still lowered.

Once they had eaten, both their moods perked up again from seeing the animals. They both walked while eating ice-cream. Matthew giggled when his father dabbed his strawberry ice-cream onto Matthew's nose. They finished the zoo visit by seeing the elephants. Matthew was fascinated by their long trunks: he stood there pointing at them. Randolph's arm never left his son's shoulders.

*

Randolph parked the Hillman Imp on Avenell Road. Highbury Stadium was a little further down on the left and they could walk from there. Randolph instinctively held his son's hand as they made their way down the road.

The stadium had recently hosted the World Heavyweight Championship boxing clash between Britain's Henry Cooper and America's Muhammad Ali — with Ali being victorious again in the second bout.

Approaching the stadium, the pair slowed down and then stopped, admiring the white façade of the East Stand of the historic stadium, containing the famous Marble Halls.

"Best stadium in the country, Son!" Randolph turned and smiled to look down at Matthew, with his arm around his shoulder. It wasn't the first time he had said it.

"Cool." Matthew continued to look. It was actually the first time he and Randolph had admired the East Stand together. When they went to the odd game, they would sit in the opposite West Stand.

"Hopefully we'll win the League again, soon," Randolph added.

It had been far too long since Arsenal celebrated a title success. It had been yet another disappointing season for The Gunners again, with pressure building on manager Billy Wright. There were rumours that the football club had run out of patience with him, and his sacking was imminent.

A man wearing a black cap and a light green jumper came out of a side entrance to the left of the stand. He plopped a cigarette into his mouth and pulled out a box of matches from his dark grey trousers. Striking a match, a strong breeze picked up. He cupped his mouth with his left hand, lighting the cigarette with his other. He then wafted the match out, dropping it to the ground. Puffing on his smoke, he nodded towards Randolph, who nodded back.

Matthew hadn't noticed the man; he was still smiling to himself and looking at the stand and at ARSENAL STADIUM in red lettering, along with the red cannon underneath. "It would have been really nice to have watched Arsenal today, Dad."

"I know, mate. We'll have to wait a few months for when the season starts up. It will soon come round." Randolph smiled over at the man smoking the cigarette.

"I wish we could go inside onto the pitch!" Matthew pleaded.

Randolph laughed. "I don't think we can do that, Matthew." He squeezed his son's small waist.

"Why not?"

"It's private. You can't just walk in uninvited or when you feel like it."

"Okay," Matthew said sadly.

"We'll soon be back in there, watching them." Randolph wasn't sure himself, when the next time would be.

"I might be able to help with that," the man wearing the black fisherman cap suddenly said.

Randolph turned his head and frowned. "Excuse me?"

He and Matthew watched the man walk over.

The man smiled and stopped in front of them. Holding what was left of the cigarette in his left hand, he held out his right hand. "I'm Rodney. I'm the groundsman here."

Randolph smiled at the man, who appeared to be in his late fifties. He shook the groundsman's hand. "I'm Randolph and this is my son, Matthew."

The groundsman, Rodney, then held out his hand for Matthew to shake.

Matthew was a little shy and looked up to Randolph as if for confirmation it was okay.

"It's all right." Randolph smiled.

Matthew reluctantly shook the man's hand back and gave a faint smile.

"I couldn't help but overhear your conversation. How would you like to come and walk on the pitch for a bit, eh?" Rodney said, mainly to Matthew whose eyes lit up. "Of course, if it's okay with your dad, that is?" He grinned, then took a drag of his cigarette. A bottom tooth was missing from his gums.

"Can we, Dad, can we? *Please!*" Matthew looked up at Randolph excitedly.

"Sure, if it's okay?" Randolph frowned slightly at Rodney.

"Ah, it will be fine," Rodney replied cockily and winked. "You're not supposed to do it, but it's only myself and a couple of others here today. They won't mind, anyway — the chairman. I get on quite well with him and his family." Rodney grinned some more. "I've been doing the ground and that for a good number of seasons now."

"Well, if you're sure it's okay, that's great!" Randolph smiled.

Rodney then escorted them to the side entrance. Before entering, he quickly finished off his cigarette, dropped the stub to the ground and squashed it out with his boot.

Matthew appeared in constant awe as they walked around the edge of the football pitch. It was a lucky coincidence that the groundsman, Rodney, had just come out of the stadium when he did. Randolph said how generous it was of him to have offered showing them in. He just hoped that Rodney wouldn't get into trouble. Rodney had laughed and said it was fine. Rodney expressed his excitement at the forthcoming World Cup that would be held in England in July. He was pretty optimistic about England's chances. They then got back to the topic of Arsenal, and how last season's campaign was highly disappointing, with the club finishing 14ᵗʰ in the First Division:

"But yeah, there's a strong chance that Billy won't be the manager here next season," Rodney said, scratching the back of his neck.

"You think the reports are true, then?" Randolph replied. "To be fair, it's not been the best four years!"

Rodney sighed. "Tell me about it! I don't know for sure, but I've heard rumours from within the club that he'll be sacked, or even that he'll resign. The club needs a fresh impetus. We really need to start challenging for the League again. Well, actually *winning* it! And trophies! It's been *far* too long since the club and fans have tasted success and silverware."

"Here, here!" Randolph affirmed.

"Morale has been pretty low for quite some time around the club. Obviously amongst the players themselves, too. I chat to them from time to time. Even Billy as well. He's a nice enough gentleman, just not the man for Arsenal, I'm afraid."

Randolph nodded in agreement. "Yeah. We definitely need a change, mate. We need the glory days brought back as soon as possible!"

"For sure!"

"Look, Dad!" Matthew said, pointing up to the West Stand. "That's where we sit when we come!"

Randolph and Rodney smiled.

"Do you come and watch The Arsenal, much?" Rodney asked.

"A few times. Perhaps not as much as I would like. But when I can. I try and bring Matthew, too, when I do."

Rodney nodded. "Same with members of my family. I can sometimes grab free tickets." He grinned. "We're all Arsenal — our family. Has been the case since the club founded in 1886. They were called Dial Square Football Club back then."

Randolph nodded again. He knew of Arsenal's history. "Pretty much the same with me. My old man was an Arsenal fan. His father, too. It runs in the family." He chuckled.

"Yep. We all bleed red and white!" Rodney laughed.

It was a pleasant and welcoming experience setting foot on the historic pitch in the sunshine, and even a little surreal stepping on the grass where so many famous names had played and become legends. Randolph was a lot younger himself, but he still remembered fondly the great Arsenal sides that dominated the 1930s before the Second World War broke out. He and Rodney spoke about how if it wasn't for Hitler and the war, Arsenal could have dominated further and won more trophies. "Bloody Nazis!" Rodney had half-joked.

Once they were done on the pitch, Rodney showed them around the old dressing rooms. He even made the three of them and another colleague a hot cup of tea and shared a pack of biscuits between them. They spent an hour with him. Rodney asked Randolph for his address and telephone number. He promised them that he would try and 'hook them up' with some free tickets if he could. Randolph and Matthew were more than grateful.

Rodney walked them out through the famous Marble Halls entrance and past the bronze bust of the legend Herbert Chapman as they left the stadium.

"Thank you again for showing us around and for doing this; it's much appreciated," Randolph said, holding out his hand.

Rodney grinned. "No worries, Randolph. It's been my pleasure! Always happy to help a fellow Arsenal fan." Rodney had since rolled up his sleeves. He had a faded Arsenal cannon tattooed on the back of his right wrist.

"Thank you." Matthew smiled, holding out his hand, mimicking his father's actions.

"No worries, Matthew!" Rodney shook Matthew's young hand and ruffled up his hair. "It's been a pleasure to meet you both as well. I promise I'll be in touch if I can get hold of some tickets. I can usually work my magic! I have some connections." He laughed and winked.

"Much appreciated." Randolph laughed back, taking his son's hand in his.

The day had gone even better than expected. Randolph and Matthew had thoroughly enjoyed themselves. At least for now, Randolph had forgotten his case and the concerns linked with it.

*

After their Highbury visit, Randolph had pulled over outside a small bakery on Albany Street to buy a loaf of bread and the pair had gone to feed the ducks at Regent's Park. It was almost four in the afternoon, when Randolph and Matthew returned to the flat on Shaftesbury Avenue. Matthew couldn't wait to tell his mother about his 'Arsenal experience.' He was also excited to tell his friends back at school on Monday.

Opening the door to his flat, Randolph and Matthew saw Thelma holding the phone receiver. She placed it back down and smiled at the pair.

"*Mum*! You wouldn't guess where we went after the zoo!" Matthew ran to give his mother a gripping hug.

Thelma held him back. "Well, you've certainly been gone for a long time!" She smiled. "I've not long been back myself, actually. I went to see Linda, then looked around some shops. I noticed that you were a bit short of toilet roll and some food, so stocked up for you."

"You didn't have to do that but thank you," Randolph replied. "How's Linda? She all good?"

"It was no bother and she is, yes. We had a good catch up! What about your day? How was the zoo and where did you go afterwards?"

Matthew excitedly explained their 'tour' around the Arsenal Stadium. His parents laughed when Matthew pronounced Rodney, "Rodmay." He told his mum how he couldn't wait to tell his friends back at school on Monday.

Thelma was really pleased that the pair had had a fantastic day out. They then sat together on the sofa, Matthew between his parents, watching *Stingray*.

"Do you want to do anything for dinner, later?" Randolph asked the two.

"Perhaps. We can see later on. I don't feel overly hungry yet. I had quite a heavy lunch at Linda's."

Matthew didn't say anything. He was too engrossed in the TV show.

"Yeah. I don't feel too hungry at the moment. We can see later on." Randolph smiled across to Thelma. This was how life should be, snuggled up on the sofa, together as a family, albeit not in this run-down excuse of a home.

The phone rang and Randolph got up to answer it. He could hear breathing down the line again like the call in his office the day before. The caller then hung up.

"No one there again?" Thelma asked. "The same thing happened just before you came back. Whoever it was hung up. I didn't hear anything."

Randolph sat back down, his forehead creased up, thinking.

Matthew continued to watch his show.

"You okay?" Thelma asked.

"Huh? Oh. Yeah. Probably just some silly sod messing about and playing games. I had the same thing happen yesterday at my office."

"More than likely. Probably some kids messing about." Thelma smiled.

Randolph wasn't sure. It more than unnerved him, along with the hooded figure.

*

Matthew had said he fancied pizza for dinner, so later on that evening, the family went out to PizzaExpress. It had been open since March the previous year, over on Wardour Street. It was the first time either of the Landons had been there. It was near the office blocks where Cheng-Lei Wu lived — the Asian man who Randolph had questioned about the Peanut case.

They were sat on a table under a coloured framed photo of the PizzaExpress founder, Peter Boizot. At the bottom of the frame, a plaque read *"I'd like to think that all things in my life are concerned with love."* — a quote from Peter himself, which Randolph rather liked.

Matthew sat next to Randolph with Thelma opposite them. They were enjoying each other's company and having a good laugh, when not for the first time that day, Matthew brought up the dreaded topic again:

"When are you and Dad, getting back together, Mum?"

Thelma looked awkwardly at Randolph.

"Are we going to move back to London? What about Nanny and Grandad and my friends at school?" Matthew seemed torn. He wanted his parents to get back together, but he had also settled in well up in Lincolnshire. He didn't want to leave his friends behind.

This made the decision even more difficult regarding their plans if they sorted their marriage out. Randolph didn't feel he had much to leave behind in London though.

"I don't know, love," Thelma answered. "Me and your dad need to talk about it."

"That's what you always say," Matthew said sadly. "Do you still love one another?"

Thelma half-smiled and looked at Randolph who returned the smile. It was the first time Matthew had asked them the question together. They no doubt both sensed that with Matthew getting a little older now, he became more aware as the months passed, starting to ask more questions.

Randolph felt uncomfortable. He waited to see how Thelma answered.

"Yes. We do," Thelma said honestly. She still looked at Randolph, then averted her eyes to Matthew.

Randolph felt a pang of joy. He had always loved her — he always would and now he knew how she felt.

"Why don't you get back together, then?" Matthew kept pushing.

"Like I said earlier, mate. We still need to discuss things. It takes time." Randolph squeezed Matthew's right hand.

"What do you need to talk about?" Matthew looked down at the table at his empty plate.

Randolph and Thelma didn't know what to say. Surely it was about time they sorted their marriage out. It wasn't fair on Matthew.

"We promise we'll sort things out soon. Okay?" Thelma promised.

"Okay." Matthew didn't look up.

The tone lightened somewhat, when Randolph suggested a large bowl of ice-cream for Matthew and made a couple of jokes about him being a 'greedy little piggy.'

*

Randolph tucked Matthew into bed. They read *The Beano* Randolph had bought almost a couple of weeks back and laughed together. When they had finished reading, Randolph kissed his son goodnight on the forehead and turned the bedroom light off.

Thelma was sat on the sofa reading *Valley of the Dolls*, by Jacqueline Susann.

Randolph walked back in and slumped onto the sofa next to her. "I fancy a brandy. Do you want one?"

Thelma placed a yellow bookmark in her novel and closed it. "I'm fine … I think it's time we had a chat about things, if not for our sakes, for Matthew's."

Randolph sighed. "It's long overdue. It's not fair on Matthew. I sense he's confused and struggling with it all. I guess you see it, too."

Thelma nodded.

"Is it true what you said, back at the restaurant? Do you still love me?"

Thelma turned so that she was facing Randolph. She nodded again. "It is. I'm still in love with you, Randolph. I'm not sure that will ever change."

Randolph felt that pang of joy again. "You have no idea how much that means to me, hearing you say that. I've doubted whether you still did. I've never stopped loving you. I guess sometimes, I try to fight my feelings, because I feel like I've lost you both."

Thelma smiled at him. "You haven't lost us."

"It's been torture, a living hell, here without you two, especially in this dump of a place I call home," Randolph semi-joked, making Thelma laugh slightly. "But where do we go from here? What do you want? I know what I want. I want you back, Thelma, you and Matthew, more than *anything*."

Thelma smiled again, her eyes filling. She held Randolph's hands. She was still wearing her silver wedding ring. "I'd like to give our marriage another go. I think we can make it work, if we take things slowly to start with. And not just because of Matthew, but for me, you, and for all of us. I want for us to be a family again. The past few months, I've thought about it so much. One of Linda's friends has just lost her husband. It makes you think: life's too short."

Randolph smiled. "How can we move forwards? What's next? I'd like perhaps, for you and Matthew to move back down here to London, although not to this flat. But I know you're both settled in Lincolnshire, especially with your folks. I wouldn't want you to move Matthew again, when he's just made friends up there. I guess the only plausible thing would be for me to move up there and for us to give it a shot."

Thelma sighed. "But I'd feel guilty. Like when I moved away. It isn't fair on you, giving up what you have here, like your work, your friends, the people you see. It's your home."

Randolph laughed and shook his head. "Other than my latest case, work has been pretty much non-existent, apart from some minor cases and most of my friends don't live in London anymore, as you know."

"I know, but you're still nearer to them down here, than you would be up in Lincolnshire. And I'm sure work will pick up for you here."

"Moving would be a small sacrifice to make and I can still find work up there. There may even be more opportunities there. Or failing that, I could start afresh and do something else. Believe me, it will be an easy transition. I know my work got in the way before, but I promise you, I won't allow it to again, just as long as we're all together again, as a family. That's all I've ever wanted."

"Me too, Randolph. We'll try harder this time, together, the *three* of us." Thelma leant in and kissed Randolph's forehead and they embraced.

"God, I've missed you," Randolph said quietly over Thelma's shoulder. "I've been so alone without you."

Thelma affectionately rubbed her hand over Randolph's back. "I've missed you, too." She pulled away and wiped tears from her eyes. "Perhaps I could do with that glass of brandy after all?" She laughed and sniffed.

Randolph smiled and got up to pour a couple of glasses of brandy.

"Thanks." Thelma took the glass, whilst Randolph sat back down. "My parents have always been fond of you; you know that. They'd be more than happy for us all to live together until we perhaps found a place of our own."

Randolph sipped his brandy and Thelma did the same. "We might have to wait a little. I've no idea how long my current case will take."

"Then I guess we'll have to be patient for now."

Randolph nodded. "I know … It's a complex one. I'm pretty much clueless on it."

"You sure you don't want to talk about it? You can confide in me. What you tell me won't leave this room."

Randolph sighed. He sipped his brandy and shook his head. "I know. It's just pretty strange, and I'm still mulling it all over at the moment."

Thelma didn't press Randolph on the matter. "Well, I'm here. I'm just a phone call away."

"I know." Randolph smiled and then held Thelma's hand. "I don't even know what the hell is going on right now."

"You're working in France, too?"

"That's right. I'm most likely going back next week, and I don't know how long for. My client is going to contact me on Monday to discuss things further."

"I'm sure you'll get to the bottom of it. There's no one better at what you do than you, Randolph," Thelma said reassuringly.

Randolph smiled; he was so happy he had his family back.

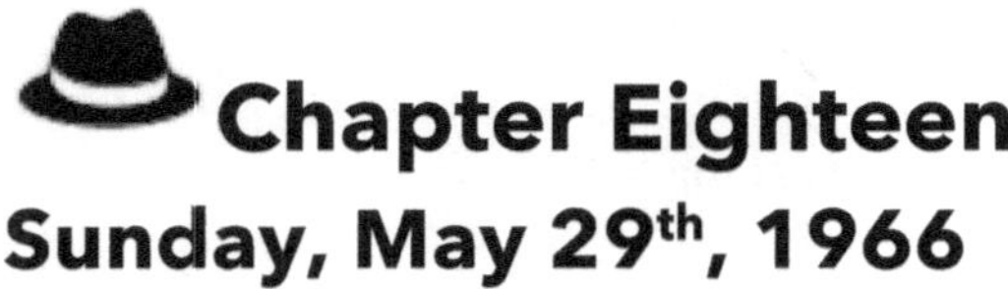

Chapter Eighteen
Sunday, May 29th, 1966

Shaftesbury Avenue, London – 7.44 am

After last night's talks and a couple of brandies, the married couple had watched some late-night television, before Thelma dozed off to sleep in Randolph's arms. Now, she groaned. Randolph opened his eyes. His head was resting on the sofa arm. He looked down at Thelma, who was still fast asleep, pressed against his body. He smiled to himself. For the first time in ages, he felt optimistic about life. Once again, there was meaning. Although Thelma and Matthew were leaving later today, the ice had finally been broken. There was now hope.

Randolph slowly got up, being careful not to waken Thelma. He checked his watch. He decided to let her sleep some more. Matthew obviously wasn't awake yet either.

Randolph boiled the kettle and made some coffee. He looked out of his flat window. He was half-expecting to see the mysterious hooded figure, but everywhere was quiet this Sunday morning. He wondered what the following week would entail in his quest to find this missing archaeologist, Natalie Conners. He wanted to get to the bottom of the case as soon as possible, particularly if Natalie's life was in danger, assuming she wasn't dead already. The sooner the case could be concluded, the quicker he and Thelma could finalise a potential move up to Lincolnshire. His family came first — naturally. But for now, at least temporarily, this case needed solving. He didn't want to let anyone down.

He finished his coffee and heard what he thought was someone slowly coming up the old staircase leading to his flat. As they only lead to his flat, someone must have taken the wrong staircase. Perhaps they were still drunk from a raucous Saturday night.

He stopped at the flat door and listened as more footsteps approached. He wasn't sure if they were coming or going. He unlocked the door and slowly opened it, expecting to see someone on the staircase. Yet there was no one there. Perhaps they had realised their mistake and backtracked. Fleetingly, he wondered whether it was the hooded figure stalking him. Just then, Thelma sat up and yawned, distracting him.

"I think those two brandies put me to sleep," Thelma joked, still fully clothed, wearing her blue Wrangler jeans.

Randolph smiled. "You want a coffee?"

"Sure," Thelma yawned again. "Thanks. Matthew not up yet?"

"Not yet. I was just about to check in on him," Randolph replied, making his way to the kitchen.

"I'll go see him." Thelma soon returned. "He's still fast asleep."

"Probably from all the excitement of yesterday." Randolph grinned.

Thelma laughed. "Yep! Bless him."

*

Matthew didn't stir until late morning. After noon, they went for a picnic in Hyde Park. A fair few others were there. Some had even brought deck chairs to take advantage of the sunshine. Rain was forecast for most of the next week so everyone was enjoying the warmth while they could. A group of people had also gathered around the bandstand and were dancing to a small band playing a mixture of songs. The afternoon was pleasant and cheerful.

Matthew became excited when Thelma and Randolph explained their plans to be a family together again and for Randolph to move up north with them. He started jumping about with joy. His parents were quick to remind him, that they'd all have to be patient, and nothing was set in stone yet. They explained about Randolph's latest case.

Randolph had brought an old football to the park. After eating, he and Matthew enjoyed a kickabout on the grass. Thelma sat on the blanket, reading on and off, smiling and watching the two kick the ball about.

"Goal!" Matthew cheered. He had kicked the ball between two trees they were using as goalposts.

Thelma looked up, adjusted her sunglasses and grinned. She noticed Randolph's grey trilby upside down on the red blanket. Resting inside it was a small brown paper bag. She reached over and picked it up. Inside the bag was a small, white, porcelain elephant. She smiled to herself, placing the elephant back in the bag.

After a short while, Randolph returned. He left Matthew kicking the ball against one of the trees, close by. "Our news has certainly perked him up. I just hope he realises it's still not going to be a quick fix."

Thelma closed her book and placed it down next to her. She took off her sunglasses. "I know." She smiled and took out a sticky bun from the wicker hamper. "He'll be fine. All three of us will be. We'll just have to be patient."

Randolph took the present from his hat. "I've brought a present for Matthew." He took the elephant out.

"It's cute. I took a peek. Sorry! I guessed it was for Matthew."

Randolph smiled. "I bought it last Monday in France, in a lovely city called Limoges. There are some really nice little shops there. As soon as I returned home, I had to go back to Paris."

"Limoges? I think I've heard of it. You've certainly been busy! It must have been nice to do a bit of sightseeing, although I know most of your time is spent working. I'm really pleased for you, Randolph, that you have something more substantial to work on."

Randolph looked down at the elephant in his hand. "Thanks." If only Thelma knew what the case involved. He didn't want to tell her. Certainly not now, whilst they were enjoying themselves. "After this case, it might be best if I give up the private investigator malarkey, if I move up to Lincolnshire with you. I don't want it to affect our relationship again, Thelma. Especially if it means travelling about and staying in places away from you."

"I don't want you to give it up for us, Randolph — I didn't before. I guess I just wanted you to take some time out sometimes. Maybe you were too committed to certain cases. Or there were some you could have declined, but then I suppose the harder you work the better your reputation and successes. I'm sorry. It sounds so selfish of me."

Randolph put the elephant back in the bag. "No. It doesn't sound selfish. I know as well as anyone, I could have taken a step back at times. I need to learn to be able to switch off more, too. But yes, the job does require dedicated commitment, which is why I'm seriously considering packing it in altogether. Family comes first. There are always other jobs available. We can see." Randolph smiled at Thelma.

Matthew came running over, carrying the football in both hands. Thelma wiped her sticky hands from the bun on a white napkin. "You all right, love?"

"Yeah!" Matthew beamed. "I'm a little hot now, Mum."

"Yeah. I'm starting to sweat." Randolph grinned. "I have something for you, Matty."

Matthew took the small bag from his father's hand and opened it. He took out the small porcelain elephant. "Thanks, Dad!" Matthew hugged his dad appreciatively.

"It's a little something I thought you'd like, when I was in France last week."

"I love it!" Matthew had always been a grateful child, no matter how small a gesture was.

*

It was after six that evening, when Randolph kissed his wife and son goodbye. He waved to them from his flat window as Thelma pulled out onto the main road. Matthew still held the porcelain elephant in his hand. The inevitable sadness washed over Randolph, but hopefully in a few weeks, they would be living together properly as a family once more. Thelma and Matthew were coming down again next weekend, which had cheered him up but of course it would depend on whether or not Randolph wasn't tied up with the case. Now they had left, he started mulling it over again in his head. It distracted him from the void created by their absence.

He lit a cigarette, put his feet up on the table and read through his notes on Natalie's case — for what use it would do. He flicked some ash into the ashtray next to him on the sofa. He wondered how Pierre and Christine were doing and the other two members of Natalie's team. He pondered again over visiting the excavation site, although he rather dreaded the thought of it. It might be risky and would probably be a waste of time. There might however, be a clue there to help resolve Miss Conners' disappearance — something that the others had missed, though it was doubtful.

Timothy might cancel the case, as there were no leads but again he doubted that. Even if Timothy did terminate Randolph's services, he wasn't sure he could let it go. Natalie could be in serious danger somewhere. He wasn't one to quit when the going got tough. He wanted to see this to the end now.

He sat a while, trying to rack his brains. He finished his cigarette and got up to pour himself a whisky. While he was placing the bottle back in the cupboard, his phone rang. "Hello?" Randolph answered abruptly; he was half-expecting it to be the bogus caller.

"Randolph, it's Timothy Andrews. I'm sorry for calling you on a Sunday evening. I hope you had a good time with your family. Am I intruding?"

"Timothy. It's fine. I had a great time with my family, thank you. We sorted out some things, so hopefully it's all looking good on the horizon, and we can move forward. They left a little earlier."

"That's great to hear. I was ringing about the case. Are you able to return to France tomorrow?"

Randolph swigged some whisky from the glass in his left hand. "Whatever you want, Timothy. You've hired me for my services, and I'm willing to do anything it takes to get to the bottom of all this."

"I admire your tenaciousness, Randolph. Thank you."

"It's all part of the service," Randolph jested, making Timothy chuckle. "What's the plan?"

Timothy cleared his throat. "We can fly down to my villa tomorrow morning. I've spoken to the gendarme who's willing to answer any questions you may have."

"I'm happy to do that. It's just difficult to see what good it will do, when they'll most likely say the same things as Pierre and Christine. It just seems like we're going over the same ground, repeatedly."

"I know. Though it could be good to get acquainted with the gendarmerie down there. They might even open up a bit more to you, if they've been holding back on anything, seeing as you're a PI."

"Possible. It could be useful to check out the dig site, too."

"That can be arranged. We'll discuss things further on the way down there. We'll pick you up tomorrow morning; would nine be okay?"

"Fine, Timothy. Would it be okay to pick me up at my office? I need to check a couple of things and catch up on the paperwork before we leave."

"All good, Randolph. Not a problem at all. We'll see you tomorrow. Enjoy the rest of your evening."

"You too."

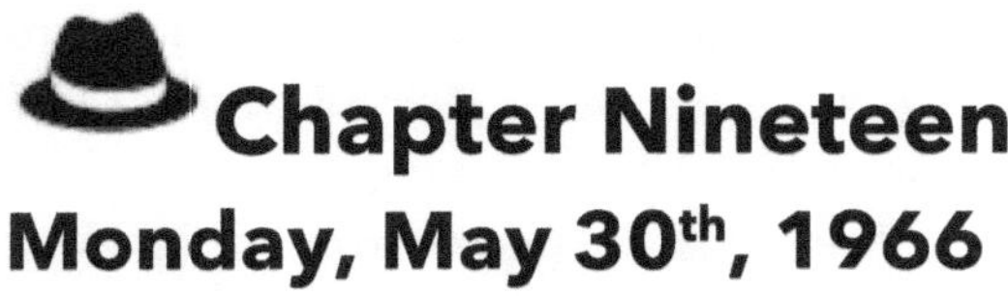 # Chapter Nineteen
Monday, May 30th, 1966

Shaftesbury Avenue, London - 7.31 am

Getting dressed that Monday morning, ready for the return to France, Randolph put on a pair of his trousers and sat in one of the armchairs, bending down to tie the laces to his black shoes. Once again, he could hear somebody slowly climbing the stairs. He crept slowly towards the door and quickly swiped it open. No one was there. Randolph stood, staring down the empty staircase. "What the hell is going on," he muttered to himself. Swallowing, he slowly closed his door and returned to his bedroom to finish packing.

*

It was a grey and drizzly morning, when Randolph walked to his office on Hopkins Street. He wore a dark grey trench coat and black fedora for a change. He turned into his office building and walked down the corridor to his office. Taking out the key from his trench coat pocket, he noticed the corridor lights dimming. Perhaps they were on the brink of failing again. *There's a surprise,* thought Randolph. He shook his head and unlocked the office door, just as the lights in the corridor went out completely, followed by the ones in the main foyer and then the other corridor beyond. Randolph stood in near darkness. The only source of light came from his right from a small window at the end of the corridor. Only a limited amount of daylight reached the foyer.

Light from his office window helped him a little. He placed his suitcase inside the room near to the door and flicked the light switch on the wall a few times, but the power was out in the whole building.

He heard nothing from inside the other offices on his corridor, although he was used to that, as they were mostly vacant. He cursed under his breath. Entering his office, he heard footsteps from the blackened corridor. He leant back to see someone standing at the other end. Whoever it was, stepped away from what little light there was in the foyer. Randolph froze. It looked like this person was wearing a hood. Shit!

The unnerving shadowy figure continued to stand there without saying a word or moving.

"Hello?" Randolph asked abruptly in a raised voice. "Is there something I can help you with?" He swallowed. He couldn't be sure, but he thought they might be holding something in their left hand. It had to be the same mysterious hooded figure he had seen in Paris and outside his flat. Surely it all had to be related.

Still the person refused to move or speak.

"What the fuck," Randolph whispered quietly. He started to feel nervous. He thought of the murders. Showing courage, he took a few steps forward as if to confront the figure. "I *said*, can I help you?" Randolph raised his voice further.

Still the figure remained still.

Randolph edged a few more steps forward. He wished Greg was about. Typical!

Eerily, the shadowy figure then began to walk slowly, one step at a time, closer to Randolph, who swallowed again.

Randolph tried to stand his ground, but he instinctively stepped back. He wasn't sure whether to lock himself inside his office, or make a run past this person to get outside. However, the figure temporarily stopped in the middle of the corridor, before continuing slowly, almost entirely embedded in the darkness of the corridor. They said nothing although the sound of dripping could be heard.

"What do you want?" Randolph tried to sound confident, but his voice was shaky and betrayed him. He backed into his office doorway, fixated on this slow-moving person. He expected the figure to suddenly dart towards him and he was ready to slam the door in their face if need be.

The figure stopped. Randolph could just about make out their outline.

The phone on his desk suddenly rang, making Randolph jump. He instinctively turned his head and looked towards the ringing. He quickly turned his attention back to the figure, still in the corridor. The phone continued to ring. Randolph started to breath heavier. What did this person want with him? What had he done? Randolph did the only thing he thought was practical. He quickly closed the door and locked it, feeling weak for doing so. The phone continued ringing. He eventually answered it.

No one replied. Randolph heard the breathing again. He never took his eyes from the door. His blinds were up. He could now see the figure in silhouette through the frosted glass, standing outside his office. Randolph swallowed again. Who the hell was this? It didn't make sense. It had to be the same hooded figure. Or could it be someone entirely different? Surely it couldn't be the same person on the phone, if they were stood outside his door! Was he being harassed by more than one person? Or was the caller just a random joker? Shit!

Still there was no voice from the other end of the line. The shadowy figure through the glass remained ... Then, the lights in the office started to come back to life. Randolph looked up; the lights came on fully. The figure had gone and the caller on the phone ended the call. Randolph slowly placed the receiver back down and stood. His heart was pounding.

He stood in the same spot for a good couple of minutes before moving slightly closer to the office door. He breathed in and out sharply. He was too frightened to open the door and in no mood to do any paperwork now. He checked the mat: there were no envelopes or notes pushed through. He reached for the doorknob and gripped it. Hesitating, he unlocked the door. He slowly opened it and stood back. He carefully peered into the corridor. It was all clear. The lights had returned to normal throughout the foyer and beyond. Randolph breathed a sigh of relief and closed his eyes. He was now in no doubt that for whatever reason, he was being targeted by someone, or *more* than one person.

After composing himself, Randolph picked up his suitcase and locked the door to his office. He didn't want to stay there now. He would wait out in the main foyer, or outside, depending on whether it had stopped raining. Halfway down the corridor, something caught Randolph's eye. He crouched down to get a better look. Dark red blood, still wet and shiny, formed small puddles. The trail started from the beginning of the corridor to around halfway down. It must have been what made the dripping sound, presumably from the figure in the corridor, perhaps linked to what they held in their left hand.

There was a fair amount of blood. Randolph thought about poor Greg having to clean this bloody mess up. The metallic scent of the blood made him retch slightly. Even during the war, he had never got used to the sight and smell of blood. Randolph slowly made his way up to the end of the corridor. There was no sign of blood in the main foyer. It was strange. Things really were starting to get weird. He looked around the foyer. Perhaps he should ring DCS Quincy, though that would mean him having to return to his office, which he didn't want to do. Instead, he waited for Timothy and his driver to arrive outside in the open, where he felt safer.

*

Randolph had waited outside in the drizzling weather, protected only by his fedora and trench coat, until Timothy pulled up in the limousine with his driver. No one else had entered or left the office block, which he thought was a little surprising. Timothy arrived at two minutes to nine. After the pair had greeted one another, Randolph told Timothy what had happened. Randolph put his case in the back of the limousine, then took Timothy to see the blood in the corridor.

"Maybe someone cleaned it up, whilst you waited outside?" Timothy said, standing in the corridor.

Randolph became agitated. "No. I know the cleaner here. We often chat. He would have seen me standing out there. No one else has entered or left since I went out. Besides, he usually doesn't work Mondays."

"You're sure you weren't mistaken about what you saw? Maybe someone else came out of their office or from downstairs, and cleaned it?"

Randolph shook his head. "No. Yes, it's possible someone other than Greg saw the mess and cleaned it, but it's unlikely. Most of the offices are vacant my end, other than mine and one other." Randolph pointed to a door to their left. "He's clearly not in today. Or not yet, at least. Whoever this person is, or *persons*, is clearly messing with me. The way the phone rang, the way they approached me in the corridor. Standing like some kind of *dummy* in the street, and in the pouring rain over in France. It could even be the same person responsible for these murders."

Timothy's expression was more than concerned. "You think it might be the killer that's been going around London? Why would they target you? This seems to have started since I hired you. Maybe it's my fault. I'm sorry for getting you involved."

"Don't be sorry. It's not your fault, Timothy. You paid for my services, more than generously, I might add. This isn't your fault at all. Besides, it kind of started before you and Claret hired me."

Timothy frowned. "How do you mean?"

Randolph told him how he had found the last murder victim.

"Shit! I had no idea. I'm sorry."

"It's okay. I'm not saying it *was* definitely the killer here this morning and stalking me, but I'm starting to lean that way. They obviously know I found that body that night. Chances are, they were watching me then, and of course, there are similarities between what was discovered in France and the inverted pentagram, with the orange and green candles."

"What? You're saying it's possibly all *linked* somehow? But how? This was miles away in another country. There have been no reports of any killings in France, like this. I would have heard about it … But yes, you're right! I never fell in, with the burning candles and inverted pentagram similarities."

Randolph sighed and puffed out his cheeks. "I honestly don't know … It would be a *very* strange coincidence. And what freaks me out even more is that I'm involved in it all. Talk about unlucky."

Timothy shook his head. "Shit. This really is all a mess. What if Natalie's already dead? Is she linked to all of this?"

"I can't answer that question, Timothy. We can speculate as much as we want and come up with all sorts of conclusions. It's certainly all *fubar* …"

Timothy frowned, looking confused. "Fubar?"

"It means 'fucked up beyond all recognition.' Or 'repair.' It was a term I picked up from some of the Americans back in the war."

"Ah, I see … I think it's best I pull you off the case, Randolph. Just leave it to the authorities. It's too dangerous. It's not fair on you or your family."

"No. I know it's risky carrying on, but I don't want to let you down, or Natalie and her team. You all need as much help as you can get. I've started, so I'll finish," Randolph replied defiantly.

"Are you sure? I don't want to be responsible for anything. You know? If anything happens."

"I'll be fine. I'll just have to watch out for myself. Hopefully this gendarme guy we're meeting will help us."

"Thank you. I admire your courage. Rest assured, you'll be given all the resources you require." Timothy put a hand on Randolph's shoulder briefly.

Randolph gave a nod. "I should call the detective in charge of the London murder case. It's best I fill him in on what's happening."

"Good idea. Then we should really get going."

Randolph rang the West End Central Police Station from his office. Timothy waited in the corridor near the door, just in case this hooded figure returned.

"Good morning," Randolph said over the phone. "Can I speak to DCS Quincy, please?" Randolph heard voices in the background, all sounding a little frantic.

The police receptionist had to raise her voice over the phone. "I'm sorry, he's not long left — an urgent matter of business to attend to. I can leave a message for him, if you like?"

Randolph introduced himself as having found the last victim on Conduit Street and explained that DCS Quincy had asked him to call if he had any more information. He described what had happened in his office block this morning and gave the address. He explained that he couldn't stay and wait for the detective, because he had a flight to catch.

"Well, I'm glad you're okay, Mr Landon. You did the right thing calling us, regardless of whether it's related to the four London murders. I'll pass your message on to DCS Quincy, and he can investigate further."

Randolph paused. "Wait a minute. What? *Four* murders? There've only been three, haven't there?"

Timothy stepped back into the office, hearing Randolph mention four murders.

"Erm. Yes. It isn't official, yet. But a fourth body has been reported this morning. I shouldn't have said anything, my mistake. You'll no doubt hear about it soon enough, once it's been confirmed. As you can hear, it's pretty hectic here at the moment. DCS Quincy has gone to the scene now, before the press are all over it."

"Shit. I guess it was only a matter of time before the killer struck again."

"Yes, Mr Landon. Awful times for the poor victims and their families. I'll be sure to pass on your message to the Detective Chief Superintendent. He'll be in contact."

"Thank you. He's obviously got enough on his plate at the minute."

"Thank you, Mr Landon. Have a safe flight."

"There's been another one?" Timothy's eyes widened, looking at Randolph as he put the receiver down.

Randolph shook his head. "Yep. She didn't say where. It's not confirmed yet, but another body was found some time this morning. DCS Quincy has gone to the scene now … It's getting worse."

"Whoever this person was in the corridor might not be the murderer. They could have just cut themselves. Maybe it was someone looking for help? Perhaps, someone high on drugs?"

"I wish I could believe that. We'd better get going. We've kept your driver waiting long enough."

On the way to Heathrow Airport, where the pair were to board a private jet back to France, they spoke very little. However, a breaking news report came over the car radio, stating that a *fourth* body, had been discovered somewhere off Great Russell Street. The police had yet to confirm the murder officially, but according to eyewitnesses, the naked body of a woman had been found with her heart cut from her chest and her throat slit. There was the usual MO involved with candles and an inverted pentagram.

Randolph swallowed and Timothy glanced back at him from the front of the car.

"And there's your next one!" the limousine driver said. "Hard to see the police catching this killer. I wonder when it will stop."

"Who knows," Timothy replied quietly.

Randolph wished he hadn't got involved in this case. It was a shame he and Thelma hadn't sorted out their differences sooner. He could already be living up in Lincolnshire by now. But then, how could he know the case would lead him down this dark and sinister road. To think that it all started innocently with a Chihuahua called Peanut going missing.

*

Sitting with a large whisky, Randolph found it hard to believe that he was on a private jet for the fifth time in just over a week. Here he was again for the third time, heading back to France. They had just crossed the English Channel.

"You all right?" Timothy asked, seated opposite him. He too, held a large glass of whisky, but with ice.

"As much as I can be." Randolph half-smiled. "Just thinking."

"I know. I'm worried for me and Claret too, now. I wonder if these London murders are linked to what's been found in France?"

"It's a strong possibility. I'll discuss it with the DCS, when I know more. They have enough going on and besides, it's not like we have anything concrete. Plus, if the French police knew anything, they'd surely have contacted the police in London, anyway."

"Very true." Timothy sipped his whisky.

Randolph did the same, just as some turbulence hit. "Never been keen on flying. I don't think it's something I'll ever get used to. Not fully. I think my fear started during the war."

Timothy gave an understanding smile.

Timothy pre-arranged for a friend, who lived not far from Verneuil-sur-Vienne, to pick them up once they had landed at the private airstrip near Limoges. Tumas, was a retired chef, who used to work in Paris and then Limoges, before his retirement at the age of seventy. His English wasn't perfect, but good enough to converse.

*

The Andrews' Villa, Verneuil-sur-Vienne – 1.01 pm Local Time

Being a pleasantly mild day, Randolph and Timothy sat outside near the pool. Timothy had earlier phoned the gendarme they were due to meet. He was due sometime this afternoon. Timothy had also made lunch earlier for the pair.

"That's one beauty of this region," Timothy said, "you can always guarantee nice weather this time of year. It can be quite a contrast compared with the weather back in London. The scenery is spectacular too, obviously. We often take time away from the UK when we can. This is probably our favourite villa. We have a few other properties around the globe – shouldn't brag I know – but this is the best." Timothy smirked.

Randolph smiled. "It's fine. If you've worked hard for it, you've earnt it. Fair play to you. It must be nice to get away, when you can."

"Yep. I was fortunate enough to inherit many things from my father, but I never took it for granted. Sure, I had a platform and was lucky — yes. More than most people. But I've never rested on my laurels or been lazy. I've worked hard to expand our company. I don't do it solely for the money, either. It's just fun to try and become more successful."

"I respect that," Randolph replied sincerely.

"I know some people hate others, who are 'born into it,' so to speak. Like I said, I was very lucky, even if it meant losing my father, which was awful. The same with my sister and mother. So, I guess you could say that I haven't always been 'fortunate …' I didn't just want to inherit fully what he left. I wanted to be successful for myself. I also believe that in life, if you get, you give."

"Yeah. I think I read how you've donated to the homeless and other charities, including ex-soldiers from the war, who were injured or needed therapy?"

Timothy smiled. "I prefer to do things under the radar, if I am honest with you. But things get out. I don't do things to look like a saint. It's not why I do it. Claret also donates to charities from her clothing business. We do it for the right reasons. We've also set up some shelters for stray animals in various countries — including France. We have one outside Paris; there are many animals without homes in the city."

"Fair play to you both." To Randolph, Timothy seemed a more sincere and humble person than he had first expected, when he had followed him to the business centre that day under Claret's instructions. An all-round nice and generous guy.

"That's enough about me, anyway. Would you like a drink? I have some good Cognac."

"Sure."

Timothy went back inside and returned shortly after carrying two tulip-shaped glasses of richly coloured Cognac. "This shape of glass can help you appreciate the aroma more."

Randolph took a glass from Timothy, smelling it. "Mmmm. I don't usually drink Cognac, but I do like it."

Timothy smiled and sat back down. "Well, here's to our health and finding Natalie! May we be *successful* in our case!" He reached out and they clinked their glasses together.

"It certainly tastes good!" Randolph appreciated the sweet, spicy taste.

Timothy sipped his own and grinned.

"You know, I was thinking something on the flight over here."

"What's that?"

"The person in the office corridor, potentially this killer. Part of their MO is removing the victims' hearts, right? What if they were holding this current victim's heart, when I saw them? It was obviously dark in that corridor, and I couldn't see properly, with the lights going out. But they could have turned up there, after they had murdered the woman."

Timothy drank from his glass. "You could be right, there, Randolph. It would make sense. It isn't too far to walk from Great Russell Street to Hopkins Street. But, wouldn't they risk being seen in broad daylight? Especially with the morning traffic?"

"It's what I'm thinking, too. Maybe they drove? And surely, they would have done their latest murder during the night or early hours when it was dark and fewer people were about."

The pair sat there in silence for a short moment.

Timothy sighed. "What have we got ourselves involved in? Or more importantly, what have I got *you* involved in?" He gulped the last of his Cognac down. "I need another." He went back inside for a refill, then quickly sat back down.

Randolph finished his Cognac, but refused Timothy's offer of a second.

*

Later that afternoon, Timothy introduced Arnaud Laurent to Randolph. He had worked for the gendarmerie for a good number of years. He took off his navy-blue hat with white rims and placed it under his left arm. Wearing his tan-coloured uniform with a navy-blue tie, Arnaud held out his white gloved right hand to Randolph, who got up from his seat.

"Pleasure to meet you." Randolph smiled, shaking Arnaud's hand.

"Oui, Monsieur," the black moustached Arnaud replied. He was in his early forties, Randolph suspected.

Timothy asked for Arnaud to sit down in the plush villa living room. Randolph sat on one of the button-tufted turquoise armchairs, in front of a glass coffee table. A matching armchair sat at the other end. In between was the two-seated sofa.

Arnaud politely asked if he should take off his shoes before sitting on the sofa. Timothy replied jokingly that it was fine if his shoes were clean. Several paintings — mainly landscapes, lined the white walls. A light mahogany mini-bar with several cabinets behind it was built into a corner of the room. The Andrews sure knew how to live. But they had earnt it, they had the money. Opposite the mini-bar on the other side of the room, was a large console television. A beige and white tiled fireplace provided warmth when needed for the cold winter months. Above the fireplace was a bronze sunburst clock and two fans hung from the ceiling.

Arnaud sat on the sofa, placing his hat down on the glass coffee table, next to a small vase of scented flowers. He adjusted his black gun holster to get comfy. Timothy asked him if he'd like a drink and he opted for only a 'small' Armagnac, as he was still on duty.

"You want one too, Randolph?" Timothy asked.

"I'm good, thank you," Randolph declined.

Rather than go to the mini-bar, Timothy walked over the hardwood flooring to a low sandalwood sideboard at one side of the living room. He slid open one of the cabinet doors and took out a near full Basquaise bottle of Armagnac, filling a glass from a silver tray on the sideboard. A few framed photographs of Timothy and Claret stood on the sideboard. Randolph noticed an older black and white one, likely to be of Timothy as a child and his younger sister who sadly passed away.

"Merci." Arnaud took the glass from Timothy, adjusting a single purple cushion behind him on the sofa.

Timothy sat on an armchair, crossing his legs. He pulled the white sleeves of his top up his arms.

The three of them began to talk about events.

Arnaud explained further what he knew of the case. As expected, it was pretty much the same recycled things that Christine and Pierre had already gone over. He was quick to state that it wasn't him who initially came across the findings out in the field, which led to the excavation, but rather another member of the gendarmerie. The discovery had disturbed everyone who had climbed down to the mysterious cave. "It was most terrible, seeing those skeletons, oui. I was a soldier during the war and saw more graphic things, but there was something *different* about these dead bodies — these skeletons." Arnaud's accent was strong, but Randolph and Timothy could just about understand him.

"No clues at all were found down there?" Randolph sat forward. "Relating to where Natalie may be?"

"Non. Not at all. Only the remains and the items you have seen with Christine, Monsieur Landon." Arnaud sipped his drink, then dabbed his thin moustache with his thumb. Like his hair, his moustache was completely black, without a single grey hair or whisker. "Even some detectives from Paris came down to check. They also checked the land and surroundings. It is a big area, oui, but they found nothing and I also found nothing."

Randolph lowered his head and shook it. He sighed through his nose. "Natalie could quite literally be anywhere and for whatever reason. Her passport was in her apartment so she may still be in France. Though, she could still be in another country."

"That is true. We have alerted other towns and cities of her disappearance, and villages, too. The authorities — police and other gendarmerie, have been informed. They have her photo and are doing what they can." Arnaud sipped some more Armagnac. "Her disappearance was also mentioned in several national newspapers and news outlets on television, oui."

"And no one has seen her? No reports, nothing?" Randolph asked.

"Non, nothing. Her apartment was checked over thoroughly countless times. There was no sign of a struggle and no clues at all. It's like perhaps she doesn't wish to be found?"

"No. I don't believe that, Arnaud. I know her. She wouldn't just disappear like that. Something has definitely happened to her or someone has taken her. Something isn't right. She's been gone for almost a month, now."

Randolph leant forwards. "Someone may know more than they are letting on. If the police and their detectives can't find anything, I honestly don't see what I can do. After all, I am just one person, compared to numerous others and their resources."

The three sat in silence for a short moment.

Randolph looked deep in thought. "There may be one slight advantage I have over the police and gendarmerie, however …"

Timothy and Arnaud both frowned, looking at Randolph.

Randolph explained the London murders to Arnaud. Arnaud wasn't too familiar with the details of these ritualistic killings but had heard of them. Randolph described the modus operandi, with the slit throats and removal of the hearts, along with the inverted pentagram also drawn and the lit candles — burning orange and green. He also told him about how he had found the third victim and about the hooded figure in Paris and London.

Arnaud listened well, yet still had a confused and disturbed facial expression. "I don't understand. There are similarities, oui? But we are talking miles away from this discovery, in another country, to where these killings are happening in London. This cave underneath the ground has also only just been discovered. How can a single person, or small group, if it is more than one, achieve this?"

"I honestly can't answer that right now, Arnaud, if we ever can. It just seems too much of a coincidence. It's certainly fucking strange, that's for sure. Pardon my French." Randolph smirked.

Timothy and Arnaud raised half a smile each.

"But Monsieur Landon, how is this an advantage?"

"I'm not sure exactly. But if this is indeed the killer I have encountered, or they are involved somehow, they are definitely interested in me. Perhaps I could, I don't know, use it as an advantage to find out who they are. I still need to talk directly to the detective in charge who is leading the case back in London. We also need clarification about the latest murder, too."

"Oui. I understand."

"Regarding witchcraft in the area of the dig site, do you know any of the history, Arnaud? Can you shed any light on the supposed orphanage?" Randolph asked.

"Only what you have already been informed, oui. There were rumours dating back over the years, centuries, of witchcraft. The residents around these parts never knew of any orphanage themselves, or encountered anything out of the ordinary."

"Yeah. I just find it all a bit difficult to understand, that. How can stories of an orphanage circulate, yet no one is alive now to tell the tale and confirm it? Even if the area is remote, you'd think more people would have known about it. What about the gendarmerie, and police? Any records?" Randolph queried.

"Non. None at all."

"Something isn't adding up. Have you lived in the area long, Arnaud?"

Timothy watched and listened. He was feeling increasingly more unnerved. He himself, hadn't heard any stories of witches in that area from when he was younger and had spent time in France with his parents and his sister, until she passed.

"I live in Aixe-sur-Vienne with my wife, Juliette. We have recently become parents for the second time, oui."

"Congratulations." Randolph half-smiled.

"Merci beaucoup." Arnaud nodded. "When I left the French military in '53, I joined the police in Lyons. After four years, I and my wife moved to Aixe-sur-Vienne, where we've been settled now for over nine years, and I became a gendarme shortly after."

"How did you hear about the stories of witchcraft in the area?" Randolph continued to ask.

"Talking to some of the locals as a member of the gendarmerie, oui. You hear stories and rumours passed down from generations. People don't like venturing too far out into the fields or warn others not to. Since the discovery, I've heard how there used to be witches who lived in the area centuries ago. They came to use the land to worship The Devil."

"And there really is no one currently alive, who can confirm the orphanage existed or who owned it?"

"Non, Monsieur Landon. Other than it was a husband and wife."

"I agree with Randolph. It just seems so odd that something like this existed, even if it was remote out there, and no one can confirm it."

"Oui. I agree. But there is nothing on record, non. No names. No anything. These people who knew the stories cannot confirm it. They never saw it for themselves."

"What of these land tremors some of the locals have been experiencing?" Randolph asked.

"It has happened several times, oui. I've encountered them a couple of times. The ground just shook for a few seconds, and then it was gone. It was only minor."

"Near to where the excavation site is?"

"Oui, Monsieur Landon. Maybe reaching out to a proximity of a couple of miles. A little more. I've felt them in my car."

"Has it happened since the discovery?"

"Not to my knowledge, non. It started a few weeks before the dig."

"This is all so messed up," Timothy said. "Fubar …" he then muttered quietly under his breath.

"I'm debating whether or not it's worth the risk to check out this cave for myself," Randolph suggested.

"But why, Monsieur? There is nothing left down there. Everything has been removed, other than the symbols."

"I know, Arnaud. But still. I am concerned though about the illness that Christine and Pierre and the others have caught. Were you ill after you had been down there?"

"Non. I've been fine."

"It might not hurt to go back down there to see if Randolph can pick up any missing clues. Though, it still concerns me," Timothy said.

"If that is what you want to do, I will accompany you, oui. I just have a couple of things to attend to first."

*

Approximately Two Miles East of Oradour-sur-Glane – 4.06 pm

Arnaud drove the three of them to the excavation site. He parked up on a mass of unfarmed land, insisting that it would be best to walk the rest of the way, due to some of the land being uneven and muddy. In spite of the nice weather of late, large areas of the rural fields and countryside never seemed to fully dry out, he explained. With the wind picking up, the further they walked, it also grew colder. Randolph was a little surprised that there appeared to be no farms nearby. All he could see were bushes, trees and hills, which were pleasant to see all the same. Some fields were less verdant than others, with a mixture of muddy earth where nothing grew at all, and yellow patchy areas of overgrown grass now dried out.

Arnaud explained that because of the stories of witchcraft down the centuries, potential farmers were too afraid to set up farms there, even to this day. The same went for the development of houses and homes. It was rumoured that many years ago, there had been a couple of farms, but each time the land was sowed, the crops failed. The gossip had spiked following the archaeological dig. Of course, some people weren't bothered by rumours and still walked their dogs across the supposedly 'cursed' countryside.

It took them roughly fifteen minutes to reach the site. Their shoes were caked in mud from where it was difficult to avoid the dank soil. Randolph was a little peeved that Arnaud hadn't driven them closer to their destination. Yes, the land was uneven and muddy, which may have made it difficult for the blue Peugeot 404 station wagon to move across with its lack of suspension and lack of grip with the old tyres, but still, he could have driven a little nearer. They would also have to walk back later.

"And this is it, Monsieur Landon." Arnaud stopped and gestured. He took off his white gloves.

While they stood there, a large grey cloud loomed over them, blocking the sunshine and darkening the excavation site.

"A suitable and ominous sign," Randolph said sarcastically, looking above.

The others looked up too. A strong breeze enveloped them, rustling the red and white cordons that went around the dig.

"I wouldn't say that the excavation site is closed off very well. Anyone can still access it easily," Randolph commented less sarcastically.

"Oui. But we don't have to worry about anyone coming out here and climbing down there, non. It's pretty remote out here. Most people don't want to come out here — especially with what was found — above and below."

"It will be dug back over but with Natalie having disappeared, it's been delayed. Apparently, she had wanted to hold off with covering it all up after the discoveries, in case further investigations were needed," Timothy added. "I certainly don't like being back here."

The excavation site was neatly dug out. Mounds of earth containing small and large stones were placed in sections nearby, ready to be replaced. Several feet below, the white and grey limestone could clearly be seen, revealing the top of the cave. To the left, a raised opening with a strong and sturdy looking wooden ladder, descended into darkness.

Randolph really didn't fancy going down there.

"It's believed there was a trap door initially fixed there, leading down. No ladder. The one you see is left from the archaeological team," said Timothy.

The dark looming cloud took its time to reveal the sun again.

"I'm ready to go down there, when you are, oui?" Arnaud pulled out a couple of chrome steel torches from his dark blue coat pockets, along with three white surgical masks he had retrieved from the boot of his car at Randolph's suggestion, just in case there was something contagious down below. Arnaud had previously gone to get some.

With their masks on, they made their way under the cordons and towards the ladder. In turn, they jumped the few feet onto the hard limestone, making a dull thudding sound with their muddied shoes.

"I'll go first," Arnaud offered, handing a torch over to Randolph. "It isn't too far down, thankfully." He checked that the ladder was firmly in place, before carefully mounting it. He placed a torch between his teeth and descended slowly and wearily.

Randolph aided him by crouching down and shining the other torch below from the top. He could barely see into the cave.

Once at the bottom, Arnaud put his left hand to the side of his mouth and called up, "It's good. Come down, oui."

Putting the torch inside his trench coat, an unsure and nervous Randolph climbed down. Mud from his shoes clung to the rungs of the ladder.

"Be careful not to slip," Arnaud called up, shining the torch to help Randolph see.

Slipping on one of the bottom rungs, Randolph stepped onto the smooth limestone floor. He took out his torch and examined the cave.

"Okay, Monsieur Andrews. Your turn." Arnaud continued to shine the torch for Timothy.

Randolph was startled by a shout and a thud. He quickly spun round to see Timothy on the floor. He rushed towards him.

"You okay?" Arnaud asked worriedly, helping Timothy to his feet.

"Yeah. Bloody foot slipped on the mud on the ladder. I'm fine. I just hurt my arm." Timothy grimaced, rubbing his lower right arm, where he had landed on it.

"You sure you're okay?"

Timothy half-smiled in the two torch lights focused on him. "Fine, Randolph. It's not broken — I can move it fine. Thankfully, I was already over halfway down when I slipped. I already feel uncomfortable down here. Let's not take too long, shall we?"

"Oui. I feel the same. Let us have a look and get back to the surface, *illico*."

Their three voices echoed around the ancient limestone walls.

The cave was imperfectly oval in shape. The temperature was colder than above. Timothy and Arnaud stood back, watching Randolph carefully and slowly move about, shining his torch. There really wasn't much to see. The only noticeable things that remained were the faded symbols drawn in blood on the limestone walls and floor, along with the inverted pentagram or pentacle — depending on the preferred terminology, according to Pierre, the expert. Again, this was perfectly shaped, including the circle. Although the floor was fairly smooth, it wasn't completely even, with bits of limestone sticking up here and there, which would have surely made the circle hard to draw. It was all very strange and eerie, accompanied by a stale and earthly smell, that filtered through the surgical masks.

Randolph walked inside the inverted pentagram and shuddered. He remembered the photographs of the skeletons, positioned where he now stood. He felt a chill. He also remembered the candles being mysteriously lit when the team had first got down there, and the sounds of children crying. He started to get goosebumps. He looked up at the ceiling where a few other occult symbols had been drawn in blood, again, neatly drawn, but faded. The height of the cave was over six feet. Had it been any lower, Randolph would have had to bend his head. Timothy could stand without stooping, but Arnaud had to, being taller than the other two.

Randolph shone the torch slowly over the floor and walls, carefully examining them and searching for any missing clues. He checked again where the table used to be and remembered The Devil figurine holding out its arms. He looked at the hole in the wall where the black cauldron used to be. The bottom of the hole was blackened where it had no doubt been used for cooking. Randolph shivered again. He touched the walls to see if anything was hidden within. He was looking for anything that had been missed. There was nothing. The limestone felt cold and strange to touch. Something didn't feel right — with any of this. He noticed a few scratches on the walls, perhaps fingernail marks.

"As you can see, Monsieur Landon, nothing is here, non? All items have been removed. All that remains are the symbols."

Randolph didn't answer Arnaud. He knew Arnaud was most likely right. It was pretty obvious that the archaeological team and police would have made sure that the cave was searched thoroughly and that everything was removed. But Randolph still hoped that there might be something that had been missed.

"Yeah. There's nothing here." Randolph scratched his left cheek behind the white surgical mask. "I guess it was pretty obvious."

"It was worth checking again, just in case. It's best if we get out of here. I'm starting to feel a cold dread." Timothy shuddered. "It's like we're not alone down here."

"Oui. You're not the only one." Arnaud looked around nervously with his torch.

"Let's get out of here." Randolph gave one last check of the cave with the torch, then followed the other two towards the ladder. Walking inside the inverted pentagram, he thought he would just check the floor, one final time …

Arnaud started to climb the ladder and Timothy looked back towards Randolph, who was crouched down, scrutinising the floor. "Randolph, have you found something?"

Randolph didn't answer.

Inside a crack on the hard surface of the limestone, there was something blue in colour. Randolph got on his knees and shone the torch. Specs of dust danced in the beam from the metal torch. He pulled out what appeared to have been a light blue, braided bracelet, dirty and small in diameter, perhaps designed for a child's wrist.

"What is that?" asked Timothy, approaching Randolph who was still on his knees.

Arnaud had stopped on the ladder and looked across. He climbed back down and joined the other two, bending his head down.

"It looks like it's some kind of bracelet." Randolph handed it to Timothy.

Timothy scrutinised it and Arnaud shone his torch on it.

Arnaud took it from Timothy's hand. "It looks like it belonged to a small child, oui."

"It was embedded in one of the cracks there. It would easily have been overlooked," Randolph said, brushing his knees.

"You think it came off one of the skeletons that was found, Randolph?"

"I don't know, Timothy. Possibly. Whether or not it belonged to one of the victims, it doesn't tell us anything."

"MB," Arnaud said, still looking at the bracelet in the torchlight.

"What's that?" Timothy asked.

"It has the letters MB stitched inside in red, oui."

"I noticed that. It could be the initials of either the person who wore it, or the person who made it," Randolph said.

Timothy took the braided bracelet and looked at it himself. "Maybe it's a lead?"

Randolph wasn't so sure. "Possibly, Timothy, but I doubt it. With no records of anything relating to this orphanage, no names, it's virtually impossible to find out more. And regardless, it doesn't help with finding Natalie. That's our main goal, obviously."

"You're right. It doesn't tell us anything," Timothy said glumly, handing the bracelet back to Randolph.

"Let's get out of here, anyway. We've spent enough time down here." Randolph put the bracelet inside his trench coat pocket.

Arnaud walked back to the ladder and glanced upwards; *"Que'est-ce que c'est!"*

Timothy and Randolph stopped. Arnaud looked shocked.

"What is it, Arnaud?" Timothy asked frantically.

"I, I saw someone, oui. They were looking down. As soon as I looked up, they disappeared."

Timothy and Randolph looked at each other.

"I couldn't see their face clearly, non. They had some black hood over their face."

Randolph's eyes grew large in the dark. "The same person I saw in Paris and London!"

"But how?" Timothy said nervously.

"We can talk later. Let's just get the hell out of here." Randolph swallowed.

"Oui!" Arnaud quickly climbed the ladder, carefully as he could, not wanting to slip. The others followed suit behind him, doing the same.

At the top of the ladder, there was no sign of anyone. Not nearby nor in the distance. The three checked behind the mounds of dirt, before setting off and returning to the car.

*

"It was a good job we got back out before whoever Arnaud saw took the ladder," Timothy said, continuing to wipe his muddy shoes clean on the grass, just like the others did.

"Perhaps I saw them just in time, non?"

The three then got back into the car.

"Was it your hooded stalker, Randolph? How did they vanish out of sight like that!" Timothy turned his head towards the back of the car to get Randolph's attention.

"It had to be. They must be watching my every move. How they're travelling with me between England and France is anyone's guess."

"Merde," Arnaud muttered. "You think that this is the killer back in London, oui?"

Randolph sighed. "I don't know, Arnaud. I'm certain it's all linked somehow. But *how* exactly? I don't think any of us can answer that. At least not at the moment. That inverted pentagram down in the cave was drawn perfectly. The same as the ones drawn in chalk back in London at the murder scenes. It can't be a coincidence. Not to mention the candles."

The three sat in the car not saying anything for a few seconds.

"I wonder if this killer is watching us right now from somewhere?" Timothy looked out. "What do we do next, Randolph?"

Randolph suddenly remembered Miss Albescu's warning. "Maybe we can look into this bracelet some more." He pulled out the bracelet to examine it again.

"You said it wasn't relevant, though?"

"I know, Timothy … Maybe there's potential there. If these initials belonged to whoever made it, they might know more about all of this. Of course, it's a bit like finding a needle in a haystack. Not to mention this bracelet could be many years old."

"It could be recent. Maybe someone has been down there since the discovery?" Timothy suggested.

"That's possible," Randolph replied doubtfully.

"I could ask about, Monsieur Landon; someone around these parts may know of someone who makes such things, oui?"

"It's worth a shot, Arnaud. Here." Randolph handed the bracelet over. "After all, it is evidence. I'm going to need to call the detective in charge of the murder case in London to fill him in on everything and get an update on the latest body."

"You can call him from the villa," suggested Timothy.

*

Arnaud had dropped the two off back at the villa.

"I'm really starting to think that we're all at risk, now," Timothy said.

"I don't know what to say, Timothy. If this is the killer, they must know that I'm looking into the disappearance of Natalie. That's evident by now. Perhaps they know I am onto them. If so, they would want to know what I do and hence check on my every move. They obviously wouldn't want me or the police to get close to them."

"And what about Natalie. Do you think her disappearance is linked to this killer? I mean, might she be dead?"

"There is a strong chance she is linked somehow. She may be dead. I'm sorry to be blunt."

Timothy sighed. "No, it's fine."

They walked over to the other side of the living room to a sandalwood telephone stand.

"Yes. Hello. Is DCS Quincy available, please?" Randolph heard a few voices in the background; it didn't seem as chaotic as earlier when he'd rung.

The same woman as before answered, "He is here, yes, though I'm afraid he's extremely busy right now. Is it urgent?"

Randolph reminded her who he was. "It's very important that I speak with him."

The receptionist went to check with DCS Quincy and then patched Randolph through to his office.

"Mr Landon. I'm very busy, so we'll have to be quick. I sent DCI Sommers and a couple of officers to check your office. They questioned some people there, including the cleaner. No one had seen anything. Nor was any blood or anything found. But you did the right thing contacting us. What can I do for you?"

"I'm not sure where to begin, or maybe I'm jumping to conclusions. But it's best I tell you what's been happening and what I know. I believe what I am about to tell you, is all related to the London murders. So, if you could just bear with me and hear me out."

"I'm listening, Mr Landon — you have my full attention. Is it related to the case, the third victim you found?"

"I believe so, yes."

"Please, tell me what you know."

Randolph started from the beginning of when Claret first contacted him. He spoke slowly and went from there, covering every bit of detail that he could. He had to repeat himself a few times so that DCS Quincy could take the information in as he wrote it all down.

Timothy walked about a little, listening on. He opened the French doors to let in some warm fresh air and stood with the sun shining onto his face.

"And you really believe this is all related?"

"I do, yes."

DCS Quincy sighed. "This just makes things even more complicated. Something that was found hundreds of miles away in another county, and has been underground for so many years, is now linked to what's happening in London with these murders. It seems too far-fetched!"

"I know. It could just be a really strange coincidence but you have to look at the facts. My gut instinct is usually pretty good too, and this person is stalking me, whether they are the killer or not, and I know what I saw outside my office. There was blood there."

"Yes, there are too many coincidences."

"What really confirms it for me, is this hooded person. Arnaud, the gendarme I mentioned, saw them at the dig. At my office, they were carrying something which was dripping blood this morning. Maybe it was the latest victim's heart? Mr Quincy, I know you wouldn't normally be at liberty to disclose information about the murders, but we need to work together on this. I've told you what I know, and I'm hoping you can tell me what you know. My life and my client's may be in danger."

DCS Quincy paused. "Yes. You're right. The latest victim has been confirmed. We don't know the name of the woman yet. There are some things we haven't disclosed to the press for valid reasons."

"What can you tell me? I need to know. Please! Another woman's life may be at risk, the woman my client is looking for, Natalie Conners. Anything you know, could help. And vice-versa."

"Okay, I agree; we should probably exchange information, but if it's all the same to you, I would like to speak to the French police and gendarmerie first, if you don't mind? Then I promise, we'll have another talk."

"That's fine with me, though time is of the essence, Mr Quincy. You know as well as I do, that another killing is just around the corner. I don't believe they are going to stop yet."

"I agree, Mr Landon."

Randolph put Timothy on the line to give DCS Quincy the numbers of the gendarmerie and the police, along with his own private telephone numbers and the one at the villa. He mentioned that he was also concerned for his wife, Claret's safety.

"What did he say?" asked Randolph.

"He's going to contact the police and gendarmerie as soon as he can. He has some things to do relating to the killings. He hopes to phone back later on. It looks like another late night for him and his team."

"Yeah. With each killing, the police are under more pressure.

They've certainly got their work cut out with this one. Me as well. I've never known anything like it." Randolph shook his head.

Timothy phoned Claret shortly after. "… I'm not sure how much longer we'll be here, but you need to be watchful," he warned her.

"I'm beginning to feel a little annoyed that you've got us involved in all this for an old flame, Timothy!" Claret chided. "Still, I wouldn't want any harm to come to her, so I guess you did the right thing." She then told him the details of the latest killing that had been all over the news.

"Claret, okay?" Randolph asked, looking out onto the bright lawn of the villa's large back garden. He had decided to hold off from telling Thelma about all this yet. He didn't want to worry her and besides, she was up in Lincolnshire with her parents. She would be safe away from London and his life.

"She is. She's a strong woman that one. She's not scared of anyone." Timothy laughed a little. He shared what Claret had heard from the news on the fourth victim found off Great Russell Street.

The unnamed female's naked body was found with her heart removed in an alleyway behind a butchers called Burton & Son. The father who ran the business, had come across the body at around 8.50 am that morning. Her body was placed in a kneeling position inside a red chalk inverted pentagram with lit black candles, burning a bright orange and green, placed on each point of the symbol. Her neck was broken. Her head was facing unnaturally backwards and as with the previous three victims, her throat was slit. Once again, what was believed to be the victim's clothes, were found folded neatly in a pile close by.

"Sick bastard, eh?" Timothy stood, shaking his head. "Or bastards, if there's more than one of them."

"I know. And what's with the killer stripping them naked and folding their clothes up? I've never known anything like it. The killer or killers, aren't done yet, either."

"I don't doubt that for one minute, Randolph."

"It will be interesting to see what DCS Quincy has to say later on. There's clearly something else that links these victims together, which the public don't know about." Randolph put a cigarette between his lips and walked out of the French doors to light it. He deemed it disrespectful to smoke indoors.

*

The pair watched French television on and off in the living room while waiting to hear from DCS Quincy. Nothing on the news mentioned anything of another murder back in England's capital. The news channels perhaps felt it had no interest to a French audience, having no connection to the French — or so they believed. Or it was too early. Perhaps, not many were aware of what had been happening in England. Timothy disappeared into his villa study from time to time to work, although he said he was finding it hard to concentrate.

At around 7 pm, just after Timothy had sat back down on the sofa, the telephone rang.

"That could be him now." Randolph turned his head, watching Timothy pick up the black and gold receiver.

"… Yes. Yes, he's here. Hold on …" Timothy gave a nod over at Randolph who got up and walked over.

Randolph took the phone receiver from Timothy. "Randolph."

"Mr Landon. It's DCS Quincy. I apologise for not phoning sooner. As you can imagine, I have been rushed off my feet."

"Not a problem. I empathise completely. Even more so after today."

"Yes. Anyway, I spoke to the authorities at the gendarmerie and Paris police. I brought them up to date on your theory. They're happy to assist us in any way and of course, if they need help, we'll do what we can. They also informed me that they are continuing to do what they can regarding the disappearance of this woman, Natalie Conners."

"That's good. We've also heard details on the fourth victim."

DCS Quincy sighed. "Yes. Another awful killing. May God rest her soul. But let me tell you everything we know so far about these four killings and how they are linked …"

It was now Randolph's turn to pull out his notebook and begin to write:

First Victim: Female – Sheila Davies – Aged 24. Body found on April 22nd 1966 at around 7 am off Margaret Street. A single woman who lived on Berners Street.

Second Victim: Male – Christophe Livingston – Aged 25. Body found on May 12th 1966 at around 7.46 am off Upper St Martin's Lane. Married and lived on Orange Street.

Third Victim: Male – Reece Brixton – Aged 23. Body found on May 16th 1966 at around 11.15 pm-ish on Conduit Street by ME! Single and lived on Suffolk Street.

Fourth Victim: Female – Unknown. Body found on May 30th 1966 at 8.50 am off Great Russell Street.

"The MO has been the same each time, as you no doubt know, Mr Landon. The victims' throats were slit, their hearts removed, and their clothes folded neatly nearby. The only differences were whether or not the body was placed on the inverted pentagram or not and the way the body was positioned and manipulated unnaturally. As you are aware, Mr Brixton did however, have his tongue removed. His body that you found and the latest victim's head were facing backwards. The murderer must be *extremely* strong to have done this. That's if they are working alone." DCS Quincy's tone sounded desperate.

Randolph scribbled his notes. "What about time of death? Any indication on what these victims were doing at the time? Were they taken from their homes? Or kidnapped in the street and taken to these specific locations?"

"Miss Davies lived alone, so we are unsure how she was taken. You heard what you believe were the screams of Mr Brixton. It's quite likely that he was taken to Conduit Street. We checked their homes of course. There was no sign of forced entry or anything like that. Everything appeared normal. The distance from their homes to where they were murdered wasn't far, neither. Friends and family had either spoken to or seen them on that day or on the day before, but not in the evening or night they were killed. In regards to Mr Livingston, his distraught wife told us that he had popped out to a friend's who was a doctor, not too far, over on Leicester Street. Their newborn son who is only a few months old, had a temperature and fluid coming from their ear. Hence, they were concerned.

"It turns out the baby had an ear infection. Thankfully, he's fine. It was around ten-thirty at night when Mr Livingston left their home. He never made it to the doctor's — they never saw him. As to why the killer is taking his or her victims to these locations before killing them, we don't really know. Especially when they run the risk of being seen, even if it is late at night."

Randolph sighed. "I can't understand any of it."

"As for their time of deaths, Miss Davies' was approximately four to six hours prior to her body being found. Mr Livingston's TOD was roughly seven to nine hours before he was found. Mr Brixton's death was less than an hour, after it was determined. You obviously came across his body almost straight after it had happened. With the latest unnamed victim, it may have been anywhere from two to four hours."

"It's all awful. The wife and child losing a husband and father, and in that manner. The boy will grow up never knowing his father. Those poor victims and their families … What about evidence? Was really nothing found? Do you believe it is just the one killer?"

DCS Quincy sighed. "We're not fully certain how many are participating in these atrocious killings, though we still suspect that it is just the one person working alone. As for the evidence, there really hasn't been anything. No weapon or fingerprints, other than the inverted pentagram, candles and the victims' clothes. Not even any footprints in the blood. The order of removing the victims' clothes and drawing the inverted pentagrams may vary. Christophe Livingston, we believe that he was alive whilst he was nailed to the wall. His throat being slit and the removal of the heart came afterwards."

"Shit … So, he was still alive when he was nailed up like that? He would have felt everything? Poor, poor man."

"That's what we believe. The killer no doubt wanted him to suffer and feel everything. I'll add too, for the record, that none of the bodies were abused sexually. No bodily fluids like semen were found."

"But how would it be possible to nail him up, when he was still alive? Surely, he would have fought off the killer? I'd imagine it would be almost impossible to nail a grown man to a wall like that, with them no doubt struggling and resisting!"

"I'll get to that, Mr Landon, if you please bear with me. The same thing most likely happened with Reece Brixton. Despite his back being broken and snapped like that, he was still alive after his body was brutally manipulated that way. He then had his throat slit, before his heart was cut from his chest. We are still waiting for more details on the fourth victim.

"The victims appeared drugged, injected into the left side of the neck with a syringe or needle, with a thick black, tar-like substance that restricted them from moving. Basically, it paralysed them, and we believe there was a strong chance that they could still feel what was happening to them. The bruising and holes were clearly visible on the victims."

"My God. That would explain it then."

"One theory is that Mr Brixton had his tongue cut out to prevent him from screaming further. His body may have been more resistant to whatever it was that was injected."

Randolph wished he'd found Reece Brixton sooner, whilst he was still alive. "What of this tar-like substance? What is it made from?"

"It's new to us, Mr Landon. We're still running checks. All we know so far is that it contains a mixture of herbs and plants. Some are toxic and dangerous, others are milder. A couple of notable ones are gelsemium, that can act as a painkiller but can also cause paralysis. Whoever did this, mixed these herbs together to make their victims helpless. Other ingredients were wolfsbane — one of the most toxic plants in the UK, which can lower the heart rate, and hemlock."

"Jesus. So whoever is responsible mixed all this together, making some kind of paralysis potion? They clearly knew their stuff."

"We've never seen anything like it. Also strange, the candles were still lit and hadn't burnt down when we reached the crime scene. We're still not sure, but they most likely include certain ingredients and chemicals. To burn the green colour that they do, also. Again, we're still running tests … Something else links these victims, something significant."

"Which is?" Randolph's heart rate increased with anticipation.

"Their birthdays; they were each born on the 6th day of the 6th month — June, albeit, with different years of birth. We suspected the link after the second victim was found. Two might have been a strange coincidence, but after the third victim was confirmed, there really was no doubt. We're still waiting for details on the latest victim. You can just bet that her birthday is the same. Why it's relevant, we don't yet know. We still don't know what the murderer's motive is."

There was a pause of silence, while Randolph made notes on all this. Not for the first time, his hand became cramped.

A nervous looking Timothy was walking around his living room, biting on a thumbnail. He could hear the sound of DCS Quincy's voice over the phone, but not what was being said.

"I'm taking it you have no real leads, no suspects?" Randolph asked.

"Nothing. As I mentioned before, when we first met, there were a few people we wanted to question. However, they aren't linked to any of this. They may be 'dodgy' individuals so to speak, but they aren't killers. The reason why we haven't disclosed all the details, especially the birthday links, is because we don't want to cause further panic to the public, particularly to people who share the same birthday as the victims. We need to know more before we release anything further. Some 'loonies' have already claimed to be the killer so the less the public know the better. When they have come in 'confessing,' we've asked how they committed the murder, and there is no mention of this mysterious substance that's been injected into the victims' necks."

"That's understandable ... They're still waiting for the results to come back on the remains found in the cave here in France. But the similarities are striking. A black substance that was found in the cauldron there. The orange and green candles were lit when the archaeological team got down there, and there was an inverted pentagram, albeit drawn in blood and not red chalk."

"Yes. It has to be related somehow. Hopefully the results will come back from Paris soon on the skeletal remains. Everything about this is all strange. My team here are all feeling extremely uncomfortable. More than with any other case we've worked on."

"Again, completely understandable. Everyone involved is unnerved by it, and there's a sensation of dread."

"I know that I can trust you, Mr Landon. Still, in regards to what I've told you, the things that haven't been mentioned to the press, please keep these to yourself for now. We don't want anything leaked to the press. They're difficult to deal with as it is."

"I won't. I promise. Apart from Timothy. He's in the room with me in his living room. He won't speak to anyone."

"Very well. It's going to be another late night for me again at the office. I doubt I'll be getting much sleep once again. Please inform me of any news. That obviously includes any other sightings of this hooded person. Watch yourselves out there. Be extremely careful. These are testing times for all of us."

"I will. And likewise. Take care."

Timothy was eager to know fully what DCS Quincy had revealed to Randolph.

Randolph explained in detail and relayed what DCS Quincy had told him. He saw Timothy's eyes become large when he mentioned about the victims' birthdays being the same. "What is it?"

"Natalie. Her birthday is also June 6th! She was born in 1922. She'll be forty-four next week."

"Shit."

"What if her body is somehow the latest victim in London, Randolph?"

Randolph noticed that Timothy seemed to care a lot about an ex, who he hadn't seen for years. He wondered if Timothy had stronger feelings towards her than he let on, yet he knew how much Timothy loved Claret. He guessed it was only natural that Timothy cared about Natalie still, particularly as they had parted on good terms. "We can't jump to conclusions, Timothy. We'll find out soon enough."

"I know. I just don't understand any of this. How can she share the same birthdays with the victims? What are the chances? The fact that she and her team found that cave? I just don't get it!"

"I know. It's a lot to take in. None of it makes any sense. This will be one case I won't easily forget and I'll be glad to see the back of," Randolph said, with a glum face.

Chapter Twenty
Tuesday, May 31ˢᵗ, 1966

Verneuil-sur-Vienne – 8.09 am

Coming down the oak staircase, Randolph could already smell the fry-up. Neither he nor Timothy got much sleep last night.

"Morning, Randolph. How did you sleep?" Timothy turned his head, attending to a sizzling frying pan.

Randolph yawned before answering, "Not great. Too much on my mind. Yourself?"

"Same. Barely got a few hours. I thought I'd cook us up some breakfast. Are you hungry? I could probably just about stomach some food."

"Yeah. Thanks. You didn't have to do that. Though I do feel hungry." Randolph stood in the posh kitchen, with its white cupboards and worktops and dark mahogany tops. The Andrews certainly didn't do anything by halves. Everything looked modern and expensive in the villa, even the fridge-freezer and oven.

"Feel free to have a drink. There's some orange juice in the fridge. Or some cans of Coca-Cola. The use-by date is still fine on them."

"Thanks." Randolph took out a can from the fridge. He plonked himself down at the solid oak table.

"You want a glass?"

"Eh? Oh. No, it's fine. Cheers." Randolph was still racking his brains about everything. He opened the can. The refreshing fizzy drink soothed his dry morning throat.

"I've got some work to do today. I'll be in my study for most of the morning at least. I'm going to at least try and get something done — occupy my mind."

"I'm just thinking about what I can do. I might give Christine a call. See how her and the others are doing. See if they're any better. It's still early, so I can try later."

"Good idea. Feel free to do what you want, Randolph. I know you're still hired, but get out and about if you want. Take my car. It's not like we can do much more at the moment and it's a nice morning again." Timothy pulled out a couple of plates from a cupboard, before filling them with hot food from the frying pan.

"I appreciate that, Timothy. I think it's best though, if I stay here for a bit, in case there are any calls and we get some more information."

"I'm here if the phone rings."

Randolph then mentioned about the corridor incident at the office block. He had been thinking how if this was the killer carrying the latest victim's heart, why would they still be carrying it, if the time of death had happened hours before?

*

Timothy went to work in his study as planned, whilst Randolph took a stroll around the garden in the warm morning sunshine. He watched a couple of birds flap and splash in the heavy stone birdbath. It was a pleasant morning with little breeze. He smelt the fresh flowers from the flower beds and from several bright and vibrant flower trellises. He looked down at some daisies which had attracted a group of buzzing bees. Although normal and tranquil, the flowers reminded him of what DCS Quincy had told him about the mysterious concoction that had been injected into the murder victims' necks. Randolph felt a brief chill run through him. He walked around the garden one more time, then returned indoors to ring Christine.

"Hello," came Christine's voice. She gave a slight sniffle.

"Christine — it's Randolph Landon. How are you?"

"Oh. Hi, Randolph. I'm still not great, but definitely improving, thank you — is there any news about Natalie?" Christine quickly asked.

Randolph could hear the small hope in Christine's voice. "Unfortunately, no. I'm still working on things — me and the police.

We've found out a little more." Randolph considered DCS Quincy's request and told Christine the bare minimum.

"You really think what the team discovered is linked to these London killings? Where does that leave Natalie, Randolph? Is she in danger?" Christine sounded more than worried.

"We believe so, yes. The detective in charge back in London has spoken to the police in Paris and the gendarmerie. Being on the same page with everything may help in our efforts to locate Natalie." Randolph tried to sound positive.

Christine sighed. "I guess so. Even if it's the worst-case scenario and she's dead, I suppose we all need closure, Mr Landon."

"Don't give up hope, Christine. There's still a strong chance that Natalie is alive and well. I'm ringing from Timothy's villa. I've met with Arnaud from the gendarmerie, so we're all working together. The more the better."

"I-I guess it can only help."

"Have you spoken to Pierre? How is he?"

"I have. He's the same, like the others. Not great, though better than last week."

"That's good. Hopefully you're all over the worst now, of whatever this virus is."

"Let's hope so." Christine coughed.

"I'll keep you updated on things, Christine. Timothy said he'll call you later on as well."

"Okay. Thank you."

After speaking to Christine, Randolph walked back onto the patio and lit a cigarette.

Timothy came out to join him. "I couldn't have one of them, could I?" He smiled. "I don't really smoke much. But sod it."

"You sure?"

"Yeah. Why not." Timothy winked.

Randolph pulled out his slightly squashed pack of Winston Lights and Timothy took one. Randolph used his Zippo to light it. "I need to pack this crap up, myself." He then told Timothy he had just called Christine.

They then heard the doorbell ring. Timothy went inside to answer the front door, wafting away some of the cigarette smoke.

"Monsieur Andrews, may I come in? I have some news regarding the bracelet that we found." It was Arnaud.

"Really? Of course. Come in!"

Arnaud stepped in and wiped his shoes on the mat. He again took off his hat and tucked it under his arm out of respect on entering the house.

Timothy led Arnaud out to where Randolph was still smoking.

"Monsieur Landon." Arnaud nodded his head. "It's good to see you again, oui."

"Arnaud." Randolph nodded back.

"Arnaud has some news about the bracelet you found," Timothy said.

"Really? Already?"

"Oui. Maybe we can sit down?"

The three sat down at a teak, cross-legged garden table.

"So please, Arnaud. Tell us what you know?" Timothy asked eagerly.

"When I left here yesterday afternoon, I got started straight away by asking people and my fellow gendarmerie colleagues. I would have come last night to tell you of the news, but forgive me, I had a headache and needed to lie down. I asked a couple of shops in Limoges that sell such things, oui — small items and trinkets. They were the first places that came to my mind. Although the bracelet you uncovered has been hidden for many years most likely, it could have been more recent, non? Unfortunately, they knew nothing of it."

"I guess it was a long shot, Arnaud."

"Oui, Monsieur Landon. However, they did recommend someone else that they knew of. One of the ladies who owns a small shop in Limoges suggested I ask an elderly woman who runs a small bakery next door to her home in Veyrac."

"Veyrac?" Randolph queried. He recalled Timothy stopping off there to buy the flowers for Tiffany's grave.

"Oui. It is a few kilometres north of here. She has lived there for many years. She used to run the bakery with her husband until he passed away a few years ago. In her spare time, she makes small items like the braided bracelet that you found and she sells them. She has also heard the stories about witchcraft and Satanism, but not of the orphanage, non."

"How long has she lived in Veyrac, for? And it was her who made that bracelet that Randolph found?" Timothy asked.

"She has lived in Veyrac for over thirty years. Non, forgive me, it was not her. But she knew of another lady who lived in Oradour-sur-Glane, who would also make these bracelets and sell them, or give them away free at times to young children in the area or who lived in the village before it was destroyed by the SS in the war, oui. Her name was Mirielle Blanchet. She would always stitch her initials of *MB* … According to Adrienne — the lady I spoke to; Mirielle was a kind-hearted soul. She had never married nor had children of her own, but the locals were always very fond of her, and particularly the children."

"What happened to her? Did she die?" Randolph asked. Although they had possibly found a clue linked to the old bracelet, he couldn't help but feel it was all futile.

"According to Adrienne, Mirielle moved in 1944 to Mont-Saint-Michel. She was well into her seventies by then, perhaps pushing eighty. Adrienne has heard rumours over the years both that Mirielle had died and also that she is still alive. The later, even recently, oui."

"Not exactly useful information, then. If she's alive, she would be pushing a hundred at least." Randolph shook his head. "I guess that the evidence further points to the bracelet belonging to one of the skeletons, no doubt a child."

"Pretty much what we know already," Timothy confirmed.

"Where is Mont-Saint-Michel? I think I've heard of it," Randolph asked.

"Claret and I have been near there. It's three hundred miles or so north-west of here — in Normandy."

Arnaud gave a nod as if to confirm.

"Quite some way. I wonder why Mirielle moved so far away at her age." Randolph looked in thought.

"I think it's safe to say that this bracelet you found moves us no nearer to finding Natalie or finding out more about the orphanage."

"Maybe, Timothy." Randolph continued to look thoughtful.

Timothy frowned at Randolph. "You have something in mind?"

Randolph let out a sigh. "I don't know … what if this woman is still alive, maybe she would know about the orphanage? If she is still alive, she's going to be really old though and we wouldn't know her state of mind, or whether she'd remember twenty to thirty years back."

"Well, there is that. It could be worth a shot. She definitely won't know anything about Natalie's disappearance per se, but she might know more about this orphanage like you say, and it would give us and the police something to move forwards with," Timothy said slightly optimistically.

Randolph rubbed his stubbly face several times. "It's a shame it isn't nearer."

"It shouldn't be too much of a problem. I'm pretty sure I can arrange a flight to Rennes."

"Really?" Randolph checked.

"Definitely. I know a bit about France, like Claret. I'm pretty certain Rennes Airport is the closest to Mont-Saint-Michel. We'd still need to travel some way to get from Rennes to there. I'll check into it all and make sure. Leave it with me."

"I'll have to check with my superiors, but I wish to accompany you. We can try contacting the police and gendarmerie near to Mont-Saint-Michel, too, to see if they can help us find Mirielle, oui."

"You're more than welcome to join us, Arnaud," Timothy replied. "We could maybe do with your services."

Randolph nodded. "Definitely. We're all out of other ideas and we could be running out of time both for Natalie and the next London victim."

After Arnaud went to attend to his duties, a restless Timothy returned to his study to work and to arrange for his private jet to take the two of them and possibly Arnaud, from Limoges to Rennes the next morning at 9 am.

*

Approaching midday, Randolph sat in the living room going over his notes and trying to piece everything together. He found it a little easier to concentrate than Timothy, though racking his brains, he came up with nothing at all. Timothy came out to pour himself a small drink, before returning to his work. Randolph declined his offer of a brandy.

Randolph closed his notebook and tapped the pen on it several times. He continued to try to develop a plausible explanation for everything. None of it made sense. It was no doubt evident that whoever ran this orphanage was now dead — along with some of its children. But why weren't there more children buried below the surface? How was the killer linked to this discovery? The cave had been hidden for years. Had someone escaped from the orphanage years ago? Why would they kill people in London, sharing the same birthdays? There were so many burning questions and few, if any, answers. Randolph plopped his notebook down on the glass table and leant back in the armchair, tilting his head back. He rubbed his face with his palms. Surely if the police back in London and here in France couldn't find out anything with their manpower and numbers, he surely couldn't. Fuck!

Randolph sat forward and began to think: *6th day of the 6th month, sixty-six, 66 …* His eyes enlarged and he stood up. He made his way to an oak bookcase in one corner of the room near to the expensive looking Venetian glass-topped dining table with its marble legs. He immediately searched for a Bible, hoping the Andrews had one. After scanning the shelves, he soon found what he was after. On the bottom shelf, was an old black, leather covered Bible. *Holy Bible* was printed in gold on the front and spine. It had faded over the years, along with the leather. The edges of the spine and some of the corners had worn away with age. On one of the opening blank pages, in faded blue ink, it read:

To Dear Claret,
Father Daley – St Bartholomew the Great – March, 1956

Randolph wondered if Claret and Timothy were religious, but it wasn't of any importance. He flicked through the pages, tinted yellow with age, to where he wanted to read: Revelation 13. Reading the passage, Randolph swallowed, standing there. Not for the first time, he felt a shiver run through his entire body …

1 And I saw a beast rising out of the sea, with ten horns and seven heads, with ten diadems on its horns and blasphemous names on its heads.

2 And the beast that I saw was like a leopard; its feet were like a bear's, and its mouth was like a lion's mouth. And to it the dragon gave his power and his throne and great authority.

3 One of its heads seemed to have a mortal wound, but its mortal wound was healed, and the whole earth marvelled as they followed the beast.

4 And they worshipped the dragon, for he had given his authority to the beast, and they worshipped the beast, saying, "Who is like the beast, and who can fight against it?"

5 And the beast was given a mouth uttering haughty and blasphemous words, and it was allowed to exercise authority for forty-two months.

6 It opened its mouth to utter blasphemies against God, blaspheming his name and his dwelling, that is, those who dwell in heaven.

7 Also it was allowed to make war on the saints and to conquer them, and authority was given it over every tribe and people and language and nation.

8 And all who dwell on earth will worship it, everyone whose name has not been written before the foundation of the world in the book of life of the Lamb who was slain.

9 If anyone has an ear, let him hear:

10 If anyone is to be taken captive, to captivity he goes; if anyone is to be slain with the sword, with the sword must he be slain.

11 Then I saw another beast rising out of the earth. It had two horns like a lamb and it spoke like a dragon.

12 It exercises all the authority of the first beast in its presence, and makes the earth and its inhabitants worship the first beast, whose mortal wound was healed.

13 It performs great signs, even making fire come down from heaven to earth in front of people.

14 And by the signs that it is allowed to work in the presence of the beast it deceives those who dwell on earth, telling them to make an image for the beast that was wounded by the sword and yet lived.

15 And it was allowed to give breath to the image of the beast, so that the image of the beast might even speak and might cause those who would not worship the image of the beast to be slain.

16 Also it causes all, both small and great, both rich and poor, both free and slave, to be marked on the right hand or the forehead.

17 So that no one can buy or sell unless he has the mark, that is, the name of the beast or the number of its name.

18 This calls for wisdom: let the one who has understanding calculate the number of the beast, for it is the number of a man, and his number is 666.

Randolph read it for a second time. He remembered this particular chapter from the *Book of Revelation*, all those years ago from school, when a religious teacher had read it out loud in class. He had forgotten all about it until years later, during a cold winter's night during the war, when he was shacked up in an old farmhouse in Belgium, with fellow soldiers, Privates Donald and Edwards — both of whom were American and religious. One of them, Edwards, had read the same extract to the group. He believed that Adolf Hitler was the 'Antichrist,' which caused a few laughs from the others. Randolph never saw them again after that following morning. He read that particular chapter for a third time, thinking …

"Randolph." Timothy had returned, making Randolph jump. "Sorry." Timothy smiled. He then briefly held the Bible, looking at the front cover. "You're reading the Bible? I guess it wouldn't be a bad thing, considering everything that's been happening," Timothy half-joked.

"Are you and Claret religious?" Randolph asked, with the Bible still open.

"Nah. That Bible was given to Claret years ago, from some priest to thank her for donating some clothes to the church charity organisation at the time. She kept it out of respect."

Randolph explained the connection of the passage he had read.

"What, you think the killer is some sort of *beast?*" Timothy laughed awkwardly.

"No. Well, not in a literal sense. But they're no doubt evil and disturbed — clearly. Like I said, I was just sitting here thinking about the dates and then it came to me about *666*. I doubt it would have crossed my mind, if witchcraft and Satan hadn't been mentioned."

"You could be on to something, there. I wonder if the police have made the link? Though it's only *two* sixes — the sixth day and sixth month."

"Yes. But think what year it is?" Randolph looked at Timothy who didn't fall in at first.

"1966."

"Exactly. Even though the nine is upside down. Is it of any relevance? Or is it all a strange and messed-up coincidence? I'm betting on the former. Despite what has happened, I don't believe in ghosts and things like that. Or 'things that go bump in the night.' But whoever is doing all of this, clearly does, and then some. They've no doubt done their research and believe something. Of course, why they're doing it, also remains a mystery, and is the biggest question of all."

The pair stood in silence for a moment, until the phone rang in the living room, startling them both. Timothy went to answer it and Randolph tucked the Bible back on the bottom shelf of the bookcase.

"Christine!" Timothy said. "It's so good to hear from you. How are you feeling? I was going to phone you."

Randolph watched on and listened, seeing Timothy's face fall serious again.

"… I see. Okay … I know. Yes. We'll talk soon … Please, take care."

Randolph watched Timothy slowly place the receiver down. "What is it? Something happen?"

"Christine's feeling better this afternoon. That's one good thing. She's just got the official results back from the skeletons from the anthropologist team. The two adult skeletons were male and female, as expected. The one wearing the torc was the female. They were both believed to have been in their fifties. Christine is going to forward me an official copy of the report with full details. The analysis was finished fully, late last night, after the delays."

"Well, is that it?" Randolph sounded annoyed.

"Huh?" Timothy turned to face Randolph. "Oh. Sorry, Randolph. There's quite a bit more. It's just … the smaller skeletons belonged to six young boys and four young girls. They believe the ages varied anywhere between six and twelve years old. The report has more specific details, in regards to each skeleton's assumed age … There was no bone damage or anything like that. They all seemed in good health with no deficiencies. The bones appeared normal and no signs of trauma. No diseases were detected.

"The adult male skeleton — the same. With the female skeleton, there were a few things detected. She appeared to have suffered from brittle bone disease for most of her adult life, combined with rheumatoid arthritis. They could determine previous signs of breakages and fractures, even more recent ones towards the end of her life — like in her arms. She also suffered from painful ankylosing spondylitis, which caused a hunched-over posture that got worse with time. Again, signs were detected on the vertebrae. There were a couple more minor things that Christine said, but I can't remember the names of the conditions. Needless to say, this woman — whoever she was, most definitely suffered in her life."

"It certainly seems it. Normally, I'd have nothing but compassion and sympathy for someone like that. But were they the reason these children's skeletons were down there in that cave with them?"

Timothy nodded in agreement. "They believe they died anywhere from around twenty to twenty-five years ago. Give or take a few years. They couldn't find any dental records on any of the victims but there were traces of a dried black substance like 'tar' on all of their teeth. It matched the substance that they scraped from the cauldron. It contained hemlock and wolfsbane."

Randolph's eyes became large and piercing. "My God. The same as in the London murders."

"I know. Frightening, eh? There really is no doubt now, that it's all clearly linked. Christine will send me the report. That's basically the crux of it all. They believe the poison most likely killed the adults and children. They are still researching further into this black substance."

"It's amazing what they can find out from skeletal remains."

"Definitely. However, there's another disturbing thing to tell you."

"Which is?"

Timothy let out a sigh. "This morning, the team working on the remains, came into work and noticed that all twelve skeletons had turned to dust. *Gone!*"

"What the hell. *How?*"

"They literally have no idea, other than maybe the humidity of the room caused it."

"If that was the case, surely the skeletons would have turned to dust before now?"

"You'd have thought so, eh?" Timothy shrugged. "I need a drink. You?" Timothy walked over to behind the mini-bar.

"Yeah — I think I do."

"At least Christine and Pierre are feeling better and the other two, apparently. Oh, and another thing, Christine informed me that Pierre had received some bad news: his friend, the witchcraft expert, had died from a heart attack."

Arnaud phoned Timothy not long after to confirm that it was okay for him to travel north to Normandy with them in search of Mirielle Blanchet. His superiors believed it would be good for him to go along, in case they learnt something to help with the disappearance of Natalie Connors or with the murders back in London. He had also queried about Mirielle Blanchet with the gendarmerie in Normandy and someone would get back to them.

*

Timothy and Randolph had gone out for a meal at a restaurant in Limoges. The pair had both needed a break from the villa and a change of scenery, though it didn't help much to clear their minds.

Leaving Limoges and driving back through the pleasant countryside in the dusk, a few dark clouds appeared on the horizon in the orange sunset. A few flashes of fork lightning could be seen. The weather forecast had forewarned thunderstorms in the area with heavy downpours lasting well into the night.

"We often get thunderstorms in the summer down here," Timothy stated. "They can sometimes get really bad. I guess it's a small price to pay when you get great weather most of the time. The winters can get bitterly cold, though."

"You can certainly appreciate the scenery, that's for sure." Randolph admired the view of fields and the foothills. He wondered if there were more caves buried underneath this vast empty land. He felt a little more relaxed when they drove past a couple of farms.

A short while later, they arrived back at the villa and the night drew in. Thunder clouds covered what was left of the sun, creeping closer to Verneuil-sur-Vienne. There was also a bite in the air and a wind had materialised.

"It's gotten cold quickly," Timothy said, locking up his Ford Zephyr. "Blowing up for something nasty, no doubt."

Randolph held onto his brown trilby when a gust of wind shot past.

Inside, Randolph made his way to the living room. Timothy went into his study to finish some work before giving Claret a call. Randolph considered calling Thelma but decided to wait for now.

When Timothy was done, he had come back out and he and Randolph shared a nightcap together.

Chapter Twenty-One
Wednesday, June 1st, 1966

Verneuil-sur-Vienne – 2.28 am

Randolph switched on the bedside lamp as another rumble of thunder sounded. He checked the time. He'd been asleep for over three hours. The storm had started not long after he went up to bed and was still ongoing. He hated waking up early for no apparent reason and then always struggled to get back to sleep. For some reason tonight, he felt especially strange.

He stepped out of the warm bed into the coldness of the room, in his white boxer shorts and vest. Standing at the window, the flashes of lightning made him squint. With each flash, he saw his reflection on the glass, along with the multiple rivulets of rain pelting against the glass. The noise of the rain was enough to keep him awake. Thunderstorms never usually bothered him. He had even fought in them during the war, with gunfire and explosions sometimes drowning out the thunder. However, this storm unnerved him. He flinched slightly when the next thunder came, vibrating the walls of the villa. He wanted to go back to bed, though he didn't feel tired. He felt alert to someone or something. He sensed that must have been a reason for him waking up randomly like this because he normally slept through storms. Randolph then smelt what he thought might be smoke. Perhaps something had been struck by lightning outside and had caused a fire. There was nothing but darkness and the intermittent lightning visible through the window — no fire or flames.

The villa had four rooms upstairs. The master bedroom where Timothy slept was across from Randolph's and Timothy's door was shut. Stepping out onto the landing, Randolph could smell the smoke more strongly. He wondered if Timothy had perhaps also woken and gone down for a snack, perhaps burning something in the process. The landing was dark apart from the occasional flash of lightning. Rather than wake Timothy, Randolph decided to check downstairs himself.

He made his way downstairs and at the bottom, stepping onto the hard wooden flooring, his bare feet stepped into something wet. He looked at the sole of one of his feet, waiting for a flash of lightning to show him what it was. He touched the wetness and smelt his hands. There was no smell. It was definitely water. Perhaps the villa was leaking. The smell of smoke grew stronger. He flicked the nearby light switch, but no lights came on. He tried a few more times. The storm must have knocked out the power. He cowered when a louder boom of thunder startled him. The sound vibrated heavily. Lightning then shimmered down the hallway. Randolph looked ahead into the living room. He saw an orange flicker and heard the slight sound of crackling, the sound of something burning. He dashed into the smoky living room towards the light.

There on the floor and burning away bright in the flames was the Bible Randolph had read from. Randolph quickly went to the kitchen. Again the light switch didn't work, but using the lightning flashes to guide him, he dowsed a tea towel under the cold tap and rushed back. He smothered what was left of the burning Bible with the wet towel, causing numerous embers to fly up into the air, before eventually putting it out. Breathing heavily in the dark, he noticed that the thunder and lightning had stopped. He stood, shocked, shivering in the dark. What the hell had just happened? After another minute or so, the lightning returned a little, but not as intense. Randolph bent down and picked up what was left of the Bible. A small burnt snippet of a page fell out and floated to the floor. He bent back down to pick it up. He read the snippet in the sporadic flashes of lightning:

18 This calls for wisdom: let the one who has understanding calculate the number of the beast, for it is the number of a man, and his number is 666.

Randolph breathed heavily and his heart rate increased. Another crack of thunder came, louder than any yet. Again, Randolph cowered, turning his head towards the French doors — his blood froze as he saw the hooded figure lit up in the lightning flashes, staring through the glass in the falling rain straight at him. Randolph dropped the remains of the Bible in shock. The hood of the dark jacket was pulled tightly round this figure's face but Randolph could still see them slowly smile before grinning sinisterly. Randolph instinctively edged back into the wet hallway. He never took his eyes from the figure as they continued to grin at him. The lightning stopped suddenly and all was dark. The hallway and kitchen lights came on and the figure was gone.

"Randolph."

"FUCK!"

"What is it?" Timothy asked frantically.

"That fucking hooded person was outside!"

"What?"

Randolph could now see what he'd stepped in: the wet footprints from someone's boots starting from the front door and leading into the living room.

Timothy was then told what had happened. With the power on now, they switched on every light in the villa and searched every room. Timothy also switched on a floodlight that lit up the back garden but neither of them dared go outside to check whether anyone was still there. Timothy then rung the gendarmerie, in case the hooded figure was still lurking outside.

"Let's just hope that they turn up soon," Timothy said anxiously. He and Randolph were pacing up and down the living room. "I don't fucking understand, Randolph. How could this person have got inside when everything is locked up? There's no sign of breaking and entering! The footprints came from the front door to here yet there aren't any prints leading to the French doors, which were locked anyway!"

Randolph's head started to hurt. "I don't know, Timothy. I can't explain it either. Maybe they can dust for fingerprints. I don't think I've ever been so scared in my life, even during the war! Maybe I spoke too soon about not believing in 'things that go bump in the night.' I was only looking at that Bible yesterday and now it's burnt to a crisp. Not to mention the fact that the *exact* snippet fell out, mentioning about 666."

"How would this person even know what you were looking at yesterday?"

"I don't know. Maybe they were spying through the window or something, watching me, whilst you were busy in your study? We still have to remain rational and realistic."

"And you say that you smelt something burning from upstairs and downstairs? Even before you saw the flames in the living room?"

Randolph swallowed and nodded. "That's correct. None of it makes sense. That grin, too — just standing there *watching* me … I'm sorry about your floor."

The wooden floor was slightly singed from the fire. What was left of the Bible was wrapped inside the now blackened tea towel on the glass dining table.

"Don't worry about that, Randolph. I'm just glad you got up when you did, and that you're okay. The whole villa could have gone up! God knows what else they could have done, if you hadn't come downstairs."

"I think they knew exactly what they were doing, Timothy. They're perhaps trying to warn us off and frighten us — I think it's safe to say they've achieved that, all right!"

"Shit. They could still be out there."

"Quite likely. At least there's two of us, the storm has passed and the power is back on."

*

It took almost forty minutes for the gendarmes to arrive; there were two officers but Arnaud wasn't with them. Timothy didn't want to call him in the middle of the night, as he'd lost so much sleep lately with his newborn son. He would find out what had happened soon enough. Timothy and Randolph both felt a little safer with the gendarmes present, especially with them both being armed. They checked upstairs and outside, front and back. The wet footprints had since dried out.

"We can arrange for a team to check for prints later today," one of the gendarmes suggested.

"Sure. If you think it's for the best. I can't see what difference it's going to make, even if there are fingerprints detected. Virtually all the ones that will come back, will be mine and my wife's."

The two gendarmes then went over the same questions about Natalie's case and the London murders that Randolph and Timothy had answered already. They were even advised to stop the investigation and leave it to the gendarmerie and French and UK police forces to deal with. Neither Randolph or Timothy mentioned their forthcoming flight to Rennes. Once the two gendarmes were satisfied with their questioning and that the area was safe, they left the villa. Neither Timothy nor Randolph felt like going back to bed.

The two stayed awake the rest of the night. They tried to focus their minds on a game of cards, sitting at the dining table. Although Claret and Timothy didn't normally smoke in their villa, Timothy let this rule slide — tonight was an exception and they smoked until dawn.

*

Arnaud was updated at work just before eight in the morning. He appreciated why Timothy hadn't wanted to disturb him but said he would have preferred to have been called. Arnaud was shocked at what he heard, particularly the '666' connection with the year being 1966. Timothy pointed out that Natalie's birthday was the same date. Arnaud then informed Timothy that the forensic team were due to arrive shortly to dust for fingerprints. Timothy and Randolph would have their own fingerprints taken for reference, narrowing the results down if more were found. It also meant their flight to Rennes would be delayed a little.

The phone rang. Timothy answered it. "… It's the DCS. He'd rather talk to you. You can fill him in on what happened last night."

Randolph took the phone from Timothy. "DCS Quincy … I'm good. Well, kind of. After what happened last night …" Randolph told of his frightening encounter during the night and how the missing Natalie Conners shared the same birthday as the London victims.

"Any news? Have they identified the latest body?" Timothy asked anxiously after the call. "What did he say about last night?"

"They have. Her name was Jennifer Grantham. She was twenty-two years old and recently engaged," Randolph replied sadly. "She was an insurance broker, working late on Great Russell Street, just a little further down from where she was murdered. She only lived around the corner on Montague Street — so close to her home. There are still a few things they are looking into, regarding the victims." Despite the news being tragic, at least there was still hope for Natalie.

"Shit. Poor woman. Poor fiancée!" Timothy's face became saddened. "And let me guess, her birthday was June 6th?"

"Yep," Randolph said, nodding his head. "DCS Quincy was informed yesterday evening about the forensic results from the skeletons in Paris, and how they had turned to dust. At least they're all trying to work together on all this now. No doubt it will all soon be in the news over here."

"That could be a good thing; more exposure could mean a better chance of capturing the killer."

"I'm not so sure, Timothy. I didn't mention the 666 and 1966 connection. I'll wait until I speak with him again, ideally in person. Hopefully we can find this Mirielle lady and get some more insight into all of this and pass that on to him, too." Randolph updated his notebook, with the other two watching on:

Jennifer Grantham – Aged 22.
Fourth Victim: Female – ~~Unknown~~. Body found on May 30th 1966 at 8.50 am off Great Russell Street. Engaged and lived on Montague Street.

When forensics arrived, they found numerous fingerprints over the French doors and front door of the villa. No fingerprints were found on what was left of the burnt Bible remains. The three didn't read too much into it; they knew that most likely the prints belonged mainly to Timothy and Claret, and none belonging to this strange hooded figure. Once finished, the three drove to the airstrip via the gendarmerie station wagon that Arnaud had parked up there until he returned from Normandy.

*

Mont-Saint-Michel, Normandy – 1.36 pm

They had landed at Rennes Airport in Timothy's private jet. Timothy had then hired a taxi to take the three of them the further fifty odd miles north to Mont-Saint-Michel. Timothy had also booked them in for at least one night at the Hôtel d'Estouteville, in case they needed to stay over.

In the overcast afternoon, the mysterious tidal island of Mont-Saint-Michel could be seen in the distance, rising from the grey-brown, sandy seabed.

"I've never seen anything like that before," Randolph said, admiring the walled island of rock as they drove closer.

"Claret and I have drove past a few times and flown over it. It's strange, but also a thing of beauty." Timothy was sitting in the back next to Arnaud and followed Randolph's gaze.

"Oui. I've seen pictures of it, though not been there myself, non." Arnaud rubbed his moustache a few times, looking on.

"What's its history?" asked Randolph.

"Legend has it that the Bishop of Avranches — Saint Autbert, had a dream where he encountered the Archangel Michael. He told him to build a sanctuary for people to pray and worship at the summit," the bearded French taxi driver suddenly said, then continued the story in impeccable English, "The bishop had the same recurring dreams yet refused to accept the command, until one morning, when he woke to find that the Archangel had burnt a hole in his head. Only then, did he build what was ordered, dedicating the island to the Archangel Michael. The Benedictine abbey itself, was built a couple of centuries later."

"Interesting." Randolph gave a wry smile, not believing the legend. "You believe the legend?" he asked the middle-aged taxi driver.

"Of course, oui," the taxi driver replied seriously, briefly turning his head to Randolph.

"Does anyone still live up there?" asked Timothy.

"There are no monks living there currently. However, a few monks from other monasteries are to be sent there during the summer, to mark its 1000th anniversary since it was built. It is rumoured that the old abbey is haunted, from the spirits of deceased monks during the centuries passed. At night, they can sometimes be heard chanting and singing, or they have been known to mysteriously ring the bell there."

"You've experienced this for yourself?" Randolph quizzed, again doubtful.

"Me? Not personally, I have not." The taxi driver gave a sniff.

"What about the population of Mont-Saint-Michel?" Timothy queried. A few old houses started to come into view. It seemed a strange and remote place for someone to live, in spite of the scenic setting.

"Over a hundred, I think," the taxi driver responded, scratching his nostrils ... "Here you gentleman are!" The taxi driver smiled, coming to a sudden stop. He pointed up further to where the hotel was. "Unfortunately, you'll have to walk the rest of the way."

Randolph thanked the driver and climbed out on the passenger side. He put on his brown trilby and looked up at the abbey, carrying his suitcase. He could just about make out a gold statue, probably Saint Michael, the Archangel, fixed to the top of the bell tower.

Arnaud got out too and Timothy paid the taxi driver his fare, insisting that he keep the change. The more than grateful taxi driver thanked Timothy and smiled warmly. Timothy put his bag over his shoulder: he'd mostly some paperwork he needed to finish, if he had the time. The three men then made their way up towards the hotel.

It felt quaint and peaceful walking up to the hotel through the streets of old stone houses. There were even some small shops and a few places to eat. A little to Randolph's surprise, it wasn't quite as desolate as he had anticipated. He smiled, seeing a couple of young boys throw buckets of water over each other outside their home. Despite the grey skies, the temperature was mild and pleasant.

It was a steep climb to the hotel, with numerous stone steps leading the way up. Hôtel d'Estouteville was one of two hotels on the island. It was built at the top of the village, with the abbey towering above.

"I'm not sure how good this hotel is. I randomly chose this one over the other," Timothy said.

"Maybe you could build a hotel of your own here, Timothy?" Randolph joked.

Timothy laughed and Arnaud grinned; he adjusted his black satchel with its brass buckle, in which he'd stored the braided bracelet to show Mirielle if they found her.

Although a little ordinary looking, the hotel was nice enough, with its brickwork and brown painted window frames. At the front of the hotel was a concrete pillar with the hotel name. Above the name was a coat of arms of a black lion with its golden claws and tongue sticking out. Arnaud told them that the coat of arms belonged to the House of Estouteville. An old outside light hung over the sign and was switched on, despite the daylight.

Inside, was a strong smell of cigarette smoke. The reception was small and the desk was unattended. On the back wall was an old wooden pigeonhole unit with slots from 1 to 16, suggesting that there were sixteen rooms in the hotel. A black and white framed photo of the Mont-Saint-Michel abbey was fixed on the wall to the left and looked like it could do with a feather duster. To the right hung a shield with the same coat of arms as on the pillar outside. A cigarette was smouldering in an ashtray on the reception desk.

"Certainly a contrast to my hotels, eh?" Timothy sniggered and hit a bell on the reception desk.

A few coughs came from inside a small room behind the desk. They heard a toilet flush and the door opened. An old woman in her late sixties emerged. She attempted to waft away some of the lingering smoke as she stood in front of the three men. Randolph couldn't help but smirk.

"Oui?" the old woman coughed at them. She noticed the smouldering butt, picked it up and squashed it out on the bottom of the ashtray.

"Good afternoon, Madam. I have a reservation for three rooms under the name of Timothy Andrews ..."

The old woman took out an old reservation book from underneath the desk and opened it up. "Ah. Oui, Monsieur. You are all on the second floor." The old woman then walked to the pigeonhole unit and took three room keys from compartments 11 to 13.

"Merci," Timothy replied. He smirked at the others, flicking his eyebrows up, handing them their keys.

"Number thirteen. Unlucky for some," Randolph jested, taking the key.

"Excuse me, Madame. Would you happen to know of an old woman named Mirielle Blanchet? She lives here or she used to." Timothy thought he'd ask.

The old woman frowned. "Mirielle Blanchet? Non. I am afraid I don't know anyone by that name."

Timothy thanked her anyway and the three gentlemen made their way up the carpeted stairs.

*

"If only the Normandy gendarmerie had responded; it could have saved us the journey up here, if she is no longer here, oui?" Arnaud said.

The three of them were in Timothy's hotel room, discussing how to find Mirielle, if she was still alive and living in Mont-Saint-Michel.

"It's not highly populated or a huge place. I'm pretty sure we could find something out." Timothy stood looking out of the window. The rooms this side of the floor, looked out to the large abbey and several tall maple trees and a large chestnut tree behind the hotel. A stone wall and steps led up to the historic abbey.

"I'm pretty sure someone will know something. It would certainly have saved us time had the receptionist known of Mirielle," Randolph replied. "Although, there's one quicker way we can possibly find out."

Timothy turned to face Randolph. "Which is?"

"Walking up here to the hotel, I noticed a small post office. There's a good chance that they would know if Mirielle still lived here."

"Great suggestion, Randolph, although they may not be authorised to give out her address."

"True, Timothy, but that's where Arnaud may be of help, as a uniformed officer."

Timothy smiled. "Very true! Arnaud, what do you think?"

"Oui — we can certainly try. It won't hurt, non?"

Timothy and Randolph waited downstairs by reception for Arnaud. Arnaud wanted to use the phone in his room to speak to his wife back home before they went out. The old woman from the reception wiped a table clean and then started dusting the cobwebs away from the picture of the Mont-Saint-Michel abbey. She looked across to Randolph and smiled.

Randolph noticed a wedding ring. "Are you the owner? Do you run the hotel by yourself?"

"Ah, oui. I used to run it with my husband. Unfortunately, he passed away almost six years ago." The old woman glanced to Randolph before continuing with her chores. She started dusting the pigeonhole unit. "We took it over back in 1948."

"I'm sorry to hear about your husband," Randolph replied sincerely.

"It's fine, Monsieur. I sometimes have my children and grandchildren to help. I also have a cleaner. It's not a big hotel, so I can mostly manage by myself." The woman looked back and smiled, before coughing.

Randolph smiled at her. Although she seemed a little rough around the edges, Randolph sensed good in her. "What does Hôtel d'Estouteville mean, exactly?"

"The hotel has been here for well over two centuries, Monsieur. It was erected in honour of Louis d'Estouteville. The shield I am dusting now and the sign outside, represent the House of Estouteville."

"Who was Louis d'Estouteville?" Timothy joined the conversation.

"He died in 1464. He was a lord and French soldier. He was Captain of Mont-Saint-Michel and Governor of Normandy, a *very* important man, oui." The woman finished her dusting and then pulled out an old spray can of polish and started polishing her reception counter. The smell of the polish was strong, prompting the old woman to cough some more. "He also defeated the English and protected the island from their sieges during the Hundred Years War."

"I think his name may ring a bell," Randolph said, thinking.

"It is said that the spirit of Louis d' Estouteville still watches over the island, guarding its ramparts today." The woman coughed again.

"Have you seen him?" Timothy asked a little sarcastically, winking at Randolph who resisted a smirk.

"Non, but I have spoken to people and guests of this hotel who have, oui."

Arnaud then appeared from the stairs.

*

The post office was on Grande Rue. It was next door to a small gift and souvenir shop. It was a pleasant but fairly steep climb down. Parts of the street became narrower, causing brushing of shoulders with others going about their business. Some of the stone streets were rough and uneven so they had to watch their footing, and it was now a little busier than when they had arrived. There were also a few museums on the island. It felt like a surreal experience, walking through the streets of Mont-Saint-Michel, with its shops, houses, inns and buildings. Some dated back centuries; its rich and timeless history could be felt deeply and not easily forgotten.

Whilst Arnaud was in the post office, Randolph popped into the souvenir shop. Timothy waited outside. Randolph returned carrying a small paper bag.

"What did you get?" Timothy smiled.

"I thought I'd buy a snow globe of Mont-Saint-Michel for my son." Randolph smiled, taking out the pretty snow globe and handing it to Timothy. "I suppose one thing about all of this is that at least I'm seeing some sights," Randolph remarked sarcastically.

Timothy shook the snow globe. "Cute. And there is that!" He handed the snow globe back to Randolph.

"I got him this, too." Randolph showed Timothy a small black and white, hand painted plastic figure of the animated character Pepé Le Pew. "I got some aniseed balls as well."

Timothy took Randolph's offer of a sweet from a separate brown bag. He started to suck, enjoying the taste. "God. It's years since I've had one of these."

"Same."

A couple of minutes later, Arnaud returned. "I've got it, Mirielle's address." He looked very pleased with himself.

"What — really?"

"Oui, Monsieur Landon. She still lives here and is a hundred and one years old."

"Were they okay giving you her address?" Timothy asked.

"Oui, I think the uniform helped? I said I needed to talk to her about something important. Mirielle, still comes down to the shops by herself sometimes. She is still very much able at her age."

"Where does she live?" Randolph asked.

"She lives further up on Grande Rue. Next door to a bookshop run by her great niece."

"Well, let's go see her!" Timothy said firmly, still sucking on the aniseed ball.

Arnaud also took a sweet from Randolph's bag.

They made their way back up Grande Rue and climbed the steps. They had passed Mirielle's home on the way down. They decided to eat after they had spoken to Mirielle. None of them had eaten since this morning, and the bakery they passed selling fresh baked goods increased their appetite.

The bookshop, called Librairie Siloë, had a turquoise painted front door, which stood open. Black bars were fixed over the windows, which had matching turquoise frames. Randolph bent down and stroked a black cat that was sitting outside. It meowed and put its tail up, rubbing itself against Randolph's trousers, enjoying the fuss. Randolph looked at the small name disc on the smart purple collar, which read *Mog*. She rolled over wanting her belly rubbed.

"This is Mirielle's house, oui," Arnaud said, hands on his hips.

The house and bookshop were built together, with the same matching brick work. Mirielle's home had painted red window frames and the front door was white. Both front doors had long black, arrow end tee hinges emphasising their age.

"I'll knock." Randolph knocked firmly using the black iron, fleur de lys door knocker. Like the others, he began to feel a little anxious. It might come across strange, having three men turning up at her home unannounced, but they were all desperate for answers.

Less than twenty seconds later, the front door opened. The lady who answered looked old, but surprisingly well for the grand age of a hundred and one. She certainly looked younger with her fluffy white head of hair and blushed cheeks. She looked quite elegant, wearing a green dress and light pink cardigan, with a white pearl necklace. A pair of reading glasses hung around her neck via a decorative beaded chain. She smiled warmly. A scent of sweet perfume surrounded her.

Randolph cleared his throat. "Excusez-moi. Are you Mirielle Blanchet?"

"Oui, je suis Mirielle, c'est moi."

"Would it be okay if we could talk with you, please?" Randolph said, feeling awkward. It seemed that Mirielle didn't speak any English.

"Je suis désolée, mais je ne parle pas Anglais." Mirielle gave another warm smile.

Randolph turned to Arnaud for help.

Arnaud smiled and approached Mirielle in the doorway. "Bonjour, Madame! Puis-je vous présenter Timothy Andrews et Randolph Landon. Je m'appelle Arnaud … Nous sommes venus de Limoges ce matin pour vous poser des questions très urgentes! Serait-il possible de venir chez, Madame?"

Mirielle's face became serious. Whatever Arnaud had said, she stood aside and beckoned them into her home.

"What did you say?" Timothy asked quietly.

Arnaud smiled. "I asked her if we could come in and ask her some questions about a very important matter." He took off his hat and then walked inside, slightly dipping his head underneath the door frame. The other two followed him.

Mirielle shuffled in her red slippers and shut the door after them.

Arnaud translated her words for the others: "She asks us to sit, please, and hopes that nothing is wrong." He continued to translate for them …

Mirielle said that her great niece had been busy and would be shutting up the bookshop next door soon for lunch, and that they would lunch together. She told Arnaud that they sometimes went out for lunch, and that even at her old age, she was still fit enough to manage the numerous steps. She joked about how it wasn't often that three handsome (beau) men turned up unexpectedly at her front door. Then she said that she felt a little unnerved to see a gendarme at her door and asked what was so urgent. Arnaud reassured her that everything was fine, but they wanted her help with something.

Randolph and Timothy took a seat on the velvet, two-seated sofa, which was covered with numerous bright-coloured cushions. Arnaud sat on a matching armchair, with Mirielle seated on the other. A white shiny coffee table sat between them on a fluffy white shag rug. A few magazines were stacked on the coffee table, with the novel, *Moby Dick*, by Herman Melville on top, face down and open. The blue hardback in French, with its golden lettering looked old and worn. Mirielle explained to Arnaud that it was one of her favourite books. She has read it before but was in the mood for reading it again. Her great niece, Margarita, had taken over the bookshop next door and lived above it with her black cat.

Getting on for six years now, Mirielle had been enjoying reading more and was getting through a lot of books — she said with a grin. She explained that she was close to her great niece, and that she never had the privilege of marriage and her own children, but she was more than happy in life.

Mirielle then sat forward and asked what the three needed help with. She was more than happy to assist, if she could.

Arnaud and the others looked at one another. They weren't quite sure where to begin. Randolph asked Arnaud to tell Mirielle exactly what had been discovered in the cave in France. The more she knew, the more she might be able to help. After all, it wasn't just about finding Natalie now, it was about finding a serial killer.

Arnaud proceeded to explain in French the reason for their visit …

Mirielle listened to what Arnaud had to say. She looked shocked as the story unfolded.

Arnaud then relayed to the others what Mirielle told him. She waited patiently for Arnaud to finish telling the others: "She says that it doesn't come as a complete surprise. She had lived in Oradour-sur-Glane her whole life, oui. She was born in April, 1865. She had moved to Mont-Saint-Michel in April, 1944, to care for her younger sister, Ana, who was sick. Ana sadly passed away two years later. Ana had lost her husband during the war only a few years before. Mirielle had moved just two months before the SS destroyed the village and massacred innocent civilians and children — some of whom had been her friends and neighbours. She had heard about the tragedy from newspapers and from other friends in the area.

"She isn't surprised by what was discovered by the archaeological team, non. She had heard stories herself growing up, of how some of the fields surrounding the area were believed to be cursed or to be what she describes as a place of power. Many people didn't like venturing too far out there, oui. She had heard stories of witches who performed rituals out there. As a young girl, she was certain that she could sometimes hear witches chanting out there in the dark, or cackling with laughter, although her parents assured her that there were no more witches and that the witch trials had ended centuries ago …"

Mirielle gave a chilled shudder.

Arnaud passed on more of what Mirielle knew: "Although it was never confirmed, Mirielle's great grandmother was rumoured to have been a white witch who practiced magic for altruistic purposes. Mirielle also heard stories of witches down the centuries being burnt at the stake in the area. Whether they were witches or not, some were placed in metal cages and burnt alive along with their cats. She believes that it is a strong possibility that their spirits still haunt the land there today, oui."

"What of this orphanage? Does she know anything about that?" asked Randolph, starting to feel uneasy, the more Mirielle told them.

Arnaud asked Mirielle of this orphanage … "Oui. She saw it for herself but from a distance."

"Really?" Randolph sat forward, eagerly awaiting Arnaud's translations.

"Oui, Monsieur Landon. She saw it a few times out there in the middle of nowhere. She says it was built sometime in the early 1930s. She thought it was a strange place to have such a building. Especially for an orphanage and the dark history of the area. There was something strange about the married couple who ran it. Regardless, she is still shocked to hear about this cave and the skeletons."

"What? Did she know them?" Timothy asked, more than intrigued.

"She knew of them, oui … The couple couldn't have children of their own, which was why they started the orphanage. For the first few years they seemed like a normal couple. They used to walk through the village with some of the children sometimes. Mirielle said that she would sometimes chat to them and the children, just as the other residents would. The children would change, as some were found homes and new children arrived." Arnaud asked Mirielle if she knew the couple's name and she responded without hesitation.

"Michael Perkins — a British surgeon, and his French wife, Gertrude. It was around the mid-1930s when Mirielle and the villagers first saw them. The couple were believed to have been in their late forties. After a few years, the village saw less of the couple and children."

Randolph was taking notes. He asked Arnaud to ask Mirielle about where the children came from and how old they were on average, and how many there usually were.

Arnaud waited patiently for Mirielle to continue … "Mirielle says that in general, the children could be between two and twelve, but rarely older. She doesn't know where they came from, non. Michael and Gertrude must have taken them in when the parents had died, perhaps? The numbers varied at times. But at most, it was likely less than twenty children."

Mirielle shrugged and began speaking again …

"From the early 1940s and up until when she moved from Oradour-sur-Glane in 1944, there were no new arrivals, except one, and the same group of children had remained there for a good few years at least. It seemed that they couldn't find homes for them, non. The numbers were less and there were around six or seven of them — including the latest arrival, though Mirielle isn't completely sure. Although her memory is still pretty good, it isn't perfect." Arnaud and Mirielle smiled as did the other two in response …

"Mirielle says that the new child arrived in maybe 1942 or 1943. He was a little boy aged between five and seven, who appeared a little different to the other children. He used to walk behind the group, dragging his feet, with his head constantly bent down. He used to wear a black hat that was pulled down over the left side of his face, covering it up."

Randolph thought about a possible connection between the hooded suspected killer and the child with a hat. He didn't say anything for now.

"Despite seeing less of them, Mirielle states that the couple began to act more aloof from around that time — the children, too. The children became absentminded and walked through the village like they weren't there, just staring into blankness. They rarely said anything to the villagers and Michael and Gertrude started to behave the same way, oui. They became less friendly as though there was some kind of 'darkness' behind their eyes. Gertrude had been quite friendly for the first few years, although she would sometimes complain to Mirielle that her back and body ached.

"As time passed, Gertrude aged rapidly. She struggled to walk, with her back arching over. Her face became gaunt and pale and her hair greyer. She started to walk with an old and strange-looking, withered cane, wincing in pain." Arnaud cleared his throat after continuing. He tried not to leave anything out in his translation, no matter how small it may be, but it was hard work.

Timothy and the note-taking Randolph sat listening intently.

"Were there any suspicions about the couple who ran the orphanage? Or about the orphanage in general — was anything strange reported?" Randolph stopped writing, flexing his right hand …

"There was one other thing," Arnaud translated. "Mirielle recalls that there was someone who she used to know, who she bumped into occasionally in Limoges. They had heard rumours that Gertrude was a witch and that she had started dabbling in the dark arts, oui. The woman had passed away, about two months before Mirielle moved to Mont-Saint-Michel … The woman was found in her bed one morning by her husband; her neck and limbs were broken and twisted in an unnatural manner. The cause of death was believed to have been a violent seizure in her sleep."

"Interesting." Randolph added to his notes.

"Mirielle hadn't heard of any other witch rumours, but this woman had told her that Gertrude had started worshipping The Devil himself. She had never said where these rumours had come from."

"Did anyone contact the police or gendarmerie? Did anyone go inside the orphanage itself?" Timothy asked.

"Let me ask, oui … Non, Monsieur Andrews. People who knew the orphanage had either moved or passed away. In fact, most were killed during the massacre at the hands of the SS in Oradour-sur-Glane. Only a few managed to escape from what Mirielle was able to learn afterwards."

"That would explain the lack of confirmed reports of the orphanage," replied Randolph.

Timothy nodded.

"Mirielle states too, that no one that she knew of contacted the gendarmerie. There was no need to and no one from the village had been inside the orphanage. People didn't like going out there anyway, because of the stories of witchcraft."

"I think it's time we showed her the bracelet, Arnaud," Randolph suggested.

"Oui, Monsieur Landon."

The three sat there in anticipation. Arnaud undid the buckle on his black satchel and took out the worn braided bracelet. He handed it to Mirielle and asked if she had made it.

Mirielle put on her glasses to examine it more thoroughly. Her eyes widened. She seemed to recognise it instantly. "*Mon Dieu*. Petite Isabelle." Mirielle's old blue eyes filled with tears.

Arnaud asked softly if Mirielle was okay. He explained that someone in Limoges had told them that she made such items. He swallowed as Mirielle explained … "She says that the bracelet is indeed hers, oui. Or rather it belonged to a little girl who lived in the village, named Isabelle. She was only four years old at the time Mirielle moved to Saint-Mont-Michel. She was the only child of Lucas and Fayette. They had only moved to Oradour-sur-Glane the previous summer. Lucas had fought in the war but his service came to an end early, after he was injured in his right leg, causing a permanent limp."

Mirielle apologised in French and she dabbed her eyes with a clean white handkerchief from her cardigan pocket.

Arnaud continued to translate, "Mirielle would sometimes make such bracelets and beaded necklaces for the young children to wear. She had even made some for the children of the orphanage early on, oui."

Mirielle recognised this particular bracelet and was quick to point out how a section of thread was a little lighter. It was the only time she had run out of thread and had used a different colour. She had given this bracelet to Isabelle.

"Mirielle says that she remembers little Isabelle vividly, oui. Like all the children, they were grateful for their bracelets, but Isabelle was her favourite. With her dark hair and blue eyes, she was such an innocent child, and she would chat to Mirielle. Mirielle even looked after her sometimes, if her parents needed her to. She remembers how upset Isabelle was when Mirielle moved. Mirielle was sad, too ..." Arnaud felt emotional himself, having to relay what Mirielle told him.

Mirielle wiped away a tear.

"The morning that Mirielle moved was the last time she saw Isabelle and the young girl's parents, or any of her friends from the village again. She was due to visit them all in the summer, but of course, the Germans arrived. Forgive me, I am sorry." Arnaud found it hard to continue the last part. He fought back tears himself. He thought of his own wife and two children, along with what had happened that tragic and awful day in Oradour-sur-Glane. It was one of the most horrific accounts of World War Two that involved the unnecessary killings of innocent civilians and children.

"It's okay, Arnaud." Like Timothy, Randolph also felt saddened. He gave a sympathetic half-smile to Arnaud and Mirielle.

Mirielle composed herself and spoke again ...

Arnaud continued, "She thought that little Isabelle had died that day in Oradour-sur-Glane, along with the others, oui. Most of the village were killed and only few survived. The women and children were locked inside the church. The SS threw grenades through the windows. Anyone who tried to escape was shot. Barns and buildings were burnt and set ablaze. The men were led to barns and shot by machine guns. Those who tried to escape were shot. A survivor had passed on that the SS shot the victims in their legs so that they couldn't get away. They even doused them in fuel. The village was burnt to the ground, but not before it was looted and ransacked."

"Bastards," Randolph muttered in reference to the SS. He fought back tears at the horror. What those poor people and children must have gone through, the sheer fear and terror of it all.

Mirielle said that although she was glad to have escaped that horrendous day by moving, she still felt guilty that she had survived and that so many didn't.

Arnaud said a few consoling words that Mirielle appreciated.

Mirielle then went on to question how little Isabelle's bracelet had somehow found its way underground and into the floor of the cave. She could only presume that Isabelle had somehow escaped the events of that day in Oradour-sur-Glane, and was perhaps taken in by Michael and Gertrude. She said how more saddened she felt, that Isabelle may have been fortunate enough to escape the Germans, only to then find herself in the hands of this couple who ran the orphanage, and die in the cave with the other poor children. The conversation was opening up old wounds for the centenarian.

Arnaud asked Randolph and Timothy if he should tell Mirelle about the linked killings in London, but Randolph said there was no need. Mirielle was upset enough as it was. Although Mirielle had helped them as much as she could, they were still no closer to finding Natalie or the London murderer.

Although bitter sweet, Mirielle asked if she could keep Isabelle's bracelet. Arnaud checked with Randolph and they agreed that it would be fine. It was the least that they could do. Arnaud gave Mirielle his phone number, in case she thought of anything else, and took Mirielle's wrinkly hand in his and kissed it. They all thanked her and promised to be in touch if they could tell her any more about what had happened to Isabelle.

Arnaud insisted on them seeing themselves out. Exiting the house, a blonde-haired woman in her late twenties was holding Mog, the black cat, in her arms.

"Bonjour," the woman said politely but curiously.

Mirielle called out from the hallway for Margarita to come in.

*

Mont-Saint-Michel was a quaint little place with numerous attractions. Other small shops and a couple of inns were tucked away behind the streets and alleyways. The three men ate a late lunch inside one of the cafés and then took a walk around the island before heading back to the hotel. The bells of Saint Pierre Church chimed four o'clock.

"I think that's the last thing Mirielle needed at her age, three men turning up to dredge up a painful past like that," said Timothy, with them making their way up towards the hotel.

"True. At least she helped us to join some of the dots together," replied Randolph, removing his trilby. His head had been perspiring in the warmth of the sun that had broken through fully in the past hour. "I'm wondering whether there's any connection between this hooded person and the child from back then who wore his hat pulled down over one side of his head."

"Shit! Yes. You could be on to something there, Randolph!" Timothy replied.

"I'll definitely inform my superiors of what we have learnt. I'll make sure we run some checks on this couple who ran the orphanage, too, now that we have their names. It can only help, oui?"

"I guess so, Arnaud," Randolph said, though not sounding hopeful.

Walking up the steps into the Hôtel d'Estouteville, they smelt the familiar scent of cigarette smoke.

The owner was sitting behind the desk reading *Le Monde*. She acknowledged the three by smiling and nodding her head. A photo of an inverted pentagram on the front page caught Randolph's eye. The headline read:

UN QUATRIÉME CORPS RETROUVÉ LORS D'UN MEURTRE RITUEL À LONDRES!!

It seemed that the French news was now covering the serial killings in England's capital. It reminded Randolph that he needed to speak with DCS Quincy again as soon as possible.

"I'm going to speak to my superiors in my room, oui," Arnaud informed the others.

"Okay, Arnaud. I'm going to try and do some paperwork for a bit, although it's hard to take my mind off all of this." Timothy shook his head.

Randolph said he would try and phone DCS Quincy back in London.

Randolph was unsuccessful in contacting DCS Quincy and told the receptionist he would call back. Arnaud updated him and Timothy that he had reported the information they had learnt from Mirielle back to the gendarmerie. His colleagues would follow through straight away and speak with the police in Paris.

*

The three men were sat out on the hotel terrace. Timothy and Randolph were smoking.

"I think it would be best for you to return home tomorrow, Randolph. I can arrange a separate flight to get you back to London. Arnaud and I will head back south. I want to check on my villa and speak to the gendarmerie regarding the prints — for what good it will bring. They'll most likely want Claret's fingerprints, too."

"Are you sure? Do you feel safe?"

"I think your work is done for now, Randolph. Now that the police and gendarmerie are working together with the police and detectives in London. We'll have to let them deal with it and hope that they can find the killer and Natalie. I feel bad for getting you involved in all of this. It's not safe for you or your family. We've done everything we can. I'll make sure you are paid well for your services."

"I understand your concerns, Timothy. But it's not about the money. You hired me to find Natalie, and I don't intend to stop until I've found her."

Timothy smiled at Randolph. He admired his determination and tenaciousness even more. "I know, mate. If it wasn't for you, we wouldn't have found the bracelet and Mirielle. You linked the discovery in France to what has been happening in London. That's *all* down to you."

Randolph appreciated the praise, though he wasn't having any of it, humble as always. "I'm just doing what anyone else would have, Timothy. A lot of it was down to chance, too. Like me coming across the third victim and Claret and you hiring me afterwards. I just can't help feel that I can or should have done more."

"You're too hard on yourself, Randolph. It was your reputation and skills that got Claret to use your services to begin with. Besides, most people would have quit a long time ago with what you've encountered."

"I guess I'm just persistent," Randolph said.

Timothy laughed. "That you are. It's a virtue and a great quality to have in any walk of life. I know as well as anyone. I've had to work and push hard for things, despite my more than fortunate upbringing."

*

As it was a warm and pleasant night, Randolph and Arnaud went for a walk before bed, after Timothy had turned in. Most of the island was now asleep. Only a few lights remained inside the homes for those up late. The Waxing Gibbous Moon was almost full, reflecting and shimmering slightly across the water of the English Channel. The island and ramparts were now at a higher tide, with half the road now being submerged by water. There was no way in or out on land by foot nor car. It certainly felt surreal and not something that Randolph and Arnaud had ever experienced before. It felt a little too isolated and somewhat creepy.

"This island is certainly unique, oui?" Arnaud said, leaning with his arms over the old stone ramparts, looking out across the moonlit water.

"It certainly is, Arnaud," Randolph replied.

"Do you think we'll ever find this killer?" Arnaud stood upright and looked at Randolph.

A few moths flew around a nearby streetlamp, catching Randolph's attention briefly. He exhaled from his nostrils. "I honestly don't know, Arnaud. I suppose there's a stronger possibility that we may now, as the British and French police are combining their efforts. I'll tell everything further to the detective in charge in London tomorrow, when I get back. Although Timothy no longer wants me to continue on the case, I still want to find Natalie, although it's like finding a needle in a haystack."

"I share your frustrations, Monsieur Landon. Oui, I do. Very much so. Let us return to the hotel. The air has become much cooler. We should sleep. It has been a long day."

Randolph yawned and followed Arnaud's lead. He then happened to look back and stopped on the spot. Something had caught his attention.

Arnaud had started talking again but Randolph wasn't paying any attention.

"Monsieur Landon. What is it?"

"Do you see that, Arnaud?" Randolph asked quietly. He had his eyes focused on one of the rampart turrets a little further away.

"See what?" Arnaud asked confused.

"It seems to have gone. There was someone standing there near to the turret looking out across the water. They turned and started to walk along the rampart."

Arnaud frowned and stared hard for a few seconds. "Non. I don't see anything."

"There! Tell me you see that?"

This time, Arnaud did see something. "I, I do, oui."

A shadowy figure that seemed to flicker and dim in the low lighting appeared to walk along the ramparts. Whoever it was stopped and looked out across the water.

Arnaud muttered something in French and then asked, "What *is* that?"

"I don't know," Randolph whispered back.

The ghostly figure walked back to the turret. Once more, it looked out across the vast waters, just as a passing cloud blocked out the moonlight. Once the moon reappeared, the mysterious figure had gone.

Randolph remembered what the owner at the hotel had said about

Louis d'Estouteville's spirit keeping watch over the island and reminded Arnaud. They wondered if this was what they had seen and that the tale was true.

Back at the hotel, the old receptionist was fast asleep behind the desk on her chair. She was snoring loudly with her mouth open and head tilted back. Randolph and Arnaud couldn't help but snigger when the woman snorted, twitching her face, no doubt dreaming.

After saying goodnight to one another, they went to their rooms.

Stripping down to his vest and boxer shorts ready for bed, Randolph went to close the window. It was approaching midnight. Closing the window, he was alerted to a sound from the old abbey, which had a faint orange glow cast from the outside lights. He could hear the soft yet pleasant sound of what sounded like monks chanting. The taxi driver had told them that no monks were currently living up at the abbey, but that the old place was haunted and the spirits of deceased monks could sometimes be heard.

Chapter Twenty-Two
Thursday, June 2nd, 1966

Mont-Saint-Michel, Normandy – 8.19 am

Before checking out that morning, Arnaud and Randolph mentioned their sighting of the ghostly figure on the ramparts to Timothy. Randolph recounted how he also heard some chanting from up in the abbey. Neither of the other two had heard anything.

Timothy insisted on covering the hotel costs. They then thanked the owner for their brief stay. She said that she was grateful for their custom and wished them well.

Timothy had already organised the travel arrangements the night before. He would return briefly to Verneuil-sur-Vienne and meet Randolph in London the next day to conclude on the case. Timothy reiterated to Randolph that he believed everything should rest solely now on the police authorities.

The three men didn't fancy any breakfast that morning. They walked straight down to the bottom of the village and through the Porte de l'Avancée to wait for their taxi. The fog was thick and heavy around the island of Mont-Saint-Michel, in spite of the sunny morning.

*

Shaftesbury Avenue, London – 12.46 pm
Local Time

After arriving back in England and home to his flat, Randolph felt a sadness and somewhat lonely. It was no doubt caused by a bit of everything, after spending the week in other people's company and with his mind occupied. The case saddened him, and he felt a failure for not finding Natalie Conners. He felt sad for her, her friends and family and her archaeological team. Although Timothy had indicated his services were no longer needed, he thought that it was possible he could still help. After a bite to eat, he would head on down to Savile Row to seek an audience with DCS Quincy in person. There was much to discuss.

Randolph was unpacking his suitcase in the bedroom, when he heard the phone ring in the living room. He went to pick up the receiver. "Hello?"

As expected, no answer came. Nothing but silence and the slight sound of somebody breathing at the other end.

"Hello …? What the hell do you want? I'm tired of this. *Say* something!" Randolph could feel whoever it was grinning to themselves on the other end of the call. "You don't scare me," Randolph lied.

"I think we both know that is not true, Randolph Landon," a voice replied coldly. "I know who you are. I've been watching you. You are *most* persistent. You've been a busy man."

Randolph's eyes grew large and he felt a chill, hearing this person finally speak. Randolph couldn't detect what accent the voice was. "What do you want? Are you behind the killings and the disappearance of Natalie Connors?" Randolph's pulse began to race. "Where is she?" Randolph's questions sounded silly to him. The murderer was unlikely to give him answers.

"You won't stop me from achieving my mission — my assignment. For now, you have been spared. However, if you don't stop now, you will have forced my hand, Randolph Landon. Take *this* as your final warning."

"Are you behind the killings in London? What about that cave in France?" Randolph said in a fluster.

The call ended.

Breathing heavily and still holding the receiver to his ear, Randolph stood frozen on the spot. Perhaps it was just as well that Timothy had ended the case. He slowly put the receiver back down. Why was he being targeted and no one else? Why not DCS Quincy or one of his team? But then, they hadn't linked the French discovery to the London killings. If it wasn't for Randolph, there'd still be no connection; maybe that was why.

Randolph took out a bottle of whisky. He gulped some down without bothering with a glass. It burnt his throat and he coughed, which made his eyes water. He considered necking another swig, but thought better of it. What good would that do? He needed to speak to DCS Quincy, *now*. In spite of the 'final' warning, Randolph rushed downstairs and outside to his car.

*

Randolph approached the front desk of the West End Central Police Station. "I need to speak with DCS Quincy — it's urgent!" he said frantically and a little out of breath.

"I'm sorry. He's currently out of office on pressing business. Is there anything I can help with, or anyone else? Or you can leave a message?" The male receptionist stood with a concerned look on his face.

Randolph paused, trying to catch his breath. "It's about the killings. He knows who I am. I've been helping him with the case."

The receptionist looked dubious. "Helping how? This is a police matter."

"I'm a private investigator. My name is Randolph Landon. I need to speak with him. When is he back?"

"I honestly can't say, Mr Landon. You're more than welcome to wait for him, or I can get him to contact you?"

Before Randolph could answer, DCS Quincy and DCI Sommers walked in, quietly in conversation with each other. DCS Quincy held an old brown envelope in his right hand. They were both dressed smartly in their trench coats and fedoras.

"DCS Quincy — we must talk." Randolph waited until the DCS and his associate were close.

"Mr Landon. It's a pleasure to see you again." DCS Quincy smiled.

"It's about the case. There's more to tell you." Randolph kept his voice down. "I've had a phone call from the killer. They spoke to me this time."

DCS Quincy's smile disappeared from his face. He looked at DCI Sommers. "We've just made some discoveries as well. Let's chat in my office."

The receptionist watched as the three made their way into DCS Quincy's office.

DCS Quincy listened intently to everything Randolph disclosed to him and his colleague. DCI Sommers took notes. Randolph told of his visit to Mont-Saint-Michel in search of Mirielle Blanchet and the names of Michael and Gertrude Perkins, along with the connection of the murders being linked to the year of 1966; 6th day of the 6th month — *666*.

The seated DCS Quincy sighed again and rubbed his fresh shaven face with the palms of his hands. "You aren't the only one to make that possible connection, Randolph. A professor who teaches at the University of Oxford, has been trying to help us, pretty much from the start, with expertise in witchcraft and occult beliefs — things like that."

DCI Sommers with his short blonde hair, stopped writing for now. He sat stone-faced, legs crossed, next to Randolph, at the opposite side of the large desk to DCS Quincy.

"What else did this professor have to say? I take it you told him about the cave in France?"

"Yes, Randolph." DCS Quincy smiled. "It's only theories, of course. He thinks that it's possible that the killer believes that The Devil himself is ordering them to carry out these horrendous murders. The reason the killings are taking place where they do, only the killer would know. It could be down to numerous things, such as London ley lines, points or places of power, perhaps previous witches' 'hotspots,' or covens, dating back down the centuries, places where witches gathered and practiced their magic and witchcraft or meetings, called Sabbaths, that were held at midnight. There may be links to certain moon phases ... I told Professor Albert in confidence about how our murders are all no doubt linked to what was found in France and the cauldron you mentioned. It's thanks to you, Randolph, that we've been able to connect the two cases."

"I was only doing my job. It was just bad luck really and a damn strange coincidence that I got involved in all of this. And others just haven't perhaps, fallen in. Either way, it still hasn't solved anything."

"We'll run a search on the names of this couple who ran the orphanage. We'll also update the French police and gendarmerie, although no doubt Arnaud will have done this already. We now feel a little more confident about catching our killer. And we believe fully now, that it is just the one." DCS Quincy gave a knowing glance across to DCI Sommers.

Randolph could tell that the two were on to something. He frowned. "You've found out something else, haven't you?"

DCS Quincy sighed. "Normally, it would be against police policy to disclose this to you, but you have proven your worth again, Randolph. I don't have any issues telling you. Earlier, a woman gave us much needed information. Although we're still not there yet, we now have a name, also."

"What? Who was this woman?" Randolph asked, looking at DCS Quincy and then to DCI Sommers.

"The English woman is called Yvonne Harrison. She has only just come back from visiting her brother and his family in America. She and her husband had been gone for two months. She wasn't aware of the murders or what had been happening here in London, until she received a letter. She was shocked, when she read about it all. She contacted me almost straight away and drove down from Northampton to London, this morning. She was also familiar with parts of the murderer's MO."

"She used to work at an orphanage on the outskirts of Châteauroux, in central France," DCI Sommers said, taking over.

"I've heard of the place. We passed through it during the war," Randolph replied. "What of this letter?"

DCS Quincy took out a large piece of paper from the brown envelope. "If you can bear with us, please, Randolph. Yvonne was kind enough to write down what she knew in advance for us. The period was from 1946 to 1952. Yvonne was married to a Frenchman at the time. He passed away in 1951 and she has since remarried an Englishman in Northampton … A young boy was brought to the orphanage in July, 1946. He was malnourished, thin, dehydrated and dirty. He hadn't eaten anything substantial — if at all for weeks. He was found walking the surrounding countryside aimlessly. No one knew where he came from nor his background. He rarely spoke and was mute."

"During the war and afterwards, the orphanage took in many children who had lost their parents and family members. It was most tragic. Some children who had been separated were reunited with their biological parents or families, those that were more fortunate. This particular boy was different. Some poked fun at him because of his appearance and because he couldn't speak much. We all know how mean and cruel children can be." DCI Sommers uncrossed his legs briefly.

"Some of the children called him a freak, odd, or *bête curieuse* — a curious beast. He always wore a hat, even indoors, covering his head and face. The other children used to laugh and pull his hat away, poking fun at him. The staff felt it was best if this boy was placed in a room by himself, away from the other children." DCS Quincy cleared his throat.

"What was wrong with the way that he looked?" Randolph asked.

"He was born with a rare form of what they believe was hemifacial microsomia of some sort. It's a congenital disorder that affects the face. For this young boy, it affected the left side of his face. He only had one fully working eye — his right one. His nose was a little skewed and the top of his face and head bulged out somewhat. It was never confirmed, but the orphanage believed his parents may have burned his face, either out of spite for looking the way he did, or because they believed it would treat his afflictions. He had scar tissue on his undeveloped side," DCS Quincy explained solemnly.

"Dear God! The poor child," Randolph responded. "And this who you believe to be the killer? I guess it matches with what Mirielle told us in Mont-Saint-Michel. There was a young boy who appeared different to the others, who wore a hat pulled down over his face."

"Yes, Randolph. There are still many questions to be resolved, of course," DCS Quincy replied.

"Why was the boy not with the skeletons in the cave? Did he leave that other orphanage before? Why was he wandering around by himself out there? Did he escape the previous orphanage? Did he ever speak at all? He's now a grown man … doing these killings. Wearing this hooded jacket to still cover his face. It's hard to have sympathy for him as a child, when he's now doing this as an adult." Randolph shook his head. "You say you have a name?"

"Indeed. So many burning questions needing answers," DCI Sommers said. "And yes, we do. *François Griffiths*. Some children were reunited with their parents, others found new families, but no one came for François for a good number of years. He was perhaps not easily accepted because of the way he looked and acted. In time, he began to speak a little more, in French. The staff at the orphanage believed he'd suffered and been through physical and emotional trauma, to become the way he was. He had told them his date of birth and first name, just not his family name nor where he came from."

"After a while at the orphanage, his behaviour grew worse." DCS Quincy took out a cigarette and offered one to Randolph, who accepted. "Sometimes, he would just sit there staring blankly into space, with a disturbed smile on his face. He was never violent with any of the adults at the orphanage, or the other children, in spite of the insults and mockery aimed at him. But he never befriended any of the other children either, and became isolated."

"Passive aggressiveness," Randolph replied, allowing DCS Quincy to light his cigarette.

The other two nodded.

"He started to twist and break toys, figures and dolls, biting them, too — all with a sinister stare and expression on his face. He possessed quite some strength for a boy his age, too. Yvonne told us that the other children stopped taking the mickey after a while as they became frightened of him. Fear also began to sweep through the staff there. They tried to find another orphanage for him — no one would take him in. He would sometimes sit by himself, making strange noises, grinning and muttering to himself." DCS Quincy flicked some ash into an ashtray on his desk, next to a small, framed photo of his wife and two grown-up daughters.

"They had even brought in psychiatrists. Even *they* were put off trying to speak to him and learn about his history. No one got anything out of him. No one knew his background," DCI Sommers stated. "The orphanage thought it would be best to have him sectioned in a mental institute for children. However, François' psychiatrists felt it would be better for him to stay where he was, around 'normal' children and a more 'normal' environment. He was having regular psychiatrist consultations at the orphanage, so being in an institution wouldn't be so different."

"Shit … You said something about a letter and the MO?" Randolph used the ashtray for himself.

"That's right … Things became worse after a few years. In 1952, they managed to find a home for François — I'll get to that," DCS Quincy replied, flicking more ash into the ashtray. "He started to get these unexpected seizures from time to time. He used to sit in his room and draw strange yet perfect symbols on the walls in crayon."

"Like a perfectly drawn inverted pentagram?" Randolph guessed.

"Exactly," DCS Quincy answered. "Things rose to a head one Sunday afternoon in early March, 1952. François was born on June 6th, 1936."

"Sweet Jesus." Randolph swallowed.

"Aged fifteen — a few months before his sixteenth birthday, he and a few other younger children were outside on the grass. There were six of them, including François. The other five children were sitting around François — who was sat in the middle of them, wearing a hat. They were all joining hands, except for François. They all had their eyes closed and François appeared to be muttering something quietly. Yvonne had gone to fetch another lady who worked there, after she had caught sight of them and watched them for a little while.

"When Yvonne returned with her colleague, the five children were passing a bowl around and drinking from it, including François, who drank last. Growing concerned, Yvonne and her colleague rushed over. François was sat holding the bowl. It had strange symbols drawn on it and his one eye was flickering. He was muttering words that neither of them could understand. It was like he was in a trance. The other five children were all looking blankly at François in the middle." DCS Quincy cleared his throat.

"God. Were they drinking blood?" Randolph guessed again.

"You are correct, Randolph," DCS Quincy replied. "The five children and François, had cuts on their left palms. A strange knife lay next to François. The staff at the orphanage had no idea where it had come from. The children had no doubt collected blood from one another, combining it into the bowl to drink. The children got up and acted as if nothing had happened.

"François' eye, then returned to normal and he stopped muttering in this strange language. He sat there with this evil and satisfied grin, which frightened Yvonne and the other lady. The staff confiscated the knife without any fuss from François and bandaged up all the children's wounds. Thankfully, the cuts weren't deep. François wouldn't answer any of their questions. When the other five children were also pressed on what had happened, they were blasé about it all, stating that they were just playing a game and didn't remember much of it, anyway."

"The children involved in this suspected 'blood pact,' left the orphanage in the weeks that followed … And here's the real *kicker*, Mr Landon," DCI Sommers said. "The other five children were born on the 6th day of June, albeit in different years. *They* were the four grown victims found around London with their throats slit and their hearts removed …"

Randolph's eyes grew large. "My God. How? I know that this victim named Christophe was half-French, but weren't the others English? If it was a French orphanage, why British surnames?"

DCS Quincy sighed, holding his cigarette. He turned the paper with Yvonne's notes on over. "It's so complex, isn't it? So unbelievable and strange — yet real. We knew of the potential Châteauroux orphanage link after the second victim, but we wanted to wait for confirmation after the latest killing. It's why I didn't mention it to you when we last spoke, Randolph. To sum up and trying to keep it brief, Sheila Davies — the first victim, was born to French parents. She was born Sheila Lavigne. She had lost both parents during the war. She was ten when she left the orphanage near Châteauroux in April of 1952. She was adopted by an English couple, who lived in France at the time. They moved back to England a year later. They lived in East London.

"Out of love for her adopted parents, Sheila changed her surname to Davies. Lavigne then became her middle name. She was also a single child from her French parents. She had a younger brother and younger sister through her adopted parents."

"Shit." Randolph shook his head. "The poor family — all of the victims."

"Christophe Livingston was born to a French mother and an English father. A single child who lost both parents, he was taken in at the orphanage. He was adopted by a French couple in April, 1952, also. When he was nineteen, he moved to England and that's when he met his wife and became a father. He still kept his birth surname.

"As for Reece Brixton, his situation was a little different and perhaps peculiar; he had been on holiday in France with his parents and brothers in March, 1952. He was joined by their cousins and aunt and uncle. The aunt, was French. Reece had ended up in the orphanage for a very short time. The Brixtons were staying in the commune of Luant for a week or so. They had visited Châteauroux. Reece, his brothers and a couple of his cousins — who were older than he was, had wandered off with the parents' permission. Reece got separated and was found by a couple of the locals and then taken to the gendarmerie.

"The upset nine-year-old Reece couldn't remember the name of the place where they were all staying, which was understandable. The gendarmerie couldn't locate his family in Châteauroux, so he ended up temporarily at the orphanage. He was soon reunited with his family, but the orphanage had some explaining to do, in regards to Reece's cut hand!" DCS Quincy said in detail.

"God. Talk about unfortunate," Randolph said, shaking his head. "Only being there very briefly and getting involved with this François boy. What are the chances of that and his birthday matching the others?"

"We know," DCI Sommers said solemnly.

"Jennifer Grantham ended up in care at the orphanage in 1951. Living in France and not too far from Châteauroux, her parents had fallen on hard times. Her mother was French and her father was English. Sadly, she was physically abused, and was taken away from her abusive parents," DCS Quincy said. "Yvonne remembers well.

She said that the parents weren't even bothered that Jennifer was taken away from them."

"Bastards. There are so many people out there who don't deserve children. It adds insult to the kind and genuine couples that can't have children of their own," Randolph replied.

"Totally!" DCI Sommers said.

"Anyhow, Jennifer was found a new home a year later. She was born Jennifer Nelson. Her new parents used the adopted father's family name of Grantham. He was English and his wife was half-French and half-English. They moved with Jennifer from France to outside London in 1954. She was their only child."

"I guess now, it makes sense somewhat, how the killer — François, was targeting these victims and obviously knew of them from his childhood and how they ended up in England … Just what was, *is*, his motive? Had he been stalking them? He's waited what, like fourteen years to commit these murders? Why now? There are still so many questions … Did François, eventually find a home, yes? And how does this Yvonne know that François is the killer for sure, responsible for these murders?" Randolph frowned.

DCS Quincy answered, "July of 1952, a married and devout Christian couple visited François at the orphanage. They were both pious and in their fifties. They couldn't have children of their own. One of the psychiatrists helping François knew of this married couple who lived in Chinon — which is about a two hours' drive away from Châteauroux. Their names were Vernon and Penelope Griffiths. Vernon was an Englishman and Penelope was American.

"Vernon was a fighter pilot for the RAF during the war. Funnily enough, I actually knew him. I met him myself in France a couple of times. He was well respected and a kind and polite man. Penelope was a map maker or cartographer. She was known as a 'Millie the Mapper' during the war, helping develop maps for battle and drafting topographic maps. With their religious beliefs and optimism, they fully believed that they could help François with his issues." DCS Quincy cleared his throat.

"Help him how? Jesus! They must have been brave. I take it this couple were told of his sinister behaviour? Why would they decide to help him?"

DCS Quincy explained further, "They were told everything, Randolph. They generally believed that they could help the teen and sensed good in him. He seemed to open up a little to the couple. Yvonne says that after three meetings, they had a trial period. François would stay with the Griffiths in Chinon for a little while, to 'test the waters.' Although Yvonne feared for the married couple, she, along with the others, were glad that François had finally been removed from the orphanage. It then became permanent after a month.

"Surprisingly, François' behaviour and mannerisms improved — particularly in time. He began to speak more. Vernon and Penelope taught him how to read and write in English, although his speaking and writing skills were still poor in French. Yvonne and her colleagues from the orphanage were pleasantly surprised when they visited François in his new home in Chinon. He seemed like a normal teenager, with the exception of his facial appearance."

"How did Vernon and Penelope help him exactly?"

"Perseverance, Randolph. They were kind and taught him their religious beliefs, even taking him to church. He never fought or became aggressive towards them. They home-schooled him because of his appearance. François never got over the way he looked. He still wouldn't leave the house or go anywhere without a hat or hood covering his face. He still had no friends and was a recluse. He would only venture out if Vernon or Penelope was with him."

"So, there were no more seizures or sinister behaviour? No strange symbols drawn anywhere?" Randolph asked.

"Not that Yvonne or the other staff were aware of. François was still a quiet and disturbed young man, but he had improved. The Griffiths never found out where he came from, though they still loved him like their own. He grew up to be a strong man physically and to be very intelligent. He could understand and make maps, thanks to Penelope's teaching. He even learnt how to fly, thanks to Vernon — although François never gained an official licence. Still, they were proud of him."

"Shit. What happened in the end? I assume that something bad happened, if this now grown-up François is our killer. Presumably the story doesn't have a happy ending with the Griffiths?"

DCS Quincy looked briefly at the still cross-legged, serious DCI

Sommers. He then looked down at the sheet of paper in front of him, before speaking again. "The three of them moved to England in 1963, when François was twenty-six years old. They had lived in Maidstone together. They had even got a pet dog, a German Shepherd named Rex. Vernon and Penelope had bought a house, on land which had been used as an RAF aerodrome. The listed building of the boxy control tower had been transformed into a house. Vernon taught flying lessons there. Penelope was semi-retired from her map making."

"I'm dreading what you're about to say next. It's clear something happened, because you're still talking in a past tense," Randolph said.

DCS Quincy sighed. "Here …" He pulled out a letter from the envelope, giving it to Randolph to read. "This is a letter dated two weeks back — written by Penelope. Yvonne only opened it yesterday evening, returning home from America. Occasionally, Yvonne and Penelope would send letters to one another to keep in touch. Or sometimes speak via telephone. The orphanage at Châteauroux no longer exists: it closed in 1960. The records are still held somewhere of all the children. Yvonne still has some of them, too."

Randolph swallowed. He squashed what was left of his cigarette into the ashtray, before beginning to read the letter addressed to Yvonne. Randolph believed that Penelope was right-handed, by the way the handwriting was tilted and the way certain strokes were cast.

DCS Quincy and DCI Sommers sat patiently, waiting for Randolph to finish reading the letter:

Peppercorn Aerodrome,
Maidstone,
Kent.

May 18th, 1966.

My Dearest Yvonne,

It has been a while since we were last in contact. I hope that this letter finds you and yours well. I did try phoning you a few times, but there was no answer. Perhaps it's easier to put what I am about to tell you, in writing, anyway.

On the whole, things had been good since we moved here over three years ago — as you are well aware. François' behaviour, attitude and intelligence, continued to improve. Since the start of the year, he also started to speak a little more, too.

However, I now write this letter with much concern. For the past few weeks now, François' behaviour has changed — it is becoming darker. I don't know if 'relapsed' is the word to use? Even Rex seems frightened of him of late, not wanting to be around him. François has become more closed off, locking himself inside his room for hours at a time. We can hear him in there during the day and at night, muttering strange words and laughing to himself. One night last week, I saw what appeared to be a glow of fire underneath the gap of his bedroom door. He has also been 'borrowing' Vernon's plane without asking and with no licence, and flying to who knows where, disappearing for hours at a time, or even days, sometimes with the plane and sometimes without.

François doesn't appear to chat much nowadays. He just grunts and glares darkly at me and Vernon. He even grabbed Vernon by the throat one day, lifting him up with such strength. Vernon had been questioning him about where he was flying off to. We are now fearing for our own well-being, especially after what I found in his room yesterday morning. Under one of the mats in his room, was a perfectly drawn inverted pentagram in blood, which we assume was his own. Some smaller symbols were also drawn nearby, next to it. We found a map he had made himself of a part of London — including Soho, scaled and designed it seems, in a very specific and intelligent way. Three points of interest were marked on it.

It wasn't until Vernon and I spoke, that we realised the possible, chilling connection to the horrific murders in London. As you are also aware, François always folded his clothes at the side of his bed before he slept. We couldn't help but make a link to the murders.

Randolph turned the letter over to read the other side:

Vernon wanted to go to the police, but I insisted on holding off until we could get some answers from François, himself. Vernon, the past few nights, has also been having these awful and lucid dreams, waking up in a cold sweat. He dreams of the two of us being burnt alive. We are scared, Yvonne. François had been fine for years but now he refuses to go to church and just laughs wickedly when we ask.

I am not sure why I am writing this letter to you, Yvonne. I guess I am just frightened in case anything happens to us. I've included a copy of François' map, again, in case something happens to us.

In spite of it all, we still love François like a son. Perhaps by the time that you read this, the police will have already been informed. We have, as always, been praying and keeping our faith in God The Almighty and His begotten Son, Jesus Christ our Saviour.

Take good care, Yvonne. Hopefully we'll hear from you soon,

Penelope

PS. Pray for us!

Randolph swallowed hard, handing back the letter. "Surely there's really no doubt now, that this François is the killer. Him being able to fly would explain how he has been getting to France and back. I take it you've contacted the police in Maidstone, about this?"

"Naturally," DCI Sommers replied seriously. "Unfortunately, the fire brigade were too late."

"Oh, God." Randolph's face was desperate.

"Their home was burnt to a cinder — completely gutted. There was no real clue as to how the fire was started and where. The remains of Vernon and Penelope Griffiths were found in the early hours of May 19th along with the dog — a day after the letter was written.

Penelope had obviously managed to send the letter the day before, the same day as she wrote it. Nothing was recovered." DCS Quincy bowed his head.

Silence fell on the room for a moment.

"We were made aware about a couple who were killed in a fire in Kent. The land was more secluded from the other houses. Some people had eventually seen the fire from afar in the early hours and there were even reports of green and orange flames burning bright. François was never a suspect initially. However, the police in Kent, had already put out a search for him — due to him being missing. They had no clue at the time, on his past and him being linked to the London murders. Just like us, until now.

"There was no sign of Vernon's plane. An alert had already gone out to track the plane at any airports or private airfields here and now obviously, in France. Everything was burnt in the Griffiths' home, but there were still records elsewhere, including the tail number of the Cessna 172 Skyhawk. Their car was left near to the house, unscathed. Neighbours and church friends who knew of the family were most saddened," DCS Quincy said. "That included poor Yvonne. She had tried phoning them upon her return, but the phone wouldn't connect."

"We will run checks on this Michael and Gertrude Perkins, Randolph. Along with everything else. Now that there are more of us looking into all of this, it can only help. Unfortunately, no one really knows what this François looks like. However, we'll now release to the press about him being the main suspect and for everyone to look out for him, wearing a hooded jacket." DCI Sommers uncrossed his legs.

"So, four of the children from that day in 1952 have already died in London, but who is or was, the *fifth* child?" Randolph suddenly realised, feeling the story was unfinished.

"According to Yvonne, it was a nine-year-old girl called Coraline Amar. She was looked after by the orphanage in, let me see ..." DCS Quincy stubbed out his own cigarette and turned the sheet of paper back over to refresh his memory. He brushed away a few dropped ashes from his cigarette from the paper. "In 1952, after Christmas. Her parents had split up in the New Year and were struggling mentally and emotionally. They had placed Coraline into care at the orphanage temporarily, whilst trying to sort themselves out.

"Four months later in May, they worked hard through their difficulties and got back together and found work. They took Coraline out of the orphanage. Yvonne says that the three of them lived in a town called Vierzon, which is about forty miles from Châteauroux. We've already contacted the police and gendarmerie over there. Hopefully Coraline is safe, and she will be looked out for, as she's obviously at high risk."

"This really is so complex," Randolph said.

"You can say that again," DCI Sommers agreed.

"There are a couple of other things ..." DCS Quincy took out another piece of paper from the envelope, handing it across to Randolph.

"What's this?" Randolph frowned, looking at the strange black drawing on a slightly yellow piece of paper. It was drawn in black crayon. Six strange occult symbols were drawn perfectly around the main image. "It looks like a drawing of someone? What are these symbols?"

The black silhouette had been drawn quite well. It seemed to depict a woman, judging by the long shoulder-length hair. Black smudges and swirls seem to cover most of her legs.

"François had drawn it in 1952. It was found a day or so after he had left the orphanage. One of the other ladies who worked there found it underneath his pillow. They had no idea who or what it represented. We have just come back from showing this to Professor Albert. Conveniently, he's in London for a couple of days, doing a lecture at the Queen Mary University of London. It has been a busy and somewhat eventful morning." DCS Quincy shifted in his leather chair.

"He's no idea who it is either. Though he believes that the smudges and swirls are perhaps flames or a fire of some sort. Maybe it's a witch or someone being burnt or rising up through the flames? As for the symbols, he looked up in a couple of his books related to Wiccan and pagan symbols, to confirm what they may mean. The triangle symbol that you see, represents fire. The stick figure with the crescent moon facing to the right on the body, represents the crone. The spiral symbol beginning from the left side, represents rebirth. And the square symbol with an X drawn inside it with a line going down the middle, represents the witch." DCS Quincy pointed respectively to the symbols in question.

Randolph focused on the symbols. He told them that the spiral one that represented rebirth matched ones found on a couple of the items from the surface and cave in France.

"He doesn't know what the other two symbols are. They weren't in any of his books, either. The symbols can be used in different ways with different meanings," DCS Quincy said. "Depending on their knowledge and skills, the symbols can be mixed and used together, even with other religions and cultures. That includes runes as well, Randolph. Runes are either letters or magic symbols."

Randolph gave a serious nod of his head.

"Professor Albert, also believes that the number six is regarded to some, as the perfect number." DCI Sommers cleared his throat, placing a fist to his mouth. "And that those born in a year ending in six, can be the type of person that immerses themselves in the more 'darker' side of life. And/or, someone that thrives for darkness. Also, possessing the capabilities of destroying someone that dares to threaten … And a year that contains sixes or ends in a six, is regarded to be a dark and powerful, meaningful year."

"Another disturbing thing … as François left the orphanage, he grinned and said to Yvonne and the other staff, something along the lines of: "At midnight, when the moon is full, the *fifth* will be done …" The way that he said it, sent chills through the staff."

Randolph looked at DCS Quincy. "You think he was talking about the potential fifth murder? But why randomly say that, when there were four other victims to come first?"

"Possibly because the fifth is key, or the last killing? He was clearly a very disturbed young boy growing into his teens," DCS Quincy said concerned. "From what you told us of the orphanage and cave in France, it's quite likely that he was brought up learning the dark arts there."

"Yes, the orphanage could have been practicing black magic and rituals. I guess we are all products of our environment and upbringing, especially in this case. The mockery that this François had to endure no doubt didn't help matters, either. Regardless, it's no excuse for torturing and murdering others."

DCI Sommers nodded in agreement.

"True, Randolph. There are two types of bad apples in this world; those born or develop that way and those who unfortunately react to misfortune to become that way, although as you say, the latter is no excuse to inflict needless pain and suffering onto others."

"It seems like François has been biding his time. Did he become better whilst living with this religious couple or was it just an act? Maybe the discovery in France triggered something? How does he know certain things, too?"

"We'll perhaps never know for certain," DCI Sommers said. "But rest assured, we are onto him and doing everything in our power to catch him, bring him to justice and get answers. We have to remain positive."

"Like I told Timothy back in France. I've never believed in these sorts of things; witches and dark magic. Maybe I will now!"

"I know how you feel, Randolph. I am open-minded — just like DCI Sommers, here. There must be a rational explanation behind it all, though."

"Timothy Andrews is closing my involvement in the case. He doesn't think there's any more that we can do. He's also worried for my well-being."

DCS Quincy gave a sympathetic half-smile. "That's a smart move, Randolph. You've done more than enough and we're most grateful for your hard work and efforts. I'm sure the French feel the same way. You have shown much courage, too. You have been a great help but leave it to the UK and French authorities now."

"I just hate failing. I set out to find Natalie Conners, and I am genuinely concerned for her. She may still be out there."

"Now that we have a name and are virtually certain that François is behind these killings — and maybe this woman's disappearance too, there really isn't any more that you can do. Just leave it to us, Mr Landon." DCI Sommers placed a hand on Randolph's shoulder.

"You should take the killer's warning and drop it — for your own good. We'll catch him. Hopefully this Coraline will be safe, too."

Randolph sighed. "I guess I have no other choice. However, there is one thing that I would like to look into, with your permission?"

"Which is?" DCS Quincy frowned.

"I'd like to investigate the property where the Griffiths lived. Yes, I know it was like two weeks ago and the police have been through everything, but if you don't mind, I'd like to check for myself, just in case something was missed. After all, I did find that bracelet on the ground in the cave."

"We're actually heading out there this afternoon to meet with the Maidstone DCS. I want to check the area for myself and to meet him in person, although everything has been checked. I guess it wouldn't hurt for you to join us. What do you say, Burt?"

"As you say, it's not going to hurt. We could use an extra pair of eyes, in case something has been missed," DCI Sommers replied.

"Very well." DCS Quincy smiled.

Finally, Randolph looked at the black and white map that François had made. Points had been marked in small dots regarding the first three murdered victims, near to Margaret Street, Upper St Martin's Lane and on Conduit Street. It was unclear whether the markings had been made before or after the killings. The map was drawn in pencil. The streets and roads were blank. In the middle of the map read *Soho*. Randolph asked if it would be okay for him to have a copy of the map so they gave him one; DCI Sommers used the Xerox 813 copying machine. Randolph then carefully added another dot to the map, indicating the fourth and latest murder location, the alleyway off Great Russell Street.

Once done with the two detectives, Randolph returned home to his flat for a quick bite to eat before the journey to Maidstone, in Kent. Thelma rang him shortly before the detectives were due to pick him up outside his flat. Hearing the phone ring, he was concerned at first that it was the killer — François, again.

Thelma wanted to know how Randolph's current case was going and if he was free for them to join him again for the weekend. Only her and Matthew would come down Saturday morning this time, due to Matthew having a sleepover at a friend's tomorrow night. She had tried phoning Randolph a couple of times during the week without luck. Randolph told her he had been in France, working on the case. Although Randolph would love to see his family again, he told Thelma he would call her tomorrow to let her know. Not only was his own life potentially in danger, but he couldn't risk getting his wife and son involved in it all. He would never be able to live with himself if something happened to either of them.

*

Peppercorn Aerodrome, Maidstone – 3.38 pm

Randolph watched DCS Quincy shake hands with the chubby DCS Turner, the man in charge of the detective department in Maidstone.

The four of them had studied the remains of what was left of the converted control tower, which had previously been the home of the Griffiths. The exterior of the building had pretty much remained intact, other than the black and green singe marks over the outside walls. Police cordons surrounded the perimeter. The front of the boxy building had a small balcony at the top to the right, with steps to the roof of the building. Inside however, was a different matter entirely.

The building had five bedrooms all upstairs. The whole inside was burnt out. The police and DCS Turner — along with the fire brigade, were surprised that virtually nothing remained, apart from a few minor items and houseware utilities. Everything had been burnt. The smell of dank soot emanated from the burnt walls and interior. Light drizzle worked its way inside via the gaps in what was left of the roof and burnt-out windows.

DCS Turner had explained that the strange green substance or residue that was most likely flammable, had been found inside and out of the gutted building. It had also been found on what was left of the two bodies and the dog. The three were found in the master bedroom together. The dog was on the floor and the bodies lay in what was left of the double bed. The mysterious substance had been sent for testing. No one knew what it was. They couldn't determine a single ingredient. Whatever it was, it had no doubt caused the green flames that eyewitnesses reported having seen.

DCS Turner had also told them that the bodies hadn't appeared to be bound, although it was possible that any ropes were destroyed in the fire. Randolph had mentioned the poisoning and paralysis of victims in the London killings. He suggested the possibility that Vernon, Penelope and Rex may have tragically been awake throughout the blaze. However, DCS Turner stated that what was left of the bodies, hadn't revealed any black like substance or poison. He reiterated again, that initially, François wasn't necessarily regarded as a suspect and responsible, more that he was just missing.

Randolph had also mentioned the similarities of the supposed burnt down orphanage in France, and how there was no remains of the building itself left. Nothing made any real sense. He remembered Christine showing him items like the toy doll found. He hadn't recalled any burn or black/green singe marks on any of them.

Randolph, standing a short distance away by himself, lit a cigarette.

DCS Turner was saying his goodbyes. He went to his black police car and drove off.

"Any other news?" Randolph asked, when the others joined him.

The drizzle now felt colder than when they had first arrived.

"Nothing as of yet," DCS Quincy replied. "As mentioned, they've put out notices to all the major airports and known private airfields. The French have also been notified. It's only a matter of time before someone sees the plane."

"François can't fly around and hide for ever. Especially when the papers come out about his appearance," DCI Sommers said confidently. "Not unless he's gone to another country."

"At least that's something," Randolph said, feeling less confident. Even if François was caught, Randolph couldn't imagine him confessing to being behind Natalie's disappearance.

"It was good to meet DCS Turner at least, although as expected, there's nothing to find here. Forensics and Turner's team have done everything they can." DCS Quincy looked up at the grey skies and drizzle fell on his face. He pulled down the tip of his grey fedora.

To the left of them, roughly a hundred metres away, a few ravens flew above the treetops of a small woodland area, croaking as they went.

"That could be worth checking out?" Randolph gave a nod of his head in the direction of the woodland.

"We could do, although DCS Turner has already searched the area. As we're here, though, we may as well." DCS Quincy started to walk.

DCI Sommers and Randolph followed behind.

Checking around the area, the three came to the centre of the woodlands where several bright flowers grew. A mixture of sweet scents filled the air around them. Some more flowers grew a little further down, surrounded by some marshy land. The three grimaced when their shoes became wet. They checked the woodlands thoroughly, coming back on the opposite side.

"Doesn't look like there's anything of interest here," Randolph said, almost tripping over a raised mound of grass.

DCS Quincy then stopped. Something had caught his attention.

"What is it?" DCI Sommers asked.

"Hold on ..." DCS Quincy walked further into the marshy part. The cold water rose up past his ankles. He grimaced some more. His black shoes squelched and became stuck in the mud. "This looks like hemlock ..."

Reluctantly and not wanting to get his own shoes and trousers wet, DCI Sommers walked over to join his friend and superior.

DCS Quincy bent down to examine the white flower heads.

Randolph stood back watching.

"I looked up the herbs in a book after hearing about the black tar-like substance that was found injected into the victims. I can smell the musty scent of it. It grows in wet areas or near water ... Don't touch it!" DCS Quincy warned DCI Sommers, whose arm was slowly reaching downwards.

"Maybe it's been grown deliberately out here," Randolph called over.

DCS Quincy assisted DCI Sommers as his right, black Pierre Cardin shoe got stuck in the marsh. Returning from the hemlock, DCS Quincy examined another small area where some herbs were growing, notably basil, rosemary, lavender and thyme. Again, he remembered reading about these herbs — including poisonous ones. As he scanned them all, he noticed wolfsbane, recognising the helmet-shaped purple flower. Careful not to touch it himself, he warned the others to keep their distance.

The other two looked on.

"These poisonous flowers are hidden amongst the more common herbs. This area is a little more drained. This too, looks like gelsemium. I recognise the yellow flowers. You'd think nothing of it unless you knew." DCS Quincy looked serious.

"It certainly looks like François has been a busy boy. He's no doubt been deliberately growing these herbs out here. Christ knows how he's mixing them all together." Randolph looked above them. A large raven caught his attention.

"Busy indeed," DCS Quincy said. "I'll alert DCS Turner, make him aware of these flowers and how dangerous they can be. The police station isn't too far from here."

*

That evening, Randolph spent a couple of hours at Teresa's, drinking a couple of whiskies. He didn't wish to be alone. He was afraid to stay in his flat with no one there with him. Randolph felt like François was watching his every move.

Max wasn't behind the bar; some young lady was. Randolph chatted briefly to a few other locals he often saw there. He checked his watch; it had just turned nine. Finishing a cigarette, he said good night and left the bar, making his way to his parked-up car, where the streets were quiet.

Randolph's nerves weren't helped further when the light on the stairs to his flat didn't come on. At least the flat lights were on and working fine. He briefly wiped his feet on the doormat and plonked himself on the sofa. He picked up his notebook and started going through his notes again. He then looked at the copy of François' map.

The map had been drawn to perfection. François certainly had a gift. Penelope taught him well. Or was 'something' else teaching and driving François? Penelope too, must have been highly intelligent and had patience to have been a cartographer. 'Have' now being the past tense; Randolph thought how their religion and faith had failed them. So much for being religious. They were not only overcome by the evil François, but suffered dreadful deaths. It seemed that evil and nasty things happened more than good in the world. Evil always seemed to outdo good. Randolph had seen it all during the war, including religious soldiers fighting courageously and praying before battle, only to die gruesome and agonising deaths. So many innocent lives lost, never to see their families again. Randolph had cursed 'God' so many times during that period. Fuck you, God!

Randolph again, wondered if the locations on the map for the first three victims had been marked before or after the acts were committed. Why these locations? How did François choose them? Was he a psychic? Randolph jumped when his phone rang. He stood watching it ring, reluctant to answer it.

"Randolph? It's DCS Quincy. I'm sorry to phone so late."

Randolph breathed a sigh of relief. "No, it's fine. Everything all right?"

"Yes. Considering. We're working late. I called you earlier. I just wanted to let you know that we heard back from the French police and gendarmerie. There have been no sightings of François, nor the plane. In regard to this Coraline, they managed to contact her parents in Vierzon. They were out for most of the day. Coraline still lives at home, though she isn't currently there. She's on holiday with a friend — in England."

Randolph sighed. "Really? Of all the places, she just so happens to be in the country where the killings are happening? I'm starting to believe none of this is pure coincidence now. It's like it's fate. François seems to have a connection with them, maybe even a link to them somehow? Maybe it was formed by the bond they created from drinking their blood together all those years back, when they were kids at that orphanage outside of Châteauroux."

"I know. We're all starting to question whether some darker power is influencing all of this, Randolph. Coraline's parents know she's at risk. I can't imagine how they felt when they were told. Naturally, they are now panicking, as they don't know where in England she and her friend are."

"How so?"

"They aren't staying in a fixed place. The two friends were staying in Felixstowe for a couple of days first, then visiting other locations around the country — including London. We're already trying to locate the girl through hotels. We found one place they were staying in. They had booked in on Monday but checked out on Wednesday."

"I can imagine that it's a nightmare. On top of trying to find this François. So much work you guys are putting in. Respect to you all."

"Thank you. We're certainly earning our crust," DCS Quincy half-joked. "It accounts for nothing though, unless we can bring François in and save Coraline."

"I hear you."

"We've also started to dig around for Michael Perkins and his wife. Nothing has come back on our side yet. According to some research from our friends over in France, there was a Michael Perkins living in Bordeaux, from 1929 to 1931. They are unsure whether this is the same gentleman who ran the orphanage with his wife, Gertrude. They can't find any records of her, although it's possible that records got destroyed during the two wars. It can be a very time-consuming process, not to mention often futile, unless they have an already criminal background on file."

"It still seems suspicious to me ... Mirielle mentioned that this Michael Perkins was a surgeon. Was there nothing on that?"

"I was going to mention that, Randolph. Unfortunately, nothing. Of course, that doesn't necessarily mean that he *wasn't* a surgeon."

"I suppose. It's not like it matters now anyway, seeing as we now know who the killer is, although it leaves many unanswered questions."

Chapter Twenty-Three
Friday, June 3rd, 1966

Hopkins Street, London – 10.04 am

"Let's just hope DCS Quincy and his team find François quickly, or else find Coraline before François does," Timothy said concerned, sitting opposite Randolph in his office. He had returned from France yesterday afternoon. He didn't wish to stay the night alone at the villa. Timothy then mentioned that the gendarmerie and French police were still looking into the fingerprints from the villa.

Randolph doubted any fingerprints would belong to François — he was probably too smart for that. There had been none at the murder scenes in London. Regardless of whether there were any prints belonging to him, it still meant nothing if he wasn't on any police records to match with. "It doesn't really matter now anyway, seeing as François is the killer. Hopefully, Coraline will be found safe and well." Randolph walked back over to the desk with two mugs of hot coffee.

"Thanks," Timothy replied. "I'll contact DCS Quincy, myself. I'll offer any support I can."

"I'm sure they'd appreciate it, Timothy. Time is of the essence. Coraline needs to be found urgently. Time is running out. As I discussed with DCS Quincy last night, as François shares the same birthday as his victims, he could have something planned for this coming Monday: it's June 6th. He's clearly removing these hearts for a reason."

"I still can't believe any of this … what you told me about this other orphanage and this François kid and everything else. That poor religious couple as well. On the one hand, it's starting to make sense.

On the other, it's even more messed up. I saw the newspaper this morning and the police drawing of the hooded figure, presumably François. At least it's all out there now."

"True. Regarding our case, it doesn't mean an awful lot, especially if François isn't found. We still have no idea where Natalie is or if her disappearance is linked to the murders. There's only her birthday as a link."

"With the British and the French all over it now, François can't hide for much longer and with the warning you got yesterday, it's a good thing we're concluding the case. And here ..." Timothy pulled out a cheque from inside his jacket pocket and handed it across the desk.

"I can't accept this, Timothy. It's way too much. I haven't even found Natalie. Besides, you already paid me in advance."

"Nonsense." Timothy smiled. "It isn't just what you've done, it's a thank you for braving it out."

Randolph shook his head and sighed. "Thank you. It just feels wrong. Natalie is out there somewhere, and I just can't let it go. It's not right. Not after everything that we've learnt."

Shortly after, Timothy left and Randolph sat nervously by himself briefly. He considered phoning Thelma to discuss the weekend plans. As he didn't wish to disturb her at work, he would call later on this evening at her parents. He locked up his office and made his way out to the main foyer. He wouldn't pay Timothy's cheque in just yet. He felt a failure for not finding Natalie and the payment was way more than he had anticipated.

"Randolph!" Greg startled Randolph, making his way down to the foyer. "You okay? I've not seen you for a while, mate. I heard about your encounter and the blood!" For once, Greg didn't seem his usual jovial self.

"Hey, Greg. You okay?"

"Sort of. I wasn't feeling too great yesterday, so came in today, instead. I've been feeling nervous, though, after your experience! The police and one of the detectives questioned me. I wasn't working that day, but happened to pop in to pinch some toilet cleaner for me flat. They didn't mention your name, but I knew it must have been you, as you're the only one using an office down that corridor. That other bloke rarely uses his. It was you, wasn't it? What happened?"

"It was me, yes." Randolph told Greg what had happened to him.

"Fuckin' hell, mate. I'm scared to do me cleaning, now! You think I'll be all right? I didn't clean any blood up. I wonder who cleaned it up? So strange!"

"I'm sure you'll be fine, Greg." Randolph smiled.

"I read the paper this morning, too. It looks like they now have a main suspect and a name for the murderer. No doubt it's the same man you saw here, wearing the hooded jacket. I would have shit meself, if it were me down there in the dark!" Greg motioned his head down the corridor to Randolph's office. "I wonder why they came here? I'm just glad you're all right, Randolph."

"Thanks."

*

Randolph smoked a cigarette and had a small whisky that night. He had called Thelma earlier, and come close to telling her everything. He still wasn't sure if it was safe for her and Matthew to come down at the weekend, although his case was now over and he had inadvertently accepted François' warning to back off. Regardless, Randolph had told Thelma he would phone her early tomorrow, claiming he might still be a little busy. He still needed to pay in Timothy's cheque; it could wait. In his eyes, it wasn't justified. He couldn't get Natalie out of his mind. Whether she was alive or not, she was out there somewhere, and apart from possibly François, no one knew where.

Randolph had browsed the newspaper earlier and also seen on the news that the hooded François Griffiths was now the leading suspect into the ritual killings in England's capital. The police still hadn't released information regarding the victims' common birthdays or about the orphanage in France. There was no need to panic the public further. Right now, all that mattered was capturing François.

Randolph again stared glumly out of his flat window. For a Friday night, it had been surprisingly quiet down below. The Full Moon was in view and the temperature inside the flat had lowered despite the heating since being turned on. He sat back down on the sofa. Sighing, he picked up his notebook and read through his notes. He then picked up the copy of François' map. He felt a sharp shiver shoot up his body. Was it the temperature, or something else? He stared once more at the four locations of the victims.

Still thinking, he got back up to grab a pencil and a wooden ruler from the holder next to the telephone. He eagerly sat back down and pulled the coffee table nearer to him. He placed the map on the hard surface. The map had been scaled to a specific size. Randolph started to draw a line, connecting the black dots marking each of the four victims' locations. His lines drew a trapezium. He sensed he was on to something …

Rubbing out the pencil shape using the eraser tip of the pencil, he started again. He created two triangle shapes and then a trapezium shape with an X inside it. "Argh. What the fuck am I doing?" Randolph said annoyingly to himself. He threw the pencil down on the table. He then got up to pour himself another whisky. He was about to take a sip, when a thought struck him. He walked back to the table, put his drink down and began again …

Starting with the Margaret Street location, he carefully used his pencil and ruler to draw a diagonal line down to near Upper St Martin's Lane, then across to the left marking on Conduit Street. Randolph was drawing the lines in order of the victims being killed. He swallowed and then drew another line up to Great Russell Street, where the latest body had been found. It lined up perfectly across from the dot near Margaret Street. Randolph already knew for sure now, what he had expected to draw. He drew another diagonal line down in the direction of St James's, then connecting finally, back up diagonally towards Margaret Street. At the lower point, he now added a fifth dot or location, completing all five points.

He got up again to fetch a pair of brass compasses from the same holder. Sitting down, he attached the pencil to the compasses. Placing the sharp point in the middle of what he had just drawn, he carefully drew a circle around the now five points. The end of the pencil had loosened, falling out onto the paper. Randolph went to fetch a pen this time. He marked the order of the murders, *1, 2, 3, 4* and then

5?. In thought, he went over each of the points with the pen, making the five dots slightly bigger. He swallowed again, staring at the map, focusing on the five key points and the pencilled occult symbol …

Randolph wondered if anyone else investigating the case had come up with the same result; he suspected not. Surely DCS Quincy would have mentioned it to him? Either way, the lower point of the inverted pentagram or pentacle, *had* to point to where the latest killing would take place — somewhere within the district of St James's. But when and where exactly? He walked over to his bookcase, where he kept a couple of atlases. Flush against them was a couple of road map books, including the *Road Maps of Britain 1964* edition, which he took out. He opened to the page of London focused on the St James's area. Babmaes Street was closest to where the fifth point was.

Ignoring his glass of whisky, Randolph paced around his flat living room anxiously. Time was of the essence. He rang DCS Quincy, hoping he would be working late. Randolph checked his watch: it wasn't far off midnight, almost a quarter to. Randolph tried several times, calling the police station — there was no answer. He considered driving there, or checking if any other police stations were open. He cursed again. If only he had DCS Quincy's private number. Yes, it was late, but the call would have been justified.

Randolph bit a thumbnail. Pacing up and down his living room further, he stopped and stared out the window again. What could he do? The moon now appeared high and full above the Shaftesbury Theatre across the street from him. The moonlight lit up parts of his window, revealing a few smudges on the glass. He sighed and turned his head slightly to the left in thought, frowning. *At midnight, when the moon is full, the fifth will be done.* Randolph remembered what Yvonne had told DCS Quincy, in regards to François' chilling last words when leaving the orphanage. Randolph looked again at the bright, Full Moon. *At midnight, when the moon is full, the fifth will be done* — he thought again. His eyes then widened. "Oh, *Fuck*! Surely not *tonight*?" He looked at his wristwatch. It had just turned ten to midnight.

Picking up his jacket from the back of an armchair, he dashed down the stairs to his flat, almost slipping at the bottom. He quickly got in his car and hurtled south to St James's; it was less than a mile away.

*

Although it was late and the pubs would be shut by now, the streets were strangely quiet, with nobody milling about, or making their way home after a night out. The night felt different. It felt similar to when Randolph had been searching for Peanut, and found the body of Reece Brixton. It seemed so long ago now. The feeling tonight felt eerier and off — stranger. Perhaps it was just paranoia playing its part. It was also similar to what Randolph had felt in France at

Timothy's villa in the thunderstorm. When he had awoken and found the burning Bible.

The temperature dropped again. Randolph did the zip up on his jacket. He became more anxious. Families in the wealthy St James's district had obviously all retired for the night as there were no lights to be seen. Randolph parked his car on Jermyn Street. He wondered at the chances of a murder happening so close to his working the puzzle out. So strange — but then this whole shit fest was! He also wondered if some unknown force was somehow guiding or 'misguiding' him. Perhaps François was luring him in — messing with him further? Or maybe he was psychic and was picking up on some hidden ability or sixth sense, which was telling him things.

Breathing heavily, he took out the folded piece of paper that had the map drawn on it, and now also the inverted pentagram. Randolph held it under an old streetlight that dimmed. He was so close to where the bottom point was shown. He swallowed. Nervously putting the map back inside his jacket pocket, he pulled up his sleeve to check the time on his watch; it was three minutes to midnight. If he was right about tonight and right now, he had to hurry. Fuck! A person's life was in danger. Maybe Coraline's? Randolph knew St James's. He'd been there before a few years back, when a fairly wealthy couple wanted his help tracking down their estranged son. Randolph had located him living in Chelmsford, Essex. The prodigal son had returned soon after.

A few more streetlights dimmed. Randolph was now on Babmaes Street. An eerie, thin mist descended on the streets, flowing slowly. Randolph checked his wristwatch again: two minutes to midnight. He came to a dead end but to his left was an iron arched gate, leading to a darkened and narrow alleyway which was becoming enveloped in the mist. Randolph winced as the black gate groaned open. With time against him, he walked hastily trying to make as little sound as possible. The alleyway was dark. It cut out the moonlight. It was the cusp of midnight — a minute to go. Up ahead at the end of the alleyway, the mist had virtually cleared. Randolph saw an orange-green and white glow and the distorted black shadow of someone cast up against a wall. A second shadow now appeared in the moonlight: it seemed to be dragged on the ground by the other.

Randolph peered his head to the left out from the wall at the end of the alleyway, that led down a small flight of concrete steps where some thin mist still hovered. He froze in shock when he saw the hooded figure standing over a motionless, naked body of a woman. They were within an inverted pentagram with the orange and green candle flames burning at each of the points. The woman's arms and legs were positioned oddly, and a small pile of clothes lay outside the circle. The hooded person — presumably François, was muttering strange words. The temperature grew colder. The hooded person's words exuded a foggy breath. The terrified woman seemed to be making slight murmurs: she seemed to be paralysed. The hooded person, tall and broad, then straddled over the naked woman with his knees either side of her petite body.

Randolph acted on impulse, stepping out onto the steps, moving down onto the small opening. *"François!"*

The hooded head moved up slowly, acknowledging Randolph's call. "Randolph Landon," a cold voice replied, followed by a gruff sound of annoyance in their throat. Randolph had disturbed the ritual.

Randolph saw their lips curl into a smirking grin.

"It is I …" François held out his gloved hands, as if goading Randolph.

Without thinking, Randolph instinctively charged over to the hooded François still straddled over the helpless woman.

François rose and grabbed Randolph with a single arm and threw him against a brick wall.

Randolph winced in pain from the force of the impact.

François started to laugh menacingly, looking down at Randolph.

Randolph's fear quickly intensified. François was six feet tall. Randolph was no match for him in size or strength. He struggled to get back to his feet. The daunting hooded figure of François made his way over. Randolph began to call for help, to wake anyone he could. He needed help to save this poor woman who was awaiting her fate, terrified. Randolph noticed a couple of tears run down her cheek. He tried throwing a punch, but the strong arm of François just swiped his own arm away.

François scoffed mockingly. He forced a large gloved hand over

Randolph's mouth, muffling his cries for help and slamming him back onto the wall. Using his other hand, he stuffed a black rag into Randolph's mouth, causing him to gag. Grabbing Randolph by the throat, he then pulled out a large metal, hypodermic syringe. "You've become *quite* the nuisance, Randolph Landon. You can helplessly watch on while I tear her heart from her body."

Randolph started kicking and punching. All he could see through the pulled in hood was a mouth and a right eye. Randolph's feet then gave way, slipping on the hard concrete with the strong figure of François now on top of him, pinning him down. Randolph tried punching with his right arm, aiming blows to the face with no effect. François tried to insert the needle into Randolph's neck. Randolph resisted, using all the strength he could muster. François was too strong for him. Randolph felt the prick of the needle press up against his neck, almost piercing it.

François laughed quietly. "I was going to spare you, Randolph Landon. Now, not only will you watch my fifth victim die, you will also join her. This won't just paralyse you, it will kill you. I warned you. You can't stop me from achieving my destiny."

Randolph closed his eyes. He tried to conjure up hidden strength before the syringe penetrated his pulsating neck. He prayed and hoped that someone had heard his calls for help. A couple of bricks lay near him on the ground. He stretched to touch one with his fingertips, flicking it. Turning the brick onto its side, he gripped it with all his strength. François noticed and pinned Randolph's right arm down. Again, mustering strength from deep inside his mind and body, Randolph let out a shout, lifting up his right arm and smashing the brick into François' head — twice.

François grunted in pain, loosening his grip on Randolph.

Dropping the brick, Randolph took the opportunity, with his right knee now free, to hit François between the legs.

François let out a groan and Randolph wriggled out from underneath him. Randolph was free — for now.

Randolph took out the rag from his mouth. *"Hey! Anyone!"* he shouted as loud as he could. François was between himself and the naked woman.

Recovering from Randolph's blows, François laughed again, still holding the syringe. He charged at Randolph and grabbed his throat, lifting him into the air, and pinning him up against the wall again, body to body, with Randolph's legs dangling. He tried again to insert the needle into Randolph's neck. Randolph began to choke, not being able to call out further.

"Stop!" a voice suddenly called from the steps.

Randolph looked over François' shoulders, to where four men were standing. They were staring at the naked woman on the ground and at Randolph with his hooded attacker.

François growled angrily and glared back with his one eye.

"What the fuck is going on?" one of the men said nervously.

François had loosened his grip a little, losing focus.

"Let him go!" another man shouted.

Randolph, still choking, recognised Cheng-Lei Wu in the group.

Cheng-Lei and another man ran to Randolph's aid. The other men dashed over to the woman and used their jackets to cover her.

François grunted in anger. He dropped Randolph to the ground.

Cheng-Lei's friend took a punch from François and fell to the ground, but Cheng-Lei; expertly blocked some attacks, countering with a few strong kicks to François' head and body. With the mist now circling again, François sensed defeat and eluded them, charging up the steps — he had been unsuccessful with his fifth victim.

*

"Thank God, all of you are all right," DCS Quincy said. He and DCI Sommers had finished taking statements. "You are all very brave."

Cheng-Lei and a couple of the others had run in pursuit of François, but lost him somewhere off Piccadilly Circus, where he disappeared down an alleyway.

Underneath the small pile of clothes, which François had set aside, was a small brown purse from which DCS Quincy was able to establish Coraline's identity. DCS Quincy explained that it was likely that François would have taken the purse and ID with him, had he not been interrupted.

Randolph was sat on one of the concrete steps leading up to the alleyway. He wiped some blood from a graze at the side of his head, where François had pinned him to the wall. DCI Sommers handed Randolph a tissue. "What about Coraline? Is she going to be okay? She was injected with the poison, no doubt," Randolph asked worriedly. "François, said that it would eventually kill me after it had paralysed me."

DCS Quincy sighed. "I honestly can't answer that, Randolph. At least she's still alive and safe in hospital. We'll have to hope for the best."

Randolph gave his sore throat and neck a rub.

Cheng-Lei and his friends had been enjoying a Friday night of poker at a friend's house in Duke of York Street. Upon leaving the expensive home, they had heard Randolph's pleas for help. Though the four of them were wary, they had hurried to help. Randolph thanked the four men and particularly Cheng-Lei. Randolph asked where he had learnt to fight like that. Cheng-Lei laughed slightly and said he had learnt a little kung fu from his father and brother while growing up. Randolph said that he would be dead if it wasn't for him and his friends turning up. They had saved Coraline, at least for the time being.

Randolph watched a couple of policemen cordon off the crime scene. The candles still burned mysteriously orange and green in the moonlight: the black candles didn't seem to melt down. Randolph wondered if all of this was fate. Out of all the people who could have turned up earlier to save him, one of them just happened to be Cheng-Lei. He had never seen him before until a few weeks back, when questioning him about Peanut. What were the chances? He was so grateful. He owed the four men his life. In spite of Cheng-Lei's dodgy background, Randolph sensed the good in him.

"Can I speak to you in private, please, Randolph?" DCS Quincy asked politely.

"Of course." Randolph got up and rubbed his neck and throat again. The two stood a little away from the others. "What is it?"

"I'd like to talk further about how you knew of what would happen tonight." DCS Quincy took out Randolph's copy of the map with the inverted pentagram. Randolph had previously told DCS Quincy how he had drawn the symbol on François' map and linked

Yvonne's words to the fifth victim. "It's so strange. I've never known anything like it, Randolph. The chances of you knowing this right before it happened. My God. It isn't normal."

"You think I'm involved?" Randolph asked half-serious.

"No. No, of course not. You did well, Randolph. Hopefully Coraline will survive and you will have saved her life." DCS Quincy gave an awkward smile.

"No one else came up with the inverted pentagram on the map, then? Even that professor at the university?"

"No, Randolph." DCS Quincy sighed. "I can't believe we missed it. *All* of us. Yes, we tried linking the dots literally, trying to triangulate and come up with a connection. *Shame* on us. We could have prevented this from happening tonight, period. We could have had some policemen patrolling the area had we known."

"Don't beat yourself up over it, Kendall. I just got lucky. It's strange that I just 'thought' of it before it happened. What the hell is going on? Hopefully the police on the street will catch François tonight."

"Hopefully, Randolph. We've also got someone keeping an eye on Coraline at the hospital. For your protection, I insist on having a couple of policemen outside your flat, too," DCS Quincy replied seriously. "And for Cheng-Lei and his friends. François can't hide from us for much longer. Hopefully you and the others have scuppered his plans. It seems that Coraline was the last victim. She was the final key."

"Possibly. Which will make him even more angry at me for stopping him."

"You should go home, try and get some sleep. There's nothing more to do here, apart from wait for forensics. I'll phone you tomorrow if there's any news on Coraline. We need to inform her parents and find where her friend is staying."

"I can't see myself getting much sleep tonight!"

DCS Quincy smiled warmly. "I'll make sure a couple of policemen are outside your place, at least until daylight. You'll be okay."

*

Randolph struggled to sleep during the course of that night. He had got up at a certain point and looked out into the dark street from his window. True to his word, DCS Quincy arranged for a policeman to patrol outside the flat, keeping watch. Randolph wondered if there was another at the back. He doubted whether they would be able to stop François, if he decided to come looking for Randolph in retaliation.

Chapter Twenty-Four
Saturday, June 4ᵗʰ, 1966

Shaftesbury Avenue, London – 9.29 am

Randolph had since picked up the early morning paper from Tom Galton before heading back home. Tom had commented on how drained Randolph looked. Randolph had no energy to share his story.

The paper hadn't mentioned anything from last night. It was too late to have been reported. Randolph had completely forgot about phoning Thelma back about arrangements for the weekend.

He got up from his sofa to pour another glass of apple juice. He still felt on edge and his heart skipped a beat when the phone rang. "Oh, shit — he we go." Randolph hesitantly picked up the phone.

"Good morning, Randolph. How did you sleep?" DCS Quincy sounded tired and downbeat.

"Not great. Thanks for posting a policeman out front."

"Not a problem, Randolph. It was the least I could do. There should have been another out there too, at the back?"

"I didn't see him. I never checked, though. Any news from last night? Judging by the sound of your voice, you didn't get much sleep. I sense only bad news?" Randolph let out a yawn. "Excuse me."

DCS Quincy paused. "You're right on both accounts, Randolph. None of us slept a wink last night. There was no trace of François, either. Unfortunately … I do have some sad news. Coraline didn't make it. She died a few hours ago."

Randolph screwed his face up, tilting his head.

"Are you there, Randolph?"

"Sorry." Randolph sighed. "It's just hard. I should have *got* there sooner. This is the second time I've reached a victim too late."

"You did *everything* in your power to save her. It isn't your fault. If anyone is to blame, we failed her — the police."

"Have you informed Coraline's parents and the friend she was travelling with yet? Do you know how Coraline was captured by François?"

DCS Quincy swallowed. "The French police and gendarmerie are going to visit Coraline's parents. Her friend, Avriel, has also been notified. She's in such a terrible, terrible state."

Randolph was angry at himself. First, he had failed to find Natalie — who could literally still be anywhere, he now had failed to reach Coraline in time.

"They were staying at Mahoney's — an old bed and breakfast on Warwick Street, not far from St James's. The friends were very close. They'd only been in London for a couple of days after visiting Stonehenge and other places. They were looking at cheap places to stay and had come across Mahoney's and liked the elderly Irish couple who ran it. The two friends had gone up to bed at around eleven. They had planned on seeing a few more attractions today. Coraline had trouble sleeping and felt restless. Avriel joked that maybe it was the cheese they had eaten earlier that evening. Coraline decided on some fresh air and a cigarette. Avriel had fallen asleep and woke up at about six, concerned that Coraline wasn't there. We turned up not long after, bearing the bad news." DCS Quincy became emotional and had to apologise to Randolph.

"It's okay, take your time …"

There was a silence for a moment, while DCS Quincy took in a couple of deep breaths. It was the fifth time he'd had to break tragic news to friends and family in the past few weeks.

"How did you know they were staying on Warwick Street?" Randolph asked dejectedly, his eyes had since pooled.

"Sorry. I was getting to that, Randolph. Coraline was conscious for a short while before she died. Through an interpreter, she struggled, yet managed to tell us where she was staying. She had even got some slight movement back in her limbs. She'd been grabbed outside the bed and breakfast by a hooded man and injected in the neck by a sharp needle. Before passing out, she said that her body became like stone, burning hot and cold. She had then woken up, cold, naked and on the ground, being unable to move."

"Jesus."

"Shortly after explaining to us what had happened, she, she had a seizure and went into cardiac arrest … She started to convulse quite violently. She started to foam white and black from her throat and mouth."

Randolph closed his eyes in despair.

"They were unable to bring her back. Her official cause of death is poisoning. François, is creating this poison to paralyse his victims before slitting their throats and removing their hearts. Though, that is obvious by now."

Randolph let out a sigh. "I wonder what happens now? François didn't get her heart."

"You're ahead of me. I got a call an hour ago. The morgue was broken into. Coraline's chest had been cut open, her heart removed, her throat slit … Her body was placed on the floor inside an inverted pentagram, drawn in red chalk. Mimicking the same posture you had found her in at St James's, François completed his ritual."

"*What?* Jesus wept."

"I know. No one saw anyone or anything."

"Why is he collecting hearts? Why the barbaric rituals? He's clearly on a mission to achieve *something*. But *what?* Have the killings now stopped?"

"I am not sure we will ever find out for certain. We just have to keep working hard to catch him. I am still optimistic we will. He's perhaps planning something for Monday — June 6th. And of course, it's his own birthday … I don't know if it's of any relevance and just a coincidence, but it's pretty much six weeks exactly, since the first murder was committed …"

"Mmm."

"The media are going to have a bigger field day once these details get out. I also spoke to Professor Albert. He believes the killings are linked to moon phases. The organs and parts of the body can be influenced by certain phases and star signs, and whether surgery can be performed. Only people with a background and knowledge of the occult and witchcraft would potentially know such things and what it all means."

"My 'non-belief' in such things is waning," Randolph admitted.

"Mine too, Randolph — and DCI Sommers.' François somehow knows things which he shouldn't. Perhaps he is being manipulated by some Svengali or darker force, something related to that cave in France?"

"If this Michael Perkins was a surgeon, he could have taught François things. However, it doesn't explain why François wasn't amongst those who died in the cave. Did he escape or was he spared?"

"Quite possible. I must go, Randolph. We've much to do. Keep safe and look out for yourself. There'll be policemen watching your flat for the next few nights at least — just in case and to be safe. Don't hesitate to call."

"I won't. Thank you, Kendall."

"Anytime."

Now that François had completed his ritual and gained his fifth heart, Randolph wondered if he would be safe. François had achieved what he had set out to do, but he clearly still had one big and final thing in store. Whatever it was, remained to be seen. Randolph doubted that anyone could stop him now; it unnerved him. He thought of Coraline, lying vulnerable on the ground last night. He had failed her — just like he had failed Natalie Connors.

Filling a large glass of whisky, Randolph's sadness turned to anger. He knocked back half the drink. He then slung the glass against the living room wall. The glass smashed into pieces, spraying the wallpaper and television.

*

Randolph sat in the hot bath, deep in thought and taking his time with his ablutions. He ducked his head under the water temporarily, before coming back up. He sat a while longer until the water became lukewarm: he then pulled out the plug and stepped out of the old bathtub. Still feeling emotional but less angry, he got dressed and slipped on an old pair of blue trousers and white T-shirt.

After a cup of tea, he took out a green dustpan and swept up the broken glass from his carpet. He was annoyed at himself for losing his temper, however justified. While he was wiping whisky off the wall and television, he heard the creak of the staircase outside his flat. Was that laughter he could hear? Randolph rose slowly and made his way to the door. Was it François? He moved his hand slowly to open the door, while the creaking continued. It now sounded like two sets of footsteps. Breathing in fully and then out, Randolph opened the door with force.

"Dad!"

"Matthew? Thelma? Wh-what are you doing here?"

Randolph stood with shock on his face. Matthew ran up to hug his father. For a second, Randolph hesitated to hug him back.

"We thought we'd surprise you. I was going to come in with the spare key that you gave me."

"You've certainly done that!" Randolph tried to smile, calming down a little.

"It was my idea to sneak up here. You had said that you were finished in France and the case was pretty much finished for now, so I assumed that you'd be home. We didn't hear back from you earlier, so we thought we'd come down and surprise you … I'm sorry, perhaps it isn't the best timing and was silly of me. If you are still working? I should have waited longer to see if you would call, or rung back myself." Thelma had a slight expression on her face, suggesting something was up.

Randolph managed to smile. "Don't be silly. It's fine! I'm touched, really." He held his son tight and kissed his head on the crown. "You've just caught me by surprise, that's all. So much has being going on – I've been very distracted. Sorry!" Randolph walked back to the living room; Matthew and Thelma followed. "I was meant to have phoned you early this morning."

"Is everything okay?" Thelma asked a little concerned.

The timing wasn't right. It was too risky for Thelma and Matthew to be here with François still at large. Randolph tried to hide his concern: "Yeah. Good." Randolph turned and smiled unconvincingly. "You want a drink? The kettle hasn't long boiled."

"No thank you," Thelma replied.

Matthew politely asked for an orange juice.

Shortly after the surprise arrival, Matthew sat sucking his thumb, watching late Saturday morning television. He was holding the small porcelain elephant he had received last Sunday at the picnic. Randolph and Thelma stood in the kitchen doorway, watching him and smiling.

"He had fun telling his friends at school last Monday about his 'Arsenal adventure.'" Thelma smiled. "He's been taking the elephant to school with him, too."

"Bless him." Randolph smiled, trying to hide his concerns, but feeling a little calmer with his family with him.

"Talk to me, Randolph … I know something's up. I could tell from the look on your face when we arrived. I know you all too well." Thelma smiled caringly and held Randolph's arm. "What happened to your head?" Thelma touched the graze tentatively.

Randolph sighed. "Not now. Not whilst Matthew is here."

"Is it about the case you had been working on? Did you not find the person you were looking for, then?"

Randolph shook his head. "No. There's a lot to tell you. Confidentiality is no longer an issue but I can't go into details whilst Matthew is here."

"It's serious, then?"

"*Very* serious. I didn't want you to come down this weekend because of what has been happening — what I've got myself involved in. I'm not sure it's safe."

Thelma held Randolph's arm tighter. "You need to tell me what's been going on. You're frightening me, Randolph."

Randolph took Thelma's hand firmly. "Let's chat in my bedroom, whilst we can."

*

Randolph had explained everything to his wife. Thelma held him tight and kissed him on the lips. Randolph appreciated the support and compassion from his wife.

"You've been through so much. I should have been here, supporting you. You aren't to blame for not finding this Natalie woman or for the other girl dying. You're so brave, Randolph. You have *not* failed them."

Randolph squeezed Thelma back. "You have nothing to be sorry for, Thelma. If you were here, it might have been dangerous for you and Matthew. It still could be, until this François is caught."

Thelma wiped tears away from her eyes. "It's so awful. It's unbelievable …"

"I, I know …" Randolph struggled to fight back his own tears. "I just couldn't get there in time. God knows I tried. I got there as quick as I could once I'd worked it out … I'm a failure, Thelma."

"Don't be silly, Randolph. *Don't* do this to yourself!"

Randolph sobbed into Thelma's chest. "If only I got there sooner, she could have made it. She must have had no idea what was happening to her. The fear and tears in her eyes."

"Shhh. It's okay, Randolph." Thelma held the back of Randolph's head. "It wouldn't have mattered. If she was already injected, there was nothing you could do."

The pair stood crying in each other's arms.

Matthew turned his head wondering why they were upset. Looking confused, he got up and walked over to his parents. He had never seen either of his parents cry before. Certainly not together. "What's wrong?" he asked innocently, holding the elephant in his right hand. "Are you not getting back together after all?"

Thelma and Randolph both looked down and smiled at their son. They wiped the tears from their eyes.

"We are, Matthew," Randolph replied, pulling his son to them.

"Why are you both crying?"

"It's okay," Thelma added. "It's just your dad had some bad news."

*

Thelma cheered Matthew up by serving strawberry ice-cream from Randolph's freezer. Randolph also distracted Matthew with the snow globe of Mont-Saint-Michel and the plastic figure of Pepé Le Pew.

Soon after, they went for a walk, to do some shopping, then have some lunch. They took their time. Matthew felt happy watching his mum and dad walk together holding hands, sometimes with him in the middle of them. They returned early afternoon and Matthew had a nap on the sofa whilst Thelma and Randolph chatted in the kitchen.

"I don't think it's safe for you two to be here, Thelma. The killer may be out to get me. We don't know what François has in store or why he's been committing these ritualistic murders. Maybe it's best if you leave before tonight?"

Thelma smiled affectionately. "I can't leave you by yourself and there are policemen keeping watch outside at night. But if you're really worried, there's a better solution."

"What's that?" Randolph scratched the graze at the side of his head.

"Come back with us, later today, or tomorrow. Get away from all of this. Try and clear your head. You're more at risk here by yourself. The police here and in France are already working on all of this. It's up to them now. You've done your part and there's nothing more that you can do. Let's all go together? At least until this all blows over. My parents would love to see you."

Randolph smiled. He held one of Thelma's hands. "Ah. I don't know. I'd love to. But I just don't think I can. Not now."

Thelma frowned. "Why? What's keeping you here right now? You've already finished your case with Timothy. Come and spend some time with me and Matthew."

Randolph sighed. "It's just … I don't know. I still think it could be risky being around you all. And it isn't just that, something might come up regarding Natalie's case. I feel it's best being in London, regardless of the risks."

"Oh, Randolph." Thelma smiled. "I've always admired your dedication, even when it put a strain on our marriage before. I just think you need to learn to switch off sometimes."

"I do know that, of course. And I *promise* I will. It's just this case is different to all the others. More importantly, Natalie is still missing. A woman's life is in danger. The police may still need my help. I just can't run away right now, as much as I would like to, more than anything!"

"I know and I do understand. I'm just worried … I don't want anything to happen to you."

"I'll be fine. Remember, I'll have the police outside. I can still look after myself. Besides, I could be all right now, as François has achieved what he set out to do." Randolph wondered if he was trying to convince himself or Thelma.

Despite going against Randolph's wishes, Thelma insisted that Matthew and her would stay the night and return home to Lincolnshire, first thing tomorrow morning.

*

That evening, the family went out for some fish and chips before heading home to watch some television and then playing *mouse trap game*, Matthew's favourite board game. Randolph brought out an old fold up table and chairs to put up in the living room, making it a little easier for the three of them to play. With the evening growing dark, Randolph and Thelma became anxious. Just after Matthew had gone to bed at 9 pm, there was a knock at the door. It was a policeman, which decreased their fears a little. Although the knock had startled the pair, the friendly policeman assured the two that they would be fine during the night. He and his colleague would keep watch around the building, "Just in case."

Randolph insisted on sleeping on the sofa again so Thelma could sleep in his room with Matthew. They first watched the night-time news: it covered the latest events of the previous night. A pressurised DCS Kendall Quincy and the Chief Constable addressed the press once more, and there were some more interviews with Cheng-Lei and his friends. Randolph had asked to remain anonymous. The last thing he wanted was to be hounded by the press at his flat or office. Randolph was happy for Cheng-Lei and his entourage to enjoy their little turn in the limelight. After all, their actions were more than admirable.

Two final interviews were with the matron from St Thomas' Hospital. An emotional and tired Susanna Jane was interviewed sometime during the afternoon, outside her home in North London. She repeatedly confirmed that she and her team, along with the doctors, had done *everything* in their power to save Coraline Amar. The last was from one of her colleagues, Samantha Perry, who reiterated the same words.

Nothing was mentioned regarding the links between the victims: the orphanage, the June birthdays, or the map and inverted pentagram.

Chapter Twenty-Five

Sunday, June 5th, 1966

Hopkins Street, London – 1.48 pm

Thelma and Matthew had left at around 11 am, shortly after breakfast. A disappointed Matthew wanted to stay for longer. Thelma had explained that Randolph had some things to do, but they'd be together again soon and possibly the next weekend. Thelma had embraced her husband, fearing for his safety. She asked him to take good care of himself and they kissed each other passionately on the lips. Neither could remember the last time they had done that.

Randolph decided against buying the Sunday paper. He didn't need to depress himself further. DCS Quincy would no doubt inform him of any updates. He still felt like a marked target. It was a chilly and windy afternoon walking up to the steps of his office building. In his fedora, with the collar of his grey trench coat pulled up, he made his way inside. The old brass key felt cold in his hand. He unlocked the office door and opened it up. He then stared in shock at what he saw, instantly feeling an electric chill run through his body.

Although nothing had been disturbed, on the light painted walls were symbols drawn in red chalk or crayon. They had been hand drawn perfectly with such precision and attention to detail. Twig bundles containing dry herbs were arranged on the light black carpet around the room. Again, placed with perfection and forming symbols of some sort. Carefully stepping over them towards his desk, Randolph saw his desk was covered in items: a black gemstone next to his telephone, some twigs and bones held together in twine, that included a small skull possibly of a rodent. Tempted to touch them, he resisted for now. He didn't want to disturb any of the evidence.

His heart skipped a beat when the telephone rang. He jumped. The door to his office was still open and he felt a draft fill the room. The phone continued to ring and ring. Swallowing, he picked up the receiver and slowly placed it to his right ear.

"I can sense your fear, Randolph Landon. I can hear your heart beat. I know you are afraid and you should be ... for what is about to come."

"F-François. What do you want with me?" Randolph did his best to sound strong.

"I warned for you to step away. You almost stopped me, thwarting my plans. The others who helped you, I will spare them, and I will also spare you, Randolph Landon. However, you must be punished. You are very smart to have found and worked out where I was to be the other night. I believe that everything is fate, and it was meant to be."

"Punished how? What is your goal, François? How did you know where the victims would be?"

"I *know* things, Randolph Landon. It was my destiny from when I was born, from before I was born. A pact was made with my victims when we were young, shedding our blood and drinking it, bonding us for when the time and *year* was right. They were chosen, long before. They soon forgot. I was patient for years, biding my time and learning along the way. I was taught well, learning the darkest forms of witchcraft and the black arts. I was spared back then at the first orphanage, for my time to die was not then. I had *bigger* plans but only when the time was right."

"Who taught you? You're talking about the orphanage back in France, ran by Michael and Gertrude Perkins — yes?" Randolph pulled out his seat and slowly sat down. He needed to find out what he could. The temperature dropped further. "Who were they? Why did they die in that cave?"

"Yes. They taught me well, Randolph Landon. They enhanced my inner intuition. I will be for ever grateful. Gertrude was like a mother. Michael was like a father. They rescued me from my earlier upbringing and pain. Now, the pain has made me *stronger*. I use my own pain to *inflict* pain. Rest assured that the five victims' sacrifices will not have been in vain. Although you disrupted my ritual the other night, I was still able to *claim* my fifth victim. It just needed a little more work and practicality." François laughed menacingly.

"You're a sick man, François. You need help."

"I have all the help that I need, Randolph Landon."

"Why did they die like they did — in that cave? Tell me."

"Gertrude and Michael could never have children of their own. They took in children who were unfortunate, helping them until they were found better homes. Gertrude suffered with her afflictions, which got worse over the years. First, they built the orphanage out on the land near to Oradour-sur-Glane. The ancient lands out there were sacred to witches: she believed that the power of the earth and land would cure her of her pain and suffering. But nothing would stop her pain or treat her weakened bones, even spells and white magic failed to work.

"With each passing year and her health only getting worse, she began to turn to the dark side, becoming angry and bitter. I had to watch on as a child, along with my own afflictions and suffering. I had to stand by and watch Gertrude in pain. We are all products of our environment, Randolph Landon."

"I understand that. That is still no excuse for what you have been doing and what Michael and Gertrude were responsible for. Where did these children come from? What happened to them?"

"Broken homes, dead parents. It matters not. In time, Gertrude used black magic to help her. It began to work, though it was only temporary. It required something more substantial and *potent*. To increase her power, the children — including myself, were involved in rituals, ceremonies and black masses. Gertrude was preparing the other children. Her and Michael stopped finding homes for them. She *needed* them."

"Needed them for what?" Randolph swallowed nervously.

"*Him*. The Prince of Darkness. The Fallen One."

"Y-you mean The Devil?"

François laughed. "Yes. Gertrude needed time to prepare not only herself and Michael, but the children, too. And me. She was preparing their souls for *Him*, the children's and their own. When she believed the time was right, she led the children down to the cave below the orphanage. They sacrificed themselves for *Him*, including Michael, her husband. What greater sacrifice, than laying down your life for the one that you love, yes? By offering their twelve souls to *Him*, Gertrude will return once again, reborn with no impurities and no afflictions, stronger than ever with the ability to reproduce powerful children of her own. Her beloved Michael will join her."

Hearing this first-hand from François scared the shit out of Randolph. Goosebumps formed on his skin and chills swept through his frame. "Wh-what of the children's souls? Will they be reborn also, to join the other two?"

"Possibly. If *He* decides to have them reborn to Gertrude and Michael, they will be their minions, at least to start with." François laughed mockingly. "The cave was already there. It was ancient like the lands out there. Sometimes, the children would be isolated in there for days at a time. Me also. It was part of our preparation. Some children were more affected than others by the rituals and dark magic.

"I know of your visit to see Mirielle. I know of the bracelet that you found. I knew the little girl who wore it, Isabelle. She and a few others had escaped from the Nazis in Oradour-sur-Glane. Michael and Gertrude took them in after they were found walking the countryside, their own parents and families killed."

"Only for them to end up dying and being sacrificed, yes?" Randolph's eyes welled up.

François chuckled nastily. "Correct. Their sacrifices will be worth it. None of them died in vain."

"And let me guess, they were poisoned, using the same concoction that you have been injecting into your victims and were going to use in me?"

"Correct again. Though it has been modified a little." François continued to laugh. "I was taught well and learnt many things, Randolph Landon. I still had to work and allow myself to be taught ... I was Michael and Gertrude's favourite."

"Hence, why you were spared?"

"Not quite. I was spared because I was chosen to fulfil my destiny. Gertrude helped prepare me separately. Michael taught me things about the human mind and body."

"What, so The Devil had plans for you? You really are crazy, François, if you believe that."

"Am I? And how do you think I know things? Is it just a coincidence? I know you doubt what you say, Randolph Landon. You are now also a believer. *He* does exist. *He* guides me. Amongst other forces. Yet, I still have to prove my worth and to do things for myself. I still need to open myself up to be taught and to learn new things. Everything was predestined before I was born. Like many things, it is all fate and destiny."

"That includes that poor religious couple who took you in? You murdered them in cold blood — burning them to death with your pet dog."

"They had served their purpose, Randolph Landon. They too, taught me all that I needed. They fulfilled their own destiny and their deaths were most fulfilling. I made sure, that they felt pain and were aware of their deaths, lying there, being burnt alive … I myself, suffered and became corrupt. I was then taught the ways of the wicked. I guess that one cannot get close to the darkness, without it rubbing off on you." François laughed evilly.

Randolph gave a shudder. It wasn't just François' confession, but the tone in which he spoke. There was no emotion. Just a calm, cold voice that shook Randolph to the bone. "And what is it you plan to achieve, François? Are you responsible for the orphanage burning down?"

"Of course. It was the final request of Gertrude, part of her ritual, to burn everything. Fire purified it all — helping to finalise her pact with *Him*."

"If you burnt everything, why did some items remain?"

"Fate. If they had not been found, it would never have led to the discovery and excavation, no?"

Randolph could feel François grinning over the phone. "You are behind the disappearance of Natalie Conners, aren't you?"

"Yes, Randolph Landon. For now, she is well. Her destiny was also set before she was born. Her fate will soon be decided. It was, it *all*, is meant to be. Know once again, that her death will not only be a painful one, it shall be one that bears fruit and will be justified — not in vain. She was chosen."

"Where is she?" Randolph asked afraid. "Tell me!"

"She is where she is meant to be. That is all that you need to know."

"What is she being saved for?" Randolph became more agitated.

"At just after midnight, the ultimate sacrifice *will* be performed. Natalie Connors shall burn so that *She* — The Great Witch, can rise and be born once more, powerful and vengeful. I will be at *Her* side, my own afflictions *cured*."

Randolph began to shake slightly. There was a short silence. His breathing became difficult. "Great Witch?"

"At least now, you will have some closure. You can pass on to your police friends what I have told you. You cannot stop me and your punishment will be met."

"What of my punishment?"

"You will find out soon enough, Randolph Landon. *That*, I can promise you."

And with that, the call abruptly ended.

Randolph dialled DCS Quincy straight away. It took a second attempt due to his nerves and shaking hand. He then phoned Thelma's parents. He needed to know Thelma and Matthew were safe but it was too early. They had probably stopped off halfway for a toilet break and something to eat. All the same, he felt worried.

*

DCS Quincy and DCI Sommers did their best to calm Randolph. He had told them everything. He had begun to pace back and forth in his office. DCS Quincy took notes. They were running out of time.

DCI Sommers then returned to the station to contact Professor Albert and relay what Randolph had explained of 'The Great Witch.' They needed information and *fast*. DCS Quincy had instructed him on what to do. DCI Sommers would get the ball rolling. He was to supervise detectives and other members of the police to research everything they could on witches and witchcraft. It would be a hectic day ahead of them. Perhaps they could still find Natalie Connors in time, if they could just find a clue, however small.

"We don't even know where Natalie is being held." Randolph anxiously smoked his third cigarette since the phone call. Although he was concerned about his own punishment and what it would be, he was more concerned about Natalie. "Poor Natalie. She could quite literally be anywhere. In France? London? Somewhere else?"

DCS Quincy tried further to calm Randolph. "We're going to do our best, Randolph. We'll have more police patrolling the streets and DCI Sommers will feed back to France everything we know. There's still time. It's good that you didn't touch anything, although looking at them, I don't think the twig bundles are poisonous. This strange item with the bones is called a witches' totem. I remember seeing something similar in a book. I know you're worried about your family, Randolph. The police will be notified up in Lincolnshire. Your family will be protected."

"It's not enough, though, is it? François has got away with all of this from the start. Right now, I just want to find Natalie and make sure that my own family are safe. I need to phone them again."

The desk telephone rang again. Randolph anxiously breathed cigarette smoke out. He looked worriedly at DCS Quincy.

"I'll answer it." DCS Quincy picked up the phone. "… Yes, Mr Andrews. Hold on. I'll let Randolph explain."

Randolph stubbed out his cigarette next to the other two stubs in the ashtray and took the phone receiver from DCS Quincy. "Timothy?" Randolph still sounded anxious.

"Randolph! Are you okay? I tried ringing your flat. I've only just seen the news and heard about what had happened. I've been busy all weekend. I have a feeling you were the unnamed party at the last victim's site?"

"Yes. I would have called you sooner but there's been so much going on. Listen, François *definitely* has Natalie. Her death is to be the ultimate sacrifice!"

"*What?* Please, Randolph. Tell me *everything!*"

Randolph brought Timothy up to date and Timothy offered his services to the police. He would check with Christine and Pierre for any stories involving 'The Great Witch.' He had spoken to Christine earlier; her and the others were now fine in regards to whatever virus or ailment that they had picked up.

*

At just after 4 pm, Randolph and Timothy were sat in Randolph's living room. They had a small pile of books relating to witchcraft and the occult on the floor. They had spent most of the afternoon reading and trying to gain any information on 'The Great Witch' that may lead to François and Natalie's whereabouts. It was Sunday, so most libraries were shut. DCS Quincy had made special requests for libraries to open in view of the emergency. Most of the police force were now reading and working on trying to find Natalie and potentially stop this Great Witch from returning. Some books mentioned rituals or witches in general or even the names of famous witches. Symbols and patterns were also illustrated, but there was nothing about The Great Witch. DCS Quincy now referred to the case as *The 666 Murders*, albeit not yet to the media.

DCI Sommers had taken a team to the London Library located at St James's Square, not far from where Randolph had found Coraline, almost two nights before. Others had gone to other libraries throughout the city, whereas DCS Quincy and some others had remained back at the station on Savile Row. Randolph and Timothy had gone to a couple of libraries and returned back to Shaftesbury Avenue with some books for themselves to peruse.

Although they were far from hungry, Timothy had suggested the pair had something to eat, to help them concentrate. He had popped out for a short while, soon returning with some Chinese food from an expensive Chinese restaurant in Kensington, not far from his London home. He and Claret knew the owners well. Down the years they had held important business meetings with dinner on the upper floor of the restaurant, hosting numerous guests and clients alike. Randolph wasn't overly keen on Chinese food but didn't mind it occasionally.

Thelma and Matthew had returned safely back up in Lincolnshire and DCS Quincy had kept his word: police were already watching her parents' home. Thelma and her parents were shocked and Matthew had asked what the police were doing there. They told him that the police were paying a friendly visit.

"I can't help but think that this is all a waste of time, Randolph. Well, I don't think. I *know* it is. There's nothing here giving any evidence of this Great Witch. There's not even any mention of her. It's not like it's going to give us any idea of where the two are, anyway. I mean, François wouldn't have mentioned The Great Witch if he knew that there was an outside chance we could find some information on her. He's far too smart for that. After all, he claims he *knows* things, and I for one, believe him!"

"I agree. Still, we have to try. I don't think I've ever read as much in one sitting as I have done this afternoon. He clearly mentioned about this Great Witch to scare me. Perhaps, even to gloat. He sure as hell isn't going to slip up now, when he's so close to achieving what he believes is his destiny." Randolph put down a book and picked up another with a green cover. He swiped away some dust from it.

"Yeah. Hopefully, Pierre and Christine might find something, or that professor bloke who's helping the police. Poor Christine was in tears. At least Claret is safe. She has a couple of business meetings this afternoon with numerous others, so she isn't alone. She's afraid, too. If François succeeds, I wonder what this Great Witch's plan is, exactly?"

"I dread to think, Timothy. I'm trying not to think about it too much. The same with my warning. We just need to focus on stopping him and saving Natalie."

The two were sat on the old sofa. The Chinese food on the coffee table had long since gone cold, barely touched by either of them.

"Maybe Arnaud and the gendarmerie might find something. Perhaps they've had more luck." Timothy looked nervously at his expensive looking Rolex.

Randolph glanced up from the musty smelling book on his lap. It had been published in 1951. The green fabric of the cover was well worn. Normally, Randolph would have felt uncomfortable with someone so rich and successful sitting in his run-down flat. Right now, he was passed caring. "We can only hope. Apart from the pentacle and inverted pentagram symbols, I can't see anything looking like what was drawn on my office walls. I recognise a couple from some of the items from the cave, like this spiral rebirth symbol. This triangle one as well that represents fire, also." Randolph showed Timothy the old stained page he was referring to.

Timothy looked at the page in question.

"They were also on that drawing I told you about, where some woman appeared to be rising up from the flames … That could have been The Great Witch, the drawing by François when he was a kid, years ago."

"Honestly, Randolph. This all creeps the hell out of me. I am so scared for Natalie and you. François has plans for you. I'm so sorry for getting you involved in all of this."

"Don't keep apologising, Timothy. You're fine. You weren't to know this would happen. Don't worry about me. It's all about saving Natalie …" Randolph scanned through a few more symbols on the current page. Below them, other symbols representing compounds were printed, such as arsenic, platinum and sulphur. Other related symbols continued over to the next page.

Timothy briefly sat forward with his elbows resting on his thighs, his hands clasped. One thumb rubbing the other. He then bent down to pick up another book from the uneven pile.

*

6.00 pm

"And that's it. A complete waste of time like we all thought." Timothy dropped the last book on the pile: it made a dull thud. "We've heard nothing from the detectives or police. There's literally *nothing* that we can do."

Randolph felt his pain and looked up at an emotional Timothy.

"Six hours from now, François will have completed his goal and Natalie will be burnt alive. That's if she isn't dead already! That *sick bastard*! Do you have something to drink, Randolph?" Timothy stood up and walked towards the window.

"Sure." Randolph got up and took out the cheap bottle of whisky from his cupboard. He poured them generous drinks.

Timothy thanked Randolph, taking the glass from his hand. He stared out to the street below from the living room window. It had begun to rain. "It's gotten cold." Timothy raised the glass to his lips.

"What are we going to do, Randolph? I hate it that Natalie is out there, awaiting her fate. She must know that something is going to happen to her. François must have been keeping her captive somewhere for weeks now. She must be so terrified."

"I don't know. There's still time. We just have to hope. I'm sorry I can't help more."

"You've already done more than enough. Not just for me, but the police, too. Whatever happens, you've done your best with everything."

Before Randolph could say anything, the telephone rang.

"Maybe they've found them or found out something," Timothy said anxiously with a hint of both sadness and hope. He watched Randolph pick up the telephone receiver.

"Randolph."

"Evening, Randolph. It's Kendall. I'll get straight to it. Professor Albert has something."

"Really? That Professor Albert has found out something," Randolph called over to Timothy whose eyes lit up. He walked over to Randolph, standing next to him. He leant his head in to hear DCS Quincy speak.

"I don't wish to get your hopes up, as it isn't an awful lot to go on, with time running out, too."

"Well, was it? Tell us!" Timothy asked impatiently, speaking into the voice piece.

"Okay, listen. Professor Albert knows something of a Great Witch or The Great Witch. She's sometimes coined as 'The Great Witch of Soho.' If this is the same witch that François speaks of, her name was *Brigitte Alarie*. According to Professor Albert, 'Alarie' means 'all power.' A name with a dark or sinister undertone."

"She was French — judging by her name?" Randolph asked.

"Correct. Professor Albert informs us that she was born in France at the end of the 16th century, from a long line of witches. It's believed that she lived half of her life there — earning the name of *La Grande Sorcière* — The Great Witch. It is just a theory from Professor Albert: he thinks that the inverted pentagram drawn on the map could be pointing down to somewhere specific in France, perhaps even an area where Brigitte was born or lived. Naturally, if true, it could quite literally be any given area and almost impossible to locate specifically … Escaping the witch hunt and witch trials in France during the 17ᵗʰ century, Brigitte fled to England. Although it states in one snippet that she may not have immediately moved to the capital, but resided somewhere in East Anglia, near to the coast."

"Why was she named The Great Witch? What made her so *great*?" Randolph asked eagerly.

"It's believed that she was more powerful than any other witch, able to perform dark spells and magic causing harm and illnesses to people, 'hexing' them, as well as being able to conjure up evil spirits. Some believed that the Great Plague of London was caused by Brigitte and the other coven of witches. There were stories that Brigitte made a pact with The Devil, having sexual relations with him. Some also believed that The Devil manifested itself in the form of a ghostly looking black dog with red eyes, known as *Black Shuck* or *Old Shuck*."

Timothy and Randolph listened intently. Timothy got as close as he could to the phone receiver, his dark hair brushing against Randolph's.

"How did it all end for Brigitte?"

"She was caught, Randolph. She may even have *allowed* herself to be captured and be burnt at the stake, knowing she would come back even more powerful, when the time was right. There are some beliefs that the Great Fire of London started due to smoking out and trying to burn and destroy the witches — including Brigitte. The story that the fire started at a bakery on Pudding Lane was just a cover story. Thomas Farriner wasn't just a baker, but also a churchwarden. According to Professor Albert and some matching reports, Thomas Farriner was in league with Samuel Pepys. Pepys is believed to have formed a secret guild, and one of their goals was to hunt down all the witches in London — especially Brigitte Alarie.

"Thomas Farriner was under orders from Samuel Pepys. Pepys was also believed to have been superstitious and had a fascination with the occult and the paranormal. It is quite possible too, that the fires got out of hand, becoming wider spread than they planned. Six women believed to have been witches, were found the next morning at daylight. Completely burnt. It's likely Pepys and Farriner, targeted a Sabbath or ritual, although it isn't fully clear. The dates of the Great Fire of London were from September 2nd to the 6th, 1666, three hundred years ago."

"666 again," Randolph said quietly.

"Yes," DCS Quincy replied. "There was a lot of fear and paranoia in London during that period. Feelings of impending doom, that awful things were to happen. On top of the witch hunt and trials, there were also two comets seen above London in both 1664 and 1665. They were believed to have been harbingers of doom, predicting the Great Plague of London and then the Great Fire of London. People also believed that the numbers 666 were magical. So things weren't helped with what happened in the year of 1666 … As for the fate that befell Brigitte Alarie, she was found by herself, on September 8th on a small patch of grassland between where Berwick Street and Dean Street are now. Put another way, practically in the middle part of the inverted pentagram that you drew on François' map."

"Shit," Randolph said. "Ironically, not too far from my flat and office."

"No one ever knew for sure where Brigitte lived in London. When they found her that night — believed to have been some time after midnight, she was standing inside the middle of an inverted pentagram made of fire. With her arms stretched out at her sides, she was muttering some strange words and appeared to have been in a trance, her eyes blinking ferociously and looking up. It's believed that she wished to be caught, in spite of what she knew would happen to her …"

Randolph and Timothy both looked at one another seriously.

"During her inquisition, she confessed to *all* charges and allegations willingly and enthusiastically, even admitting to having sex with The Devil. Nothing though, was mentioned of this Black Shuck during these interrogations or was witnessed at her death. There was no wasting time with her execution, either. The following day on September 9th, at just after 10 am — she was stripped fully naked and led back out to that same patch of grassland. Her third nipple was also revealed. Back then, it was a telling sign that someone was a witch and dabbled in witchcraft."

"Jesus," Randolph muttered.

"At first, she was pressed and crushed, then she was hung, before finally being burnt alive at the stake. With the flames growing and reports of the smell of her burning flesh, she laughed, promising her return and revenge for when the time was right, to the goading crowds. It is believed that she was in her seventies at the time of her death. She is the only witch in England, believed to have suffered all three methods of execution."

"God … Although it's an awful lot to take in, I guess certain things make more sense now. Why has this not been recorded more, though? This is a big thing to have happened in England. Why haven't more books covered it?" Randolph asked.

"Even Samuel Pepys' diary never confirmed a hint of all this. According to Professor Albert, many witchcraft and trial records were never preserved, or most people were too scared to mention it, write Brigitte's name, or say it out loud, for fear of something bad happening to them. The less said about her, the better. Particularly those directly involved in her trial and sentencing her to death. That no doubt included Thomas Farriner and Samuel Pepys."

"This Professor Albert," Timothy asked, "can he be trusted? What are these sources he has read from, portraying these events which not many — if anyone else, knows about?"

"The records belonged to his father who studied the occult and things like that. They were passed down generations and are believed to be *very* expensive and rare. He has numerous times, turned down lucrative offers for his prized possessions. And yes, I do trust him. Most definitely. Although this was before the events of 1666, he has in his possession one of the first editions of *Daemonologie* by James VI, first published in 1597. So, Professor Albert certainly knows his stuff. It's why we turned to him for help."

Randolph couldn't help but think to himself that the professor had failed to work out the inverted pentagram on the map. He still wasn't sure, like any of them, how this information would help in finding Natalie or stopping The Great Witch from returning. "I guess that François was the 'chosen one,' to bring The Great Witch back somehow, for whatever reason unbeknown to us."

"Professor Albert never brought up about this Great Witch, previously. There was nothing to suggest that she was linked to what François was doing. At least not specifically. He also had to refresh his memory of her … He also mentioned that in the 17th century, 'Soho' was possibly used as a hunting cry for witch hunting."

"This still doesn't help us find Natalie, does it?" Timothy said dejectedly. "All it does is make for a depressing history lesson. It's basically over." He necked back the whisky.

Randolph's own glass remained untouched on the telephone stand.

"I already spoke to the French. Something may fall into our laps. We have police out on the streets, too, wearing down our shoe leather. A group have also gone to check where Brigitte was reported to have been killed. Albeit, the grassland area has long since gone. We're certainly not going to lie down on this. I can assure you both of that."

"We respect that," replied Randolph, looking at the disheartened Timothy.

*

7.18 pm

Timothy had not long got off the phone with Claret. Her business meetings had finished a short while back. He had been torn whether to suggest she go to stay with friends, go home to be with her himself, or stay with Randolph. In the end, Randolph insisted that Timothy should be with his wife. A policeman would be outside Randolph's flat within another hour or two, so he wouldn't be alone.

Randolph soon became anxious once alone, however. He sat on the edge of one of his armchairs. His left leg started to shake and he felt emotional. Natalie Connors was just a few hours away from a horrifying death. "Please, God. Just give us something. Even if you have to make it hard for us, don't make it impossible," he said aloud. Tears ran down his worried face; his leg still vibrating on automatic.

He felt a hypocrite for asking God for help, when he was quick to criticise others who were religious, like the poor Griffiths.

He sat there for another ten minutes or so. His leg finally returned to normal. He pondered on leaving his flat, checking the area where The Great Witch had been sentenced to death. The phone then rang and he jumped up quickly to answer it.

There was silence on the other end of the call.

"Hello?" Randolph asked again.

"Hello. Randolph Landon."

"François!"

"It's a pleasure to speak with you again. I hope you had fun learning of The Great Witch."

"*What*? How on earth do you know that?"

"I told you before; I *know* things. Everyone who has tried getting in my way will be spared for now. I killed who I was meant to kill. Everyone else will have their fate bestowed upon them by The Great Witch, when *She* returns. It shall be *Her* choice, what *She* wants done with you all, including Professor Albert. But you will still face your punishment from *me*."

"What the hell do you want from me?"

"You will find out soon enough, Randolph Landon. We shall speak again, shortly."

Randolph swallowed and placed the receiver back down. He stood nervously biting his nails. The first thing that came to his mind was his family. He must check on Thelma and Matthew … Everything was fine. A policeman had joined the group of them in the living room and they were sat watching television together. Another policeman had gone to check the perimeter of the house. Thelma said that Matthew was feeling tired and she would take him upstairs to tuck him in soon. He had been giggling when one of the policemen let him try his police helmet on. Randolph was relieved that at least his family up in Lincolnshire were safe for now.

Within the past hour, there had been two more phone calls. The first was from Timothy who was still at home with Claret. He had wanted to check whether there was any news and that Randolph was okay. Randolph told Timothy about François' brief call. Timothy had invited Randolph to join them at Chelsea, but Randolph didn't want to put them further at risk, so he declined. He also wanted to stay in his flat in case Thelma or DCS Quincy called him with any updates. And of course, that included François.

The second phone call came from DCS Quincy, about ten minutes after Timothy's call. There had been no updates nor further developments. Again, Randolph had told of the call from François. DCS Quincy was also concerned for Randolph's safety, insisting he shouldn't be alone. Randolph stated that he was fine.

Shortly after, there was a knock on the door of Randolph's flat. With his heart skipping a beat and beginning to race, Randolph asked who it was before opening it. It was a policeman from the street. He wanted to introduce himself and reassure Randolph of his safety. He told Randolph that another policeman was due shortly, which made him feel a little more secure.

*

10.22 pm

It was now just over an hour and a half before Natalie Connors would meet her terrifying fate. Or she could even be dead already, if she was in another country. They still had no idea if François had returned to France to proceed with this ritual of bringing back Brigitte Alarie — The Great Witch. The anxiety was too strong for Randolph. He hadn't felt this bad during the war. The thought of Natalie being sacrificed while they were all sitting ducks was too much. Knowing that something awful was about to happen and they weren't able to prevent it was torture, not to mention what the return of The Great Witch would mean. Randolph wasn't sure what to believe anymore. Was François for real? The clock ticking down became excruciating. Randolph couldn't sit down. He resisted cigarettes and alcohol. Returning from the bathroom after a nervous leak, he heard the phone ring again.

"Randolph! He's gone!" Thelma was hysterical and in complete tears.

Randolph's heart sunk. He felt his chest drop. He knew instantly who Thelma meant. "Matthew …" Randolph said quietly and despairingly. "Wh-what happened?" Randolph asked anxiously. Tears formed in his eyes.

Thelma tried to compose herself. She couldn't find the words. "H-he …" She burst into tears again.

Thelma's mother took the receiver from her daughter. "Randolph. It's Lorraine." She also found it hard to talk.

"Lorraine, please tell me what's happened to Matthew?" Randolph tried to ask calmly.

"He … he went up to bed a couple of hours ago. Thelma had checked in on him several times. He was tucked up and fast asleep. Ten minutes ago, she went upstairs to check again, and he was gone. His window was wide open."

"*What*? He was upstairs? How would he have got out? He surely couldn't have jumped!" Randolph began to lose his composure.

"We … we don't know." Lorraine began to cry.

"Lorraine! Where is my son? Where are the police?" Randolph half-shouted. He had tried to remain calm for Thelma and Lorraine's sake.

Thelma took back the receiver. "They're still outside looking for him, with Dad," she managed to say. "One of the policemen was outside the front, and the other at the back. The one out the back came in to use the toilet. He then spoke to us for a short while."

"*Useless bastards!*" Randolph spat over the voice piece.

Thelma winced from the shout.

"I'm … I'm sorry, Thelma. I didn't mean to shout."

"It's okay. It's possible that he was enticed out through the window. Maybe someone caught him below. It isn't that high. There … there's something else."

"What is it? Tell me!" Randolph began to break down, setting Thelma off again too.

"There … there was like a black gemstone on the window sill. We don't know how it got there."

Randolph recalled Christine showing him some black gemstones and the one left on his office desk.

"F-François has taken him, hasn't he, Randolph?"

"We don't know that for sure," Randolph replied calmer this time. He knew full well that François was responsible. It was payback and the punishment François had promised him, but he needed Thelma to keep calm. He had to reassure her.

"Wh-who else would it have been? He surely wouldn't have just jumped out from his room and run off. He wouldn't do that." Thelma sniffed. "What are we going to do? It's not far off midnight. That Natalie lady ... wh-what if Matthew ends up the same!" She broke down again.

"We can't jump to conclusions, Thelma. Let me speak to DCS Quincy. Okay? I'll call you straight back."

"O-okay. *Please* hurry!"

A frantic Randolph immediately and anxiously rung the police station on Savile Rowe. He had no idea what else to do. Despite trying several times, the line was engaged. That was when he just lost it. He slammed the receiver back down and sank to his knees and sobbed uncontrollably and shouting: *"God. Why! Not my son. Not my Matthew! Not my little boy! What have I done?"* Within seconds, Randolph stood up, raw with rage.

Shouting, he grabbed the telephone stand and slung it to the floor. The phone remained connected to the wall, but fell to the ground. He punched the wall with his right fist full on a few times, hurting it. *"Fuck!"* He went over to a cupboard and smashed it repeatedly, kicking it with his right foot. He then pulled it to the floor. A mirror on the wall was the next victim of his rage. He punched it repeatedly. It cracked and broke into several pieces. Randolph's knuckles bled. Blood dripped over his hand and splashed against the wallpaper. He had never shown such rage.

Almost immediately, guilt hit him. He tried to calm himself, taking in deep breaths. He needed to contact DCS Quincy — for what good it would do, then phone Thelma back. Thankfully the phone wasn't damaged. Using a kitchen towel to stem the bleeding, the phone began to ring.

"H-hello?" Randolph cleared his throat. He sat on his knees on the carpet.

Silence.

"François. I know it's you, you bastard."

"Enjoying your night, Randolph Landon?" François laughed loudly.

"Where's my son?"

"I don't know what you are talking about, Randolph Landon."

"Please. It's me that you want. If you want for me to be punished, that's fine. My son hasn't done anything. Please. Don't hurt him. He's just a child." Randolph knew full well what François was capable of.

"What? Is he missing?" François mocked further.

"*Tell me where my fucking son is*! If you hurt him, I *swear*!"

"That is quite a temper that you have there, Randolph Landon. It's a horrible feeling, isn't it? Loving someone and not having any control over them or the situation, not being able to save them. Feeling *so* helpless. I warned you to step away or face the consequences. You are fortunate — at least for now, that I haven't taken your wife, too."

Randolph swallowed again. "Wh-what do you want? *Please*. Just let my son go. You already have Natalie. You've already won and you're on the verge of achieving your destiny."

"How would you like to see your son? One final time."

"Wh-what are you talking about? I'm just tired of all this. I just want Matthew back and for it to be over."

"And it shall be. Soon. However, I think that it is only fair, that you and Timothy Andrews witness what is about to happen. He got you involved in all of this. He should see his old flame, Natalie Connors, again. It will be a chance for him to say goodbye." François chuckled briefly.

"Just. Just save the games. Just tell me!"

"I will let The Great Witch choose your son's fate for Herself, when *She* rises from the flames. The fate for you and Timothy Andrews will also be for *Her* to choose, when you bear witness to this glorious and defining act. A kind of fitting offer."

"I don't understand?" Randolph now sat on the carpet with his back against the wall. His bloodied knuckles throbbed.

"I want you and Timothy Andrews to join me. I think that you could *just* about make it." François laughed again. "No matter if you don't … but if you don't make it before midnight, the chances of seeing your son again are less. Come alone — *no one* else. No police. No detectives. I will know if you fail to comply and I will *end* your son's life straight away in the most *horrific* way. Do we have a deal, Randolph Landon?"

Randolph sighed. "We do."

"Very well. The place is directly south from London. I shall give you the co-ordinates. It is best that you write them down, Randolph Landon."

Randolph quickly picked up a pencil. He tore a piece of paper from the note pad on the floor. He retrieved the receiver.

"These co-ordinates will only take you close by. You will have to work out for yourself *exactly* where I am." François laughed.

"Please. Just stop with the games. Just tell me already!"

"Things should be worked for in life, Randolph Landon. Even *I* had to work things out and be patient for *my* destiny. Once you arrive at the co-ordinates, it shouldn't be *too* hard to find me. Remember, you *must* come alone. Do *not* think that you can fool me. I suggest that you hurry. The clock is ticking — tick tock."

"My son. Can I talk to him, quickly? Please. I just want to hear his voice."

"Not a chance." François ended the call.

Randolph jumped up and became flustered. He didn't know what to do first, phone Thelma, call Timothy or work out the co-ordinates. Calling DCS Quincy was now not an option. Randolph dashed across the living room to where the small bookcase was. He quickly flicked his left forefinger across some larger stand-alone maps that were propped-up at the end of the shelf next to the two road map books, until he found the one that he wanted. He pulled it out and unfolded it. He opened up the large map of England and placed it down on the carpet, trying to press out the creases and make it flat with the palms of his hands as best he could, smudging blood from his injured knuckles onto the paper.

Randolph was no stranger to co-ordinates and finding locations; he had done enough of it during the war. He looked at the bloodied piece of paper with the co-ordinates written on it:

51° 3' 24" N, 0° 8' 14" W

On his knees, he used a pencil and ruler to work out the location. He drew two lines that were slightly uneven due to the carpet. They crossed at a place called Balcombe. It was a village in West Sussex. Randolph had never been there, though he was aware of it. It was directly south of London as François had said. Randolph didn't have time to check, but it was quite possible that Balcombe was where the bottom point of the inverted pentagram from François' map pointed down to. He hurried to find the piece of paper with Timothy's number, which was also on the floor.

"Timothy!"

"Randolph. You have some news?" Timothy answered anxiously.

"François has my son!" Randolph blurted out.

"What?"

"There's no real time to explain. We *have* to hurry. We can just about make it."

"Randolph. Slow down. What are you talking about?"

"My wife, Thelma, phoned me in hysterics. Matthew — my son, has been taken. François phoned me. He wants *only* me and you to meet him. Natalie is there, too, Timothy. He gave me the co-ordinates for Balcombe. It's directly south of London — we can just about make it if we hurry!"

"Randolph. I don't understand. Why does he only want *us* to be there? Aren't your family up in Lincolnshire? What about the police up there? Was François calling from up there? How is he planning on getting down south before midnight? We need to tell the police!" Timothy said flustered and all at once.

"*No*! He said strictly for only *us* to come alone. Otherwise, he'll kill Matthew. He said that he'd know if we disobeyed him and I believe him. Perhaps he's flown? I don't know but we need to go, quickly!"

"Okay — I'll come and pick you up in my car. I've heard of Balcombe."

"Please hurry, Timothy. And do *not* tell Claret where we are going to!"

"I, I won't."

Randolph dialled Thelma. "Thelma! There's no time to explain. I know where François is —"

"Where is he?" Thelma interrupted.

"There's no time to explain. François phoned me straight after you did. He wants for me and Timothy to go alone — no police. Otherwise, he'll kill Matthew. I can't go into it all. Timothy is on his way right now to pick me up —"

"I don't understand, Randolph. Wh-where are you going?" Thelma started to get hysterical.

"*Listen*. Please. Are the police near you now?"

"N-no. They are still outside with some others that have turned up. The neighbours heard the sirens and flashing lights, too. They're still looking for Matthew."

"Okay. François gave me some co-ordinates. I found the place we need to go. Write these co-ordinates down, in case you don't hear back from me or Timothy within a few hours. Whatever you do, do *not* tell the police these co-ordinates — at least not for a few hours. By then, if we haven't been able to stop François, it won't matter. Matthew still has a chance, as long as we do what François says. Do you understand?"

"Y-yes," Thelma replied emotionally. She then asked for Randolph to wait, whilst she quickly fetched a pen and piece of paper. She nervously wrote down the co-ordinates. "I can't lose you both, Randolph." She burst into tears.

"I promise I'll do my best to save Matthew. I love you, Thelma."

"I love you too, Randolph. Please get Matthew and come back safe, I beg of you."

"I'll try, my darling. I have to go. Remember what I told you. I love you."

"I love you, Randolph."

Randolph hung up the phone and tried to compose himself. Timothy would arrive any minute. He quickly went into the bathroom and washed his bloodied hand. He was fortunate he hadn't broken any of his knuckles. He winced as the soap stung his wounds. After drying his hands, he took out a bandage from the bathroom cabinet and wrapped it tightly around his right hand. Seeing it was beginning to rain outside his flat window, he put on his long, grey trench coat and matching fedora. He folded the map. Along with the small piece of paper with the co-ordinates on, he placed them both into his pocket.

Looking around his flat with the telephone table still laying on the floor and the items strewn across the carpet, he wondered if he would ever see this dump of a home again. He looked at the clock on the wall. If Randolph and Timothy were to make it before midnight, they would certainly be cutting it fine. They still had to find the exact location too. Randolph made his way down the stairs to the drizzling rain.

"Mr Landon?" one of the short policemen out front said in a Cockney accent, turning to see Randolph walk out onto the pavement. It was a different policeman to the one who had introduced himself to Randolph, earlier. "Where are you off to at this time of night? You should be indoors. Me and my colleague out the back have got your back covered," he said cockily.

"Mr Andrews is picking me up in his car. We thought it would be best if we were together, with midnight coming up, just in case."

"Ah, I see. Are you going to his home, then?"

"We are, yes," Randolph lied. "Look on the bright side, you and your colleague out the back won't need to stay here for the rest of the night." He tried to smile.

"I guess there is that!" The policeman who was only in his twenties, laughed back.

Randolph soon saw fast approaching headlights to his right.

Timothy's black BMW 507 pulled up at the side of the pavement.

"Good night," Randolph said to the policeman, opening the car door and getting in.

The policeman nodded back and watched the BMW speed off.

"Shit, Randolph. I can't believe we're doing this. I told the policeman outside my home I was going to drive to yours to see how you were. I didn't know what to say! I kind of panicked. I couldn't just say I was just going out for a drive. They're going to know that something is up when I don't return."

"I wouldn't worry about it, Timothy. It's the least of our worries right now, as long as they don't know we're heading for Balcombe. What did you tell Claret?"

"I told her I didn't have time to explain, just that François wanted us to go somewhere alone but we weren't to say where. She started to get upset and angry ... I think I calmed her somewhat. I tried convincing her that I'd be fine. I didn't know what else to say!"

"Thelma was in pieces, too. I told her the co-ordinates in case something happens to us. She won't say anything to the police. She won't risk Matthew's life. I wonder if François only has the one chance tonight of bringing back The Great Witch?"

"Maybe he's just a delusional psychopath — wrong about The Great Witch? If it's just us and him, maybe we can save Matthew and Natalie. We should be able to make it, especially in my BMW."

"Hopefully. We certainly have more chance than in my crappy Hillman Imp." Randolph tried to smile nervously.

Timothy glanced back and did the same. "Once again. I am so sorry for getting you involved in all of this, Randolph ... Your family and poor little boy, too. I'll never forgive myself, if, if —"

"Don't, Timothy. This is all my own fault ... I should have taken François' warning. It's what caused a strain on my marriage – not being able to let go. Now Thelma and I have decided to get back together, and I've got us into all this."

"You're a good man, Randolph. Whatever happens tonight, I'll be for ever grateful for your help and tenaciousness in trying to find Natalie. You're courageous and I've got your back tonight."

"Thank you. And me, yours. I don't know about being courageous. Right now, all I'm thinking about is trying to save my little boy and Natalie. I'm just doing what any other father would do. You're brave, too, Timothy."

Timothy smiled. "There you go again, being humble as always. I promise you this, Randolph. If we make it through tonight and somehow manage to end this, you and your family will be set up financially for life. You have my word on that."

"I honestly don't know what to say to that, Timothy. I don't think I could accept such generosity. Anyway, let's save my boy and Natalie first ..."

Driving through the dark and empty streets, not a soul was to be seen. Timothy made his way to the outskirts of London. Their nervousness started to grow, along with their darkest fears. It would soon be time to face François. Not only did they have to save Randolph's son and Natalie Conners, who Randolph had never met, he and Timothy would have to somehow prevent The Great Witch from returning. How? They had no fucking clue.

*

11.43 pm

It was roughly forty miles down to Balcombe. Much to the pair's nerves and frustrations, late night road works had slowed parts of their journey south. Randolph wondered if François had flown over them during their journey. Though François was most likely well in front of them, or even at his destination already. Randolph imagined him menacingly looking down at the two, smiling to himself. Assumably he was in his Cessna. There was no other way that he could have snatched Matthew from Lincolnshire and made it down to Balcombe in the time. Of course, that was if François was being honest about the co-ordinates. Randolph felt a shiver as it occurred to him that François might just be tricking him into believing there was a chance of seeing Matthew and potentially saving him and Natalie.

Having a light aircraft too, meant it would be possible and easy to land on grass and potentially anything other than a hard service of an airport or airstrip. It would also make sense why François' plane was never detected by the authorities or airports. He could sneak in and out without anyone knowing or seeing him. That included France and other countries too. Especially if he wasn't flying in restricted airspace. Timothy even suggested that maybe François could 'somehow' avoid detection and being spotted, due to some 'supernatural' gift, power or influence.

Timothy and Randolph would reach Balcombe in time, but still needed to find the exact location. They were now just a couple of miles outside the small village. A white fingerpost with black letters read *BALCOMBE* and pointed ahead. Timothy had broken a few speeding limits on their way down, yet he was still careful, especially on the wet road surfaces, with the rain pelting down hard. The two kept fidgeting nervously on the maroon-coloured leather seats.

"Balcombe ..." Timothy said quietly, slowing down and seeing the village sign to his left.

Neither of them said anything for almost a minute. Timothy carefully made his way through the wet village. The only sound came from the pouring rain falling onto the black canvas roof of the car, along with the sound of the window wipers, fighting a losing battle with the onslaught. With the time fast approaching midnight, village residents all appeared to be in bed and asleep — completely unaware of what was about to happen so close to them. No lights could be seen shining out from any of the homes.

The night had a strange and eerie feel to it. The village seemed dark and gloomy. Even the few streetlights did nothing to repel the timorous darkness. They saw a church light. The BMW's headlights revealed the spire and other distorted silhouettes from the building and its surroundings.

Timothy drove on to the end of the village, passing the old village train station. He stopped again, the engine of the car still running. He reached back at the small gap behind the leather seats and retrieved a small torch. "We'll probably need this." He shone the torch briefly over the car clock: it was ten to midnight. "Where the hell are we supposed to go, Randolph?" he asked anxiously. "We have ten minutes! There's no clue or anything of where we are supposed to go."

Randolph looked around.

"François really said nothing else?"

Randolph shook his head. "Nothing. Just that we would need to work out for ourselves where we needed to go. He said that it shouldn't be difficult to find ... Shit!"

"We don't stand a chance!" Timothy seemed to be losing his calm.

"We can't give up now, Timothy. There's still time. Whatever ritual François has planned may only start at midnight. Even if we arrive later, we could still save them. François must know that we're here. We're going to have to park up somewhere and search on foot."

"Okay. Whatever you say. I'm with you." Timothy sounded more positive.

Randolph shone Timothy's torch over the large map he had brought with him. Timothy held one end of it.

"What happened to your hand?" Timothy frowned, noticing the bandage on Randolph's right hand.

"It's nothing. I just had a run-in with a wall and a mirror." Randolph was fully focused on the map. "There's so much land around the village. They could be anywhere."

"It's hopeless, Randolph. Are we expected to go banging on doors in the middle of the night?" Timothy breathed a little heavier.

"I don't know why, but my gut feeling is telling me to go north of the village. Don't ask me why. I just have a hunch. There seems to be a circular area here on the map."

Timothy was slightly relieved to have a plan, however flimsy.

They returned the way they had come. On the left side of the road, exiting Balcombe — less than a couple of miles further on, Randolph instructed Timothy to pull over. Timothy then turned off the ignition.

"We'll go on foot, to reach this circular area on the map." Randolph folded the map and put it back into his trench coat pocket. He swallowed. "Let's go!" He opened the car door.

Timothy reluctantly opened up his door and followed Randolph out into the rain.

"It looks like the moon is trying to break through," Randolph said.

"It's certainly turned colder." Timothy zipped up his coat.

The two walked through an opening in some bushes. Randolph suspected that they were following a footpath. Up ahead in the torch light, they noticed a wooden gate, leading out onto a large field. The gate was padlocked. Randolph noticed something and shined the torch on the gate.

"We need to hurry, Randolph — what is it?" Timothy said impatiently.

"Look. Although it isn't inverted, it's a pentagram."

The middle of the gate had the symbol carved into it.

"I guess we're on the right track, then," Timothy said nervously.

Randolph climbed over the gate and Timothy followed.

They dashed across the wet grass of the field to where some more trees lined the other side. The rain slowed. They made their way through the wet leaves and branches. Timothy grimaced when a large wet leaf wiped his right cheek. After making their way through the trees, Randolph stopped to look at something. It was virtually midnight. Timothy then saw it too.

Further up and a little to their left, on a hill, an orange and green flame could be seen, burning bright in the wet night. Edging closer, the hill became illuminated by the Waning Gibbous Moon that now shone brightly, where some of the dark rain clouds made way. The rain was now only a wet mist. Stars could now be seen in the night sky.

"What is that?" Timothy asked quietly. He was referring to the stone structure positioned on top of the hill. It was shaped like a circle and had a hole in the middle. The flame they had seen in the dark, was burning in the hole. The bright moon that could be seen, also shone directly through the hole at its centre. A strange coincidence?

"It's a circle of some sorts, no doubt representing something." Randolph swallowed nervously. "We're definitely on the right track. Judging by the map, the circular area of land I was aiming for is just beyond this hill. Let's hurry. It's about to hit midnight." Randolph glanced at his wristwatch in the moonlight.

As they were about to pass the looming stone structure, Randolph felt a strange sensation in his head. It wasn't a pain, just something that he had never experienced before. He grimaced, and stopped to tilt his neck to the side. He then heard a voice in his head: *Remember the symbol. The circle — the eye. Trust your intuition, and you will be fine.* " It was the voice of Miss Albescu from the palm reading.

"Randolph! What is it? Are you okay?" Timothy asked worriedly.

"I'm fine. Just a sensation. We need to move."

Chapter Twenty-Six
Monday, June 6ᵗʰ, 1966

North of Balcombe - Midnight

Past the hill and its strange structure, they came across a pathway of concrete steps lit up by a row of burning logs on either side, which were sprouting orange and green flames. The moon lit up the surrounding land like a floodlight showing the trees and in the middle was a circular clearing. More burning logs lit the perimeter of the circle but strangely, the middle remained pitch black.

Both warmth and coldness could be felt from the flames. With fears intensifying, the two descended the steps, with no idea what ill fate or dangers waited for them at the bottom.

"I don't like this one bit, Randolph. I've never been so fucking scared in my life."

"I know. After everything I've seen in my whole life, nothing has ever compared to this. And believe me, I've seen some awful things. Just stay alert. As long as we keep together and watch out for each other, we *do* stand a chance. Remember, there are two of us." Randolph's words of optimism did nothing to waive his own fears.

At the bottom of the steps, outside the blackened circular piece of land, the rain had completely stopped. There was nothing but black in front of them. Even the surrounding orange and green flames burning from the logs failed to cast any form of light within the circle. There was nothing but silence now that the rain had stopped.

"Now what? Shall we walk into the blackness?"

Randolph didn't answer straight away. "We're not alone. François is here. He *knows* that we're here, too …"

"*Correct*, Randolph Landon. You managed to find your way here, to me, albeit, a 'little' late. You have not missed anything." François' voice seemed to come from all around the two men.

The pair spun their heads around.

"Where are you?" asked Randolph. "Where is my son!"

"He is where he needs to be, right now."

"Let me see him!"

"All in good time, all in good time. I am glad that you kept your side of the deal by not telling others where I would be on this glorious night. I knew that you would put your son's life first." François laughed mockingly.

"What is this place?" Timothy called out into the darkness.

"It is nice to see you again too, Timothy Andrews. You have joined your friend and will bear witness to what will soon be fulfilled. This place is ancient, like many places in France and around the world. It is a place of power for only those who have knowledge and who are wise enough, or bear the gift, those who know how to use and harness it. To *embrace* it. Many do not know the powers that the land here possesses in its evil valleys and woods. People in the sleepy village of Balcombe are blissfully ignorant. They will awake to a new dawn, when The Great Witch returns. The structure that you saw on that tumulus up there is known as The Witches' Eye. It is centuries old, marking this sacred and ancient land, particularly this darkened area that lies in front of you."

"Why here, specifically? What does it have to do with bringing back this Brigitte — The Great Witch?" Randolph called out.

"Brigitte Alarie lived here many centuries ago before moving up to London. Before that, *She* lived on the East Anglian coast, before the witch hunters closed in. *She* founded her own coven of witches, teaching and sharing *Her* wisdom and power amongst *Her* followers. It became *Her* settlement and community. The villagers here are completely unaware of the history relating to The Great Witch.

"Brigitte Alarie's coven became known as The Bal Maiden Witches in the 17th century. A small group of women had escaped from the manual labouring life of mining in Cornwall, eventually setting up a new life in Balcombe. The term Bal Maiden was believed to have started from the early 18th century. It was in fact, earlier. I bet that this wasn't mentioned in Professor Albert's 'history' lesson?" François laughed.

"*She* took them under *Her* wing. They became *Her* apprentices — *Her* neophytes. *She* taught them the ways of witchcraft and black magic. Until one day, after many years, the witch hunters eventually caught up with them. Brigitte Alarie had left one night to be alone, to worship her own Master, the same *Master* that I also share. *Her* coven was caught and tortured. Refusing to betray their powerful Mistress' whereabouts, they were hung in the centre of the village.

"It is here that Brigitte Alarie wishes to be resurrected, a place that *She* held special in *Her* blackened heart. *Her* initial and favourite coven are also awaiting *Her* return tonight. They have waited for over three centuries. My adoptive mother, Gertrude, knew of The Great Witch's history. She helped prepare me for this moment before she sacrificed her own life to *Him*."

"If this Brigitte — The Great Witch, was so great and powerful, why couldn't she stop these witch hunters? She could perform spells and conjure up evil spirits, yet couldn't do that? Why the need for you to help bring her back? She doesn't seem all that powerful to me, François." Randolph tried to sound strong, mocking François.

François' annoyance echoed around them. "Such ignorance, Randolph Landon. *Fool!* Brigitte Alarie was the most powerful of *Her* kind. Yet, *She* still allowed Herself to be captured and tortured, before being burnt alive, to rise again *more* powerful. You will see. Natalie Connors will be the conduit — my *sixth* and final victim. She will provide her own body which will in turn become Brigitte Alarie's. The flames will burn away her flesh, regenerating new skin. *New life*."

"Where is Natalie!"

"Patience, Timothy Andrews. For the ritual and Sabbath is about to begin."

"Show yourself!" Randolph called out, again, trying his best to sound strong and be brave.

François quickly clapped his hands twice.

The darkened circular area lit up. The moon then cast its light down upon them. The flames burning outside the circle shot up higher and burned more brightly. A mixture of white, orange and green filled the previously darkened area. François was standing on top of a large, ancient, stone dolmen, in the middle of the grassed circle. His face was still covered by the hood from his dark jacket. Only his right eye could see out. In the centre of the dolmen, was a large black gemstone placed in a hole at the top of a large runestone.

Next to François, was a large pyre with a wooden stake rising up from it. The naked body of Natalie Connors was tied tightly to it, her hands bound behind her back. Her exposed skin had black symbols marked on it. Her mouth was gagged and her desperate eyes begged to Randolph and Timothy. She looked terrified beyond belief. To the other side of François on his right, was a stone table with a square and cylinder base. A heavy looking spell book was supported on a stone plinth. Four other large runestones rose out of the ground, each having their own symbols carved into them. A red and black heart-shaped object was positioned at the top of each of them.

"Natalie!" Timothy shouted.

François laughed and looked down at the two men. "An old flame that is about to go up in 'flames.'"

Randolph and Timothy remained frozen. They looked on in shock. Randolph had no idea what to do. Matthew wasn't to be seen. They needed to stop François somehow and rescue Natalie before it was too late. Timothy made a charge into the circle. As he did so, a snapping sound was heard and the ground gave way, causing him to drop down a couple of metres or so below. He let out a painful scream.

François laughed further with more menace this time. "Ah. I see that you have found one of my traps. My *trou de loup* — my wolf hole …"

Randolph — aware there may be more traps, carefully walked over the soft ground to where Timothy had fallen. With each step, he first checked the ground was safe by pushing firmly down with his foot.

"Careful, Randolph Landon. I wouldn't want anything to happen to you too, not before you have witnessed The Great Witch's return," François jeered.

A more than worried Randolph got down on his knees and looked into the hole. "Timothy! You okay?"

"I landed on a wooden spike down here! It's gone through my left foot." Timothy cried out in pain. He tried pulling his boot away where the spike had pierced through. *"Shit!"* He managed to succeed, but his foot gushed blood where he had freed it.

François laughed again. "I wouldn't want anything too bad to happen to you *just* yet. Pull him up, Randolph Landon, so that you can both watch Natalie Connors' destiny …"

Randolph laid flat on his stomach on the wet grass and stretched a hand down for Timothy to grab hold of. Timothy struggled to reach it. He tried to climb up some of the soil. Dirt made its way underneath his fingernails.

François on the dolmen continued to watch and laugh.

"I've got you …" Randolph grabbed and strained, eventually pulling Timothy to the surface.

"Bravo!" François clapped. "Now, we can start. I can already feel the power building from within, and the presence of The Great Witch …"

A brief, sharp and sudden breeze filled the circle.

François then began to read aloud from his spell book in an ancient tongue.

"What are we going to do, Randolph?" Timothy asked anxiously. His left foot was still bleeding. "It's too high for us to get up there and stop François!"

Randolph knew that Timothy was right. "I, I don't know, Timothy."

"We can't let Natalie burn alive!" Timothy winced in pain when he tried to put weight on his left foot.

The ground then started to vibrate. The black gemstone began to glow a shade of red, along with the heart-shaped objects on each of the other runestones. The Witches' Eye that looked down from the tumulus behind them, grew red also.

"We need to get out of the circle!" Randolph advised, sensing that something was about to happen. He helped a limping Timothy across the grass, being careful where they stepped. They moved back out to the perimeter, keeping a little away from the burning flames that had increased in temperature and height.

Timothy stumbled and fell, taking Randolph down with him. They lay there, both watching on. The black gemstone and four heart-shaped objects of the other runestones glowed stronger along with The Witches' Eye. François was still calling out in an incomprehensible language. Natalie, with her dark tousled hair down to her shoulders, looked even more terrified.

The now red gemstone, then shot out fiery, red electrical rays through the gaps of the dolmen. By joining all the runestones together at their tops via the heart-shaped objects, the rays formed a symbol, surrounding the dolmen: a square with an X inside it. A line went straight down the middle through the gemstone of the dolmen runestone.

"Wh-what is that, Randolph?"

Randolph suddenly realised what the symbol represented. "It's the witch symbol."

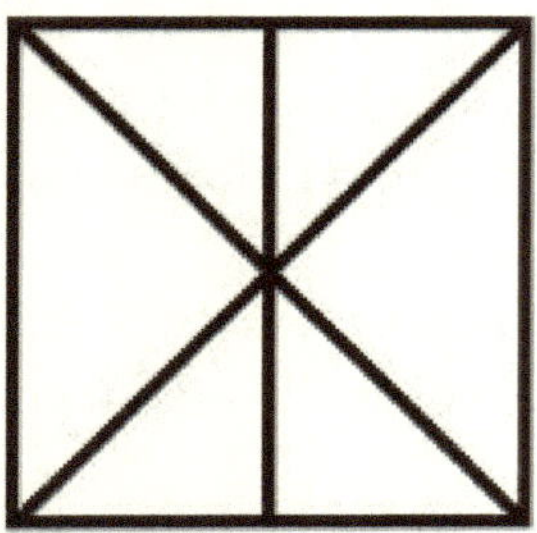

François, standing behind the table, carried on with his ancient dialect, holding his arms and hands out below him.

"Oh my God. *Look*!" Timothy said, his eyes wide.

Each of the runestones began to form an outline of a person in front of them. Gradually, five ghostly figures of women appeared.

"My God!" Randolph swallowed.

The ghostly figures each wore a black coif on their heads and long black tunics with red-tapered V-necks and sleeves draping down. Around their spectral necks, they each wore a necklace with a large silver circle glowing in red, resembling The Witches' Eye structure up on the tumulus. The translucent women looked to be in their twenties.

"Wh-who are they?" Timothy asked quietly.

"Brigitte's coven, I'd expect," Randolph replied nervously.

François stopped. All became quiet. "It appears that my Cornish language is quite good after all," he said sarcastically, grinning inside his hood. "Behold *The Bal Maiden Witches* — for they have joined us in helping bring back their Mistress. They have waited for over three hundred years for this moment. I have been chosen and am honoured to be their servant and the chosen one. I shall be the *seventh* … Those two men, have been a thorn in my side — especially *that* one there, on the left!" François was addressing the ghostly figures, nodding his head towards Randolph and Timothy and pointing specifically at Randolph, who nervously gulped.

The two ghostly figures nearest to Randolph and Timothy slowly turned their heads to glare at the pair, who were standing outside the circle. The glares chilled them to the bone.

"Sensing their capture and deaths, The Bal Maiden Witches had already set in motion their return and resurrection. Six children were specifically chosen and prepared from the village of Balcombe. For when the time and year was right, their bloodline and descendants would eventually produce offspring, worthy and acceptable for sacrifice. They would be the five victims from London. As Brigitte Alarie's body was completely destroyed, *Her* rebirth will take form from the burning flesh and body of Natalie Connors. She will be the sixth victim …

"After these five witches were tortured and hung, they were buried and preserved here, right where their spirits now stand, and they have been waiting for their time to be reborn. Only The Great Witch has the power to fully achieve that. I played my part, by taking the hearts of the chosen victims. Those hearts have been placed at the top of the runestones and one inside the gemstone. I showed my worth. When The Great Witch has risen again, *She* and *Her* coven shall live once more, more *powerful* than ever …" François laughed.

The five spirits of the witches continued to glare at Timothy and Randolph.

"My victims had to be killed in a specific place. Also linked to where The Great Witch was burnt alive in Soho, London. Now, it shall be reversed. Natalie Connors shall perish. Her burning at the stake will create a new life. It is my *Master's* and *Brigitte Alarie's* will ..." François took a burning torch from the stone table on the dolmen. He held out his arms, speaking once more in the strange language.

Natalie was about to be burnt alive.

The ghostly spirits of the five witches turned their attention back to François on the dolmen. They eagerly awaited.

"Randolph! We need to stop him! What do we do?"

"I don't know," Randolph replied desperately. It was perhaps too dangerous to get near to the electric and fire rays and even if they did, they wouldn't be able to get up to the dolmen without François preventing them.

François walked up a small platform in the pyre to be closer to Natalie. He said several more words, in what sounded different to the other ancient language.

Randolph and Timothy watched helplessly with despondent faces.

François pulled the black mouth gag from Natalie's mouth. He turned to Timothy and Randolph. "I want you to hear her screams of agony."

They could see his evil grin from under his hood, lit fiercely by the torch he was holding.

Natalie cried out, screaming for help. She begged for her life. She tried to wriggle free from the wooden stake but it was no use.

François stepped towards the edge of the dolmen. Arms aloft and outstretched, holding the torch in his right hand, he shouted loudly. The fiery, red electric rays grew and pulsated stronger together with the surrounding flames and linked up to the flame François held ...

Out of nowhere, a gunshot was heard and the gemstone shattered. The electric fire disappeared abruptly and the flames dwindled. The five spirits of The Bal Maiden Witches howled in anger. Slowly, they began to fade. Out of the darkness near the bottom of the steps, a man emerged pointing a pistol up towards François on the stone dolmen.

Timothy and Randolph stood in shock. It took them a moment to recognise him out of his usual gendarmerie uniform.

"*Arnaud.* How are you here?" Randolph asked bewildered.

"*You!*" François said angrily and then grunted.

Arnaud swallowed. Still aiming the pistol at François, he said, "I'll explain everything later."

François laughed. "You won't be able to. Do not think that you have stopped me. This is just a temporary irritation ..." François laughed hard and confidently.

"I, I don't understand," Timothy said.

Arnaud didn't say anything. He dropped to his right knee, still taking aim at François, kneeling just outside the circle. He adjusted his grip on the pistol, his left elbow resting on his left knee.

"Arnaud Laurent. I *know* that you have never shot an unarmed man before. You won't be able to now." François continued to laugh. He then stopped and became serious, muttering something. He quickly turned to throw the torch onto the kindle of the pyre.

Arnaud fired three shots from his Modèle 1935A pistol, straight into the back of François, who let out a groan and threw the burning torch onto the pyre. Green and orange flames rose instantly and the wood began to crackle as it burnt. François turned back around and roared, holding his arms aloft. Natalie began to scream. Arnaud fired four more shots into François' broad chest. Roaring further and taking the pain, François seemed resistant to the bullet wounds, until he finally toppled off the dolmen, falling face first onto the ground.

"We need to get up there!" Randolph shouted. "Watch out for the traps in the circle. Quick! We need to get up on the dolmen and free Natalie ..."

They checked the ground ahead of them for traps with their feet before proceeding. Randolph had suggested it would be best to walk to the left of the circle more, rather than in the middle, as the traps may have been placed more centrally leading up to the dolmen. All the time, Natalie was screaming with the flames and smoke growing higher — the heat intensifying.

Timothy left a trail of blood as he limped along, before slipping. It was difficult to put weight on his left foot.

The other two looked back.

"*Go*! Go save her!" Timothy shouted. He took off his left boot and stuffed a handkerchief down inside to stem the blood flow. He watched Randolph and Arnaud reach the dolmen. François still lay face down on the ground. He hadn't moved.

Arnaud counted to three in French and hoisted Randolph up onto the dolmen. Randolph sprung in the air and clung on with both hands to the ledge. Grunting, he tried to use his shoes to push him up further, scraping his soles on the stone surface. With some effort, he managed to pull himself fully up on top of the dolmen.

"*Help me!*" Natalie screamed in pain. "*My legs!*" The orange and green flames had reached higher now. She began to cough from the thickening smoke. Her legs were blistering. She was twisting her head and neck from side to side. The flames rose around her naked body. Her screams grew louder.

Randolph took off his wet trench coat to swat at the flames. The torch from Timothy flew out somewhere from a pocket, onto the grass below. Green and orange embers danced around them, floating high into the moonlit sky. Randolph started to kick away some of the kindle, singeing his shoes. Burning wood flew from the top of the dolmen. Randolph's efforts started to work and the flames began to die down. Randolph's trousers started to burn so he had to pat the flames out with his bare hands.

In the meantime, Timothy had carefully followed the route the other two had taken to avoid any traps, limping as best he could. He helped Arnaud climb up onto the dolmen, shouting in pain when he put weight on his wounded left foot. Arnaud joined Randolph and together they kicked away as much of the burning wood as they could from the pyre.

Natalie had stopped screaming. Her head fell and her eyes closed. Her chin rested above her cleavage. Her black and sooty, naked body was sorely red. Blisters had formed on her feet and legs, including some on her hips. Surrounding kindle continued to burn below her feet but she was safe.

Randolph dropped what was left of his trench coat. It had done the job but was badly burnt and not worth keeping.

"Is she alive?" Arnaud asked anxiously, pulling out a sharp pocketknife. He began to cut away at the coarse rope binding Natalie to the stake. It had cut into her skin.

"I, I think so," Randolph said breathlessly. His throat was rough and dry from the smoke. He could see Natalie's chest moving with her breathing. He then checked for a pulse in her neck. "She's still alive. Unless … unless the ritual worked and it isn't her." Randolph was worried. "I think that we managed to stop it. We need to get her safe and out of here. Her legs and feet are badly burnt. I still need to find my son!"

With their blackened faces, Arnaud freed Natalie and he and Randolph caught her body as it fell forwards from the stake.

"What now?" Arnaud sounded more anxious. "I'm sure he is dead, oui? He took several rounds in the chest and in the back; I can't see him getting up from that."

Randolph glanced down at the body of François. He hadn't moved an inch. Was he dead? Was it over now? Where was Matthew? "We can't be too sure, Arnaud. We need to get Natalie away from here."

Without the screams of Natalie and the burning and crackling of the pyre, all became quiet. Perhaps *too* quiet. Randolph had the feeling that this was far from over.

Arnaud lowered himself down from the dolmen and Randolph carefully lowered the still unconscious body of Natalie. Timothy took off his coat and placed it gently around Natalie's sore and naked body. He slowly zipped it up, trying not to catch her blistered skin. Natalie stirred, reviving consciousness and pulled the coat down modestly.

Randolph lowered himself to the grass. "You two need to get out of here. Take Natalie back up the steps and get help. She needs to go to hospital for burns treatment, before they get infected." He felt the cold of the night grow on him, without his trench coat.

"What about you?" Timothy asked worriedly.

"I need to find my son. He must be around here somewhere. I just need to find out *where*."

"I'm not leaving you, Randolph," Timothy replied adamantly.

"I'll be fine. Just get out of here. I fear it isn't over yet and you need to get your foot treated, too. Let's get out of this circle."

Arnaud and Randolph made a chair with their hands to carry Natalie, who was drifting in and out of consciousness. Timothy found it easier to walk on his left heel, rather than put his weight on the full sole. At least the bleeding had stopped. Once more, they first checked the ground carefully for any hidden traps.

"What now?" Arnaud asked, swallowing.

Before anyone else said anything, a bright light appeared. It was The Witches' Eye. The stone structure started to grow bright red again. The flame in the middle burnt and shot out another ray of fiery, red electricity. It moved quickly down the steps, creating a barrier at the bottom.

"I guess we aren't getting out that way!" Arnaud said.

"The only other way is through the woods," Timothy said, nervously looking around their surroundings.

The hearts at the top of the runestones began to glow red once more, even the shattered gemstone. Numerous female voices whispered all around them ... *"François. François. François. Wake up, François, She needs you. We need you ..."*

"Where do we go!" Timothy said in a raised voice.

"Th-there's another way out of here," Natalie suddenly said, opening her eyes. "Th-there's a passageway that leads underneath the ground."

"What's that?" Randolph quickly asked. "Do you know if my son — *Matthew* is here?"

Natalie wearily looked up at Randolph; her eyes were half open and trickled tears down her fuliginous face. "I, I think so. I don't know if it's him, but there is a young boy being kept in some cave near here. There is some water there. My legs, th-they hurt so much. There are some plants there that can help me."

"Where is this cave, Natalie? Can you show us? We need to get away from here," Randolph said trying to remain calm, with the whispering still continuing around them all.

Natalie half-heartedly pointed ahead of them. "I ... I can show you the way. We need to hurry."

"That we do!" Timothy said quickly. "They're returning!" Timothy was referring to the five ghostly witches, who slowly began to reappear in front of the runestones.

"It's, it's this way. Just down past the trees …" Natalie's throat was parched from the smoke inhalation. She coughed.

The four of them looked back to see the ghostly spirits of the fallen witches hover and glide over the still François.

"Wake up, François! We need you. Wake up! Fulfil your destiny!"

Through the trees and down a slope, a little further was a small glade with only a few sparse trees. At the end was the entrance to a cave. Two large fire logs burnt green and orange flames, positioned to either side of the yawning opening. Natalie didn't think that there were any traps in the ground there, but they still watched where they trod. Randolph and Arnaud continued to carry her.

"I still have my pistol. I will go back and finish the job," Arnaud said nervously.

"I'm not sure that's a good idea, Arnaud. It might be best if we stick together, find Matthew and just get out of here. If François survived the previous shots, further shots may make no difference anyway."

"H-he isn't normal," Natalie struggled to say.

"I understand, Monsieur Landon. But he is coming for us. I will help you get Natalie inside the cave; then I shall go and finish the job, oui." Arnaud sounded defiant. "We *must* hurry."

The limestone cave was lit up by a mixture of white, orange and green. Their four shadows cast eerily on the creviced ancient walls.

Randolph and Arnaud still carried Natalie. Although she was light, she was beginning to make both their arms ache.

"Where is my son, Natalie?"

Timothy limped behind the three, nervously looking back behind them towards the entrance, which was soon disappearing from view.

Natalie began to cough again. "He should be down here, further up on the left. I … I need water."

Their voices echoed in the cave. In spite of the flames giving them light, it appeared to get darker the further they went in and it felt much colder than outside. An earthy scent filled the air and grew stronger. What had been a wide passageway became narrower and lower so that the men had to dip their heads at times. Numerous carved symbols lined the walls either side of them.

"He ... he should be up here on the left." Natalie coughed.

"Matthew?" Randolph called out in a harsh whisper. He was worried about alerting anyone else in the cave to their presence.

"Dad!" Matthew's familiar voice cried out.

A little up ahead, Matthew was in a room off the passageway. He was still in his pyjamas and wearing a red pair of slippers on his feet. The room had a large metal grated door.

Randolph carefully let go of Natalie. *"Matthew!* Thank God — are you okay?" He tried to push the door open — locked. Randolph placed his arms and hands through the grates of the door to hold his son.

"What's happening, Dad? Is that lady poorly? Why are her legs bad, and why isn't she wearing any shoes? Is she okay?" Matthew asked innocently.

Despite her pain, Natalie couldn't help raise a slight smile at the young boy's concern.

"A hooded man called out to me in my bedroom. He threw a black stone up for me to catch. He said he wanted me to jump out to him and he promised to catch me. He said that we were going on a trip and you would be joining us and that you'd sent for me. We even went on a plane and I sat up front next to him. It was really cool, Dad ... He told me that we would be meeting his friend, a very special lady, and that I would be special, too. He showed me this stone eye. I'm sorry, Dad. I know you and Mum always told me not to trust strangers. It's just that he seemed so nice and exciting, and I felt I could trust him. Am I in trouble?"

"It's okay, Matthew. It doesn't matter. We just need to get you out of here." Randolph let go of his son and tried the door again.

"He locked it, Dad. Are we in danger?" Matthew frowned in confusion.

"I still have some ammunition, Monsieur Landon. I can shoot the lock." Arnaud took the pistol from its holster.

Matthew's eyes lit up in the gloomy light. "Is that a real gun, Dad? Is that man French?"

The others couldn't help but smile. That soon changed when they heard a voice echo down the musky passageway. Footsteps were approaching:

"Make the most of your time with your son, Randolph Landon. For it shall be the last moments that you ever spend with him. You continue to be a *thorn* in my side. I am now done with being lenient. I am *coming* for you all. You will *not* stop me from fulfilling my destiny. Natalie Connors will burn and *perish* tonight. You have prevented nothing, only delayed the inevitable. You have angered The Great Witch and *Her* coven; they lie in wait out there. They will make your punishment even more painful."

"What does he mean, Dad?" Matthew asked worriedly.

"Shoot the lock!" Randolph ordered Arnaud. "Step back, Matthew — away from the door!"

Arnaud aimed the pistol and fired at the lock. Sparks flew and the shot echoed around and down the passageway.

Randolph kicked open the door, smashing into the limestone wall. He grabbed his son and scooped him up.

François' footsteps were nearer.

"I'll stay and finish it. I can at least slow him down and spare you some time, oui. Being in a confined space may help. The rest of you, get out of here!" The empty magazine dropped to the ground and Arnaud reloaded.

"We need to stick together, Arnaud," Randolph said.

"Non, Monsieur Landon. I have the weapon. You need to hurry. Go!"

"I'll stay with you, Arnaud," Timothy said solemnly. "It isn't fair you stay on your own. Two is better against one. I feel responsible for getting you both involved in this. Randolph can take Natalie and his son out of here."

"I can't let you two do that," Randolph said.

"Decisions, decisions." François' voice came again before a reverberating laughter moved down the passageway.

"There is no time to argue — he's coming! Both of you, go — *now!*" Arnaud snapped.

Randolph let go of his son and got Natalie to climb on his back.

"Good luck, Arnaud. Thank you!" Randolph gave a nod and a slight smile.

Arnaud nervously returned the smile. "It's been a pleasure meeting you all, oui."

"Thank you too, Arnaud. For everything." Timothy placed a hand on Arnaud's right shoulder.

Randolph asked Timothy to hold onto Matthew so he could hold Natalie on his back. She winced as he moved.

They left Arnaud with his pistol aimed in front of him, trying to steady his trembling hands. He was ready to confront the approaching François …

After leaving Arnaud, the remaining four passed other empty rooms similar to where Matthew had been kept. One was where Natalie had been imprisoned. She had been kept there for around two days and nights, after being held captive in a smaller cave somewhere in France. She told them that François had injected her in the neck with something. It had prevented her from speaking or being able to move. Randolph was relieved that whatever she'd been drugged with hadn't had the same result as with Coraline and the other London victims.

They walked down a small set of steps to an opening in the cave. Spring water flowed out from an aperture to form a circular body of water that trickled down and across a line of rocks, acting as a short pathway to the other side, before flowing into another gap. The pathway lead down another passageway which Natalie claimed would serve for their escape to the south. She believed it was how François had brought her in, although she had been somewhat disoriented.

The moonlight from above filtered in rays through a metal grate at the top of the opening. The white and blue of the water shimmered over the old limestone. Shades of green flickered through where patches of dank moss grew. At the edges of the flowing water, numerous flowers grew. Some appeared more vibrant than others. Some burning torches helped light the cave and water.

"I … I need water," Natalie said.

"I know that you are in pain, Natalie, but we can't waste any time. We need to get out of here." Randolph understood Natalie's pain; it was just too risky to stop. They could hear nothing from Arnaud or François back up in the passageway.

"Please?" Natalie begged.

"Okay." Randolph gave in, carefully placing Natalie down near the water.

Timothy gave a slight nod, still holding Matthew's hand tightly.

Natalie winced as she quickly splashed cold water over her blisters. She then cupped her hands and drank the water desperately, slurping as she did so.

"It may not be safe to drink this water," Timothy commented, nervously looking behind him at the entrance they had come through.

"I … I believe so. François told me that it was clean. He gave it to me to drink while I was held captive …" Natalie continued to drink excessively. She seemed to be struggling to abate her thirst.

Randolph wanted her to hurry up. Come on Natalie! Then something caught his attention.

Built into the limestone on one of the walls, was an old stone table covered with cobwebs. A black cloth was draped over it. Two red symbols were printed on either side and two black candles burnt orange and green flames. Placed on top of the cloth were three ceramic bowls with symbols etched into them. The middle one was filled with a tar-like substance, thick in texture. Two metal syringes were laid in front of it. A wooden pestle and mortar with an inverted pentagram carved into it sat by the syringes. It was stained black and contained plant and herb remains. Another pot nearby contained a mix of black and green powder with a hint of purple. Three other bottles containing coloured liquids stood in a row, with a pair of black gloves.

Randolph noticed some purple and white flowers on the ground: he recognised them as wolfsbane and hemlock, both highly poisonous. He returned his gaze to the metal syringes on the table. He suddenly heard Miss Albescu's words again: *"Trust your intuition."* Without thinking, he picked up the two syringes and placed one into his left trouser pocket, then his right.

"Th-there might be some flowers here that can treat my burns.

François spoke of them having healing properties. He told me that he applies them to his face when it hurts." Natalie slowly stood up and stumbled slightly.

"Easy, Natalie!" Timothy supported her.

"We don't have time to check. We need to move fast!" Randolph hurried back over and Natalie climbed onto his back again.

"What's going on, Dad?"

The sound of two gunshots in quick succession rang through the cave.

"Arnaud!" Timothy said with concern. "He could be in trouble, Randolph!"

"We have to go to him. We should never have left him."

"No!" Timothy snapped. "I'll go. I'm responsible for all of this. Get your son and Natalie to safety. I'll try and gain you some time. It's the least that I can do, Randolph."

Randolph hesitated.

François' voice then came from the passageway. "That is one of you down. Now I have the Frenchman's pistol." His laughter and footsteps grew closer.

Timothy turned to the others with desperation on his face.

"Let's go! There's nothing that we can do for Arnaud, now," Randolph said.

Timothy gripped Matthew's hand tightly and limped as fast as he could behind.

They made their way across the line of rocks and flowing water, picking up their pace.

Approaching a couple of passageways, Natalie insisted that they should head straight on.

"How far is it, Natalie?" Timothy asked, a little out of breath.

"I … I don't know. I don't think it's too far." Natalie coughed.

Timothy stumbled and fell, letting go of Matthew's hand.

Randolph stopped and looked back. "Timothy!"

"I'm fine." Timothy quickly got up.

Randolph's eyes widened. There was a large dark shadow on the wall behind Timothy in one of the passageways, where the sound of water came. *"Behind you!"*

Before Timothy could react, François grabbed him from behind, squeezing tightly across his throat, choking him. Timothy tried in vain to remove François' stocky arm but it was no use. He began spluttering.

François laughed and took Matthew's hand in his.

"Matthew!" Randolph shouted.

"D-Dad?" Matthew looked bewildered.

"Come!" François ordered. He pulled Matthew back in the direction of the passageway he had come from, still with his grip around Timothy's throat.

Timothy's heels scraped on the ground as he was dragged backwards.

Randolph, with the terrified Natalie on his back, followed François.

They were led to an old wooden bridge with fast-flowing water six to seven feet below. The bridge led to another stone passageway, where a fire pit burnt brightly against the natural rock formation.

"The cave has several passageways," François said, stopping halfway across the bridge. "Some parts are formed naturally and others are man-made."

Randolph swallowed and Natalie started sobbing again. François held all the cards. He was also armed.

"I am through playing games, Randolph Landon. You two have cost me much time, tonight. The Great Witch should already have been resurrected. Regardless, you have failed in your pathetic attempts to stop me. I will win. And you will lose."

"What happened to Arnaud?"

"You should be more concerned about your own fate, Randolph Landon. He is spared for now. He is locked away and The Great Witch will decide his fate: most likely, a painful death, although it won't be as tortuous as your own. As for your beloved son, I will insist The Great Witch spares him. And *She* will …"

Matthew, holding François' left hand, looked up innocently at the daunting hooded figure of François, then back to his father. "Dad?"

"*She* will take him under *Her* wing along with *Her* coven. *She* will teach him the ways of the wicked. He will become a master of the dark arts and will be taught well, eventually becoming a powerful warlock in his own right. He will learn from the *best*. He will grow to call The Great Witch, his *Mother*."

"Never!" Randolph spat.

François roared with laughter. "At the very least, you will die knowing that part of you will live on in your son. You can take consolation in that, Randolph Landon."

Timothy was now on the verge of losing consciousness. He could barely breathe with François' stronghold round his throat.

"I wanted Timothy Andrews to watch Natalie Connors burn, but it matters not. They can be together in the next world. He can't take his wealth with him, though ..." François laughed wickedly. "It looks like he would like to say something ..." François temporarily released his hold slightly on Timothy's throat.

Timothy gasped for air and struggled to speak. "L-let the b-boy go. At least, s-spare him."

"Not a chance," François replied abruptly. "Do you have any last words, Timothy Andrews?" François squeezed Timothy's throat again, before releasing the pressure.

"T-tell C-Claret th-that I love her ... and th-that I'm s-sorry ..." With his eyes watering, Timothy looked straight at Randolph and Natalie.

Natalie sobbed and Randolph looked on in horror.

"How touching," François mocked. He then squeezed Timothy's throat until he fell unconscious. He then flung Timothy over the bridge railings by his neck. Timothy's body splashed down below.

"No! You bastard!" Randolph shrieked, darting towards François with Natalie still on his back.

François quickly whipped out the pistol from the back of his jeans and aimed it straight at Randolph. Randolph halted instantly. He wouldn't be able to help Matthew or Natalie if François shot him.

Matthew didn't say anything. He looked on in shock as Timothy's lifeless body was swept away with the gushing water into a dark gap in the rocks.

"There he goes ..." François laughed with delight.

The laughter enraged Randolph. He felt helpless.

"Don't do anything silly, now. I can shoot you in a second. I know you want to hurt me, Randolph Landon. Perhaps, kill me? Unfortunately, we can't always get what we want!"

Randolph saw numerous bullet wounds in François' broad chest. He wondered how on earth François had survived them. Was he indestructible?

François made a quiet grunt. Randolph wondered if François could read his mind.

Natalie was still sobbing quietly.

"Let's go. We do not want to anger the witches and their Mistress by keeping them waiting any further. There is a fresh pyre to burn. The stake remains fine." François gave a little chuckle. "Move!" He gestured with the pistol.

François led them back to the opening with the spring water, with the pistol still pointing at their backs. "I prepared some of my special black potion, in case I needed it for tonight. I don't think that will be the case. Certainly not now. I can feel the witches' impatience growing. The ritual will *not* be stopped again."

"You're a fucking sick man, François."

"You shouldn't swear in front of your boy, Randolph Landon. It could have a lasting effect," François teased. "Your failed intervention earlier means Matthew will now witness Natalie Connors' sacrifice. He can begin his tutelage early."

"I guess you would know. We are all products of our environment, aren't we?" Randolph tried to distract François. "Your own birth parents set the ball rolling, eh? What happened to you as a child, François Griffiths? Were you just an innocent boy born with such horrific afflictions that your parents burnt your face and disowned you? You've spent your whole life covering your face. Are you too afraid to show it? Too *ashamed*?"

François stopped and grunted in annoyance. "It was my —"

"Destiny." Randolph turned to face François. "Yeah, yeah, so you keep saying. Maybe it was just a coincidence? Being such a *freak* inadvertently led you to the orphanage run by those other two nutjobs, Michael and Gertrude. Even the other children at that other orphanage thought you were freaky. *Freaky François*, eh?" Randolph laughed and goaded François. "What a freak. Always wearing a hat."

"*Silence!* You know *nothing*, Randolph Landon! Don't you *dare* to speak of my parents. Gertrude and Michael loved me." François' rage intensified.

Randolph had him right where he wanted him. "Is that what happened to your face, François Griffiths? Your birth parents burnt your face because you were a *freak*. Or were they trying to treat your affliction? Where did you come from? What was your original family name? You're a fucking *freak*, François Griffiths. *Freaky François, freaky François.* You going to be a coward and shoot me? Or can you fight like a man, you fucking *freak*!" Randolph knew what was coming. Ready to take the hit, he dropped Natalie to the floor. She squealed from the pain.

"You!" François took a swing at Randolph's left cheek with the pistol, cutting his flesh.

Randolph fell to the ground, his fedora flying.

"Daddy!" Matthew cried out.

François let go of Matthew's hand, pushing him away harshly so that he landed on the ground with a whimper.

Randolph began to laugh. "Such anger, *François Griffiths,*" Randolph continued to mock François' way of repeating full names. He stood up, his cheek and lip bleeding. *"Come on, destiny guy —* let's see what you've got!" Adrenaline was now pumping through Randolph. He had nothing to lose. He'd won an advantage destabilising François. Now, he needed to make it count. "You don't need the pistol, you *freak*!"

François roared and swung the pistol backhanded. It cut Randolph's other cheek.

Randolph continued to laugh through the pain.

Natalie sat listening to each of Randolph's clever taunts.

Matthew started to cry, calling, "Daddy."

Randolph needed to wait for his moment. Continuing to goad him, he ran away from François towards a burning torch.

François shoved the pistol into the back of his jeans and ran after Randolph.

Randolph grabbed the flaming torch from its metal holder and swiped François with it, who leant back. The flame swished across François' upper torso. Randolph tried a second attack.

François caught Randolph's wrist and pinned him up against the wall by his throat, lifting him up easily with his other arm, rendering him helpless. "Just like before, Randolph Landon. Only this time, you won't have anyone come to your aid. You have angered me for the *last* time."

Randolph began to choke. He could feel the pure strength of François. It would only be a matter of time before François snapped Randolph's wrist. Then, over François' broad shoulder, Randolph saw Matthew get up and slowly creep up behind François.

Matthew reached towards the black pistol. His tongue was sticking out as it always did when he was focusing. His hand hovered over the pistol grip. He then quickly whisked it out and ran back, putting some space between him, his father and François.

François spun round and grunted. "Crafty boy!" He smiled wryly from under his hood.

Matthew was holding the heavy pistol in one hand, pointed at François. His hand shook with trepidation.

François continued choking Randolph up against the wall with one hand. His other hand still gripped Randolph's wrist with the torch in it. "You are a very brave boy, Matthew Landon, if you choose to pull that trigger. The safety is off. All you have to do is *squeeze* the trigger. Be careful, though, you might shoot your father." François laughed heartily.

"D-do it, Matthew. *Shoot* him. Just b-breath s-slowly. Focus y-your aim."

"Shut up!" François turned his head back briefly and shouted straight into Randolph's face. His breath smelt stale and bloody.

"D-dad. I can't." Matthew started to cry again, terrified.

"F-focus. You can d-do it." Randolph was beginning to lose consciousness.

Matthew's finger slowly pulled on the trigger and François grinned.

"We'll make a man out of you yet, boy. You have much to learn," François said.

Matthew pulled fully back on the trigger and a loud bang echoed around the cave. Matthew jolted back, his eyes opened wide and his mouth dropped open. The pistol gave off a hint of smoke.

François let out a grunt of pain: the bullet tore the hood and grazed his right cheek. He instinctively jolted back also, loosening his grip on Randolph.

Randolph seized the advantage and kicked François between his legs — not for the first time. François groaned and again lessened his grip on Randolph. With his left hand, Randolph yanked down on François' hood, revealing his face. He thrust the burning torch into the left side of François' already scarred face.

François let out a horrific roar, dropping Randolph immediately.

Randolph looked in shock at the disfigured face of François. François' one eye grew large in pain. His nose was small and screwed up to one side. The left side of his face was severely scarred from when he was a child. It appeared hollowed and the top of the left side of his forehead bulged out. His left ear appeared small and shrivelled.

François took his face in his hands.

Just for a moment, Randolph felt sad for François, seeing him like that, but he couldn't afford for his feelings to cloud his judgement. He needed to finish the job now.

François ran past Natalie to the shallow circular pool of water and splashed his face, still crying out in pain. He then quickly stood back up and turned to face Randolph. His rage had escalated and he let out another huge roar.

François and Randolph charged towards each other. François grabbed Randolph and tossed him like a ragdoll into the pool of water. He repeatedly punched Randolph in his face and nose. Randolph did his best to block the violent attacks.

"Daddy!" Matthew cried, looking on in shock. He dropped the pistol and tried to help his father by pulling off the strong body of François. François easily threw the eight-year-old away from him.

Natalie tried to get to her feet to help but with all her burns could hardly move. She managed to crawl over to Matthew who was whimpering on the floor.

François gripped Randolph's throat with both his hands. Throttling him, he started to bang the back of Randolph's head onto the hard surface at the bottom of the water. *"Curse you to hell, Randolph Landon!"* François shouted with aggression and rage. He held Randolph's head underneath the chilling water.

Randolph did his best to resist though felt his life being choked away. He was praying in his head. He couldn't wrestle François' grip away from his throat, but his hands were free. He reached inside his trouser pockets for the two metal syringes, gripping them tightly. Randolph then let out a powerful roar of his own, gurgling underneath the water. He threw up his two arms and plunged the syringes with force into either side of François' thick neck. He pressed to release the contents of the black tar-like substance into his enemy.

The attack took François completely by surprise.

For a brief moment, there was no effect. François then started to make disturbing sounds and his body went rigid. The syringes protruded out of his neck. *"C-curse you, to h-hell …"*

Randolph managed to get out from underneath François' tightening body. He stood up, dripping, with the other two watching on.

François fell onto his back into the water, struggling to move his limbs and body. His breathing became laboured.

Randolph had a feeling that this would not be enough to thwart François' strong body. He thought about the poor victims and Coraline — and of course now, Timothy. Fuelled further by adrenaline and revenge, Randolph made his way over to the stone table. He put on the pair of black gloves and picked up the ceramic bowl with the black substance in. He bent down and scooped up some of the purple and white flowers. He walked back to the pool of water where François lay. François' right and only eye looked up helplessly at Randolph. François tried to say something but he couldn't.

"This is for all the victims, you sadistic bastard and for Timothy, and everyone you hurt or killed to fulfil your 'destiny.' *This* is your fate, François Griffiths. Have a taste of your *own* medicine …" Randolph pried open François' mouth and poured the thick black substance in.

François gurgled and choked.

Natalie told Matthew not to look and held him in her arms.

Randolph stuffed the poisonous flowers into François' mouth and closed it shut, placing a black glove over it.

"Happy birthday, François." Randolph took off the gloves and slung them into the water.

The three of them watched François take his final breath.

Randolph then retrieved his fedora and placed it firmly on his wet head of hair.

"Dad!" Matthew leapt up and embraced his father. "I could have shot at you, Dad. I could have killed you. I couldn't use the gun again."

"It's okay. You saved us, Matthew. You are such a very brave boy. I'm so proud of you. I love you, Son." Tears ran down Randolph's cut and beaten face. His nose dripped with blood.

"I love you too, Dad," Matthew cried into his dad's midriff.

Randolph kissed his son on the top of his head. He then went to pick up the pistol and switched on the safety.

"Are you okay?" Randolph asked Natalie, bending down to help her up.

"M-my legs still hurt the most. Thank you," Natalie said, trying to smile.

Randolph tried to smile back. "We still need to free Arnaud and get out of here. We're not safe just yet."

They then heard a cough. Randolph instinctively turned and aimed the pistol up at the top of the steps leading into the passageway. "Arnaud!"

Arnaud stood there with his hands up. He noticed the still body of François in the water.

Randolph lowered the pistol. "What happened?"

Arnaud gingerly walked down the small set of steps to the other three. He was wincing and held the back of his head. "François, got the better of me, oui. He came out of nowhere and grabbed me. I fired two shots. However, he was much too strong for me. He bashed my head against the wall and it knocked me out. I woke up in one of the locked rooms. It took me a little while, but I managed to pick the lock with my pocketknife, oui."

Randolph smiled. "I am so glad you're alive." He placed a hand on Arnaud's shoulder.

"Merci. I am glad to see you, too." Arnaud smiled back. He then frowned. "Where is Monsieur Andrews?"

Randolph sighed and shook his head. "He didn't make it. François knocked him out and threw him into the water in this other passageway."

Arnaud's face fell. He muttered something in French. "He was a good man. Kind and generous, oui."

"I know," Randolph replied, giving a squeeze of Arnaud's shoulder. "Here." Randolph handed back Arnaud's pistol.

"What happened, Monsieur Landon. Is François dead?"

"I'll explain once we get out of here. We're not safe yet. I don't know if those witches are still outside or not. Let's check on François before we leave."

"*Oh no!*" Natalie suddenly shouted.

"Dad!"

An alerted Randolph and Arnaud looked over to where François was moving in the water.

François slowly stood up and gave his head a shake, trying to find his bearings. He then stared over and gave a wry grin.

"Oh, God. What is it with this man? Why can't he just *die*," Randolph said dejectedly.

François stepped out of the water. "I am *not* done yet, Randolph Landon."

Arnaud walked forward with his pistol and removed the safety. Just as François was about to charge at him, Arnaud once more fired several rounds into his chest. The bullets caused François to drop to his knees this time. He then staggered back to his feet. Arnaud raised the pistol higher and aimed straight for the middle of François' forehead. François was about to say something. Before he could, Arnaud pulled the trigger. The bullet pierced François' skull: his one eye looked up and he fell back into the water. Black and red blood flowed out of the bullet wound. Arnaud walked over to the lifeless body of François and aimed again at François' head.

Randolph held his son's head to him so that he couldn't watch further.

Arnaud stood over the body of François. He fired the last round into the head of François, blowing out fragments of dark bloodied brain matter and bone into the water. François was dead. Now completely out of ammo, Arnaud placed the pistol back into his holster …

The four of them winced when high pitched angry screams filled the cave. Arnaud nervously stepped back from the dead body of François. Five transparent, ghostly faces of the witches hovered above the body of François, glaring sinisterly. They were joined by a sixth, a haggard old woman, who hovered above the other five. She too, let out a loud scream. François' body then began to omit a strange looking white and black light. This ray of light joined with the others next to the old hag. The light began to materialise into the disfigured face of François. François gave one last evil grin before the old hag let out a final deafening scream. Suddenly, the now seven ghostly apparitions were gone and everything became quiet and still.

Arnaud noticed something floating on the surface of the water next to François' dead body. It had perhaps fallen from the hooded jacket. Arnaud bent down and picked it up. The others joined him.

It was a sepia-toned photograph of eleven children and two adults, a male and a female. There were seven boys and four girls. They were outside what appeared to be a black building made of wood. There were two rows of five children sitting down. Standing up over them were the man and woman. The man looked tall and slim and was wearing a suit and tie, whilst the woman next to him appeared hunched over and frail-looking. Next to them on the left, stood a young boy wearing a black hat pulled down at the side of his head: he was facing down from the camera. Apart from this young boy, everyone else stared blankly and without life towards the camera. Their stares gave Arnaud and the others the jitters. One little girl at the front, Randolph noticed, wore on her left wrist, a dark-coloured bracelet. A date written in faded black ink read *5 juin 1946.*

*

The four exited through a stone passageway that opened to the outside through some overgrown bushes. The night was now completely cloudless with the bright moon and stars in the sky. The air was still cold. Randolph began to shiver. They were by a large body of water. It was where the water from the cave collected. Arnaud was now carrying Natalie on his back. They were all tired and exhausted and Natalie was finding it hard to stay awake. She urgently needed medical attention for her blistered and burnt skin.

At the edge of the lake, Matthew noticed someone in the moonlight. "Dad, look! It's that man ..."

There by the water edge was the lifeless body of Timothy, lying half out of the water.

"My God. Timothy!" Randolph rushed over. He dragged the frozen Timothy by the arms onto a flat piece of ground, turning him over. "He's not breathing! There's no pulse ..." Randolph started performing CPR.

Arnaud carefully placed Natalie down and rushed over to assist Randolph.

"Come on, Timothy. *Breath*, dammit!" Randolph shouted.

A couple of minutes passed but Timothy remained lifeless. Arnaud took over with the chest compressions whilst Randolph tried blowing air into Timothy's water-filled lungs.

"I ... I think that he is gone, Monsieur Landon," Arnaud said quietly.

"I'm not giving up, Arnaud!" Randolph replied sharply. "Come on, Timothy. Claret is waiting for you to return. Don't give up now!" He took over from Arnaud, alternating the chest compressions and breathing into Timothy's mouth ... Finally, Timothy's chest began to move on its own. His cold and staring eyes came back to life in the moonlight. He blinked, turned his head to the side and spluttered out the water that he had ingested.

Randolph and Arnaud laughed with emotional joy. Arnaud wrapped his arm around Randolph's shoulders and gave him an affectionate shake. Natalie and Matthew hugged and she kissed the little boy on his head.

"Easy, Timothy. Easy," Randolph said, gently holding Timothy's head.

Timothy retched a final time. "Wh-what happened? Where am I ...? *François!*"

Randolph helped Timothy sit up, so that he could compose

himself and breathe better. "Easy. It's okay. It's over now. Welcome back to the land of the living!" Randolph smiled warmly.

"I remember standing on the bridge with François and then being in the water. I was never a good swimmer. Is he dead? What happened?"

Randolph and Arnaud helped Timothy to his feet and Randolph explained it was all over. He explained how he had goaded François and how Matthew had stepped in.

Timothy limped over and gave Matthew and Natalie a hug, and congratulated the boy on his bravery.

Matthew thanked Timothy sheepishly.

"My foot is still killing me and we need to get Natalie to hospital."

"We're not too far from the village. We'll seek help there. A phone box, a resident's home. Somebody will help us," Randolph replied.

Arnaud carried Natalie on his back again and the group set off south in the direction of the village.

"Arnaud, how are you here and how did you know where we were?" Timothy coughed.

Arnaud smiled in the moonlight. "Mirielle."

"Mirielle?" Randolph said confused and frowned.

"Oui. Early evening at my home, I had a telephone call from her. She was quite frantic. She had awoken from a nap. She had dreamt of her great grandmother, who was a white witch, warning Mirielle about what was going to happen. She was told to contact me straight away. She said I needed to help my two friends and to stop The Great Witch from returning. She told me to come to Balcombe in England, and not to alert anyone else, for it was less chance of François knowing and becoming aware, oui. She had also mentioned how she had seen the spirit in her dream of that little girl, Isabelle."

"Jesus," Randolph said. "You obviously flew over here?"

"Oui, Monsieur Landon. It took us a few hours. A friend has a private plane — a GY-80 Horizon. He flew me over. Lucky, oui? He lives not too far from me."

Timothy laughed and shook his head in disbelief as he hobbled along. "What are the chances?"

"Oui!" Arnaud grinned. "I saved his life during the war. It is the first time I have ever asked anything from him. He was happy to help me. We checked and found a small private airstrip about seven miles from Balcombe. He landed us there and I arranged for a taxi to bring me to Balcombe … I saw across the landscape, an orange, red and green glow in the distance, in the moonlight. Thankfully, I arrived here just in time, oui!"

*

Timothy and Natalie were taken by ambulance to hospital. Timothy promised Randolph that he would keep true to his promise of setting him up financially: Randolph had also saved his life. He made the same promise to Arnaud. He had also asked Randolph to check on his car where they had left it.

The sleeping village of Balcombe began to awaken with the breaking of dawn. The police and ambulances with their blues and twos swamped the small village and to the north. François' Cessna was found in a field — a short distance from the circular piece of land and The Witches' Eye. The body of François was found and taken away. An exhausted Randolph and Arnaud spent a few hours talking to the police with warm blankets draped around them. Randolph had refused to go to hospital. He argued that his cuts and wounds were only superficial. Randolph apologised to DCS Quincy for keeping the rendezvous with François secret. DCS Quincy understood. He was just glad François' dark and evil plans had finally been halted.

Randolph had phoned Thelma from a village phone box. She had driven down from Lincolnshire with her parents. She was proud of her son and relieved that her family had survived.

"You really think that it is over, Monsieur Landon?" Arnaud sat on a bench near the phone box. He let out a large yawn. His tired face had dark stubble growing around his moustache.

Randolph was sitting next to him and sighed. "I honestly don't know, Arnaud. We can only hope and pray that it is." He looked down and stroked Matthew's hair. Matthew had fallen asleep on his lap, sucking his thumb.

Arnaud looked down and smiled at Matthew. "What a brave little boy you have, oui."

"I know." Randolph glanced over and smiled.

Thelma, who was seated next to Randolph at the other end, with her head on his shoulder, added, "He really is. I still can't believe it all." She then looked up at Randolph and they kissed each other on the lips. "I love you, Randolph."

"I love you too, Thelma."

They heard the slamming of a white van door. It looked like the first of the press had arrived.

Epilogue

It was reported as London's — if not the country's, biggest and most abhorrent of crimes. Although a lot of people hadn't believed the more supernatural aspects to it all or that 'The Great Witch' was returning — many still did. One of those who did believe was Miss Albescu. She contacted Randolph after the events in Balcombe. Randolph thanked her for her guidance and for the palm reading. Without her help, events may have turned out differently.

Randolph was naturally lauded for his heroics, along with Timothy and Arnaud. None of them cared much for the publicity. Randolph certainly didn't like being in the public eye, although he was appreciative — as were the others. He did his best to shun the limelight in the weeks that followed and in particular to protect Matthew and Thelma from it. Timothy paid for Randolph and his family to get away for a short while, so they took Matthew out of school. Although *The 666 Murders* case — the official label now — had coverage in France, Randolph opted to take his family, including his in-laws, to Limoges. He had experienced an instant fondness of Limoges from the very first moment he had walked the streets there. They also met up with Arnaud and his family.

After being in Limoges for a couple of days, Randolph spotted the same black Scottish Terrier he had seen before and it was still homeless. Matthew fell in love straight away with the little dog and there was a mutual connection between them. Matthew pleaded for his dad to bring it back home with them to England. With some help from Timothy and his 'connections,' 'Rufus' soon found his for ever and loving home.

Randolph and the others weren't the only ones in the crosshairs of the press and media. They got their clutches into everyone involved. It would take a fair few weeks and months for things to return to normal, but they eventually did. Natalie Connors made a full recovery, although her lower legs and feet had some scarring.

Randolph and Arnaud both rejected Timothy's life-changing financial offer. They didn't feel it was quite right to accept Timothy's generosity, but Randolph managed one life-changing achievement: he gave up smoking.

Even long after, Randolph couldn't get the image of François' ghost out of his head, or the wry smile before he and the witches had disappeared. What of the return of Michael and Gertrude Perkins too? Perhaps, that would be someone else's problem to deal with later in time — another story for another time.

*

Saturday, July 30th, 1966, Lincolnshire - 2.53 pm

Thelma and her mother were preparing food in the kitchen.

"Do you really think that we will win, Dad?" Matthew asked excitedly. He was sat on the sofa between his grandfather, Terence — Thelma's father — and Randolph. Rufus was fast asleep on Matthew's warm lap.

Randolph was upbeat about England's chances of winning the World Cup before the tournament had even started, especially with England having home advantage throughout. "I really think that we will, mate! The Germans are a strong and talented team, but I think we'll do it!" He put a loving arm around his son and squeezed him affectionately.

"Me too!" Matthew beamed and looked up happily at his father. "What about you, Grandad?" He then looked at Terence.

"I'm with your father, Matthew. England all the way!" Terence winked and grinned warmly back at his grandson.

ACKNOWLEDGEMENTS

Many thanks to David Crinnion and especially Steve Christopher for their answers to my police and crime related questions and queries. Much appreciation to Pierre Laurent Faure at www.chapuis-armes.com and www.gendarmerie.interieur.gouv.fr for answering my gendarmerie related questions. Many thanks to Marcus Faulkner and Ashley Jackson from King's College London and Rob Palmer from www.britishmilitaryhistory.co.uk for their military advice and feedback. Kind thanks to Milsurp Mike Channel for my pistol/gun queries (www.youtube.com/channel/UCf9zoZ1b5OzhaXxTNIcYiFA).

Warm thanks to Ellie Howorth from www.archaeologyuk.org, Nick Barton from the University of Oxford, Rebecca Whiting from the British Museum, and Theya Molleson from the National History Museum — who were all kind enough to get back to me regarding my archaeological research.

Thanks too, to Phillips Stevens from the University at Buffalo and Jean La-Fontaine at the London School of Economics for answering my witchcraft related questions. Thanks to Christopher Partridge at Lancaster University and Jesper Petersen at the Norwegian University of Science and Technology for their help on inverted pentagrams/pentacles.

Thanks to Eric at www.xeroxnostalgia.com for his advice and help regarding photocopiers in the 1960s. Further thanks to Alex Clark from www.thg.org.uk and Bob from www.britishtelephones.com for their help and advice on using telephones back in the 1960s.

Much thanks also to David Forrest at the University of Glasgow and to Laragh Quinney from the National Library of Scotland for help on the map co-ordinates. Appreciation to Cllr Jenny Edwards for a couple of Balcombe related questions.

Thanks a lot to Edward Cerullo from www.timeanddate.com, Vanessa Couchman (www.vanessafrance.wordpress.com), Raluca Barett from www.greenwichmeantime.com, Mark Benson from www.rmg.co.uk, and in particular Mike Todd (www.miketodd.net) for their help with the UK and France time zones back in 1966.

Once again, huge thanks both to Ken Dawson from www.ccovers.co.uk and to my editor Kirstie Edwards (www.kirstieedwards.org.uk) for their patience, hard work and dedication. That also includes Jason Anderson from www.polgarusstudio.com for his hard work and commitment.

Finally, much appreciation goes to any readers/customers who have taken the time out to read my novel. If you enjoyed it, please feel free to leave a review and recommend it to others.

ABOUT THE AUTHOR

Alan Golbourn was born in Essex, England. He has enjoyed writing stories since a young age, when he was recognised early for his writing abilities. Amongst several interests and hobbies, including football and computer games, he holds a love and compassion for animals. *The 666 Murders* is his second novel.

ALSO FROM ALAN GOLBOURN

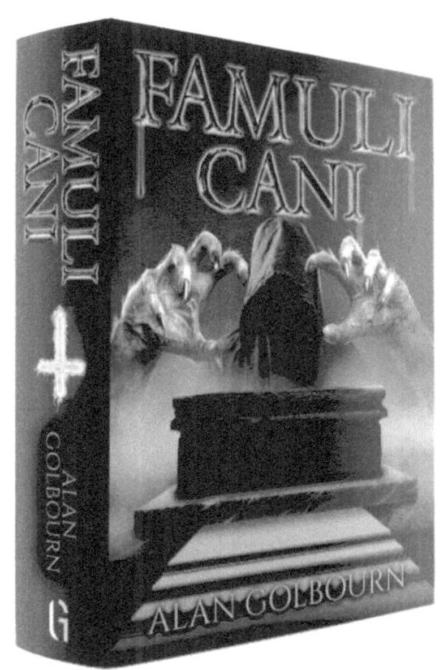

EVIL IN THE FOREST ...

www.ingramcontent.com/pod-product-compliance
Lightning Source LLC
Chambersburg PA
CBHW032141050726
47591CB00001B/42